Take Me, I'm Yours

ELIZABETH BEVARLY

AVON BOOKS

An Imprint of HarperCollinsPublishers

This is a work of fiction. Names, characters, places, and incidents are products of the author's imagination or are used fictitiously and are not to be construed as real. Any resemblance to actual events, locales, organizations, or persons, living or dead, is entirely coincidental.

AVON BOOKS
An Imprint of HarperCollins*Publishers*
10 East 53rd Street
New York, New York 10022-5299

Copyright © 2002 by Elizabeth Bevarly
ISBN: 0-380-81960-0
www.avonromance.com

First Avon Books paperback printing: April 2002

Avon Trademark Reg. U.S. Pat. Off. and in Other Countries, Marca Registrada, Hecho en U.S.A.
HarperCollins ® is a trademark of HarperCollins Publishers Inc.

Printed in the U.S.A.

10 9 8 7 6 5 4 3 2 1

For Laurie Jones,
a friend across both years and miles.
Thanks for being there, no matter what.

Acknowledgments

$\mathcal{A}$s always, many thanks to Lucia Macro for her patience and guidance and tolerance. Thanks, too, to Damaris Rowland for her knowledge and experience and perseverance. And thanks to all the good people at Avon who have been so wonderfully enthusiastic and hardworking on my behalf. It's *very* much appreciated.

Thanks to Teresa Medeiros, Teresa Hill/Sally Tyler Hayes, Barbara Samuel/Ruth Wind, and Christie Ridway for being there through both literary and personal tribulations. Thanks to Toni (Herzog) Blake and Barbara Freethy for watching *Survivor*. And thanks to Maggie Wilkins/ Margaret Moore for using the words "wiener dog" just when I most needed to hear them.

Thanks to Natural Wonders for making some naturally wonderful environmental CDs, like *Ocean Moods*, the one that's nothing but an hour of surf sounds. Thanks to my U.S. Coast Guard husband, David, for letting me steal the name he's always planned to give to the sailboat we still don't own, not to mention for answering all my nautical questions. (And before I get clobbered for using all the wrong nautical jargon—like "door" instead of "companionway" or whatever—it's because the bulk of this book is told from the point of view of someone who doesn't know boats, so she wouldn't use the proper lingo.) Any mistakes are mine.

And more thanks—and love—to David and Eli, who continue to love and tolerate me, despite my bad writer's habits of hiding in my office for days on end, drifting in and out of reality, and saying things like, "Hey, how about we get take-out tonight?" way more often than I should. You guys are swell. I owe you big. Thank you.

Chapter 1

*T*here were only two things in the entire world that Keaton Danning abhorred. One was tiny, rodentlike dogs with nasty dispositions, and the other was Teutonic chefs with overblown egos. Or was it Teutonic dogs with overblown egos, and tiny, rodentlike chefs with nasty dispositions that he abhorred? Ah, well. No matter. Because today Keaton was having to deal with *all* of them.

"Kurt, listen to me," he said to the chef in question, using the most placating tone of voice he could muster. Which, granted, ended up being not especially placating, seeing as how there was a miniature dachshund whirling around Keaton's right ankle, whining like a garbage disposal, trying to turn his pants leg into Sauerkraut. "Kurt," he tried again, shaking his leg gently in an effort to dislodge the odious little dog, "put down the meat cleaver."

Of course, it went without saying that the odious little dog belonged to the odious little chef. In fact, Kurt's revolting little wiener dog was also named Kurt—which

just went to show how overblown the chef's ego was—
something that caused no end of confusion on board the
yacht where Keaton and the human Kurt worked. And, as
was usual for both dog *and* chef, they completely ignored
Keaton when he made his request . . . uttered his plea . . .
whatever. As Kurt the chef lifted the large—sharp—meat
cleaver higher above his head, Kurt the dog hurled his
quivering little body forward again, attaching himself to
Keaton's trouser leg by, appropriately enough, his front
canines.

"Kurt, please," Keaton said again, running a restless
hand through his dark brown hair. Though, truly, at this
point, he wasn't sure whether he was directing the en-
treaty to the man or the animal. The meat cleaver under-
standably troubled Keaton the most, but right now the dog
seemed by far the more reasonable of the two. "Just calm
down," he added further.

"*Nein*," Kurt said—the chef, not the dog—reverting to
his native tongue, which was always a good indication
that he was very, very angry. Not that the raised meat
cleaver wasn't also a good indicator, mind you, but Kurt's
use of German did grab Keaton's attention. The chef
pointed to the man who stood cowering behind Keaton
and said, thankfully in English—sort of—"Not until you
tell that *Kotzbrocken* to get out of my kitchen."

Technically, of course, the room where Keaton and
Kurt—and the *Kotzbrocken*, for that matter—were having
their, oh . . . "international incident" seemed like an appropriate enough term for what was going on, should be
referred to as a "galley" and not a "kitchen," seeing as how
they were on a boat. A really big galley, too, seeing as how
it was a really big boat. But Keaton, smart guy that he was,
figured now was probably not the best time to school the
chef in matters of nautical jargon. So he only lifted both

hands in the internationally recognized gesture of *Please, for God's sake, don't hurt me*, and repeated, "Kurt, I'm begging you. For the last time, put down the meat cleaver."

But the chef ignored the appeal again, and pointed over Keaton's shoulder at the man who stood behind him. "He said my *Pflaumenkuchen* tasted *beschissen. Er ist ein Kotzbrocken!*"

This pronouncement was followed by a long stream of invective hurtled in rapid-fire German. Keaton knew it was invective, because he was fluent in six languages, one of which happened to be German. And even if he hadn't been fluent in German, the fact that Kurt punctuated his monologue by slamming the meat cleaver into a wooden cutting board on the counter beside him would have indicated fairly well that whatever the chef had just said was, you know, not good.

Keaton waited until Kurt was finished, relieved that, if nothing else, the chef had been disarmed, then settled one hand loosely on his Brioni trousers-clad hip and wiped the other over his damp forehead. The temperature in the galley must have been approaching triple digits, what with all the cooking—and shouting—going on. And the opened windows—or rather portholes, Keaton nautically corrected his jargon—helped not at all. Because beyond those portholes lay the city of Miami Beach, which in August wasn't exactly chilly. So, after a ruthless tug on his Hermès necktie, Keaton unfastened the top two buttons of his Pierre Cardin shirt. Then he shook his leg again, in an effort to dislodge the added accessory of miniature dachshund that was still attached to his trousers, and which complemented his ensemble not at all.

He was just about to mutter a sigh of relief that the situation seemed to be under control when "Well, your

Pflaumenkuchen does taste *beschissen*," the *Kotzbrocken* standing behind Keaton said, and up went the meat cleaver again.

"*Schweinehund*!" cried Kurt.

"Reynaldo!" growled Keaton to the *Kotzbrocken*.

"What?" Reynaldo asked. "It's true! Have you ever tasted his *Pflaumenkuchen*? *Beschissen* doesn't begin to cover it."

"Just knock it off," Keaton told Reynaldo. "Now, Kurt," he added, turning back toward the chef. He thrust his thumb over his shoulder, toward the man hiding behind him. "Reynaldo is not a *Schweinehund* or a *Kotzbrocken*. He's the crown prince of Pelagia. Granted, he doesn't exactly have a country to be crown prince of anymore," Keaton hastily interjected when Kurt appeared ready to take perfectly well-founded exception, "but he is still a member of the royal family, and he deserves the respect due his position."

"Yes, I am," Reynaldo said from behind Keaton. "And yes, I do. And it would serve you well, my good man, to remember that. My people *adore* me."

"Your people revolted and prevented your ascension to the throne," Kurt retorted. "They adored your *father*, not you. You they knew would turn their country into Disneyland."

Yeah, an R-rated Disneyland at that, Keaton couldn't help thinking. Then he remembered that, as Reynaldo's chief adviser, he was supposed to be on the prince's side. He opened his mouth to say something on Reynaldo's behalf—something like, "Hey, at least Cinderella and Snow White would look great in those thong bikinis," but Reynaldo stepped in to speak for himself. Sort of.

"Oh, yeah?" the prince shot back wittily.

"*Jah*," Kurt returned, just as wittily.

"Well . . . well . . . well . . ." Reynaldo sputtered. "Well, just for your information, I was thinking about abdicating and granting them their independence anyway. So there."

Keaton rolled his eyes heavenward. Oh, yeah. That was Reynaldo, all right. Mr. Altruistic. Mr. All-I-Want-Is-What's-Best-for-My-People. Mr. I'd-Never-Think-of-Using-My-Position-as-King-to-Live-Wastefully-and-Self-Indulgently-for-the-Rest-of-My-Life. Mr. All-I-Ever-Wanted-Was-a-Country-to-Call-My-Own-So-I-Could-Run-It-into-the-Ground. Mr. Don't-Tell-Me-How-to-Live-My-Life-Keaton-or-I'll-See-You-Put-in-the-Stocks. Mr.—

Well, suffice it to say that there wasn't a selfless bone in Reynaldo's body. Had he indeed become king of Pelagia, Pelagia would have been flushed right down the royal commode. Even with Keaton advising the prince on world affairs, as he had advised the prince's father. Mainly because the prince ignored pretty much everything Keaton said. The *beschissen Kotzbrocken*.

Nevertheless, had he been half the man his father was, Reynaldo would have fought to keep the throne. And he really hadn't given a thought to abdication—until he'd been awakened in the middle of the night and told that the royal palace was under attack by a band of rebel forces who were looking to make princemeat out of him, and if he valued his freedom and his life, not to mention the family jewels, he'd best be on his way.

Reynaldo had had just enough time to gather up a few belongings, including the family jewels, incidentally, and to collect some of his favorite courtiers—Keaton, of course, had been the one to alert Arabella, Reynaldo's fiancée—and escape onto the royal yacht by the skin of his teeth.

It was shortly after that, as Reynaldo had called his

court together in his pajama bottoms—Reynaldo had been in his pajama bottoms, of course, and not his court—that the prince had decided it might not be a bad idea to abdicate the throne and grant his people their independence.

"You would never have granted your people anything," Kurt replied snottily. "They took their independence for themselves, as was their right."

"They've only taken it for a little while," Reynaldo retorted. Every bit as snottily, too, something that Keaton wouldn't have thought possible. "Soon they'll realize how much they need me. Soon they'll see what a terrible mistake they made in asking me to leave. Soon they'll be begging me to come back and be their king."

Right, Keaton thought. That was why the Pelagian parliament had plundered the royal charter in the prince's absence, revoking all royal privileges and any claim he might make to the throne, and then torched what was left of said charter at a public weenie roast afterward. It was rumored they'd even hired assassins to make sure Reynaldo never set foot in his homeland again. They'd made it more than clear that if he ever returned to Pelagia, he'd be welcomed home with open fire.

Until a year ago, Prince Reynaldo Michael Julian David Lorenzo Constantine del Fuego had indeed been the crown prince of the tiny island nation of Pelagia, all set to take over for his father, King Francisco Reynaldo Phillip Teodor Enzo Nicholas del Fuego, upon the elder's death. But when King Francisco had gone to that big, bejeweled throne in the sky, instead of crowning Reynaldo their new king, the Pelagian parliament and the Pelagian people had, oh . . . taken exception. Then they'd taken to arms. Then they'd taken over.

They had later justified their actions by pointing out

that it was a new millennium, and that by the time of his death, King Francisco had become little more than a figurehead, anyway, had mostly been a local attraction aimed at bringing in tourist dollars. Of course, Reynaldo had tried to argue that he himself had always been a big attraction, too, even bigger than his father, really—why, he graced the pages of the *National Enquirer* and *People* magazine nearly weekly, and E! Entertainment Television devoted entire "Reynaldo Watch" minutes to him during commercial breaks. As king, he had told his revolting parliament and people—revolting in more ways than one, really—he could potentially bring in even more tourist dollars than his father had.

But the members of parliament had retorted, quite truthfully, that Pelagia's beaches and resorts and casinos were the biggest moneymakers on the island these days— not to mention the Pelagia Film Festival—and really, the people of Pelagia had been waiting for their independence for a long time now, and this was as good a time as any.

And since Reynaldo was a profligate, and a spendthrift, and a blowhard, they just didn't see any reason that they should keep him on. And since he wouldn't be living on Pelagia anymore, he wouldn't be needing any of the del Fuego real estate holdings, so they'd just keep those for the people, too. They had reminded the prince that the del Fuego family had hundreds of millions of dollars buried in Swiss bank accounts, so it wasn't like Reynaldo would starve.

More was the pity.

In the end Reynaldo had had little choice but to do as his people commanded and, you know, turn tail and run screaming like a girl—which pretty much covered what had happened that night when he'd been forced to abdicate the throne, the palace, and all personal dignity. Then

Prince Reynaldo Michael Julian David Lorenzo Constantine del Fuego had packed up the favorite members of his court, had loaded them onto the royal yacht, *Imperial Majesty*—whose name he immediately changed to *Mad Tryst*—and, literally a man without a country now, had set sail to find one.

That had been almost twelve months ago, Keaton reflected. Twelve long, tedious months, and God only knew how many thousands of miles. Reynaldo seemed to think he had all the time in the world to spend sailing the seven seas. Then again, Reynaldo *did* have all the time in the world to do that. Keaton, on the other hand, had better things to do with his life than spend the rest of his days being Julie-Your-Cruise-Director. Unfortunately, some misguided sense of loyalty—more to the late King Francisco than to the living Prince Reynaldo—kept Keaton pinned to the prince.

Well, a misguided sense of loyalty did that, and also the fact that all Keaton's financial assets in Pelagia had been frozen the moment he set foot on the yacht with Reynaldo.

"In any case, Kurt," he now told the chef, "Reynaldo is still a prince, and, as he said, he's still quite liked by some of his people." *At least five or six of them*, Keaton added to himself. "More importantly, he's your employer."

That, if nothing else, seemed to make Kurt think twice about hacking the other man to bits. Slowly he began to lower his arm, and after only a slight hesitation, he set the meat cleaver back down on the counter. The moment he did, Keaton lunged forward to claim the utensil himself. He had half a mind to use it to dislodge the disagreeable little wiener dog still attached to his pants leg, but instead he only held the meat cleaver firmly at his side. Still, he gripped the handle forcefully. You just never could tell with wiener dogs.

"Down, Kurt," he said sternly to the dog. And although the dog ignored the command, surprisingly the chef took a step backward. Keaton sighed silently. Whatever worked.

"Thank you," he said to the chef. "If you'd carried out your threat to cut off Reynaldo's—" Here he deliberately blurred his earlier translation of the chef's invective. "That part of him which most men consider exceedingly important," he continued, "and tossed it overboard for the fishes' lunch, then many of the people of Pelagia—"*at least five or six of them*—"would have been very unhappy."

"Damned straight," Reynaldo muttered.

"Reynaldo," Keaton muttered back, "you're not making this any easier."

It was all Keaton could do not to grab *both* men by the ear and drag them off to their rooms and send them to bed without any supper. Honestly. The chef's behavior was bad enough, but at least he had some small reason to behave badly—he had been provoked. Keaton had, in fact, tasted Kurt's *Pflaumenkuchen*, and although it wasn't by any means his favorite of the man's dishes, it did *not* taste *beschissen*.

Reynaldo, on the other hand, had no excuse for his bad behavior. His was the ideal life. Even if he had been chased off his homeland a year ago, he was still an idle, rich, handsome, twenty-six-year-old man who had absolutely no responsibilities, a man who, if he chose to, could spend the rest of his life simply being idle, rich, handsome, and irresponsible.

A man who had been educated at all the best schools, who had traveled to all the most romantic countries, who counted among his friends and lovers some of the most celebrated, beautiful people on the planet. A man who, until twelve months ago, had been in line to rule his very own country, for God's sake. Okay, so it had been only a

tiny little island nation in the Mediterranean Sea whose
chief source of income was tourism—and, of course,
Prince Reynaldo—but that was beside the point. The point
was . . . The point was . . . The point was . . .

Ah, dammit.

The point was that Keaton was getting sick and tired of
being Reynaldo's baby-sitter. He had talents and gifts that
were being wasted in his current capacity, and prospects
he would never have the opportunity to take advantage of
if things kept up at this rate. He'd been King Francisco's
chief adviser once upon a time, and had fully expected to
be Prince Reynaldo's, too, when the younger del Fuego
assumed the throne.

Hell, had things gone differently in Pelagia, Keaton
was confident that he would have one day been prime
minister of the country himself—in the not-too-distant future, too. But *noooooo*. Now, here he was, at thirty-six
years of age, having grown up primarily in Pelagia, as the
only child of the American ambassador to that country.
From the time he was a schoolboy until leaving for college, he'd called Pelagia home, and he'd returned after
earning his degrees to work for King Francisco.

Now here he was, having been virtually groomed
throughout his life to rise to the position of prime minister
of Pelagia. Here he was, with advanced degrees in political science, economics, and international affairs. And here
he was, instead of performing remarkable feats of detente
and diplomacy, having to intercede in kitchen disputes.

Dammit.

Then again, he thought, gazing at his two companions,
maybe a little detente and diplomacy wouldn't be out of
place here.

"All right, here's what we're going to do," Keaton began in his best prime minister voice, the one he had practiced since he was a teenager. "Reynaldo," he said, turning his attention fully to the dark-eyed prince.

Immediately, though, he found himself wishing he hadn't looked directly at the man, due to the danger of going blind. Not because of some ancient Pelagian mojo about looking directly upon a member of the royal family being some kind of mystic taboo or anything, but simply because Prince Reynaldo was a walking, talking fashion *don't*. His short, dark hair was swept straight back from his face with enough hair oil to keep Wishbone salad dressings bottled for years to come—had they used hair oil instead of salad oil, Keaton meant—and as for the other man's outfit . . .

Keaton didn't know if it was because Reynaldo was accustomed to viewing himself as omnipotent, so he just didn't give a damn what people thought of him, or if it was simply that the man had absolutely no taste whatsoever. But, true to his, ah, sartorial distinctiveness, the man was dressed today in a bright yellow, ruffled poet's shirt, with strings instead of buttons to bind the gaping neck—not that the gaping neck was in any way bound, mind you— baggy, lime green trousers, and purple huarache sandals. And call Keaton whimsical, but thanks to the prince's position standing in front of a refrigeration unit that was topped by a basket of fruit that hovered just above and behind his head, Reynaldo currently bore an uncanny resemblance to Carmen Miranda.

"Reynaldo," Keaton began again, doing his best not to look at the blinding combination—or the basket of fruit— "you're going to go up to the Jacuzzi deck, you're going to find the Countess Arabella, and you're going to ask her if she'd like to take a stroll around the upper deck. And no, you can*not* take supermodel Dacia with you," he added when the prince opened his mouth to object. "It would hurt the countess's feelings."

Not that the countess hadn't already had her feelings hurt countless times by Reynaldo over the last twelve months. And not just where supermodel Dacia—who seemed not to have a last name, because Keaton had certainly never heard anyone use it, unless "Dacia" was her last name and "Supermodel" was her first name—was concerned, either. In spite of the prince's clear preference for Supermodel Dacia, Reynaldo had also temporarily invited dozens of other women aboard *Mad Tryst* since beginning this fateful trip, not caring for a moment that the woman he was supposed to have been married to by now was there to watch his antics.

The man really was a *Kotzbrocken*, Keaton thought. No two ways about that.

"And, Kurt," he continued, turning to the chef, "you're going to go over to that counter, and you're going to . . . to chop up some garlic or something. And you're going to *like* it," he stated adamantly. Then Keaton shifted his gaze from one man to the other before asking both, "Is that understood?"

"Yes," grumbled Reynaldo.

"*Ja*," mumbled Kurt.

"Good," Keaton said. "And *you*, Kurt," he added, jerking his leg again in another effort to rid himself of the vicious little dachshund—to no avail. "You're going to release my pants, or else I'm going to put you on a bun, cover you with mustard, and feed you to Muffin. Got it?"

Mention of the Countess Arabella's cat finally got Kurt the canine's attention. He stopped snarling, stopped nipping at Keaton's ankle, and sat back on his haunches. But he pulled back his lips—or whatever it was dogs claimed for lips—to bare his teeth, and growled.

"Don't even think about it," Keaton told him, bending over—*way* over—to get in the nasty little dog's face. "I have it on good authority that Muffin missed breakfast this morning. She'll swallow you in one bite."

Kurt the dog narrowed his beady little eyes at Keaton, but offered nothing more by way of a comment. So, just to reinforce his position, Keaton narrowed his eyes right back at him. "Two words, Kurt," he told the dog. "Wiener. Schnitzel."

With one final snarl, Kurt turned tail—quite literally—and trotted off, his annoying little toenails tapping out a staccato *click-click-click-click-click* along the tiled floor as he went.

It was all Keaton could do not to hurl the meat cleaver after the malevolent little cretin. Instead he placed it gently on the counter—well out of Kurt the chef's reach—and having successfully mediated all the kitchen politics a man could handle for one day, he strode out of the galley to see what other matters of bureaucratic importance awaited him aboard *Mad Tryst*.

There were countesses to console, supermodels to keep an eye on, crew members to keep sober . . . bars he needed to make sure were stocked, towels he need to make sure were by the Jacuzzi, saunas whose temperatures he needed to gauge.

Keaton sighed heavily at all the responsibilities that awaited him. Honestly, his work was never done.

"So what's up with that aisle in the grocery store that's labeled 'Feminine Needs'?" Ruby Runyon asked the room at large, shoving a handful of damp, dark brown bangs out of her eyes. She couldn't see anyone out in the vast blackness that sprawled beyond the stage—the bright lights overhead prohibited it. But she knew they were out there. She could hear them breathing.

"I mean, feminine *needs*?" she asked again, gripping the mike in her other hand more forcefully. "Come on. What could be down that aisle that women *need*? Equal pay for equal work? Men who cook? Two size eight dresses that fit the same way? What?"

A ripple of laughter drifted up from the crowd—all of it feminine, Ruby noted—and she smiled. This was her favorite part of her monologue, the woman-to-woman part, and even if the male portion of the audience didn't get half of it, Ruby knew the female portion would go home tonight smiling.

And for the first time in a long time, so would she.

Because Ruby Runyon—miracle of miracles—had a date. Even more miraculous, it was a date with a nice guy. Most miraculous of all, it was their *second* date—Jimmy Golden hadn't taken a powder after the first, which was what usually happened with the guys Ruby dated. Of course, that was probably because guys who dated girls like Ruby—girls who worked in bars, and who'd grown up in trailer parks, and who'd never known their fathers, and who had figures that were way too voluptuous for their own good, and who had names like, well, Ruby— usually did so because they only wanted one thing. And when Ruby didn't give them that one thing on their first date, those guys lost interest. Fast.

And no, it wasn't the top-secret recipe for her Grandmother Pearl's famous, award-winning dump cake that those guys always wanted, either.

"And speaking of grocery stores," Ruby continued, shoving her tattered ponytail back over her shoulder before segueing into her next bit, "what is it about the phrase 'frozen niblets' that just makes a woman want to flinch, huh?"

More chuckles, more smiles, and more jokes from Ruby Runyon. She'd written her material herself, of course, from the heart, and she delivered it with the earnestness that came after a lifetime of wanting to share bits of herself with others, only to have others take no interest. And even if that sharing only came in darkness these days, and only with faceless strangers, Ruby would take it anyway. Hey, it was more than she'd ever gotten anywhere else.

She finished up her eight-minute monologue, smiled at the smattering of—almost enthusiastic—applause, waved to her good buddy, the faceless darkness, then spun around and jogged offstage. Just as she passed through the kitchen door, through which the comics always exited and entered at Frank's Funny Business, she ran into her boss, Frank Tedescucci. He wore his standard owner/operator uniform of synthetic V-neck pullover in an indeterminate shade of brown, with synthetic, plaid, sans-a-belt trousers. His dark, shaggy hair was damp and curlier than usual, due to the soggy South Beach heat that always pervaded the club, and his round face was set in its usual expression of total and complete ennui.

"Very funny," he told Ruby blandly. "Ha ha ha." Then he thrust a tray at her and nodded toward the kitchen door through which she had just passed. "But don't quit your day job, honey. Get back to work. I'd say you have roughly seven minutes of fame left. Make the most of 'em."

All right, all right, so Ruby Runyon wasn't exactly a headliner at Frank's Funny Business. She wasn't even a footnote there. What she was was one of Frank's waitresses, and had been for more than ten months. Every now and then, the tiny ice cube Frank claimed as a heart melted just enough that he'd allow one of his employees a chance at stardom—or, at the very least, a chance at eight minutes onstage. Tonight, finally, that employee had been Ruby. Now, however, her eight minutes were up, and Frank wanted her back in the capacity for which he'd hired her—serving drinks.

Expelling a long, frustrated sigh, Ruby took the tray he'd thrust at her, then the apron he likewise offered. Tucking the tray under one arm, she tied the apron over her khaki shorts and the navy blue polo shirt that was emblazoned with the words "Frank's Funny Business" over her left breast. Fame was going to have to wait for another night, evidently. Because, even four full minutes after the conclusion of her monologue, no talent scouts were bursting through the kitchen door screaming, "Baby, I'm gonna make you a star!"

Boy. There was nothing Ruby hated more than when real life wasn't like the movies. Because that, she was certain, was where she wanted to be. Movies, not real life. In fact, she'd left her not-so-happy home in the Happy Trails Trailer Park when she was eighteen years old for that very reason—because she wanted to be a star. Well, that and because there hadn't been a whole lot of prospects—professionally *or* personally speaking—in her tiny hometown of Appalachimahoochee in the Florida Panhandle. Now, eight years after striking out for superstardom, she'd had a total of eight minutes in the spotlight.

Eight years for eight minutes, she reflected again. Then she shrugged mentally. All in all, she supposed, it hadn't been such a bad trade. Some people lived their whole lives without a single second in the spotlight.

Resigned to her fate, Ruby finished her shift and, at ex-

actly ten o'clock, made her way to the locker room to
shower and change. At least the night wasn't a total loss.
Because Jimmy Golden would be meeting her in a half
hour. And tonight he was taking her out on his yacht for a
midnight cruise with another couple—his partner in the
pharmaceutical company he owned, along with the partner's wife.

Sometimes, Ruby thought, things really did work the
way they were supposed to. Not often. But sometimes.

Meeting Jimmy there at the club two weeks ago had
been the first stroke of luck she'd enjoyed in a long time.
The guy was just too good to be true. Jimmy Golden had a
good job—a *great* job, she quickly corrected herself—and
she could tell he really liked her. He'd brought her flowers
on their first date last weekend. And he called her Venus.
If things kept up the way they were promising to keep up,
Ruby might even kiss her dreams of Hollywood goodbye.
Hey, there were worse things in life than being Mrs.
Jimmy Golden.

And even if she didn't become Mrs. Jimmy Golden,
there were other benefits to dating him for a while, not the
least of which was being introduced into the social circle
Jimmy called his own. He had a lot of money, hence, she
figured, he must run around with other people who had a
lot of money. And people who had a lot of money also had
a lot of connections. Connections to, oh, say . . . the entertainment industry, for example. Lots of movies were
filmed in Miami. Well, some were. And in other parts of
Florida, too. All Ruby had to do was meet one person who
knew someone who knew someone who knew someone at
the Florida Film Commission, and she could be in like
Flynn.

So to speak.

And if all else failed, maybe she could at least meet

somebody who could land her a job at Disney World. Hey, it had worked for a couple of the guys in *NSYNC and Backstreet Boys, hadn't it? And Brad Pitt had started off wearing a chicken suit for a local restaurant. Ruby didn't think she was too old to play Snow White. Today Snow White, tomorrow the Academy Awards.

Hey, it could happen. It could. All she had to do was meet the right people. People with connections. And Jimmy Golden knew people like that. Or at least he knew people who knew people who knew people like that. And that was how things worked in the entertainment business.

As quickly as she could, she shrugged out of her waitress clothes and jumped into the meager shower stall to wash away the stale smell of cigarette smoke mixed with garlic mixed with bar slime that normally accompanied her home at night. She even washed her hair and blew it dry, brushing the long, razor-straight, espresso-colored tresses until they gleamed. Then she hurriedly dressed in her little black dress with the spaghetti straps, smoky black stockings, and black high heels, and fixed black, beaded drop earrings into her ears. Compared to her earlier persona, she thought, she looked *fabulous*. Pretty much.

She was just putting the finishing touches on her makeup when another of Frank's waitresses, Lorraine McCuskey, still wearing her uniform, came into the dressing room at the end of her own shift. "Hey, you did real good onstage tonight," she told Ruby as she flopped down onto the exhausted sofa tucked into one corner of the tiny, poorly lit room. She pulled the rubber band from her own ponytail and began fluffing out her riotous auburn curls. "But I still don't get why you're so het up to do stand-up. It's a hard life. And you probably make more now as a waitress than most of those comics do."

"Actually," Ruby said as she plugged the cap back onto her tube of Coral Punishment lipstick, "what I really want to do is act in movies."

"Oh, yeah, and that's just *so* much easier to break into," Lorraine said with a laugh.

Ruby shrugged. "One way or another, I'll get there," she vowed. "Someday my name is going to be right up there with Carole Lombard's."

"Who?" Lorraine asked.

"Carole Lombard," Ruby repeated. At Lorraine's obvious mystification, she added, "Oh, come on. She was a huge comedic movie star."

"Who?" Lorraine asked again.

Ruby frowned at her. "Don't tell me you've never heard of Carole Lombard. She did some of the best comedy in the history of the cinema."

"Yeah, well, you're certainly funny enough to be in movies," Lorraine said, "and pretty enough, too. But I sure wouldn't hold my breath on that stardom thing if I were you."

Ruby used her pinky to swipe a stray bit of mascara from beneath one slate gray eye, then squared her shoulders to check the final product in the mirror. And as she always did when assessing herself, she found herself wishing for a body that was slimmer and not so bumpy. Even if she did look *fabulous*. Pretty much.

No wonder she hadn't been discovered, she thought morosely. She didn't have any of the most desired features for superstardom—no blond hair, no blue eyes, no body like one of those emaciated orphans from *Oliver Twist*. Damn her luck anyway. She supposed she could color her hair and go the blue contact lens route, if she had to. But there was no way she'd ever be emaciated. Not while

Edy's Dreamery Chocolate Peanut Butter Chunk Ice Cream and crème brûlée existed in the world, anyway.

Truth be told, though, Ruby thought further, she didn't even look good enough to be going out with Jimmy Golden. What she looked like was a woman who had been raised in a trailer park and worked as a waitress and who was trying, with lousy results, to pass herself off as high society. Because Jimmy Golden was most definitely high society. He had Class with a capital C. Ruby still couldn't figure out what he saw in her.

"So," Lorraine said, wiggling her eyebrows playfully, her brown eyes filled with not-so-idle speculation, "you got a big date with Jimmy Golden tonight?"

"Yes, I do," Ruby replied with a smile.

"So," Lorraine said again, "have you and Jimmy done the dirty deed yet?"

"Of course not," Ruby said, her smile falling some. "This is only our second date, Lorraine."

"What's that got to do with anything?"

Ruby gaped at her. "That has everything to do with it. I'm not going to . . . you know . . . with a guy on the second date. That's way too soon."

Lorraine expelled an incredulous little sound. "Yeah, well, suit yourself. Some of us prefer a trial run before we get involved with a guy."

Ruby shook her head. "Gee, Lorraine. Some people would consider getting sexual with a guy being involved."

"And some people wouldn't," Lorraine countered.

Fair enough, Ruby thought. But she was definitely one of the former. Which was why she had only been *involved* with a couple of men in her life.

She dragged her brush through her hair a few more times, and checked her makeup once more to make sure everything was where it was supposed to be. All in all, she decided, Jimmy could definitely do worse. Because—had she mentioned?—she looked *fabulous*. Pretty much.

And maybe if she kept telling herself that, Ruby thought, eventually she'd believe it.

As if conjured by her thoughts of him, Jimmy Golden himself appeared then, in all his blond, blue-eyed, all-American boyishness, striding through the dressing room door without even knocking. That was Jimmy, Ruby thought. He knew what he wanted, and he didn't bother to ask anybody if it was okay. And she told herself she didn't mind, because it just went to show how much confidence he had in himself, and *not* how he seemed to think of himself before he thought of others. Because he also held a single, long-stemmed rose in one hand, and he smiled at her as if he knew something she didn't.

"What?" she asked playfully. "What's that little grin all about?"

He extended the rose toward her. "You'll find out soon enough," he said.

And Ruby told herself she didn't mind that he seemed to like keeping things to himself. It was just his way of teasing her, she assured herself, and *not* because it put him in a position of having control.

"Ready for a special night?" he asked further. "A *very* special night?"

There was something distinctly lascivious about the way he asked the question, and Ruby couldn't quite halt the shiver of apprehension that shimmied up her spine in response. But she shook off the sensation and took the rose from Jimmy, holding it up to her nose to inhale the sweet, intoxicating scent. And she told herself he only sounded lascivious because he only *hoped* that things might take a sexual turn tonight, and not because he *intended* for them to.

"Mm-hm," she told him, ignoring the thread of uneasiness that tried to unwind inside her. "Tonight, Jimmy, I'm ready for just about anything."

Chapter 2

They made the short drive to the yacht club in Jimmy's bright red, two-seater roadster, and met with the other couple for drinks at the bar before getting under way. While Jimmy talked business with his partner, Dennis Duran, Ruby made herself content by getting to know the other man's wife, who had been introduced to her simply as Georgia. She was easily twenty-five years younger than her husband, probably not even Ruby's age, really. Her blond hair was swept up in back, and her pale rose cocktail dress and pearls were understated, but elegant. She smiled frequently and drank her Bourbon straight up, and Ruby liked her immediately.

"So how long have you and Dennis been married?" Ruby asked her at one point.

Georgia laughed. "Oh, I'm not Dennis's wife," she said. "I'm his girlfriend."

Ruby touched her fingertips to her lips in embarrassment. "Oops. I apologize. I could have sworn Jimmy said

you and he were married. I distinctly recall him saying
that he and I were going out with Dennis and his wife
tonight. Guess I misunderstood."

"Yeah, well, maybe that was the original plan, but it
would be kind of tough now," Georgia said. "Lynn is out
of town this weekend."

Now Ruby was really confused. "Who's Lynn?"

Georgia threw her a funny look. "Dennis's wife," she
said.

"But . . . you said you're his girlfriend," Ruby objected, her brain not quite able—or willing—to process
the information it was receiving.

"I am his girlfriend," Georgia said.

Ruby narrowed her eyes at the other woman. "But he's
also got a . . ."

"A wife, yes." Georgia laughed. "Don't looked so
shocked," she said. "Hey, it's not like you're in any different position that I am."

"Whoa, whoa, whoa," Ruby said now. "I'm not
Jimmy's mistress."

"Well, you're sure not his wife, either," Georgia replied
mildly. "Her name is Barbara."

Ruby was silent as she gazed back at Georgia, having
no idea what to say. Jimmy was *married*? But how was
that possible? It wasn't possible. She must be mistaken.

But at Ruby's silence, the other woman emitted a single, humorless chuckle and said, softly, pityingly, "Don't
tell me you didn't know."

Instead of answering, though, Ruby could only continue to stare at the other woman in silence.

"Hell, even *I* knew Jimmy was married," Georgia told
her. "Next you'll be telling me you didn't know about his
three kids, either."

Oh, no, Ruby thought, a sick feeling washing over her. *No, no, no, no, no.*

"But he can't be married with children," she said, her voice sounding weak and pathetic, even to her own ears. "He can't be."

"Why not?" Georgia asked.

"Because . . . because he didn't tell me he was married with children, that's why." Even as she said it, though, she knew how ridiculous that sounded.

Georgia seemed to agree, because she laughed without inhibition. "Oh, honey, have you got a lot to learn. Next you'll be telling me you believe him when he tells you his name is Jimmy Golden."

Ruby glanced down into her wine, then back up at Georgia, a rapid, unpleasant heat spreading through her midsection at yet another revelation. "You mean it's not?"

Georgia shook her head. "Of course not. What kind of a name is Jimmy Golden? That's not a real name."

"Then what's his real name?"

"I have no idea. Guys like him don't usually give it out."

"What do you mean, 'guys like him'?" Ruby asked. "What kind of guy is he?"

Georgia shook her head slightly, as if she couldn't believe how stupid Ruby was. "A wise guy," she said flatly.

"Oh, he's not that bad," Ruby said. "I mean, some of his jokes are kind of dumb, but . . ." Her voice trailed off when Georgia began to laugh harder.

"Not that kind of wise guy," the other woman said. "The kind of wise guy who's connected. To the mob, I mean."

"The *mob*?" Ruby gasped. She glanced nervously over her shoulder, saw that Jimmy was still mired in conversation with Dennis, and said, more quietly this time, "Jimmy's involved in organized crime?"

Georgia gaped at her for a moment, then shook her head slowly. "I cannot believe you, honey," she said. "Just what turnip truck did you fall off of anyway?"

"The one from Appalachimahoochee," Ruby replied mechanically.

The other woman sipped her Bourbon and smiled. "Yeah, well, lucky for you, you got Georgia here to teach you the ropes. Stick close tonight, you hear? I think you're going to need me."

But Ruby didn't want to learn the ropes. And she certainly didn't want to stick close—to Georgia or anyone else in their party tonight. The last thing she needed was to get herself any more involved with Jimmy and his band of merry mafiosos than she already was. Even if he wasn't a mobster, he was a husband. A father. A liar.

Although she couldn't quite bring herself to believe that he was connected—it did seem kind of silly to think of Jimmy in such a way—Ruby sure wasn't going to take any chances. In all his other incarnations, Jimmy Golden was still a man to be avoided. Here she'd been thinking she might someday become his ties-that-bind. Now, however . . . Well, suffice it to say that she didn't want to use the words "Jimmy" and "ties" and "bind" in the same sentence.

"You ready to go, ladies?"

Ruby turned automatically at the question, and found Dennis Duran gazing at Georgia, and Jimmy gazing at her as if . . . Oh, God, she thought. As if the two women were a couple of big ol' bloody steaks in the meat case at Tony Roma's. Jimmy's blond, blue-eyed, all-American boyish features—the ones that, before, had always seemed to Ruby so open and affable—suddenly seemed so ugly and sinister. Even his smile was different, she thought. And she couldn't help wondering if this was the way he had looked all along, but she'd just been too lonely and desperate to see him for what he really was. Not high society, and Class with a capital C. But lowbrow, and Creep with a capital C.

Before she could stop herself, she circled her fingers around Jimmy's wrist and blurted out, "Are you married?"

His expression changed immediately, from excitement about a good, juicy piece of meat, to revulsion at how that piece of meat had suddenly turned rancid. "What the hell difference does it make if I'm married?" he asked coolly.

Ruby gaped at him. "Jimmy, how could you?"

He jerked his arm free of her grasp and immediately caught hers instead. Hard. "We'll talk about it later," he told her in a voice that brooked no argument.

She was about to reply the hell they'd talk about it later, she wanted this straightened out right now, but his grip on her arm tightened then. *Very* hard. So hard that her hand began to tingle at the loss of circulation. And his expression changed again, too, to something deeply and profoundly troubling.

"O-okay, Jimmy," Ruby said in as obedient a voice as she could manage, considering how much she wanted to deck him one. "Whatever you say." *You creep*.

Ruby might have been accused of many things in her life, but stupidity was not one of them. The way Jimmy was looking at her now, she knew better than to argue with him. But she'd be damned if she was getting on any boat with him, either. Even a luxury yacht. So she allowed him to lead her out of the bar and down into the marina, thinking all the while that she'd simply take advantage of the throngs of people that would be crowding the yacht club this late on a Friday night, and make herself disappear among them when Jimmy wasn't looking.

No problemo.

Until the small group wandered out into the marina, and Ruby realized that the throngs of people crowding the yacht club were already on their boats this late on a Friday night—and that a good many of those boats were flat-out gone, cruising the waters of Biscayne Bay or points beyond.

Grande problemo, she thought. *Muy grande problemo.*

Only one of the sleek white vessels currently in port showed any significant sign of life. But the activity—nay, the utter pandemonium—that that one vessel claimed more than made up for the dearth of life anywhere else in the marina. And the vessel itself—nay, the mini–ocean liner itself—more than made up for the dearth of boats anywhere else in the marina.

It was a massive yacht the length of which Ruby couldn't even begin to hazard a guess. Big. That was what it was. Really, really big. To her untrained eye, it appeared to be three decks high—four, if you counted the little one on top—the majority of which looked to be open to the balmy night air. And it was populated by scores of people, all of whom seemed to be having a very good time.

To put it mildly.

Mad Tryst, it said on its . . . whatever the back of a big boat like that was called, Ruby noted as she and Jimmy and the other couple drew nearer. She recalled the phrase from one of her favorite stories by Edgar Allan Poe and smiled in spite of her situation. *Mad Tryst* indeed. No doubt the yacht was playing host to dozens of them at that very moment. Live salsa music erupted from one of *Mad Tryst*'s decks on the side facing away from Ruby, but the raucous melody couldn't quite drown out the squeals and peals of laughter flowing over the side nearest her. Whoever owned the piece of floating real estate certainly knew how to throw a party.

To put it mildly.

Even Jimmy couldn't hide his awe of the vessel, and he eyed it with open admiration as they drew nearer. Ruby was grateful for his preoccupation, too, because it caused him to loosen what had been a much, *much* too possessive—and much, *much* too painful—hold on her. Although, once they were right alongside the yacht, she realized it might have been one of the guests that Jimmy was actually openly admiring. Because a tall, breathtakingly beautiful redhead stood on the deck immediately above them. And she appeared to be drunk enough to fall overboard any minute, right into Jimmy's arms.

Though, on second thought, Ruby noticed, it wasn't the redhead herself who was going overboard. No, it was actually only the woman's breasts that were going over the side, something that Jimmy also seemed to notice. And to openly admire.

"Ahoy there," the redhead said with an inebriated giggle, wiggling her fingers in something akin to a greeting when she saw Jimmy gawking at her.

And immediately any distaste Ruby might have been feeling for the woman totally evaporated. "Hello!" she called back to her new bestest buddy in the whole wide world, waving vigorously in return. Hey, any port in a storm, right? Or, at least in this case, any yacht in a port. "What a lovely boat!" she added. Then, shamelessly, "Can we come aboard for a look around?" she further invited herself.

But Jimmy, smart—if contemptible—guy that he was, would have none of that. "We have plans, Ruby," he reminded her, tightening his arm around her wrist again to urge her forward, away from the big, beautiful yacht—and the big, beautiful redhead—that had promised sanctuary.

Oh, yes, they most definitely had plans, Ruby agreed silently. Unbeknownst to Jimmy, however, his plans bore absolutely no resemblance to her own.

And now, she decided, was probably the time to make that clear. With another quick survey of the yacht's exterior, she saw that the gangplank—which in this case was more like gang*stairs*—was still down, and that party-goers were coming and going pretty freely. Whoever had been minding the door—or whatever a door was called on a boat—had probably relaxed the rules by now. The party was in full swing. Anyone who'd been invited was probably already on board, so if it was an invitation-only bash, maybe she could sneak and/or fast-talk her way into it. She was dressed perfectly appropriately for the occasion— that occasion apparently being partying until everyone aboard was blind—so she'd blend right in with the crowd.

Even if Jimmy managed to follow her aboard, she could probably lose him among all those people. At the very least, she could find someone on board to help her. Best case scenario, though, she could spend a few hours pretending to be a guest, then slip off the boat unnoticed later and call a cab to take her home. Or, better yet, she could hook up with a nice couple on board who might be able to escort her safely home. At the moment, all Ruby wanted to do was be rid of Jimmy. She'd worry about what came later, well, later.

Without even thinking about what she was doing, she surreptitiously guided both herself and Jimmy closer to *Mad Tryst*'s gangplank. And the Patron Saint of Women with Icky Boyfriends—St. Trixie, if Ruby remembered correctly—was most assuredly watching over her that night, because just as she and Jimmy were close enough to the gangplank that she might leap aboard it and run for her life, a large, boisterous group of people singing an off-key rendition of "La Vida Loca" came spilling down it. Better yet, that large group crashed right into Ruby and Jimmy, separating them from each other.

Immediately Ruby hastened up the gangplank and, looking around only long enough to determine where the largest group of people was malingering, fled in that direction. She took great care to make her moves as smooth as she could, and pretended she knew exactly where she was going. She strode with purpose and determination and a keen sense of freedom.

And, as had been her practice for the last eight years of her life, she didn't look back once.

Keaton was contemplating the pros and cons of chucking a miniature dachshund overboard without a Coast Guard–approved life vest when he saw the bumpy brunette in the skinny black dress. Of course, there were probably fifteen or twenty brunettes in black dresses aboard *Mad Tryst* tonight, but he'd only noticed this one. The one with the rich, dark hair that tumbled to the middle of her back like a spill of French roast coffee. The one with dark eyes of indeterminate color at this distance, though they somehow reminded Keaton of a Scandinavian sky in the winter. The one whose numerous—and quite impressive—curves put to shame the hills and valleys of an alpine landscape. The one whose full, ripe, coral-colored mouth evoked a memory of one singularly spectacular sunrise off the coast of Madagascar. The one who—

And what in *God's* name had come over him tonight to turn him into such a frigging poet? Keaton wondered. Worse, a frigging bad poet. Worst of all, a frigging bad poet who had minored in geography. And frigging failed it. Frig, for being such a pragmatic, intelligent man, sometimes Keaton turned his own stomach.

At any rate, the woman was exceptionally attractive—not to mention, uh . . . abundantly . . . er . . . endowed—and she put all thoughts of vicious, malignant little dachshunds out of Keaton's head, so he immediately felt indebted to her. Among other things.

As he watched her move gracefully through the crowd, smiling at several people but stopping to chat with none, his curiosity was instantly aroused. For lack of a better word. Then again, there were things other than his curiosity that were being, uh . . . provoked, incited, riled, titillated—dammit, where was a thesaurus when you needed one?—so maybe he shouldn't be surprised by his word choice.

At any rate, Keaton couldn't recall ever making the woman's acquaintance before, and Reynaldo hadn't mentioned inviting anyone special aboard for tonight's celebration. Of course, to Reynaldo, "special" meant "producing estrogen," and the prince tended to pick up women the way some people picked up cold sores—though that probably wasn't the best analogy to use—so Keaton knew he shouldn't be surprised that he hadn't met this one.

Yet.

He straightened his sand-colored silk tie, buttoned his beige linen jacket, and swiped his damp palms over his buff-colored trousers. It was actually too hot to be wearing a jacket, even over the lightweight ensemble Keaton had chosen, but Reynaldo's parties were always semiformal. And, hey, *some*body had to blandly counter the prince's wardrobe preference—even if tonight Reynaldo was wearing a surprisingly low-key dark suit . . . with a, um, a pattern of flames leaping up from the cuffs of his trousers and the hem of his jacket, and no shirt to speak of, and orange shoes. And even though Keaton attended these parties less in the capacity of guest and more in the capacity of nanny—dammit—he was still inherently averse to gross sartorial lapses such as removing one's jacket at such an occasion.

Besides. He had discovered a few moments ago, when he'd removed his jacket due to the heat, that Kurt had chewed a hole through the seat of his trousers—the canine Kurt, not the culinary Kurt—at some point after Keaton had laid out his things for the evening. He'd discovered this because Supermodel Dacia, with her inane giggle, had pointed it out to him. To him and approximately eight other people who had been standing near him. He'd been about to head below to change when he saw the sumptuous brunette come aboard. Now, suddenly, Keaton had other more important things to occupy his pants.

Mind, he quickly corrected himself. He had more important things to occupy his *mind*. Among other body parts.

He ran a hand through his dark hair a few times in what he was certain was a totally futile effort to dispel the effects of the humid sea air, and pinpointing the last place he had seen the brunette, headed off in that direction. He caught up with her at the Jacuzzi bar, where Gus the bartender was handing her a short glass filled with something clear and fizzy, adorned with a wedge of lime.

Gin and tonic, Keaton deduced. Such a refined, elegant spirit, gin. Perfectly suitable for the woman. He hoped she drank lots and lots of it tonight.

But she only sipped daintily at her drink and continued to glance about, as if she were looking for someone particular. Well, then, hey, he thought, he'd just go right up and introduce himself. Because, as anyone on Pelagia would tell you, they didn't come any more particular than Keaton Hamilton Danning III. So he sidled up to the bar, asked Gus for a Bombay and tonic for himself, and turned to the brunette, who was still scanning the crowd and had yet to note his presence.

"Hallo," he greeted her in his best Cary Grant voice.

And much to his surprise, she responded by nearly jumping right out of her skin. Fortunately, when she landed, she was on her feet. Better still, she was facing Keaton. And his breath nearly left his lungs when he saw that, up close, she was even more stunning than she had been from a distance. Her eyes were enormous and thickly lashed, their darkness resulting from a dense, sooty gray he'd never seen on another human being before. And they reflected a keen wit and intelligence that took him by surprise.

Maybe she wasn't one of Reynaldo's collectibles after all, he thought. Because if there was one thing the prince abhorred in a woman, it was wit and intelligence. All right, *two* things the prince abhorred in a woman. And he also abhorred a fondness for cats in his women. Unless, of course, it interfered with him getting laid, in which case, he could tolerate it.

"H-h-hello," the woman stammered, clearly a little breathless herself. Then, to Keaton's even greater surprise, she immediately followed up with "I have to go now. Bye." And then she was off like a shot, disappearing into the crowd.

Okay, so maybe he'd been a bit hasty on the keen wit and intelligence thing. Still, she was very intriguing. Even more so now than before. She was also very fast on her feet, he soon discovered, as he snatched his drink from the bar and made to follow her. But that was okay. Keaton had learned long ago that the things that came easily in life usually weren't worth having.

When he finally caught up with her, she had covered *Mad Tryst* from stem to stern. Or, rather, from stern to stem, seeing as how he finally found her in the forward saloon. The saloon was Keaton's favorite place on the yacht. Not just because of its sophisticated Art Deco styling, and its radiant hardwood paneling, and its gleaming brass detailing, and its splendid, cream leather furnishings, and its baby grand piano where Omar played all Gershwin, all the time, even when he didn't understand the words. But also because you could always find someone in the saloon to fix you a good stiff belt when you needed one. And, for some reason, Keaton had needed a regular dose of good, stiff belts since undertaking this cruise with Reynaldo. Not that he had become a habitual drinker. Just a chronic one.

The intriguing brunette had seated herself in one of the overstuffed lounge chairs near the starboard windows, where she appeared to be—it went without saying—lounging. But still she had her eye on the crowd, still she seemed to be looking for someone particular, and still Keaton couldn't rid himself of the notion that he was perfectly suited to whatever role she wanted that someone to play. Provided, of course, that role was sexual in nature.

So he approached her again, and when she wasn't looking, he snuck into the chair beside hers. He said nothing this time—obviously she wasn't a Cary Grant fan—and decided it might be best to wait and take a cue from her. He wasn't prepared, however, when that cue turned out to be her shifting her body toward him, and being so surprised by his appearance that she jerked forward with a start and spilled her entire drink over both of them.

As cues went, this wasn't one with which he was familiar. So it went without saying that he had no idea how to react.

"Oh. Oh, my," she said as she and Keaton both leaped up from their chairs. Okay, so far they were in sync, he noticed. That was good. "Oh. Oh, I am so sorry," she added as she set her now empty glass on the nearest table. She grabbed a stray cocktail napkin and began to dab hastily at his jacket, as if a four-inch square piece of tissue paper was going to do any good in blotting up half—or more— of a gin and tonic.

Still, that wasn't Keaton's biggest worry at the moment. No, his biggest worry was trying not to notice how the other half—or more—of that gin and tonic had splashed onto the creamy, and quite ample, flesh that was spilling from the top of her dress, and how he had to keep reminding himself that it would *not* be a helpful gesture for him to lean forward and lick away the dampness with his tongue, even if that was precisely what instinct was commanding him to do. Because clearly it wasn't any kind of hosting instinct that was commanding him to do that. No, clearly it was *another* instinct entirely that was kicking in just then.

Good thing he noticed the difference between the two. Boy, could that have been embarrassing.

"Are you all right?" he asked the woman who was still dabbing futilely at his chest, his words coming out a little ragged for some reason. Probably because his gaze was focused on one little trickle of her spilled drink that wound leisurely from the small divot at the base of her neck along the soft skin over her collarbone, then downward, disappearing into the deep valley between her—had he mentioned they were ample?—breasts.

He wrapped the fingers of one hand loosely around the woman's wrist in an effort to stop her futile—though, he had to admit, surprisingly arousing—efforts to clean him off. Vaguely he heard the piped announcement from *Mad Tryst*'s captain that everyone who was going ashore should go ashore now. But since Keaton would be staying aboard, and since the brunette was still futilely—and arousingly—trying to clean his jacket with her other hand now, he decided he wasn't going to go anywhere.

And since she paid no heed to the announcement herself, only continued with her futile—and arousing . . . did he mention that it was arousing?—cleaning, he assumed that she, too, like many of Reynaldo's guests tonight, would be remaining aboard for the cruise.

Oh, goody.

And then Keaton ceased to think at all, because the woman's futile—and oh, boy were they getting arousing now—gestures were becoming rather distracting. So Keaton circled her other wrist with the fingers of his other hand, and drew her arms gently apart, away from himself. Unfortunately, such a posture left her wide open—if one could pardon the incredibly tacky pun—to his gaze, and he noticed again the gin that had splashed across, and between, her breasts and the upper part of her dress. And as much as he would have loved to aid her in the same way she had just aided him, he instead urged her hands gently to her sides, withdrew his handkerchief from the inside pocket of his jacket, and extended it toward her.

She seemed not to understand why he was making his gesture at first, until he dipped his head once toward her— quite delectable—torso. Then, when she glanced down to see that she, too, had been a casualty of the spilled drink, she blushed furiously and hastily accepted the proffered handkerchief, and began dabbing at her damp—and quite delectable—skin with it.

And then Keaton found himself praying to every avail-

able god that she would return the square of silk to him
when she was done, because he planned to sleep with it
under his pillow that very night. And also to carry it with
him like an enchanted talisman for the rest of his natural
life.

"I am so sorry," she said again as she finished tending
to herself. Then, much to Keaton's delight, she did indeed
begin to pass the handkerchief back to him. At the last moment, though, she jerked it back toward herself. "Oh, I
should have this laundered first, shouldn't I?"

He swiped a hand airily in front of himself. "Oh, it's
not necessary," he told her. "I'll take care of it." Boy,
would he. He was already mentally designing the holy
shrine he planned to build for that handkerchief.

She smiled shyly—*shyly*, he remarked, in that dress—
then handed the handkerchief back to him, and Keaton
sent up a silent ode to joy as he accepted it, tucking it reverently back into his pocket.

"Aren't you going to . . . ?" she began. But she never
finished her question.

"Aren't I going to . . . what?" he asked.

She pointed toward the wet stain that had spread over
parts of his jacket and shirt. "Use your handkerchief to
wipe yourself off?"

What, and pollute her essence with his? he thought.
Not bloody likely.

Though, actually, when he thought more about mingling their essences, the idea wasn't so very off-putting.
On the contrary, the idea was pretty incendiary.

Later, he promised himself. But not too much later.

Providence interceded before his thoughts could become too salacious, in the form of a waiter who passed by
with a tray that was loaded down with delicate champagne
flutes. Keaton halted the man, then divested him of both

the linen towel draped over his forearm and two of the champagne flutes. Then he handed one of those flutes to the still-flustered brunette, kept the other for himself, and used the towel to dab at his own clothes.

"I'm really sorry," she said for a third time.

"It was an accident," he told her. "Don't give it a second thought."

"I hope I didn't ruin your clothes."

"Etiènne will take care of it," Keaton said easily, thinking how delighted the yacht's valet was going to be to have something to clean up that didn't require donning medical quarantine gear for a change. "In fact, Etiènne pretty much lives for this sort of thing."

"Etiènne," the brunette repeated. She seemed to be eyeing him warily for some reason. "Is that your . . . wife?"

Keaton halted his dabbing and studied the woman curiously. "Etiènne is a man," he said.

She blushed again. "Oh. Oh, I'm sorry. I didn't mean . . . I mean . . . I didn't realize . . . I just assumed . . . Not that there's anything *wrong* with that," she further assured him, though Keaton couldn't imagine why she would want to assure him that there was nothing wrong with a valet who enjoyed his work, provided it didn't, well, gross him out too much. "I totally respect alternative lifestyles, really I do," she added. "It's just . . . Oh . . ." She sighed fitfully, then bit her—quite delectable—lip, as if that were the only way to keep inside whatever other nervous words were about to spill free.

Now Keaton studied the woman even more curiously. "Etiènne is the yacht's valet," he told her. "It's his job to take care of things like this, not an alternative lifestyle. Unless, of course, he begins to enjoy fondling other people's clothing *too* much. Then it's time to call Dr. Drew."

The woman opened her mouth to say something,

seemed to think better of it—which was probably for the best, Keaton couldn't help thinking—then quickly sipped her champagne. Finally, though, she replied, "Oh."

The remark seemed to invite no response, so Keaton dabbed at his jacket and shirt with the towel a few more times, disposed of it on the tray of another passing waiter, and turned to the brunette once again. "So," he began.

"So," she replied, sipping her champagne nervously once more. Before Keaton had a chance to say anything further, however, she added, "Are you, um, are you the host of this party?"

"Oh, God, no," he told her, thinking it odd that she would ask such a question. She must know Reynaldo. Otherwise, what was she doing on board? Unless she was the escort of one of the prince's male guests. In which case, she should still know Reynaldo. Everyone knew Reynaldo. In spite of his doubt, however, Keaton added, "No, I only work here."

For some reason she seemed relieved by his revelation, something that intrigued Keaton even more. Most women came aboard for the owner of the yacht. They couldn't be bothered with the hired help, even when the hired help pulled in a *very* nice annual income, thank you very much—or at least *had* pulled in a very nice annual income, before the hired help had lost his job, which, essentially, meant that Keaton wasn't exactly *the hired help* anymore, but was simply *the help*, and he couldn't keep himself from wondering why he had stayed on for the last twelve months when he had yet to see a paycheck, something he should probably think about later, when he was alone in his stateroom.

Unless, of course, he wasn't alone in his stateroom later, which, looking at the brunette again, he decided was a prospect he very much wanted to turn into reality. And not just because he didn't want to think about being nothing but *the help*, either.

So he was about to expound on his position as the prince's right-hand man—and nanny—even if he wasn't being paid for either position, when the woman's attention was caught by something out the window. Her mouth dropped open a little in response to whatever it was she saw there, and her face went a bit pale.

"What's wrong?" Keaton asked, alarmed.

Now she pointed out the window, too, looking very confused. "We're moving," she said.

He nodded. "Yes, Reynaldo likes to get under way at exactly midnight."

"Reynaldo?" she asked, still gazing out the window. Still looking very confused.

Which made Keaton very curious. "Yes, Reynaldo. He always pulls out of port at midnight. He likes the drama."

"But . . . but . . . but . . ." the woman said. "But where are we going?"

Now Keaton was very, *very* curious. "Didn't you know?" he said. "We're leaving Miami tonight. Tomorrow evening, we'll be putting in at Nassau. In the Bahamas."

Chapter 3

Ruby had thought she was scared before, when Jimmy had been dragging her through the marina toward her certain doom—or, at the very least, an *extremely* unpleasant midnight cruise. But now . . . Now she was really scared.

She was on a moving yacht—uninvited, no less—that wouldn't be stopping until it pulled into port in a foreign country—sort of—and she had nothing more with her than the clothes on her back—which barely covered her back, by the way—and the few things she had been able to fit into a purse that was roughly the size of an electron.

Granted, one of those few things was a major credit card, which would definitely come in handy once she reached the Bahamas—*if* she reached the Bahamas before she was forced to walk the plank at corkscrew point.

Thank God she never charged more on her card than she could pay for in one month, so the balance was, at the moment, zero. Of course, that wasn't going to be the case for long now, was it? No, it was probably going to take her the rest of the year to pay off this little unexpected excursion.

Still, this wasn't the worst situation in the world, Ruby tried to tell herself. Hey, it was a really, really nice yacht, and the guy she was talking to was really, really cute. And it was a gorgeous, clear, balmy, star-spattered night.

And they were, after all, headed for the Bahamas ... hundreds of miles away from where she lived, and unconnected to where she lived in any solid, geographical manner. Still, as bad situations went, this was far better than, say, oh ... Than, say, gee ... Than, say, gosh ... A dinner date with Hannibal Lecter, for example.

Hey, it was something.

Then again, Ruby hadn't exactly been invited aboard the really, really nice yacht, which pretty much made her a stowaway, which, who knows, might potentially be in violation of some maritime law. And anybody who owned a yacht like this had to have more money than God, which, it went without saying, equated to having more power than God, so if she was discovered aboard said yacht, she might end up with her keester thrown in jail—or the brig, whatever the hell that was—due to that aforementioned stowaway thing.

And the guy she was talking to, although really, really cute, worked for the yacht owner, which meant that his loyalties were with the one who signed his paychecks and *not* with the stowaway who hadn't been invited aboard and had spilled her club soda on him.

And seeing as how Ruby wasn't known for her nerves of steel—no, hers were more like nerves of air—then the longer she stood talking to him, the greater her chances became of blurting out something foolish like, "Hey, I'm a stowaway, but don't tell anyone, 'kay?" Because cute guys always made Ruby blurt out foolish stuff. And *do* foolish stuff, too, as evidenced by her current predicament.

And, of course, the Bahamas were a foreign country—sort of—so she wasn't entirely sure that she would even be allowed into port, because a passport was much too large for a purse the size of an electron. Which wasn't really pertinent anyway, seeing as how Ruby didn't have a passport to begin with, which might *really* pose a problem once she got to the Bahamas and was either turned away because she had no proof of citizenship, or had her keester thrown into jail, or the brig, or shark-infested waters, depending on the mood of the yacht's owner.

Okay, so maybe this was right up there with having a dinner date with Hannibal Lecter, she reluctantly amended. At least she was going to her death looking *fabulous*. Pretty much.

The only thing that kept her from shouting, "Stop the boat! I wanna get off!" was that an image of Jimmy Golden—or whatever his name was—popped into her head. In her mind's eye, she saw him standing on the dock, with a suspicious-looking bulge under his jacket, surrounded by a group of mean-looking men with names like Vito and Sal and Rocco, all of whom reeked of pesto and Aqua Velva. And even if that last part was just embellishment, Ruby could still easily see Jimmy giving her a rough time of it, once he caught up with her again. And she wouldn't be surprised if he brought a few of his favorite thugs with him.

Gee, she thought. What a choice. Stowed away on a luxury yacht headed toward the Bahamas with a cute guy, or marooned ashore with a potentially dangerous, and certainly creepy, jerk who might do her bodily harm. Luxury yacht with cute guy . . . creepy jerk and bodily harm. Luxury yacht . . . creepy jerk. Cute guy . . . bodily harm . . .

All in all, not a difficult decision to make.

"Uh . . ." she began eloquently. She turned her attention to the cute—but sort of soggy—guy again and remembered that he had asked her some questions that needed answering. "Ah . . . of course I knew we were leaving Miami tonight. Of course I knew we were headed for Nassau. Of course I know that Nassau is in the Bahamas. Of course I was invited."

He eyed her curiously, and for the first time, she realized that his eyes were a lovely shade of green almost the exact same color of the kudzu that grew all over everything back home in Appalachimahoochee. Lots of people thought kudzu was annoying as hell, but Ruby had always been impressed with its ability to overrun everything in its path. And say what they would, there was no stopping kudzu once it got started. No, sir.

"I, um . . . I don't recall asking anything about whether or not you were invited," the cute guy said.

"Ah . . . right," she replied. "Right. Because that wasn't necessary, was it? It's obvious, isn't it?"

"What's obvious?"

"It's obvious that I belong here."

And oh, Ruby hoped God didn't strike her dead for that one. This was the last kind of place she belonged. And not just because she hadn't been invited, either.

"Yes, well," he said, "in any event, we have a pretty long cruise ahead of us." He smiled, albeit a bit guardedly, and extended his hand. "We might as well get acquainted. I'm Keaton. Danning. Keaton Hamilton Danning the third, if you want the full list," he told her, smiling. "And you are . . . ?"

Ruby smiled back as she took his hand in hers, but she couldn't quite bring herself to tell him her name. Mostly because, as she took his hand in hers, she couldn't remember her name. Or her location. Or her current activity. Or her species of origin. Or much of anything beyond the jolt of heat that scorched her from her fingertips to her toes, and all points between. Wow. That felt really, really good. Something about the way he held her hand—not to mention the way he sent heat sizzling through her entire body—made Ruby think of nights in white satin, and stars falling on Alabama, and hot, hot, hot, and bang-zoom-straight-to-the-moon.

And then, when she looked into his eyes, she realized she wasn't the only one thinking of hot, hot, hot and bang-zooming. Because his green eyes now were less like kudzu and more like fire, though the promise of overrunning and no-stopping-once-he-got-started was even more apparent. More persistent. More exacting. More . . .

Oh, boy.

And when, eventually, Ruby did remember her name, she realized she still didn't want to give it to him. Something told her she'd be better off if she just kept a low profile while she was on board, though Keaton Hamilton Danning III was giving her the impression that a low profile was going to be difficult to manage, seeing as how he was undressing her with his eyes, and seeing as how she wasn't exactly minding.

Still, they wouldn't be able to process her into jail or the brig if they didn't have her real name, right? Of course, those sharks wouldn't care what her name was when they threw her overboard, would they? But once the yacht made it to port in Nassau, she could slip off—she hoped—and make arrangements for her return to Miami—she hoped—and no one would be the wiser that a stowaway had been on board for the duration of the trip—she hoped. So she figured she'd be better off keeping her name—among other things—to herself.

Therefore, looking Keaton Hamilton Danning III right in the eye, and figuring she should probably have a name as hoity-toity as his if she wanted to fit in, she said, "I'm Euphemia Philippa Wemberly-Stokes." Wow, she thought. Where had *that* come from? That was *good*. She pumped his hand with as much confidence as she could muster, and hoped her palms weren't sweating too much. "So nice to make your acquaintance," she added.

He eyed her a bit warily. "Euphemia?" he asked. "That's kind of an unusual name, isn't it?"

Was it? Ruby wondered. She'd figured everyone in the upper echelons of society had such names. Maybe she could have done this a little better, if she'd had more prep time. She scrambled for something more acceptable. "Well, ah, everyone calls me, um, Babs."

Now he really eyed her warily. "Babs?" he asked.

She nodded vigorously and was somehow able to look him in the eye when she repeated, "Yes, Babs."

"How do you get 'Babs' from Euphemia?"

"It's, um, a long story."

"We have a long cruise ahead of us."

She laughed, hoping to sound carefree, but fearing she came off sounding, oh . . . horrified instead. "Not that long we don't," she told him.

"But—"

"Now if you'll excuse me," she hurried on, thinking now was as good a time as any to start that low-profile thing, and wondering if maybe there was an empty apple barrel on board someplace where she could hide—hey, it had worked for Jim Hawkins. "I really do have to go."

And before Mr. Keaton Hamilton Danning III had a chance to object, Ruby spun around and began to walk away. Unfortunately, she forgot that she was still grasping his hand—or perhaps it was that he was still grasping hers—so she didn't get far. In fact, she'd completed only one step when he tugged her back toward him, with just enough force to make her lose her balance and go toppling toward him. The good news was, she didn't spill her drink on his shirt and jacket this time. The bad news was that that was because it went crashing to the floor between them instead.

Well, shoot. What a waste of good champagne, Ruby thought as she continued to topple. Not to mention she was reasonably certain that hadn't been Anchor Hocking glassware holding it. Not to mention those looked like *very* expensive shoes Keaton Hamilton Danning III was wearing.

The worst news, though, was that when she toppled toward him, she just kept toppling until there was no more *toward*, and plenty of *against*. For one long moment, all she could do was stand with her body pressed flush to his, her free hand splayed open over his chest, her mouth scant inches from his own when she glanced up to gauge his reaction.

Vaguely she noticed again that his eyes were a marvelous deep green, that his mouth was quite sexy, and that his heartbeat beneath her fingertips accelerated wildly when she looked at him. Vaguely she noted that his breathing was a bit irregular, and that her own was none too steady. Vaguely she realized that, instead of pushing herself away from him and righting herself and making some lame excuse like "I meant to do that," she was curling her fingers more intimately into the fabric of his shirt, and pushing her body closer to his, even though they were already about as close as two people could be without being arrested for public indecency.

And vaguely she decided that she would much rather do the indecency thing with him in private.

"Oh," she said softly when she realized that the avenue of her thoughts had suddenly become the main thoroughfare through the red light district.

Hastily she pushed herself away from him and righted herself, but she couldn't quite bring herself to say, "I meant to do that." For some reason her subconscious wouldn't let her. Probably, she thought, because her subconscious didn't want anyone to know that it had planned the action all along.

And her, ah . . . undisciplined . . . subconscious wouldn't let her release Keaton right away, either. Instead Ruby continued to curl her fingers into the fabric of his shirt, as if she had every intention of . . . of . . . of . . . Good heavens, she thought. As if she had every intention of ripping the garment wide and pushing it from his shoulders, then leaning in to press her open mouth against his naked chest, tasting the damp, salty skin beneath, licking away the beads of moisture, pushing her curved fingers into the ripples of musculature beneath, then driving her hand downward, toward the waistband of his trousers, freeing the button with deft, swift fingers and then—

Ahem.

At any rate, Ruby's thoughts rather got away from her. But she couldn't help herself. Her subconscious made her do it.

Somehow, though, she forced herself to turn loose of Keaton's shirt, and she tried to ignore the flicker of heat in his eyes that had amplified into a conflagration the longer she'd held on to him. Hastily, to take her mind off of Keaton and his hot green eyes, she stooped to pick up the broken pieces of glass at her feet, because that was what she always did whenever a drink went down at Frank's Funny Business. It was second nature to Ruby—once she got her mind off tasting damp, naked skin, anyway.

She realized right away, however, that she shouldn't have reacted the way she did. Not just because it *wouldn't* be second nature to Euphemia Philippa Wemberly-Stokes, but because this new position put Ruby in a pose that was in no way, um, socially redeeming. On one's knees in front of a strange man was a position that might make a woman twenty bucks, but it *didn't* make a good impression. Everyone in the lounge seemed to agree with that assessment, too, Ruby noted when she looked around. As did Keaton, she noted further when she looked up.

His jaw clenched, he lowered his hand in a silent indication that she should take it. So Ruby did. Then he pulled her to her feet, signaled wordlessly to a waiter to clean up her mess, fetched her a new glass of champagne from another waiter, steered her away from the spilled champagne, and proceeded to pretend that the last several minutes of his life had never happened.

Ruby had to concede that his was an excellent idea. So she stood, thanked the waiter for cleaning up her mess, sipped her new glass of champagne, followed Keaton, and pretended that the last several minutes of her life hadn't happened, either.

Still, she couldn't quite keep herself from gazing into his deep, fathomless green eyes. And as she did, she felt herself being pulled lower still into those emerald depths, drowning really, in what felt like some hot, wet, wanton sort of whirlpool that just kept spinning her around and around, going deeper and deeper. And gosh, he really did have *the* most gorgeous eyes, and his smile was nice, too, and his chest had felt so warm and firm beneath her fingertips, and he really did have a nice body all around, and . . . and . . . and . . .

And what was it they had been talking about a few minutes ago? she wondered as she felt herself wanting to take a step forward and press her body intimately to his again, forgetting, momentarily, that that was what had caused her—most recent—problem to begin with. Almost immediately she remembered that, oh, yeah, they'd been talking about how she needed to be going. Yep, that was it. Going fast, too, if she had any hope of saving herself from further humiliation and certain drowning.

"Well . . . thanks," she said impulsively, offering him a brief toast with her glass. "But now I really do have to go."

Instead of moving out of her way, however, Keaton took a step to the left to match the one she took to the right. Then, when she took a step to the left, he moved right. Call her crazy, but either he was trying to prevent her from leaving or he wanted to mambo with her. In any event, she tried not to interpret his action as a romantic overture. Because it really was much too early in their relationship for that. Not too early for kneeling before him in a suggestive position, of course. But way too early for romance.

Ruby made herself stop mamboing with him long enough to meet his gaze, but then she felt herself being drawn back into that hot, wet whirlpool again. As a result, she had no idea what to say, so she was left with standing there staring at him, which made her feel woozy and lightheaded . . . and very, very hot.

Evidently, though, Keaton seemed not to share her problem. Because he immediately asked, "Go where, Miss Wemberly-Stokes? It may have escaped your notice, but we are currently under way on a boat, and there's no place to go until we reach our destination."

Oh, that hadn't escaped Ruby's notice *at all.* "Ah, I know," she said. "But I think I need some fresh air, that's all."

Keaton nodded agreeably. "You know, I think I could use a breath or two myself," he said. "I'll join you."

Great, Ruby thought morosely. "Great," she said brightly.

He helped her cut a swath through the crowd—and truly, cutting a swath through a crowd was something Ruby had always aspired to do—and opened the door to the lounge for her when they reached it. Then he smiled and swept his arm forward, silently indicating she should precede him, and looking unbearably handsome as he did so.

Such a gentleman, she thought. But then, what had she expected from someone with a name like Keaton Hamilton Danning III? She took a moment to curse the fates that she would finally meet a man like him, only to have it be under less than ideal circumstances. Circumstances like, she was illicitly aboard the yacht where he worked, she had spilled her club soda all over him, she had intimated she thought he was gay, and she had positioned herself to perform an act on him which would cost him at least twenty bucks on the street.

Oh, and also like she would be obligated from here on out to lie to him repeatedly, she had given him a phony name, and she needed to ditch him at the earliest possible opportunity. But if it hadn't been for all those things, he might just be a potential boyfriend.

Outside, the night wasn't quite as humid and uncomfortable as it had been in Miami Beach, thanks to the fresh ocean breeze that immediately encircled them. Nor was the air tinted with the scents of exhaust fumes and rotting waste in the gutters, which were the smells that always hit Ruby first when she left Frank's at night—and also when she awoke in the morning, because she lived in a tiny South Beach apartment a few blocks from work, one that faced the alley behind the building. So, actually, now that she thought about it, Ruby's whole existence in Miami Beach was tinted with the scents of exhaust fumes and rotting waste. Funny how she was worried about getting back to all that.

Outside on deck, however, even though the yacht hadn't quite cleared Biscayne Bay, the air was touched with the aroma of dark night, broiled shrimp, and the fresh, salty scent of the sea. Oh, all right, and there was just a hint of exhaust fumes, too. But they were coming from a luxury yacht instead of a metro bus, so they were considerably easier to tolerate.

The sky above was black and limitless, spattered with stars like diamonds on velvet, and the Miami Beach skyline looked like a bejeweled fortress rising against that vast darkness. From a distance, the city seemed fantastical and magical. Would that it seemed that way up close, too, she thought sadly.

Ruby had left home when she was eighteen years old because she had wanted to be a star. Well, that, and because no one in Appalachimahoochee had much wanted to keep her around. But eight years later, here she was, still living in Florida and working as a waitress. She hadn't come close to seeing her dreams of stardom become reality. Nor, come to think of it, did anyone much want to keep her around. Gee. She supposed some things really didn't ever change.

She hadn't even made it to Hollywood, which was where she had told herself she needed to go to become a star. But when she'd said, "Happy trails" to the Happy Trails Trailer Park, she hadn't had enough money to go across country to California, so she'd taken off for Miami instead. Hey, they filmed things in Miami, she'd told herself. They did. Lots of things. And the acting competition was way, *way* less fierce than it would have been in LA.

But shortly after Ruby had arrived in Miami she'd discovered that the acting opportunities were way, way less than they would have been in LA, too. By then, though, she hadn't had enough money to get back home. Not that she had wanted to go home, really. Not that Appalachimahoochee had ever felt like home to her in the first place. There had been even less for her there than there was in Miami.

So she'd stayed. And although one or two opportunities of the acting persuasion had come her way—mostly in the form of badly sung singing telegrams and badly dressed stage dressing—she had yet to land a significant part in anything.

Instead she had spent the bulk of the last eight years doing anything *but* acting. Like working in boutiques. Like tending bar. Like waiting tables at Frank's Funny Business, where she'd used most of her time over the last ten months begging and pleading and cajoling Frank Tedescucci to win the eight minutes on stage she'd had tonight.

And look how that had turned out. Just like everything else in her life had turned out. Not at all the way she'd planned.

She glanced over at Keaton Hamilton Danning III and wondered who his employer was, and what, precisely, he did on this yacht. Had he left home at an early age, too, in the hopes of following a dream? Despite his name—which might very well be as phony as the one she'd given him, Ruby thought, because who had a name like that, really?—had he come from meager beginnings and striven to become something more, something real, only to see his dreams dashed? Was he doing little more than going about the motions of life these days because he just didn't know what else to do? Did he feel as lost and disoriented as she found herself feeling these days?

She noticed then that she was still carrying the slim flute of champagne he had pressed upon her, and she lifted

it to her lips for an idle sip. She'd had champagne only a
few times in her life, mostly at friends' weddings, but it
hadn't tasted quite like this. She wasn't sure if that was because the quality of this champagne was better, or if the
luxuriousness of her surroundings enhanced the flavor, or
if the company she was keeping might have something to
do with it. Ultimately she decided it was a bit of all three.
And she wondered again why she was so worried about
getting home.

Keaton led her toward the back part of the boat, where
several couples had retreated to enjoy the night. Some
were in the large Jacuzzi, laughing and splashing one another. Some were seated at a dimly lit bar, enjoying a
drink and one another's company. Some of them were
standing very close together along the rail—some were
even entwined, Ruby couldn't help noticing—their heads
bent close in intimate conversation.

Keaton came to a stop at the rail, too, though well away
from the nearest couple, something for which Ruby was
thankful, seeing as how that couple was one of the entwined ones. Very entwined. So entwined, in fact, that she
couldn't quite make out where one person ended and the
other began. And speaking of making out, that was what
the two of them were, in fact, doing. Making out, and
making . . . Hmmm . . . Making what sounded like animal noises.

Keaton seemed to notice that, too, because he didn't
stay long at that first spot, and instead ventured to the opposite side of the boat, where he found another empty spot
well away from another couple who were, uh, involved in
some nautical exploration. Or at least naughty exploration. At any rate he was clearly trying to ignore them as
he leaned against the rail with his back to them. Ruby
made sure she continued on for a step or two beyond

Keaton before striking a pose similar to his own. He smiled at the way she had left so much distance between them, and suddenly she wished she hadn't.

Until he said, "So, Miss Wemberly-Stokes," and she remembered that she had been lying to him from the get-go, and she shouldn't have stopped at a few steps, should have just kept on walking until she went over the side of the boat. "Or may I call you Babs?" he asked further.

Gazing into his kudzu eyes, and thinking she'd never seen lashes quite that thick on a man before, and deciding she must be falling under some kind of odd kudzu mojo because something warm and fizzy chose that moment to go whizzing throughout her entire body, she said, "Hmmm?"

He gazed back at her in silence for a moment, and for that moment, Ruby thought he might be experiencing the same kind of warm, fizzy whizzing that she was experiencing herself. Because his voice sounded kind of funny when he said, "Babs. May I call you Babs?"

She nodded. At this point he could have called her Poopoo Head and she would have called him sweetheart in return. "Uh-huh," she told him. "You can call me . . . that."

"So. Babs," he began. "Tell me about yourself. Babs."

Ruby enjoyed the odd sensation of floating for a moment longer, then, with a quick shake of her head, forced herself back down to earth. "Oh, gosh," she said. "What's there to tell?"

He shrugged. "I don't know. Babs. That's why I'm asking. Babs."

Gee, something about the way he kept saying "Babs" made Ruby think he might not have believed her when she'd told him that was her name. Hmmm . . .

"I, ah . . . I'm an actress," she told him. Which was entirely the truth, because if this wasn't a People's Choice Award–winning performance she was giving right now, then she didn't know what was. "In fact, I just came here from the theater." And that wasn't too far a stretch, either, Ruby thought. You could consider Frank's Funny Business a theater. Sort of. After having a few drinks. Or ten. Hey, it had a stage.

"An actress," Keaton repeated. Doubtfully, too, if she wasn't mistaken.

"Mm-hm," she assured him. Less than assuringly, she couldn't help noticing.

"I see. Babs. Interestingly—Babs—I'm not familiar with the work of Euphemia Philippa Wemberly-Strokes."

"Stokes," Ruby quickly corrected him. "Euphemia Philippa Wemberly-*Stokes*."

"Right. Babs. Of course. Babs."

"That's because I use a professional name when I work."

He arched his dark brows in silent query. So Ruby responded by arching her dark brows in silent query, too.

"And your professional name would be . . . ?" he asked.

"Oh," she replied. "Oh, that." But she said nothing further. Mainly because she had no idea what to say. Hey, she'd already come up with one good name tonight. She didn't want to push her luck.

"Yes, that. Babs," Keaton said when he realized she wasn't going to elaborate. "What's your professional name? Babs."

"Rita," she told him off the top of her head. "Rita, ah . . . Moreno." Then she groaned inwardly.

"Now I have heard of Rita Moreno," Keaton said. "But I was under the impression that she was a bit . . . older than you? Babs?"

"That's a different Rita Moreno," Ruby said.

"I see. Doesn't the Screen Actors Guild sort of frown on two actresses with the same name? Babs?"

Ruby nodded. "They do indeed. Which could be what's hindering my progress on the road to superstardom, now that I think about it. But I only gave you part of my name. I actually go by Rita Q. Moreno."

"Rita Q. Moreno?"

She nodded. "Like Michael J. Fox. He put that J. in there because there was already an actor named Michael Fox."

"Yes, but it's my understanding that Michael J. Fox's real name is, in fact, Michael Fox."

"I believe you're right."

"Then why did you choose Rita Moreno?"

"Rita Q. Moreno," Ruby corrected him.

He nodded impatiently. "So why did you choose Rita Q. Moreno, when you could have chosen something else?"

"I thought it was catchy," she told him.

"Catchy," he repeated.

"And pretty."

"Pretty."

"And memorable."

He seemed to give the matter some consideration. "I see," he finally said. "I'm sorry, but I'm still not familiar with your work."

"Well, no, of course not," she told him. "You were obviously only visiting Miami. But I assure you, I'm very popular here. On the fringes," she added, just to be on the safe side.

"The fringes?" he asked.

"The fringes," she confirmed.

"What fringes?"

"Only the best fringes, I assure you."

He studied her in silence for a moment more, then, "I see," he said again.

Somehow, though, Ruby suspected he really didn't, and was only trying to be polite.

Had he said the cruise would be a long one? she wondered. She glanced down at the slim gold-tone watch encircling her wrist. How long could it take to get to Nassau? she wondered. Fifteen hours? Sixteen? Okay, so, at the most, she only had fifteen hours and forty-six minutes left. She could do this, she told herself. She could.

If only she could find an apple barrel to hide in.

Chapter 4

*K*eaton eyed Euphemia Philippa Wemberly-Stokes, AKA Babs, AKA Rita Q. Moreno, and wondered what kind of an idiot she thought he was. A very stupid one, obviously. Not that there was a lot to be said for being an intelligent idiot, he reminded himself. Still, she must think him utterly void of gray matter to be feeding him all this— At this rate he was going to be so full of— Actually, it was she who was so full of— Well, anyway, at this rate *both* of them were going to be too full for Kurt's midnight buffet. And rumor had it that the *Pflaumenkuchen* was unusually good tonight.

He wondered who Euphemia/Babs/Rita Q. really was and why she was lying so flagrantly to him. Was she indeed one of Reynaldo's stray bimbos, fearful of repercussions from the countess or any number of other women aboard? Or was she simply one of Reynaldo's guests who was trying to give Keaton the brush-off as politely as possible and just not doing a very good job of it? In which case he should just leave her alone and be on his merry way.

Granted, women did usually enjoy his company, but there was the odd one—and by God, she must be odd if she didn't want his company, right?—who would just as soon he leave her alone. Maybe Euphemia/Babs/Rita Q. just wasn't interested in continuing with this conversation and was hoping to let Keaton down easily. Or maybe she was just—

Oh, God. It hit Keaton then like a ton of *beschissen Pflaumenkuchen.* What if she was that most deadly of creatures, one of those vicious, malicious, poisonous monsters hired by others for the sole purpose of committing mayhem and carnage and devastation? What if she was one of those malignant fiends who made a career out of killing and maiming and exterminating? What if she was being paid by a higher political power to take Reynaldo *down*? What if she was, no, not an assassin, but something far, far more heinous. What if she was—gasp— —*a tabloid journalist*?

Was it possible? Keaton wondered. Could this dazzling, tempting woman actually be a menacing reporter? A sinister correspondent? A putrid freelancer? Had she come aboard looking to do a story on Reynaldo? They'd had some trouble with that almost every time they'd put into port on this trip. Yes, Reynaldo might be a man without a country these days, but he was by no means a man without an audience. As a result, he was still hounded by the paparazzi wherever he went, to the point of being harassed. Too often the correspondents were just flat-out mean, with a total disregard for anything other than their own interests.

That must be it, Keaton thought. It was the only thing

that explained her nervousness, and her unfamiliarity with the situation, and her unwillingness to be honest with him. Euphemia/Babs/Rita Q. was after a story. She had probably slipped aboard in Miami—whether invited or not—to dig up some dirt on Reynaldo. Which, of course, wouldn't be hard to do, because Reynaldo's entire lifestyle was filthy. He thrived in the mud. Ask anyone. Forget about fame. What the prince lived for was infamy.

A story for the tabloids. That had to be why Babs was aboard. It was either that, Keaton thought with an internal chuckle, or she really was an assassin. The real kind of assassin, not the tabloid journalist kind. The kind who carried around an aluminum attaché case and wore wraparound sunglasses and went by code name: The Badger or something. As ridiculous as it sounded, there were still a handful of fascist hard-liners on Pelagia who wouldn't mind seeing Reynaldo dead, even if he had given up the throne. Rumor had it that there was, in fact, still a price on his head, though certainly that rumor had never been verified.

Keaton's inward chuckle became an inward laugh as he considered the idea of Euphemia/Babs/Rita Q. packing a piece and gunning for Reynaldo. Until he looked at Euphemia/Babs/Rita Q. again, and saw how she was scoping out the layout of the yacht. Nah, he immediately countered himself. There was no way. She was too luscious. And too . . . unpolished. And too clumsy, too. And much too bad about drawing attention to herself, giving out names like Rita Q. Moreno—not that The Badger would have been any more convincing—and spilling her drinks into the laps of those closest to Reynaldo, and positioning herself in a way that would cost Keaton at least twenty bucks from a woman on the street. Plus she couldn't possibly be hiding a high-powered rifle under that dress. Not with scope and silencer, too.

Unless, of course, she was planning to give Reynaldo a lethal injection when he wasn't looking, Keaton thought further. That purse she was carrying was just about the right size for a hypodermic needle—and little else.

Oh, stop it, he admonished himself. *You're getting delirious*. Too much salt air, he thought. Clearly it was drying his brain.

The tabloid journalist, though . . . That was certainly well inside the realm of possibility. And really, when all was said and done, the paparazzi and assassins were pretty much on the same social level, pond scum–wise. And neither was welcome aboard *Mad Tryst*.

"Okay, look," he said to the woman—whoever, whatever she was. "Let's just cut to the chase, all right? Who are you, and what are you doing on board?"

Her storm-cloud eyes widened in surprise at his frankness, her mouth dropped open, and her lips pursed a bit to form an almost perfect little O. And something about seeing her lips do that made Keaton want to lean forward and cover her mouth with his own little O, just to see what she tasted like. Again and again and again.

Ooo, not good, Danning, he told himself. *No sleeping with the enemy, understand*? Then again, when he looked at her, or, more precisely, when he looked at her mouth, sleeping was pretty much the last thing on his mind.

"I-I-I . . . I don't know what you're talking about," she said. "I told you who I am."

"But you didn't tell me what you're doing on board," he pointed out, ignoring, for now, the fact that she was lying about that first part. Somehow the second part seemed far more important at the moment.

"I-I-I . . ." She held up her glass. "I'm enjoying the party. To which I was invited," she added meaningfully.

"Then you won't mind showing me your invitation, will you?" Keaton asked. "I'm sort of in charge of making sure this party goes off smoothly. I hope you'll understand. And I just don't recall sending an invitation to a Euphemia Philippa Wemberly-Stokes. Or to a Babs Wemberly-Stokes, for that matter," he added when he saw her open her mouth to take exception. "Or to Rita Q. Moreno, either," he concluded, before she had a chance to stall in that direction, as well.

Keaton was bluffing, naturally. Reynaldo never sent out invitations to his parties. It was all performed by word of mouth—along with a few other body parts when it came to potential female guests. Well, by word of mouth—and other body parts—and a nod to the bouncer manning the companionway when guests started to arrive. If Reynaldo liked the looks of whoever wanted on board, he nodded to whoever was in charge of the door. When Reynaldo didn't like their looks, a shake of the head would keep the person off. Obviously Reynaldo had liked Babs's looks. Then again, that didn't surprise Keaton at all. He liked Babs's looks, too. A lot.

She studied him in unmistakable terror for a moment, then cleared her throat. Then she cleared it again. And again. And again. "I, ah . . ." she finally began. "I didn't bring my invitation with me," she told him. "It, um, it wouldn't fit in my purse." She held up the accessory in question for his inspection. "Perhaps you've noticed that it's roughly the size of an electron."

Or a hypodermic needle, Keaton thought. Or one of those little tape recorders that would be just perfect for a tabloid journalist. "But you did receive an invitation, right?" he said.

She nodded vigorously. "Of course I received an invitation."

Now Keaton was the one to nod. Though not vigorously. "Funny," he said, "but the host didn't send out any invitations for this party. So it surprises me that you received one."

She opened her mouth to comment, but all that emerged was a single, humorless chuckle, and something that sounded like "Ah . . . ah . . . ah . . ."

"Do you even know the host's name?" Keaton asked further.

"Of course I do," she said, clearly panicking. "It's, um . . . Well, he *told* me his name was, um, Bob. But I sort of thought he was misleading me." She sounded just a tad bitter when she added, "Then again, men so often neglect to give their real names to women. Funny, that."

"Isn't it though?" Keaton said. "You women would never do that, would you? Give a man a phony name, I mean."

She swallowed with some difficulty. "Never," she told him. "I'd never do that."

"I see. Well then. Babs. Perhaps I should take you to, um, *Bob*, and we'll see if he remembers inviting you. Babs."

And before she could escape, Keaton took her elbow gently—but firmly—in his own and began to lead her away.

Countess Arabella Magdalena Sophia Victoria Genevieve Eugenie Wilhelm of Toulaine watched the byplay between Keaton and the stowaway with much interest. From her vantage point on the deck above them, she decided that this was, without question, the most entertaining thing that had happened since she had been dragged aboard *Imperial Majesty*—she did not care what Reynaldo was calling the royal yacht these days; it was and always would be *Imperial Majesty* to her—and forcing her to become a part of this excruciatingly embarrassing cruise.

She still could not understand why Reynaldo had even bothered to bring her along on this ship of fools when Pelagia fell to those rabble-rousers a year ago. Now that he was no longer in line to become king, he was no longer obliged to continue with the engagement that his parents had arranged with hers two decades ago, when Arabella was not even three years old.

And it was not as though he had ever cared one whit for her anyway. Of course she had never cared one whit for him, either—how could she care for him when she barely knew him?—even though she had been fully prepared to go through with the marriage. What else could she do? Her parents had promised his. She had no choice in the matter.

She knew that many people—people not of her or Reynaldo's countries—considered arranged marriages to be archaic and unnecessary, even foolish, in this day and age. But the countries of Pelagia and Toulaine were steeped in traditions that were hundreds of, perhaps even a thousand, years old. And particularly where the royal families were concerned, those traditions might as well have been engraved on stone tablets and presented by a burning bush. There were political and economic considerations, as well, though granted, those considerations were not so considerable as they had been twenty years ago, especially now that Reynaldo had been dethroned.

But Arabella still intended to honor her obligation to marry him, whether he became king or not. Because Countess Arabella Magdalena Sophia Victoria Genevieve

Eugenie Wilhelm of Toulaine was, above all, an honorable woman. And she also intended to honor that obligation because Reynaldo refused to dissolve their engagement, no matter how many times she had asked him to. He would return to Pelagia to be king one day, he insisted. And he, too, would honor all his obligations, including the one that required him to marry the Countess Arabella of Toulaine. What else could he do? His parents had promised hers. He had no choice in the matter.

Besides, what else was there for either of them? They had each spent their entire lives being groomed for their positions. And, at least early on, Arabella had not objected to the union. Although she did not meet her intended face-to-face until she was thirteen, she had learned enough about him and his family and his background to fall girlishly in love from the start. And when she had made that first trip to Pelagia, she had seen how handsome and regal the young prince was, and had fallen in love with him all over again. Of course, they had not been allowed to see more of each other than on superficial, well chaperoned occasions, but what little Arabella had seen of Reynaldo then, she had liked very much. She had never objected to marrying him.

Now, however . . .

Well, she would not think about *now*, she told herself. Just as she had not allowed herself to think about *now* for more than a year. Because thinking about *now* made her feel things she knew she should not feel. She was a Wilhelm, born to privilege and wealth and spotless reputation. And people born to privilege and wealth and spotless reputation, she knew—because she had been told so again and again, since she was a child—had certain obligations. And one of her obligations was to marry Reynaldo. Just as one of his obligations was to marry her.

Then again, she reminded herself when she recalled the night that they had fled Pelagia, it had been Keaton, not Reynaldo, who had awakened her and told her they must leave immediately. Reynaldo had no doubt forgotten all about his fiancée, sleeping in an entirely separate wing from the one he occupied at the palace—their wedding was not to have taken place for several weeks. It would have been unseemly for them to share quarters before then—not to mention illegal, because the future queen of Pelagia must, by law, be a virgin. No, Reynaldo had come aboard *Imperial Majesty* that fateful night with Supermoron Dacia, he wearing nothing but his silk pajama bottoms, and she wearing nothing but his silk pajama tops.

Oh, yes. Quite the devoted husband-to-be had Reynaldo been during her time on Pelagia. And he had only become more devoted over the last year during his exile. Devoted to Superninny Dacia, at any rate. He scarcely paid Arabella the time of day.

And Arabella had passed her time of day pretending she did not mind, pretending that everything was just fine. She did not know any other way to react to the parody her life had become. She had spent every single day of that life being groomed to become Reynaldo's wife and Queen Arabella of Pelagia. And rule number one of being Reynaldo's wife—and queen of Pelagia—was that she never, ever took exception to what her husband did. Even if it meant he humiliated and hurt and ignored her.

Truly, though, Arabella could have tolerated it, except that his treatment had made her a pariah on this boat. No one wanted to be around her, because everyone felt awkward and never knew what to say. They all knew that Reynaldo was about as faithful as a pig. Actually, come to think of it, pigs were infinitely more faithful than Reynaldo. Would that she were engaged to a pig, her life would be much, much brighter.

She watched Keaton and the stowaway on the deck below, cocking her head in an effort to better hear their conversation. The wind was in her favor, and she caught the occasional sentence or two. Mostly, though, it was the expression on the young woman's face that allowed Arabella to know she was in trouble. She had been watching from the upper deck when the woman came aboard, had seen her being mistreated by a deceptively handsome man on the pier who had clearly not had her best interests in mind. The two women had something in common, Arabella had realized then. Both of them were involved with . . . oh, what was that enchanting American word women used for such men? she wondered, searching her brain. Ah, yes. *Scum.* That was what it was. She and the stowaway were both involved with scum.

It was as good a reason for sympathizing with someone as any, Arabella thought.

Truly, she probably should have said something to someone when she had seen the woman sneak aboard, but the woman had obviously been harmless and in trouble, and the intrigue of the situation had appealed to Arabella. It had been such a boring, lonely cruise until now. What she needed, she thought, was an ally, someone who would understand what it was like to be associated with scum.

Poor thing, she thought as she gazed down at the lower deck, watching the young woman begin to flounder. She clearly needed help very badly. And if there was one thing Arabella had been trained to do since birth, it was to see to the needs of poor, unfortunate people who would some-day become her subjects.

Making her decision, she turned and made her way toward the companionway.

Ruby had pretty much given up hope of deceiving Keaton Hamilton Danning III, and was about to tell him truthfully what she was doing on board the yacht—and was hoping like hell he wouldn't throw her overboard when she did. But she was prevented from doing so by the appearance of a young, slim, blond woman who gave off the aura of a czarina, a woman whose very presence somehow demanded reverent silence. Ruby was simply struck dumb. So majestic was the woman's entrance, in fact, that Keaton himself released Ruby and straightened, then dipped his head forward in acknowledgment, as if the woman in question were a queen.

She did give the impression of royalty, Ruby thought, in spite of her youth. In fact she looked much like a young Grace Kelly, with her pale tresses wound up the back of her head in an elegant French twist, her bright blue eyes, and her classic cocktail ensemble of a simple, powder blue sheath and bolero jacket, fashioned of some shimmery fabric that gave off a silver sheen in the moonlight. A strand of pearls encircled her throat, and a pair of the luminous little perfections dotted her ears. When the woman lifted a hand to brush back a stray strand of windswept gold, Ruby noted that even her hands were elegant—gracefully manicured with perfectly lacquered pink ovals at the end of each finger. She wore only one ring, on the ring finger of her left hand, a gargantuan emerald swimming in diamond baguettes.

She approached Keaton, her bearing regal and her smile knowing, but her eyes twinkled almost mischievously. "Good evening, Keaton," she said in as lyrical a voice as Ruby had ever heard.

"Good evening, Countess," he replied formally, dipping his head in that reverent way again.

Countess? Ruby thought. *Countess?* Holy cow. Just whose yacht had she wandered onto?

"It is a beautiful evening, is it not?" the woman asked further. "The air is quite lovely here. Much warmer than at home." Ruby noticed then that the countess had an accent, though none that was readily recognizable. To Ruby's admittedly untrained ear she sounded as if she were from some Eastern European country, maybe even Russia—did they still have countesses there?—though her looks were decidedly Scandinavian.

Much to Ruby's surprise, the woman turned to her and smiled very warmly, as if she were delighted to find Ruby on board. Then she strode forward and took Ruby's hand in her own, grasping it with much affection. "And how are you, my darling? Are you enjoying the cruise?"

"Uh, yeah," Ruby said, puzzled by her familiarity. "I mean, yes. Yes, I'm enjoying it very much."

"You are having none of the *mal de mer* that used to bother you when we were children?"

Ruby's eyes widened in surprise. Just what was the countess up to? "I . . . ah . . ." she began. But she had no idea what to say. Not just because she was totally confused by the other woman's behavior, but because she wasn't completely sure what *mal de mer* was. Was it any relation to *fruit de mer*? They'd had that at one of the restaurants where Ruby used to wait tables.

"You do appear to be a bit pale," the other woman said with much concern. Then she glanced at the champagne flute in Ruby's other hand and uttered a soft *tsk*. "Well, it is no wonder. You know you are not supposed to be indulging. Not in your condition."

"Her condition?" Keaton echoed.

But the countess only lifted her elegant hand to her elegant mouth and blushed elegantly. "Oh. I was not supposed to say anything to anybody yet." She dipped her head conspiratorially toward Ruby's. "I am sorry. I will not say another word. But come. Perhaps you should lie down in our cabin for a little while. Until you feel better."

Ruby opened her mouth to speak, but still honestly had no idea what to say. Who was this woman, and why was she lying on Ruby's behalf? Should Ruby play along, or should she admit that she had no idea what the other woman was talking about? Since the other woman was a countess, if Ruby spoiled whatever game this was, would *she* throw Ruby in the brig? Was the other woman even sane? Would it be detrimental to her mental health if Ruby *didn't* play along?

Keaton seemed to be thinking along the same lines—though maybe not the mental health part, because he probably knew the state of the woman's mind . . . maybe—because he turned to face the countess fully then, something that caused him to turn his back completely on Ruby. "You two know each other?" he asked the other woman. Very skeptically, too, if Ruby wasn't mistaken.

"Of course we know each other," the countess said. "We have known each other since we were children. She is on *Imperial Majesty* as my guest."

"Then who is she?" he demanded.

"She is my friend Tatiana."

From her place behind Keaton, Ruby shook her head fiercely and opened her eyes wide at the countess, trying to alert her that she should *not* pursue this line of conversation. Then, to emphasize the point, Ruby slashed her index finger across her throat in the cinematic signal for "knock it off," hoping that might work. But the young woman only narrowed her eyes in confusion, clearly having no idea what Ruby's efforts meant. And when Keaton spun around to see what the countess was reacting to, he caught Ruby in mid-slash, so she immediately stopped the motion of her hand, quickly turning it so that she was raking three fingertips lightly across her throat.

"I, ah, I think I felt a raindrop," she said.

Keaton looked up at the—very clear—sky, then back at Ruby. "Oh," he said.

Then he turned his attention back to the countess. Ruby couldn't see his face, but she would have bet good money he was eyeing the woman suspiciously. Or else eyeing her as if she'd lost her mind. Certainly Ruby was suspicious of the woman, thinking perhaps she'd lost her mind. Not that she didn't appreciate the woman's intervening on her behalf. She just had no idea why she would want to bail out a perfect stranger, not even knowing the particulars of said stranger's situation. Not unless she'd, you know, lost her mind.

"She told me her name was Euphemia," Keaton said.

The countess glanced quickly at Ruby, then back at Keaton. "That is what I said. Euphemia," she stated in no uncertain terms.

"You said Tatiana," Keaton insisted.

"No I did not," the woman said.

"Yes, you did."

"No, I did not."

"You did."

"I did not."

He began to object again, but the woman cut him off with a very chilly look. "Are you calling me a liar, Keaton?" she said coolly.

Ruby could see his entire body go stiff, and she noticed

that his hand curled into a loose fist at his side. Clearly he didn't enjoy being challenged. But whoever this woman was, he deferred to her immediately.

"No, of course I'm not suggesting that," he said.

"Good." The woman squared her shoulders and lifted her chin in what looked to Ruby like a very queenly fashion. "What I meant was that Tatiana is her middle name, of course."

Again Ruby shook her head, again she made the slashing motion across her throat, again the woman gazed at her in confusion, and again Keaton spun around to see what was going on.

"Ah . . . another raindrop," Ruby said as she again turned her hand against her throat.

This time Keaton didn't even try to hide his skepticism. Instead he only turned back to the woman and said, "She told me her middle name was Philippa."

The woman laughed musically. "No, no, no. That is just what she tells people. It is a little joke for her, you see."

"A very little joke," Keaton muttered.

"Besides," the countess continued quickly, "we all call her by her nickname, of course."

"Babs?" Keaton asked.

"No, not Babs," the countess said. "How does one get Babs from Euphemia? And what kind of name is Babs? It is silly. We call her Tutu."

And that wasn't silly? Ruby thought.

"She said her nickname is Babs," Keaton said.

"That is the family nickname," the countess replied easily, having evidently forgotten that she had just dismissed the name as silly. "Her friends call her Tutu," she added.

"Friends don't call friends Tutu," Keaton said.

"Tutu's friends do."

"Tutu needs new friends."

"You can call me Babs," Ruby piped up then.

Keaton opened his mouth, seemed to think better of whatever he had intended to say, and closed it again. Ruby was glad. She wouldn't have believed there was a name worse than Babs. But the countess had managed to find it.

"Actually, I prefer Tutu," the countess said. And something in the young woman's voice warned Ruby that she'd better not argue. Well, that and the fact that she'd just seen the young woman put Keaton Hamilton Danning III in his place. But good.

So Ruby only replied brightly, "Okay." Then, smiling, she added, "And I'll call you by your nickname."

The young woman looked at her in surprise. "My nickname?"

Ruby nodded. "Cha Cha."

She wasn't sure, but she thought the woman smiled at that.

"I've never heard anyone call the Countess Arabella Cha Cha," Keaton said.

Ruby remembered then that she was messing with royalty here and was about to backpedal—and apologize—when the woman said, "Fine." Then she smiled again. "You know how much I have always liked it that you called me Cha Cha. So, Tutu, would you like to go to our cabin for a rest? Or do you think it would make you feel better to join me for a walk?"

"Aaahhh," Ruby began, stringing the comment out over several time zones. Because she still wasn't sure what the rules were of the game they were playing. Mostly because she wasn't even sure of the game itself.

"Kurt has laid out the buffet, if you would like to put

something in your stomach," she added. "Including his fa-mous *Pflaumenkuchen.*"

"Oh, I love *Pflaumenkuchen,*" Ruby said eagerly. "My Grandmother Pearl had the best *Pflaumenkuchen* recipe."

"I remember," the countess said, smiling a secretive little smile. "How is your grandmother, by the way?"

Ruby smiled back. She still had no idea what the two of them were doing, or why, but gosh, she was having a good time. "Grandma Pearl is doing great," she said. "Still working down at the auto parts store and giving Harry over at the Dew Drop Inn a hell of a time about cutting off her Jack Daniel's and Lucky Strikes. But her parole offi-cer said he's seeing real improvement in her attitude. I think that month working on the chain gang really opened her eyes."

The countess smiled. "She was always such a charming woman."

"Now about that *Pflaumenkuchen* . . . ?" Ruby asked.

The countess nodded once and crooked her elegant arm, indicating that Ruby should take it. Strangely, Ruby felt totally comfortable doing so. "Shall we, Tutu?" she said.

"Thanks, Cha Cha," Ruby responded. "I thought you'd never ask."

Chapter 5

*R*uby let the Countess Arabella Cha Cha lead her to wherever the buffet had been laid out, all the while biting her lip—literally—to keep inside all the questions she wanted to ask. Why had the other woman come to her aid with Keaton? How had she known Ruby was floundering in their conversation in the first place? Why was she pretending the two of them not only knew each other, but were childhood friends? Did she honestly think anyone would buy such a story, let alone Keaton, who, even after only one idle conversation, Ruby could see was smarter than the average bear?

For now, though, she said nothing, being at a complete loss as to what she should say. Arabella seemed not to mind, however, because she strode along in silence, too. But the countess seemed to feel none of the awkwardness that had washed over Ruby. Ruby, after all, had never been in the presence of royalty before. Not unless you counted Burger King and Dairy Queen. Then again, maybe being a countess wasn't the same thing as being royal. Maybe being a countess was just being noble. Unless of course being royal and being noble were the same thing. Ruby wasn't really up on her peerage these days. Whatever the hell *peerage* was.

Nevertheless, she was reasonably certain that being a countess *was* the same thing as being rich. Extremely rich. And Ruby had never been around rich people much, either.

Oh, wait a minute. Yes, she had, she recalled. Jimmy Golden was rich, wasn't he? And look how that had turned out. All the more reason to feel awkward right now.

Fortunately their trip was none too long, because, soon enough, Ruby found herself right back in the room where she and Keaton had had their earlier, um, interlude. But where before the lounge had played host to only a handful of couples, now the place was full of people, and the long dining table was laden with more food than Ruby had ever seen in her life.

Actually that wasn't quite true, she amended. She had seen this much food on a few occasions back in Appalachimahoochee, whenever someone got married, had a baby, or died. But the food back home had come from a slightly different socioeconomic background—not to mention a slightly different cholesterol level. Where was the fried chicken so essential to a spread like this? Where were the deviled eggs? Where was the corn pudding? The potato salad? The molded green Jell-O with little chunks of canned pineapple, mini-marshmallows, and mayonnaise?

Oh, well, Ruby thought as she followed Arabella's lead and reached for a plate. She'd just have to make do with the fat, pink shrimps; the succulent lobster tails; the red, ripe raspberries; the six—count 'em, six—different varieties of cheeses; some of those little crackers—they sort of looked like mini-marshmallows—and was that caviar? Red *and* black. She'd never tasted it before. Had to have some of that. And also some of the pâté, because she'd never tasted it before, either. And some of that brown bread. And some of that cold fish thing, whatever it was, because it did look sort of tasty. And blueberries the size of marbles, and those little oranges that had always been so good in the school lunches and would, she was pretty sure, taste even better here. And maybe just a little bit of that—

She glanced up then to find the countess gazing at her as if Ruby were about to say, "Moo." And when Ruby looked down at her plate, she had to concede that there might be a reason for Arabella's reaction. Ruby sort of felt like mooing when she realized she couldn't even find the gold trim around the edge of her plate anymore, so heaping was it with food.

Okay, so maybe she hadn't *quite* followed the other woman's lead. Because Arabella's plate barely held enough food to keep a gerbil alive: carrot sticks, crackers, something that looked suspiciously like cauliflower, and three—count 'em, *three*—blackberries. Then she looked back at her own plate again, and realized she could probably feed a small sovereign nation with what she had there.

"I, uh . . . I'm kind of hungry," she told Arabella in her defense.

"So I see," the countess replied without a bit of censure.

Ruby nodded toward Arabella's plate and asked, "Is that all you're going to eat?"

The countess nodded.

"You're not hungry?"

Arabella gazed wistfully at her plate. "Actually I have not eaten since this afternoon," she said.

Ruby frowned. "Then eat," she said. "Have some of those chocolate-covered strawberries. They look great."

The countess sighed as she gazed at the confection in question. "Yes. They do."

But she didn't reach for any of them. In fact she stepped away from the buffet completely. Ruby shook her head, piled more chocolate strawberries onto her own plate—hey, if the countess didn't want them, she was sure she'd find *some* use for them—and then followed once again in the other woman's wake.

Arabella approached a small bar on the other side of the lounge, then stood in stoic silence until the couple seated there glanced up and saw her. Immediately after the two recognized her, they gathered up their drinks and plates and, with a profusion of bowing and scraping, abandoned their seats entirely. The countess then perched herself comfortably on one of the vacant stools, set her nearly empty plate and nearly full champagne flute on the bar, and bid Ruby to do likewise.

Unbelievable, Ruby thought. What must it be like to go through life getting absolutely everything you wanted, without even having to voice the desire for it?

With a mental shrug she imitated Arabella's motions, seating herself at the other bar stool. Well, maybe not quite *imitating* the countess's motions, because where Arabella had seated herself with much effortless elegance, Ruby had . . . not. Consequently, she found herself tugging awkwardly at the hem of her dress in an effort to push it back down over her thighs, hoping nobody saw. Unfortunately she glanced up in time to find that Keaton Hamilton Danning III had entered the room, and that his gaze had been fixed entirely on her. Or, more specifically, on her thighs.

She did *not* want to know what he was thinking.

Which was just as well, because she saw him frown and turn away, and cut another one of his distinguished swaths through the crowd, toward the buffet.

Not far from her and Arabella, a dark-eyed, dark-haired man played and sang "The Man I Love" at a baby grand piano. Sang it with much feeling, too. But he'd interpreted the lyrics in a way that was, oh, interesting, so what he was really singing about was the, ah, the *Spam* he loved. Still, Ruby found herself fervently believing that someday it would come along, the Spam the piano guy loved, and it would be big and strong, the Spam the piano guy loved, and the piano guy would do whatever it took to make the Spam stay. It was really very touching.

She listened to the song for all of one minute before turning to Arabella. Her curiosity finally getting the better of her, though, Ruby asked, "So why did you do that back there?"

The other woman's elegant blond eyebrows arched elegantly in question. "Why did I turn down the chocolate strawberries? Because I have a wedding gown I must be able to fit into. Eventually."

Ruby's inelegant, dark eyebrows arrowed down inelegantly in confusion. "Hold that thought," she said. "First I want to know why you bailed me out with Keaton Hamilton Danning the third back there on deck."

"Oh, that," Arabella said. She lifted a tiny pretzel to her mouth and nibbled elegantly. "I know that Keaton can be a very formidable person. Especially on first acquaintance. I could see that you wanted to be left alone, but that you could not convince him of that. And I understand how that feeling is, so I stepped in to help you. I assure you, however, that you do not need to be afraid of Keaton. He is a pussycat."

That, Ruby decided, was a matter of opinion. Although

she could certainly see some potential for feline qualities in the man—mostly snarling, hissing, and growling . . . and maybe tearing a woman's clothes, though perhaps she should leave that last one for when they were better acquainted—she couldn't imagine him curled up in a woman's lap purring. As erotically appealing as such an image might be. Especially coupled with the clothes-tearing one. Hmmm . . .

"But why did you help me?" she asked again, shaking off both images. Honestly, as if it weren't already warm enough in there. "You don't know me from Adam," she pointed out. "Or Eve, for that matter. You don't even know what was going on back there. And you're a countess, for criminy's sake, and I most obviously am, uh . . . not," she finished with profound understatement. "We have nothing in common, and we're total strangers. So why did you help me out?" she asked again.

The countess eyed her thoughtfully for a moment. "Actually that is not quite true," she said. "We do indeed have something in common, you and I."

Ruby sincerely doubted it but asked anyway, "What's that?"

"I believe you American women call it man trouble."

Gee, that was kind of a broad statement, Ruby thought. No pun intended. "I don't know what you mean," she said. "We've never met before. How could you know anything about me?"

"I saw you when you came aboard *Imperial Majesty*," Arabella told her.

Ruby eyed her with confusion. "I thought the name of the boat was *Mad Tryst*."

The countess made an elegant fluttering motion with her elegant hand. Damn, she was elegant, Ruby thought.

"Reynaldo has changed the name of the yacht to *Mad Tryst*, but I shall always think of it as *Imperial Majesty*, which is the name with which his father christened it."

"*Imperial Majesty*?" Ruby repeated. "Boy, that's pretty presumptuous. I mean, who did the guy think he was, the king of France?"

"No," Arabella said. "He was the king of Pelagia."

Ruby studied her in silence for a moment, trying to decide if the woman was telling the truth or just pulling her leg. Ultimately deciding that Arabella was far too elegant for something like jerking people around, Ruby only replied, "Oh."

"You have heard of Pelagia, yes?"

Instead of answering that question, Ruby asked one of her own. "I, uh . . . I-I'm on a . . . a king's . . . yacht?" A cool lump settled uncomfortably in the pit of her stomach as she put voice to the question, and she was pretty sure it wasn't from the chocolate-covered strawberries.

"No," Arabella told her.

Oh, thank God, Ruby thought.

"You are on a prince's yacht."

There was another moment of silence from Ruby, then, "Oh," she said again.

"You are familiar with a country called Pelagia?" the countess asked again.

"Well, sorta," Ruby conceded, still feeling a little light-headed. Had she caused an international incident by stowing away on this yacht? she wondered. Was her butt/arse/derrière/*Hintern really* going to land in the slammer/gaol/Bastille/hoosegow once they hit Nassau because of this?

Then an even worse thought struck her. Did princes still have the authority to behead people these days? Or was it just hands they cut off the people who offended them? Either way, it was going to be kind of hard for Ruby to return to work.

"I mean, I'm not into the royalty-watching thing," she continued, her voice sounding a little thin, "but I've seen those 'Reynaldo Watch' minutes on E! Entertainment Television. I really like *True Hollywood Story*," she added by way of, oh, nothing. "The one they did on Lisa Whelchel was riveting."

For some reason Arabella opted not to focus on the last part of Ruby's comment. Instead she said, "If you have seen Reynaldo's minutes, then you know everything the American people know about Pelagia. And about Reynaldo."

"I guess so."

"Which means you know very little."

Ruby shrugged. "I guess that's true, too."

"Well, it is rather a small country," Arabella conceded.

The countess said nothing more for a moment, so Ruby took that moment to . . . well, to panic, actually. Holy cow, she thought. In her effort to escape Jimmy Golden's *Some Abhorrent Evening*, she had landed herself squarely in *The Prince and I*. No, she'd landed herself in *The Beheading Prince and I*. No, *The Beheading*, Behanding *Prince and I*. Could this evening possibly get any more abhorrent?

"So you see," Arabella said, "you and I do have something in common."

Ruby shook her head. "I'm sorry, but I still don't follow you on that."

Arabella sighed elegantly as she reached for her champagne, enjoying an elegant sip. "Before you boarded *Imperial Majesty*," she said, elegantly, too, Ruby couldn't help noticing, "I saw you on the dock with a man. He was a very handsome man, but he was holding you in such a way that I knew you did not like it. That you did not like him. In fact you looked as if you were afraid of him. Much more afraid than you looked with Keaton."

Ruby dropped her gaze to her lap. "It was a different kind of afraid," she said. "But yeah. I was kind of scared of him. Jimmy, I mean. The guy on the dock. Keaton, on the other hand, was . . ." Boy, was that a loaded way to start a sentence, she thought. Keaton was too many things for her to start listing, too many things she couldn't quite define. "I wasn't scared of Keaton like I was Jimmy," she finally said, confident that that, at least, was true. "Anyway, you're pretty observant if you figured out I wanted to get away from Jimmy."

"Yes. I am very observant," Arabella agreed. "And you see, I understood your need for escaping this man. I understood, because I have wanted to escape a man myself. Not a man who frightens me, but a man who offends me greatly. So I said nothing when I saw you steal aboard the yacht. I *wanted* you to escape from that man."

"I, uh, I appreciate it," Ruby told her, not sure what else to say. She wanted to ask about this man that Arabella had wanted to escape in the past, but the other woman's demeanor prohibited such prying. In fact, the other woman's demeanor prohibited a lot of things. In spite of the countess's warmth toward Ruby, there was something distinctly standoffish in her bearing. Of course Ruby supposed that wasn't surprising, all things considered.

"I also said nothing," Arabella continued, "because I am tired of having no one to talk to on this cruise. It is boring. Watching you come aboard was the first interesting thing to happen in many months. I thought it would be entertaining."

Entertaining, Ruby reflected. Wow. What a coincidence. That was exactly what she'd always wanted to be—an entertainer. Somehow, though, this wasn't quite what she'd had in mind. Still, it could work. Maybe. For a little while. Hey, at least until they reached Nassau. She hoped. Unsure what else to add—for now, at any rate— she continued to sample the variety of foods on her plate and let her gaze travel around the lounge.

Boy. Talk about being among the beautiful people. There wasn't a single person on board who wasn't flagrantly attractive. In fact . . .

"Omigosh," Ruby said suddenly, stunned. "Isn't that Supermodel Dacia over there?"

"No," the countess replied immediately, without even glancing in the direction Ruby indicated. "It is not Supermodel Dacia. It is Supernitwit Dacia."

"Oh," Ruby replied with as much equanimity as she could manage. "Well. How about that. Um, who's the guy with her? He's gorgeous. And he looks sort of familiar, but it's hard to tell from his profile."

And also from the way he was sucking on Supermodel Dacia's neck, she couldn't help noting, as well. But she decided it probably wasn't necessary to voice that part of the description. Seeing as how it was so obvious and all. *Jeez, people, get a room!* she wanted to yell. She could practically hear the slurping all the way over here.

"The *guy*," Arabella said, again without turning her attention to anything other than the scant food on her plate, "is my fiancé."

Now Ruby's eyebrows *really* shot down inelegantly. "But . . . but he's nibbling Supermodel Dacia's neck," she objected.

Finally Arabella did turn her head toward the spot Ruby indicated. She surveyed the scene for a moment, her expression completely blank. "Yes, he is, is he not?" she remarked indifferently. "The midnight buffet is seldom enough to satisfy him. Even though he is quite full of other things."

"Aren't you going to do something to stop him?" Ruby asked, thinking it a very good question. "I mean, if he's your fiancé, shouldn't he be nibbling on *your* neck?"

Arabella considered the scene on the other side of the room again, just as dispassionately as she had the first time. "My neck is not to his taste, I think," she finally said. "Still, I suppose I could go over there and shoot him. Do you think that would be effective?"

Ruby widened her eyes. "Ah . . ."

"Or I could shoot Superhalfwit Dacia. That, I think, would be infinitely more gratifying."

"Ah . . ."

"Or perhaps I could shoot them both," the countess further proposed, brightening. "Yes, I believe I like that idea best of the three. What do you think?"

"Ah . . ."

Arabella nodded. "It is settled then. I will—how is it that you Americans put it in your charming old films?— 'fill them both full of lead.' "

Ruby halfway expected her to stand up then and whip out a Saturday night special and open fire, but instead the countess only plucked a chocolate-covered strawberry from Ruby's plate and enjoyed a generous bite.

"I will see to it after we have finished eating," she added. She consumed the last of the strawberry, dropped its leftover crown onto her own plate, then scooped up a slice of the brown bread from Ruby's and smeared it liberally with the oily pâté. "First I wish to find out more about you," she said as she lifted it to her mouth. "Tell me your real name, and tell me where you come from," she stated further before taking a big bite.

There was no way Ruby could protest such a royal—noble? peerly?—decree, so she told the countess everything about herself that was worth relating. "My name is Ruby Runyon. I live in Miami and work as a waitress at Frank's Funny Business, which is a comedy club on South Beach. And I grew up in Appalachimahoochee, Florida, which is in the Panhandle. My mom and grandmother still live there, in a trailer park called Happy Trails. That's where I lived, too, until I was eighteen. I've been on my own for eight years now."

When Ruby was finished, Arabella only continued to look at her expectantly, as if she were anticipating much more. She even enjoyed another bite of pâté-coated bread as she waited.

Ruby shrugged. "That's it," she said.

"You have nothing more to say for yourself?" Arabella asked after she'd swallowed—elegantly—the bite she had taken.

"There's nothing more for me *to* say," Ruby assured her. "That's my life. You got the whole thing right there."

Arabella said nothing for a moment, only studied Ruby in silence. Then, "What is a trailer park?" she asked.

Reminding herself that this woman was European, and that they probably didn't have trailer parks where she came from, Ruby replied, "Um, it's a park full of trailers."

As the countess continued to study her in silence, Ruby recalled at the very back of her brain how her high school French teacher had once told the class that French was the international language of diplomacy. So, proud of herself for retaining not only that scrap of knowledge, but a bit of French too, she added, "*C'est une parc du trailer.*"

The countess smiled, though something told Ruby it wasn't so much because she'd been enlightened by the

French. Must lose something in the translation, she thought.

"And what is a trailer?" Arabella asked, still smiling.

"Well, I guess the politically correct term now is 'mobile home,' " Ruby told her. "I'm not sure how else to describe it. *La maison mobile*," she endeavored anyway.

" 'Mobile home,' " the countess repeated, smiling again, something that suggested that, likewise again, Ruby's translation had been a bit off. Maybe she should just stick to English in the future. "That indicates a home that moves, yes?" Arabella asked. "Your home was movable?"

Ruby shrugged again as she thought about it. "Well, actually, it was up on cinder blocks, but, yeah, I guess *technically* it was movable. If the right tornado came along or something."

The countess studied her in silence for another moment. "I see. That is very interesting."

Says you, Ruby thought. The Happy Trails Trailer Park had been about as interesting as a squished bug as far as she was concerned. Aloud, however, she only said, "Where is it that you call home?"

The countess reached for one of the peeled shrimp on Ruby's plate, swirled it in cocktail sauce a few times, then popped it into her mouth. She closed her eyes as she savored it, as if it had been a long, long time since she'd enjoyed such a treat. Finally, though, she opened her eyes and said, "I am from Toulaine. It is a very small country between Austria and Czechoslovakia. And if you have heard of it, you are unlike most Americans."

"Actually I have heard of it," Ruby said, surprising them both. "I think they mention it on those 'Reynaldo Watch' minutes sometimes."

Arabella nodded. "That would explain it," she said. "Because, you see, Prince Reynaldo is my fiancé."

"Whoa," Ruby said.

"Yes, that is a good way to put it," Arabella agreed.

"No, I mean . . . you know . . . *whoa*. On all of it. It's just amazing. All of it. You're supposed to marry a prince? This is his yacht? And he's nibbling on Supermodel Dacia's neck? Right in front of you?"

"Yes, yes, yes, and yes," Arabella replied without looking up, helping herself to yet another chocolate-covered strawberry from Ruby's plate.

"Well, well, well, and well," a third party interrupted before Ruby had the chance to say another word. "If it isn't the princess herself brightening and enlightening my evening."

Ruby glanced up at the masculine, and not a little flirtatious, voice, and discovered that the previously deserted bar at which she and the countess were sitting was now being commandeered by a bartender who was wearing a pleated tuxedo shirt on the half of his body she could see, along with a bow tie that had evidently been fashioned from a very obnoxious Hawaiian shirt. He was slim but solid, and looked to be a few years younger than Ruby— early twenties, probably. His sandy, sun-streaked hair was swept straight back from his face and caught in a short ponytail at his nape. He'd obviously enjoyed some time in the sun—which, she supposed, wasn't hard to do when one worked on a yacht—but not so much that he appeared to be a candidate for melanoma. His eyes were the most arresting color she'd ever seen on a human being, reminding her of the extremely expensive cognac that they kept on the tippy-top shelf behind the bar at Frank's and poured so infrequently.

Even having heard only one complete sentence fall from his lips Ruby detected a tinge of a northeastern accent in his voice—New Jersey, perhaps. Or New York

City. Her exposure to such things was limited to television and tourists, so she couldn't have said which state precisely. He was most definitely a Yankee, though, she thought with a smile. And a very good-looking one at that.

Then again, that was par for the course here on *Mad Tryst*, wasn't it? She wondered briefly if, when Prince Reynaldo discovered her stowaway status, he'd add to her other crimes the charge of being nonslender and average-looking. And she couldn't help thinking that those two offenses probably carried the stiffest sentences of all.

"Oh, my. It is Gus the bartender," the countess replied coolly, turning her head to look deliberately in the opposite direction. "I did not see you approach. And do not call me Princess," she added in the same frosty tone.

"Yeah, it's obvious you didn't see me coming," the bartender replied jovially. "If you had, you would have jumped up and gone running off before I got here, wouldn't you, Princess?"

"Yes. I would," she admitted readily, still ignoring him from a visual standpoint. "In fact, I think it is time for my friend Ruby and me to leave. And do not call me Princess," she repeated, her voice carrying even more of an edge this time.

The bartender turned to Ruby then and smiled, the gesture making him look even more handsome, if such a thing were possible. He jutted his thumb toward Arabella. "Don't buy the ice princess act," he said. "She's *totally* hot for me. She won't admit it, but she is." He propped his elbows on the bar and leaned over it, pushing himself as close to Arabella as he could. With his mouth only inches from her ear, he said softly, "Aren't you, Princess? Aren't you *hot* for me?"

Arabella glanced down at her lap and went to great lengths to smooth out a wrinkle in her skirt that Ruby sure couldn't see. And it didn't escape Ruby's notice, either, that where everyone else on board the yacht seemed to automatically bow and scrape and defer to Arabella—all the while keeping their distance—this bartender had absolutely no qualms about getting right in her face. Literally. Even more fascinating was the fact that Arabella seemed disinclined to move away from him. Nor did she silently command any obeisance and genuflection from him the way she had the couple who had evacuated these very seats for her not long ago. Nor the way she had commanded it from Keaton Hamilton Danning III earlier, either.

However, Arabella did still speak in that same icy tone when she replied, "Oh, yes, I do so admire a man who has made it his life's ambition to pour liquor for other people. And do not call me Princess," she said for a third time, her voice still level and controlled.

This, Ruby thought, was getting interesting. Gus the bartender and Arabella the countess clearly had some kind of *thang* going here. And Ruby would have paid good money to know just what, precisely, that *thang* was. If she'd had any good money, that was. Or any bad money, for that matter.

"No problem, Princess," Gus murmured with a smile, still hovering close. "If you don't like it, I won't call you Princess anymore, Princess. 'Cause I know how much it gets to you when I call you Princess. Princess." He winked at Ruby as he withdrew from Arabella and went back to his bartenderly duties, and she smiled at him in return. She couldn't help herself. He was just so charming and adorable.

When she turned her attention to Arabella, however, her smile fell again. The other woman's jaw was clenched tight, and pink had bloomed generously on the cheek that Ruby could see. The countess was obviously either very angry, very embarrassed, or very turned on. For the life of her, however, Ruby couldn't possibly have said which.

Knowing what little she did of the Countess Arabella Cha Cha, however, Ruby was reasonably certain it was embarrassment. She seemed much too elegant to get angry or turned on. After all, this was a woman who'd watched her own fiancé nibbling on the neck of a supermodel, and had reacted with only the merest sort of disdain for both of them. Obviously Arabella just didn't get very worked up over too many things. Embarrassed, yes. Worked up? Never.

The countess stood then, very elegantly, and ran a hand over her hair, further ignoring the bartender. "Walk with me, Ruby," she said in that no-nonsense voice that forbade protest.

Not that Ruby wanted to protest. But she would have loved to know more about this *thang* between countess and bartender. Unfortunately the countess's voice forbade asking about that, too.

Ah, well, she thought. What difference did it make, when all was said and done? She was only a passenger on board the yacht for a little while. By sunset tomorrow she'd be bidding sayonara to *Mad Tryst* and all the little mad trysts its inhabitants were enjoying. She'd be better off not involving herself any more than she had already. She had a plane to catch tomorrow, after all.

She hoped.

Chapter 6

It was somewhere around four-thirty in the morning when Keaton came to the conclusion that the wiener dog must die. Kurt evidently still carried a grudge against him over their earlier altercation, because he had hounded him—no pun intended—throughout much of the evening, ever since the two of them had run into each other on the forward deck. Canine Kurt had been trying to get a little shut-eye—as well as one could get shut-eye during one of Reynaldo's parties, anyway—when Keaton had stumbled upon him, quite literally, in fact, and very nearly turned him into *Schinkenpastete*. Kurt had taken offense—again—even though it had been an accident. And he'd retaliated by trying to turn Keaton's pants leg into *Schinkenpastete*, too—again.

Fortunately Keaton had managed to find a secluded little spot to himself in the yacht's library—God knew none of Reynaldo's guests would ever be caught dead *here*. *Un*fortunately, however, Kurt had followed him in—

oh, all right, if you must know, Kurt had *chased* him in—more than likely to, just a shot in the dark here, make Keaton's life as miserable as possible.

At the moment, the ghastly, abominable little vermin was making himself content by sitting on his haunches at the foot of the library ladder where Keaton had seated himself—oh, all right, if you must know, where Keaton had *retreated* himself—glaring and snarling (the dog, not Keaton, though he was sorely tempted), his little pointed rat-dog teeth looking as sharp as sabers. Tiny sabers, to be sure, but sabers nonetheless.

Not that Keaton was in any way intimidated by the revolting, horrific little beast. Not at all. He *wanted* to be sitting this way on the top step of the library ladder with his feet drawn up as far as they could get. And he was *glad* the only books within his reach were the Marcel Proust. He was looking *forward* to reading *Remembrance of Things Past*. In its eight-volume entirety. In one sitting. In French. He *liked* sitting here thumbing through those books, looking for the good parts. It was *very* comfortable. And *very* interesting. He actually felt *indebted* to Kurt for putting him in such a position.

Loathsome, obscene little reprobate.

He was about to utter those very words to the detestable, scurrilous little creature when he heard a soft sound and glanced up to find that the library door was slowly opening. And then who should appear but the *other* little creature who had been giving Keaton fits all night: Euphemia Philippa "Babs" Wemberly-Stokes, AKA Rita Q. Moreno, AKA Tutu, AKA the mysterious woman in black. That last moniker Keaton had added himself over the last few hours, because it fit her much better than the ones she and the countess had awarded to her. She was mysterious. And she was wearing black. And she was most certainly a woman, something that once again did *not* escape his notice.

She looked a little more bedraggled now than she had a few hours ago, though. Her hair was sea breezed within an inch of its life, though something about the carelessness of the long tresses tumbling over her shoulders was kind of attractive. Her mascara was slightly smudged, giving her the look of a waif from an old silent film, but again, there was something oddly appealing about the look. Even the scant circles that seemed to be forming under her eyes gave her a strangely engaging appearance, because with her looking as fatigued as she did, Keaton found himself wanting to approach her, and then pull her into his arms, and then silently encourage her to lean her body into his for a little rest.

Or something.

He was right there with her on that fatigue business, too. He'd moved past weary some time ago, and, if it were up to him, he'd be in bed fast asleep right now. Unfortunately, someone had to stay conscious and coherent during these parties, in case one of the guests went overboard. Or, worse, in case one of the crew went overboard. God knew Keaton couldn't trust them any more than he could the guests. They partied as much as anyone. Hell, there had been times when the crew were even *more* likely to go overboard than the guests were. Reynaldo really should have used more discretion in hiring them, because there was more to being an effective crew member than the prince's dual requirements of "familiarity with *Chapman Piloting* and big hooters."

Ah, well. At least Captain Cooki and First Mate Mimi seemed to know what they were doing, even if they both preferred doing it in thong bikinis most of the time. They'd both been members of the Royal Pelagian Naval

Guard before the prince's ouster, as had the rest of the crew. Not that anyone would guess such a thing from looking at any of them, seeing as how Reynaldo had let the rules lapse a bit with regard to uniform code—namely in the sense that there was no uniform code any longer. Nor, apparently, were there any uniforms any longer. In more ways than one. Nevertheless, the crew members were all fully qualified—if not always fully dressed— because Reynaldo had chosen each individual himself for duty as royal crew members, and he'd picked them all from the Royal Pelagian Naval Guard. Handpicked them, in fact. Or perhaps the more accurate word choice would be hooter-picked them, Keaton couldn't help thinking. From the *Navel* Guard.

Whatever.

"Oh, I'm sorry," Euphemia/Babs/Rita/Tutu said when she saw Keaton sitting where he was. She halted half in and half out of the library, seeming uncertain about which way she should go.

At the sound of her voice Kurt, who had been content enough to simply sit at the foot of the ladder snarling at Keaton, began yapping again. Loudly. Euphemia/Babs/Rita/Tutu started at the sudden racket, and all four of them took an involuntary step backward. Nevertheless, something prevented her . . . them . . . whatever . . . from retreating completely. Silently, she . . . they . . . whatever . . . looked at Keaton, seeming to ask for instruction.

"He's harmless," Keaton lied, calling out over Kurt's din. "Just ignore him. He wants to be a pit bull, but falls short in many areas, not the least of which is in the canine department. He's more suited to being a member of the rodent family. *Rattus odious,* I think, would be the appropriate genus and species for him."

Kurt set to a more furious yapping at having his dogness impugned in such a way, but Euphemia/Babs/Rita/Tutu, God love them, were in no way cowed. Instead they took a few experimental steps back into the library, closing the door behind themselves. Then they peered over the sofa that stood between them and the *Rattus odious* specimen and smiled—actually *smiled*—when they beheld the malicious, grotesque little monster standing there.

"Oh, he's so cute," they gushed, rushing around the sofa to scoop the execrable, ill-favored little fiend into their arms. "What's his name?"

"Kurt," Keaton replied automatically.

Then he watched in amazement as the supercilious, malignant little traitor ceased his turbulent arf-arf-arfing and began to tremble with excitement, laving Euphemia/Babs/Rita/Tutu's face with exuberant doggie kisses.

Boy, talk about your mood swings, Keaton thought. Then again, he supposed he could hardly blame the offensive, hateful little barbarian for his ardent reaction to the woman. Had she scooped *him* into her arms, Keaton would have been trembling with a lot more than excitement. And he would have been laving a lot more than her face.

Oh, stop, he told himself. Unfortunately, although he did indeed manage to put a halt to his sophomoric, hormonal thoughts—pretty much—he couldn't quite pull his gaze away from the spot where Kurt had nestled himself. Because Kurt had nestled himself at exactly the place where her plump breasts exceeded the fabric of her tiny dress. Oh, *boy*, did they exceed the fabric of her tiny dress. Keaton was, after all, only human. A *male* human, one who had gone way too long without any kind of meaningful—

read: sexual—interaction with a female human. In fact, the last time he'd had any kind of meaningful—read: sexual—interaction with a female human had been—

Oh, surely it hadn't been *that* long ago, he thought when he recalled the episode in question. Then again, it *had* happened in Pelagia, hadn't it? Meaning a full year, and then some, had passed since he'd—

Well, hell. No wonder he was thinking about laving Euphemia/Babs/Rita/Tutu's—

"I'm sorry. I didn't mean to disturb you," she said then, dispelling his unforgivably errant—and utterly erotic—thoughts. "I didn't realize anyone was in here. I was looking for someplace quiet. This party is starting to get a little, um . . ."

"Debauched?" Keaton supplied helpfully. "Aberrant? Twisted? Perverted?"

"Ah, actually, I was going to say 'out of hand,' " she replied, giving Kurt a good rub behind his ears, something that caused the rancorous, vindictive little demon to expel air in such a way as to make him sound as if he'd sprung a leak. "But those are all good words, too," she hastened to add. "Very appropriate, now that I think about it."

"Reynaldo's parties always eventually become debauched, aberrant, twisted, and/or perverted," Keaton told her mildly. "In fact, I can't remember the last one that didn't get out of hand, as you so politely put it."

She nodded, and although she said nothing, she looked as if she very much wanted to.

"What?" Keaton asked.

She hesitated for a moment, running her thumb anxiously over Kurt's collar again and again. For one brief, electric moment, Keaton fixed his gaze on that thumb, and wondered what it would feel like to have it running over something else instead. Something like, oh, say, his—

"There are naked people in the Jacuzzi," she announced suddenly, sounding a little scandalized by the fact.

Keaton jerked his attention back to the matter at hand. Unfortunately, when he recalled that the matter at hand involved naked people, his attention slipped right back into salaciousness again. "Mm," he replied noncommittally nonetheless. "Just naked people?"

She nodded, still looking anxious.

"No animals?" he asked.

Her eyebrows disappeared beneath her bangs in her obvious surprise at hearing the question. "Um, no. None that I could see. Unless you count the floaty toy shaped like a duck that someone was using for a . . . ah . . . that someone was using," she finished diplomatically.

Keaton waved a negligent hand before himself. "That's nothing," he told her. "You should have been here when they brought the squid aboard."

"Squid?" she echoed. "You mean, like, calamari?"

He shook his head. "No, I mean a squid. An actual, living, breathing—if squid do actually breathe, I mean— squid. Reynaldo emptied the Jacuzzi and refilled it with salt water, and kept the thing as a pet for days. Then, during one of his parties, some drunken fool got the great idea that the squid would make a good samba partner. For several people."

"Several?"

"It had quite a few . . . appendages," Keaton said. "They wrapped a hula skirt around the squid—don't ask me how they managed it—and tucked a hibiscus blossom somewhere that *might* have been an ear, and named it Carmen. Then someone put on a Trini Lopez CD, and, well . . ." He shook his head ruefully. "It was tragic, really. Frankly, calamari would have been a much more noble end for the poor animal. The squid escaped with his life, but I hope all his little squid friends didn't laugh at him when he finally managed to make it over the side of the yacht wearing the get-up."

Euphemia/Babs/Rita/Tutu narrowed her eyes at Keaton now, as if she weren't sure she should believe him. Oh, if she only knew, he thought. She couldn't imagine some of the deviant behavior he'd witnessed on this lunatic cruise. If she was shocked by the squid samba incident, then there was no way he was going to tell her about the nude crustacean wrestling incident.

She moved around to the front of the sofa, still snuggling Kurt, tossing her little black handbag onto the cushion beside her before seating herself there as well. "I also noticed a local actor up there at the party," she said with *much* interest, in a low voice, as if she were discussing a conspiracy theory.

"Yes, Reynaldo always manages to nurture friendships— or something—with actresses and actors and directors and other film types. He's always been a big movie buff. Ingratiates himself with members of the industry whenever he can."

"*Really?*" she asked, sounding infinitely more interested in that than any normal person would be.

"Ye-es," Keaton said cautiously. "Why does that interest you so much?"

"No reason," she said quickly, punctuating her answer with a hasty shrug that was in no way careless. "Just . . . I find it . . . you know . . . interesting, that's all."

Keaton was about to say something else, but she cut him off with an offer he couldn't possibly refuse.

"Look, do you think we could start over, you and me?" she asked him. "We kind of got off on the wrong foot earlier, I think."

"That might be because you told me a pack of lies," Keaton said pointedly.

Her gaze ricocheted to the other side of the room at that. "Well, yeah, there is that, I guess."

He was surprised to hear her admit it so freely, even if he did have her dead to rights. "So do you want to start off by telling me the truth this time?"

She nodded, then set Kurt carefully on the sofa beside her. Immediately he plopped onto his little haunches and gazed at her in frank adoration. Keaton took advantage of the abominable, horrid little villain's preoccupation with her to extend both of his legs down the length of the library ladder, biting back a wince at the needly pinprick of feeling that plagued him when the blood began to circulate to his lower extremities once again.

"My name isn't really Euphemia Philippa Wemberly-Stokes," she said, sounding tired.

Keaton rubbed his calf in an effort to urge the blood flow along more comfortably. "Imagine my shock to hear it," he said blandly. "Next you'll be telling me no one calls you Babs, either."

"No, no one does," she told him. "My name is really Ruby. Ruby Runyon. Everybody calls me, um, Ruby. And I'm not an actress, either."

"*No,*" Keaton replied in a scandalized voice. "Do tell."

"Not yet, anyway," she quickly amended. "I will be someday, though."

Hence the reason she found Reynaldo's movie connections so . . . interesting, Keaton thought. "And what are you now while awaiting this amazing transformation to thespian?" he asked.

She expelled a frustrated sigh and avoided his gaze. "Right now I'm just a waitress."

It wasn't what Keaton had expected her to say. He'd

pretty much convinced himself that she really was working for some cheesy tabloid. To hear that she wasn't the opportunistic yellow journalist he'd thought her to be was almost a letdown. He'd had all kinds of accusations and insults ready to hurl at her. Now, though . . . Well, how could you accuse and insult a waitress? They put up with enough in their jobs. They didn't need someone making things worse.

"I see," he said. "Can I also assume then that you weren't actually invited aboard *Mad Tryst* tonight?"

She nodded. "You can assume that, yeah."

"Then how—and why—did you come aboard?"

She said nothing for a moment, as if she were trying to decide how exactly to phrase her words.

Or else as if she were trying to come up with a new pack of lies to tell him, Keaton couldn't help thinking.

Well, he did kind of have reason to feel wary around her, didn't he? He wasn't completely stupid. She'd lied to him once already. Several times. There was no reason to think she might not try it again, since, obviously, he hadn't believed her that first time. And she'd had a few hours to perfect a story this time, where before she'd only had a few minutes. He wasn't about to give his credibility over without hearing a reasonable explanation first.

Finally she said, "I'm sort of, um, stowing away?"

Well. So much for reasonable explanations, he thought. If this was the best she could do after hours of planning, no wonder her first set of tales had been so outrageous.

"Stowing away," Keaton repeated blandly. "I see. Do people still do that these days? Stow away, I mean? I kind of thought that had stopped when, say, travel became affordable, safe, and convenient."

"I'm not stowing away because I can't afford to travel," she said. "I'm stowing away because my boyfriend got a little . . ." She sighed again. "Debauched. Aberrant. Twisted. Perverted."

"Out of hand, you mean?" Keaton asked mildly, thinking this story was going downhill fast.

Ruby shook her head. "He was *way* beyond out of hand. He was *married*. With children," she added hastily, just in case that first revelation wasn't enough to sway him around to her way of thinking.

Oh, yeah, Keaton thought. This story was definitely headed for a crash landing any minute now.

"*And* I have reason to believe he was connected to the mob."

Crash and *burn*, Keaton thought. So much for that.

He eyed her with much suspicion, and not a little confusion, wondering just how she planned to connect all these wayward details. "I'm sorry, but you just made a leap with those last disclosures that's left me hanging in midair, grappling for purchase."

In return she eyed him with much suspicion and not a little confusion, too. Instead of enlightening him, however, she said, "You know, I don't think I've ever met anyone who talks the way you do."

"What way is that?" Keaton asked, surprised by her response.

"Like . . . I don't know. Like someone just whacked you upside the head with a brick and made all the normal words get stuck in your brain."

He gazed at her for a moment with frank befuddlement. "Ah. Yes. Well," he finally said. "I, ah, I hear that a lot, actually."

She sliced a hand through the air and smiled. "Well, there you go," she said in a voice of discovery, as if that explained everything. "Just what is it you do on this boat, anyway?" she asked further. "Something that requires a lot of words, I'll bet."

That, Keaton thought, was a very good question. He wished he *could* tell her exactly what he did on *Mad Tryst*. Other than baby-sit, at any rate. "Mostly," he said, "I guess it's my job to take care of the prince. Prince Reynaldo of Pelagia," he clarified. "Your host." He couldn't quite keep himself from adding, "Or at least he *would* be your host. Had you, in fact, been invited to his party."

"And what," she said, ignoring his comment, "does taking care of a prince involve?"

Mostly it involved making excuses for the prince's egregiously bad behavior after Reynaldo did something stupid and/or repugnant to offend a foreign government in just about every port they'd visited, Keaton thought. But there was no reason that Ruby Runyon, waitress, had to know that. "I handle foreign affairs," he said vaguely. "Much as I did before we left Pelagia. Before the prince was, ah . . ."

"Chased out of his own country by an angry, torch-bearing mob?" Ruby supplied helpfully.

Keaton said nothing in response. Well, he couldn't exactly disagree, could he?

"The countess told me all about it," she said.

"Yeah, well, there may be one or two things that the countess left out," Keaton said.

"I doubt it," Ruby replied. "She was pretty thorough. The prince sounds like a royal pain." She grinned. "No pun intended."

"None taken," Keaton assured her. "At any rate, were the prince still in a position of power, I would be his chief adviser in Pelagia, handling any number of matters of national and international importance."

Ruby nodded sagely. "Instead you hide out in the library while the prince's party guests teach squid to samba."

"Well, I wouldn't exactly say I'm hiding out," Keaton denied.

"Then what are you doing here?"

"I was, ah . . . looking for Marcel Proust," he lied. Immediately he spun around on the library ladder he still claimed as his seat and plucked *Swann's Way* from the shelf. "And lucky me. I found him."

"Lucky you," Ruby replied sardonically. "Wait till you get to volume six, *The Captive*. It's riveting."

Keaton did his best to hide his surprise that she would be so familiar with *Remembrance of Things Past*. Good God, did anyone read Proust who didn't have to? He was only familiar with the author because Proust had been required reading at Oxford. "Funny," he finally said to Ruby, "But I'd think you'd prefer volume seven, *The Fugitive*. It's much more like you."

"You think?" she said with a knowing smile. Obviously he hadn't hidden his surprise very well. She knew he was astounded by her knowledge of the series, and she clearly liked having put him in his place. Just what kind of requirements were demanded of a waitress these days, anyway? he wondered. Or had she, in fact, read Proust simply because she wanted to? In which case . . .

In which case, he thought, she was nuts.

Either that or she was lying about being a waitress.

"Mm," he replied pithily. He replaced the book on the shelf behind him—clearly she hadn't bought his excuse about looking for Proust any more than he bought her explanation for being aboard the yacht—and continued with their previous line of conversation. "At any rate, I'm still not sure what your boyfriend being married and, um, connected to the mob, you said?"

She nodded vigorously.

"Right. Well, I'm still not certain what those things and you being aboard *Mad Tryst* have in common."

She sighed. "Long story short," she said. "I was supposed to go boating with him and another couple tonight—or rather *last* night—but I found out just before we were supposed to board his friend's yacht that he was married. And also that he might be, you know, connected. When I asked him about it—the being married part, not the being connected part, because I don't want to wake up in cement overshoes, you know?"

"No, of course you don't," Keaton replied obligatorily, wondering why he was encouraging her this way.

"Anyway, when I called him on being married, he got kind of . . . unreasonable? Kind of threatening? Kind of scary?" She was clearly nervous now, Keaton noted, because every sentence in her story suddenly came in the inquisitive tense. "And suddenly?" she continued. "I didn't want to be out on a boat with just him and a couple of other people? But he wouldn't let me leave? In fact? He wouldn't let go of me at all? And then? When we were passing this yacht? And I saw the party going on? I saw an opportunity to lose myself in the crowd? So I did?"

If credibility were a Thoroughbred, Keaton thought, hers would be limping toward the glue factory about now.

"And if I'd known you guys were planning to leave?" she continued, her voice still questioning, but taking on a more desperate note, one that almost convinced Keaton . . . she was lying, "Believe me? I never would have come aboard? But I figured I'd just hang out here? With the madding crowd? Until Jimmy—that's my unreasonable, threatening, scary ex-boyfriend—was gone? And then I'd slip back off? And go home?"

Keaton was surprised by how much he genuinely wanted to believe her preposterous story. Not because it seemed especially credible—au contraire—but because she had recounted it with such an earnestness that he wished he *could* find it difficult to disbelieve her. And also because when she got to the part about the notorious Jimmy, she did seem to grow genuinely frightened, as if she had indeed feared for her safety.

Now, if it weren't for that troublesome credibility problem . . .

Despite that, however, Keaton found himself thinking that if he ever discovered who this unreasonable, threatening, scary, out-of-hand—and maybe even existent—Jimmy was, he was going to sic Reynaldo's bodyguard Zolton on him, and have him beat the ever-loving life out of the man. Or, better still, sic Kurt on him. Both Kurts, as a matter of fact. That ought to do the trick.

And God, where had *that* impulse come from? Keaton wondered. He'd never been compelled to willingly provoke violence in his life. Not even on someone who was nonexistent. Well, except for canine Kurt, but he was asking for it. Nor had Keaton ever used the phrase "ever-loving" before, which was even more troubling. But the thought of Ruby Runyon, waitress—or even Ruby Runyon, media jackal, seeing as how his suspicions were leaning once again to the tabloid journalist thing—being bullied by such a man made Keaton want to strap on a pair of brass knuckles and go looking for trouble himself.

How very, very odd.

"So are you going to throw me overboard?" she asked softly, scattering his thoughts. He could tell by her tone that she was only half joking, and he marveled again at the thread of concern for her that wound through him.

He shook his head. "No, of course I won't throw you overboard." He forced an almost genuine chuckle before adding, "You're the first halfway reasonable person I've met on board in months." And even though he still didn't think she was being honest with him, he couldn't deny that what he said was the truth. She was *halfway* reasonable. "There's no reason why Reynaldo has to know anything about this," he added. "Not that he'd remember any of it in the morning, anyway."

"Thanks," she said. "I appreciate it."

Then another thought occurred to Keaton. "But if you were running from your boyfriend, then you must have come aboard with nothing but the clothes on your back. Not that they aren't very nice clothes," he hastened to add. *What little there are of them*, he couldn't help thinking further to himself. Not that that was such a bad thing, necessarily. "But you're going to look a little out of place on Nassau tomorrow. And how *will* you get back to Miami?"

She seemed to be battling an almost convincing panic as she replied. "I can handle looking out of place— wouldn't be the first time. And I have a credit card and a little cash in my purse," she added. "And some ID. I can get back home once we land at Nassau. I think. I hope."

So do I, Keaton thought. Because there was no way he was letting her aboard *Mad Tryst* again. He just couldn't take the chance that she might not be who she said she was. And if she *was* who she said she was, the point was moot, because she wouldn't want to come aboard again. She'd be itching to go home as soon as possible.

"As long as you have a credit card, you shouldn't have any problem," he told her.

"Not until the bill comes in anyway," she muttered. Before Keaton could comment further—not that he had any idea what to say—she added, "I'm sorry about stowing away without telling anyone. I just . . . I didn't think anyone would notice me, that's all."

Keaton almost laughed outright at that. Not notice *her*? In *that* dress? Not bloody likely. Aloud, however, he only said, "No harm done." And to himself he added, *Yet*.

He was surprised to realize how very little bothered he was by what she had done. He told himself he should be outraged by Ruby Runyon's behavior, that she had lied to him, had violated Reynaldo's privacy, had taken advantage of all of them, had misrepresented herself, and could have potentially been a security risk. Chances were good that she was still lying and misrepresenting herself and taking advantage of all of them and being a security risk. Not to mention she'd helped herself to a midnight buffet that had run more than two hundred dollars a head, *and* taken the last of the *Pflaumenkuchen* before Keaton could get to it.

Somehow, though, he just couldn't get all that worked up about it. Not even the part about the *Pflaumenkuchen*. Maybe he was just too tired. Maybe a part of him did believe her fantastic tale about running away from her mob boyfriend. No harm had been done. Yet. And with her looking the way she did—as if she were about to fall asleep sitting right there on the sofa—he doubted sincerely that she posed any risk between now and tomorrow afternoon. There were too many other things Keaton had to worry about than having inadvertently picked up a nautical hitchhiker who might or might not be a privacy invader. In a matter of hours he'd see to it himself that she was removed from the yacht, and *Mad Tryst* would continue on in the same manner it had for the past year.

More was the pity.

And why did it suddenly bother him so much that Ruby Runyon would in fact be leaving the yacht tomorrow? Could it be because she really was the first halfway reasonable person he'd met for a long time? Or could it simply all go back to that male animal/female animal thing that Keaton had been missing out on for far too long?

"So then you and the countess aren't childhood friends?" he asked, even though he already knew the answer to the question.

"No, of course not," she said, sounding as amused by the idea as he was. "I just met her tonight."

"Which means there's no . . . condition . . . any of us needs to be concerned about?" he asked further.

He hadn't quite been able to shake the idea that she might be, ah . . . off-limits. Not that he could figure out for a minute why he would even be afraid that she might be, ah . . . off-limits. Of *course* she was off-limits, he told himself. She was a stowaway. A liar. A waitress. Even if it *had* been a year since he'd engaged in that male animal/ female animal thing, Keaton could do a hell of a lot better than Ruby Runyon. He didn't care how luscious she was.

She seemed not to know what he was talking about for a moment, and he was about to jog her memory when she began to laugh. And quite a nice laugh it was, too, almost musical in a way. He smiled involuntarily and felt a little pop of something warm and wistful go whizzing through his midsection, a not unpleasant sensation.

No, not unpleasant at all.

"Oh, gosh, no. No," she said, still chuckling. "There's no condition. That was just something Arabella made up to help me out when you were giving me a hard time. I'm still not sure why she did that. The helping out part, I mean. But it was nice of her."

"Arabella?" Keaton repeated, surprised to hear the name slip so easily from Ruby's lips. No one on the yacht ever called the countess by her first name except for Reynaldo. Not because of any social rule, though certainly there were rules in place under normal circumstances— they simply weren't adhered to on *Mad Tryst*. Probably because *Mad Tryst*'s society was so, well, debauched, aberrant, twisted, and/or perverted ninety percent of the time. There *were* no rules here, social or otherwise. Nevertheless, no one other than the prince addressed the countess so familiarly. No one except the waitress, evidently.

"Mm-hm," the waitress replied now to his countess reference, sounding even more tired than she had before. As if illustrating that very thing, Ruby lifted her hands to rub her eyes and added, "She went to bed a little while ago, after I promised her I could look after myself. She was pretty tired."

Keaton was about to nod when the other part of Ruby's statement struck him. "Giving you a hard time?" he echoed belatedly, not quite able to hide his offense. "Well, of course I was giving you a hard time," he told her. "It's my job to make sure Reynaldo is safe and left unbothered. I didn't know who you were, and your behavior *was* a little suspect."

Now she turned both hands palm out, in a gesture of surrender. "Look, I said I was sorry."

He opened his mouth to say more, decided it wasn't worth the effort, and noticed that Kurt had snuggled up beside her thigh and was lost in doggie dreams. Amazing. Keaton would have sworn the vicious, reprehensible little savage never slept, something that only contributed to his malevolence. In sleep, though, Kurt looked almost . . .

Well, actually, he still looked like a noxious, terrible

little heathen, as far as Keaton was concerned. But at least he was a *quiet* noxious, terrible little heathen.

When Keaton glanced back up he saw that Ruby Runyon, too, had become quiet. In fact she'd stretched her arm along the back of the sofa and had twisted her upper body, then tilted her head to lean it upon her shoulder. She, too, seemed to be drifting off to sleep. For a moment he said nothing, only watched as little by little, her body relaxed and her breathing grew deeper. She must have been exhausted to nod off so quickly, he thought. He supposed he should wake her, if for no other reason than that she was going to have a pretty bad crick in her neck in the morning.

But, unlike Kurt, Ruby didn't appear to be a noxious, terrible little heathen in sleep. No, in sleep—as in wakefulness—she appeared to be a beautiful, desirable woman.

It really was a shame she'd be leaving tomorrow, he thought. And it was also a shame that she lied so flagrantly, too, he reminded himself, in case he forgot that, which he kept doing for some reason. And, of course, she was a waitress. Still, he would be strangely sorry to see her go once they reached Nassau. In just a few short, illicitly gotten hours, she'd already injected a new kind of life to *Mad Tryst*. She'd brought the Countess Arabella out of her funk, if only temporarily, and had made the normally sober woman smile, laugh even. It had been a long time since Keaton had seen the countess happy. Yet Ruby Runyon had made the other woman feel happy only minutes after meeting her. And Ruby Runyon had made Keaton feel—

What? he wondered. Different, certainly. Never in his life had he experienced such an immediate physical reaction to a woman. Never had he been attracted to one so completely without even speaking to her at length. And he couldn't recall ever experiencing the warm, wistful sensations that had run through him when the two of them finally had gotten around to talking. She made him feel happy, too. Animated. Almost human. Not like a nanny. Not like a statesman. Not like a referee. Not like a cruise director.

Like a man, he realized suddenly. For the first time in a long time, Keaton felt like a man. And he had Ruby Runyon to thank for that.

Oh, yes. It really was too bad she'd be leaving tomorrow. And also that she lied so flagrantly, he hastened to add. And, too, there was that waitress business to contend with. A shame, all of it.

As quietly as he could, he tiptoed to the door and eased it open. He could wake her once they were closer to the Bahamas, he thought. Find her a cab once they reached Nassau. Maybe even escort her to the airport himself. It was the least he could do after the ordeal she'd endured tonight, being witness to one of Reynaldo's parties. That could scar anyone for life. Anyone sober, at any rate.

Yeah, maybe he should accompany Miss Ruby Runyon to the airport, Keaton thought as he closed the library door softly behind him. It would be the polite thing to do. And it would ensure that she did in fact board a plane, leaving *Mad Tryst*, and its occupants, behind. It wasn't at all because he just wanted to spend a little more time with her.

Because the truth of the matter was, he *had* no time to spend with her. His work was never done as it was. And he had a million things on his long-term agenda. Make sure Reynaldo stayed out of trouble, which in itself was a full-time job. Keep Kurt the canine off his case—and trouser leg. Lie flagrantly to the countess about how Reynaldo really did love her, honest he did, he was just frightened by the depth of his emotions. Keaton's responsibilities were endless. There was no way he could fit "have a fling with a waitress/maybe media jackal" into the mix.

So, silently, Keaton made his way back to his state-room, thanking every god available that he didn't have to pass by the Jacuzzi deck to get there. Who knew what they were doing up there by now? He just hoped there was no marine life involved this time.

And he wondered why, even though he was so tired, he suddenly had no desire to go to bed.

Probably, he thought, it was because he would be all alone once he got there. And where for the past several months, solitude had been the one thing he had craved above all else living on this floating dormitory, suddenly isolation felt like a curse.

He scrubbed a hand over his face and rubbed his eyes. Sleep, he commanded himself. He needed sleep. Hopefully, in the morning, he'd start making sense again.

Chapter 7

"**W**ell, how was I supposed to know I needed proof of citizenship to enter the Bahamas?"

Ruby, still dressed in her black cocktail dress at three o'clock the following afternoon, sat outside on the forward deck of *Mad Tryst*, ignoring the gin and tonic she didn't recall ordering, but which a steward had placed before her only moments ago. No matter where she'd wandered on this boat since coming aboard, someone always seemed to be bringing her something: drinks, food, more drinks, more food, more drinks, more food, and more drinks. Even Kurt kept dropping little rubber squeaky toys at her feet, before falling back onto his little haunches and gazing at her with frank doggie adoration. Only Keaton Hamilton Danning III seemed uninterested in bestowing gifts upon her. No, all he'd bestowed upon her for the last few hours had been bleak, black looks.

Much like the one he was gifting her with now.

The table at which they sat was shaded from the sun by

a massively oversized umbrella, but it did nothing to protect Ruby from the hot glare of his scowl. Which, now that she thought about it, was probably infinitely more dangerous than the melanoma-inducing waves radiating from the sun.

"*You* didn't know I needed proof of citizenship to enter the Bahamas, either," she charged, "and you're a *lot* better traveled than *I* am. And it's not like I left my apartment last night thinking, 'Okay, let's see, I need my driver's license and my credit card and a little cash, and oh, yeah, a copy of my birth certificate, just in case I wind up stranded on a luxury yacht headed to Nassau.' It just sorta slipped my mind to tuck proof of citizenship into my purse," she told him, smacking her forehead with the flat of her hand for emphasis. "The only time I've ever been out of the country was to go to Key West. And you don't need proof of citizenship to go there. Just a certain way of thinking, that's all."

Keaton continued to eye her mutinously as he said, "Key West isn't a foreign country."

"Oh, well, obviously you've never been to Key West," she responded. Maybe a change of subject would do them good.

"No. As a matter of fact I haven't," he told her.

"Well, trust me. It's a totally foreign culture down there. Especially during Mardi Gras."

"Which still doesn't help us figure out what we're going to do with you," he said.

So much for changing the subject, Ruby thought.

"Because *Mad Tryst* will be leaving Nassau tomorrow morning. And you, Ruby Runyon, waitress—if in fact that's who you really are—are not going to be aboard when it does."

"What do you mean 'if in fact that's who I really am'?"

she demanded, trying to sound as indignant as he did, but falling short. "Who else would I be?"

"That," Keaton said caustically, "remains to be seen."

She gaped at him, unable to believe he was unable to believe her, but she said nothing in her defense. What could she say, after all, that she hadn't already said? If he didn't believe her, he didn't believe her. And all things considered, she supposed she couldn't really blame him. How often did something like this happen, after all? It wasn't exactly believable. If this were in a book, the reviewers would say it had an insubstantial, and sometimes downright silly, plot.

She sighed her frustration and eyed the gin and tonic with more interest. Maybe a good, stiff drink was just what she needed right now. She felt more than a little uncomfortable dressed as she was, especially since Keaton looked so breezy and carefree—well, except for the malevolent expression he wore as an accessory. He had given himself the day off, he'd told her as they'd left the yacht earlier, because the prince and his cohorts—as opposed to the prince and his court—would no doubt spend the day in their respective, and sometimes shared, beds.

And he had insisted he didn't mind accompanying her to the airport, had assured her that he wanted to see a bit of Nassau before the yacht set sail the following morning. So he was dressed for an afternoon of casual sight-seeing— and ridding himself of a pesky stowaway—in loose-fitting ivory linen trousers and a pale green, short-sleeved shirt that enhanced the green of his eyes to a dangerous extreme.

Unfortunately the afternoon of sight-seeing—not to mention the ridding himself of the pesky stowaway—had been put on hold shortly after they'd entered the customs house. Because the customs official had informed them that they would need proof of citizenship to enter the Bahamas. For Keaton that wouldn't have posed a problem, as he claimed not one but four passports. His father was American, his mother was French, he'd been born in Germany, and he had been granted Pelagian citizenship after spending most of his life there, during his father's tenure as the American ambassador to the country. Ruby, however . . .

Well, all Ruby had carried in her microscopic purse was her Florida driver's license—which proved she knew how to drive—her Visa card—which proved she knew how to shop—her lipstick, which proved she preferred the shade of Coral Punishment—her collapsible hairbrush—which proved she had good grooming habits—and two breath mints—which proved she practiced good oral hygiene. But there was nothing there to prove she was American. The Florida State Lottery ticket she had also discovered among her effects, the customs official had assured her, wasn't enough.

Hence she and Keaton had been turned away from the Bahamian port of Nassau and had been forced to return to *Mad Tryst*, where the entire population of the vessel, save she and Keaton and a couple of crew members, still seemed to be asleep. Not surprising after the party she'd witnessed last night, but awkward in the sense that she had absolutely no one to turn to but Keaton Hamilton Danning III.

She'd lied to him earlier that morning in the library when she'd told him she didn't mind feeling out of place. She did mind it—*a lot*. Not the part about wearing a tiny black cocktail dress at four o'clock in the afternoon in a place where bikinis and jams were more the norm, though certainly she felt rather uncomfortable—and not a little stinky—about that. But the part about being light-years away from Keaton socially and geographically . . . *that* bothered her. Enormously. Because a part of her couldn't help wishing that the two of them had hit it off a little better during her brief—though it was looking to be less brief now—stay on *Mad Tryst*.

She told herself these feelings were ridiculous. The man was a total stranger, and they were almost literally the proverbial two ships passing in the night. Except that there had only been one ship involved. And it hadn't really been a ship; it was more of a boat. And they hadn't quite passed; they'd stopped and talked to each other for a little while. And now it was daytime.

Okay, so they weren't even close to being the proverbial two ships passing in the night. The point was that this incident, however harrowing, would stay with Ruby for a long, long time. And she was certain that memories of Keaton Hamilton Danning III would stay with her for a long, long time, too.

It was just odd to think that this incident, so far, had only commanded a handful of hours from her entire life. Something told her she wasn't likely to ever have another experience like it again.

Nor, she felt certain, would she ever meet another man like Keaton.

He had awakened her in the library shortly after noon, with a gentle shake and a tenderly offered "Ruby, wake up." When she'd sleepily opened her eyes, she had found him bending over her, his dark hair still damp from a recent shower that had left him smelling citrusy fresh, his green eyes filled with amusement. Amusement and something else, something warm and wistful and wanton, something that had sparked a little flame in her belly, fanning heat slowly through her midsection, to points beyond. Something that had made her, in her state of semiconsciousness, reach up and thread her fingers through his hair.

And then the amusement in his eyes had turned into something else entirely, something hungry and frantic and hot. Something that had made her feel hungry and frantic and hot herself.

For a moment, before consciousness fully claimed her, Ruby had been sure she was still dreaming, because she never woke up to such sensational stimuli. Normally what woke her in the morning was the sound of the Dumpster beneath her bedroom window being clattered about by the garbage truck, or the sound of a police siren screaming by in hot pursuit, or the shout of one angry alley dweller competing with another for a square foot of untenanted, unwashed ground. No one ever tenderly whispered, "Ruby, wake up." No one ever touched her gently. No one ever smelled or looked as good as Keaton did. No one ever gazed at her with hunger and desire.

And when it *had* finally dawned on her that what she was awakening to wasn't, in fact, a dream, Ruby had experienced one sharp, scintillating moment of thinking in her sleep-scattered brain that Keaton was a part of her normal, everyday reality. And in that sharp, scintillating moment, she had known more joy than she'd ever experienced in her entire life.

Until he had told her, "You need to eat before we get to Nassau. And then we'll see about getting you back to Miami."

And then, still not quite awake, Ruby had shuddered with a burst of repugnance unlike anything she had ever felt before. She didn't want to go back to Miami, she'd thought in her state of drowsy discontent. There was nothing for her in Miami, save a dead-end job, an almost non-existent paycheck, and an apartment the size of a bottle cap with too many six-legged roommates to count. Why in God's name would she want to go back to Miami?

"You need to get home," Keaton had then said softly.

Oh. Right. That was when she'd remembered. Miami was her home. It was where all her stuff was. It was where she lived her life. Day in and day out. Until the end of time. As it was in the beginning, was now and ever should be. World without end. Amen. Amen. That was why she had to get back to Miami. Not that remembering any of that had made her *want* to go back to Miami. But she'd understood then why she had to.

Dammit.

"So what are we going to do now?" she asked Keaton, reaching for the gin and tonic that was suddenly too tempting to ignore, and trying to forget about the heat and hunger with which he had looked upon her that morning, heat and hunger that had only mirrored the feelings winding through her—both then and now.

"What are *we* going to do?" he echoed.

She nodded halfheartedly as she enjoyed a long, savory sip of her drink. Oh, yes. She definitely needed that.

"Well, *I'm* going to go ashore and enjoy Nassau while I still have a little time to do it," he said brusquely. "I have no idea what *you're* going to do. Except finish your drink and go."

She nearly choked on the long, savory sip that was suddenly not what she needed at all. "But . . . but . . . I don't have anyplace *to* go," she reminded him once she managed to clear her throat and her thoughts.

He lifted a hand to rub his forehead. Hard. "I'm sorry. That's not what I meant," he said. "But you know, maybe you should have thought about that before you came aboard last night, now that you mention it."

She gaped at him. "Oh, come on, Keaton. All I could

think about last night was getting away from Jimmy. I couldn't have planned this. This situation defies planning. Hell, this situation defies reality."

"Oh, yeah, Jimmy," Keaton said, ignoring the last part of her outburst. "The amazing vanishing boyfriend. Maybe you could call him. If he's connected to the mob, as you claim, then he probably knows someone in the Bahamas who could help you out. Don't they do a lot of money-laundering here?"

Ruby sputtered indignantly for a moment before she finally managed to say, "You didn't believe me about him being connected, did you? You thought I made it up."

He eyed her with something she decided not to ponder too much. "Well, can you blame me?" he asked.

She expelled a soft sound of incredulity. "No, I guess I can't," she finally said. "Because no one as suspicious and cynical as you are would ever recognize the truth, even if it jumped up and bit you on the tushie."

As if conjured by the suggestion, Kurt, who had, until now, been snoozing comfortably at her feet, jumped up and ran out from under the table, then began to bark wildly at Keaton, as if he was angry that the man would insult Ruby in such a way. Keaton rolled his eyes in response and growled out an exasperated sound.

"Who says I'm suspicious and cynical?" he demanded over the dog's din.

"Well, you certainly seem to look for the worst in everyone," she told him. "You thought I was a tabloid journalist at first."

"No, I didn't," he told her. "Not at first. My initial reaction was that you were one of Reynaldo's stray bimbos."

"*What?*" Ruby cried.

"I thought you were some woman he'd picked up for the night," Keaton clarified.

"Oh, well, thank you so much for having such faith in my morality," she muttered irritably.

He frowned, but she wasn't sure if it was in response to his feelings for her or for himself. "Yeah, well, of course that was before I realized you were a pathological liar," he said blandly. "Once I got to know you . . ."

"Ha ha."

"And I also briefly entertained the notion that you might be an—"

"Might be a what?" Ruby demanded when he halted mid-sentence, blushing a bit. "You briefly thought I might be a what?"

"An assassin," he admitted. But his blush deepened and he looked away as he said it, obviously realizing now just how foolish the assessment had been.

"An *assassin*?" Ruby exclaimed. "You've got to be kidding. I can't even assassinate someone's character. What did you think I was I going to do? Climb up to the crow's nest and open fire on the party crowd? Where did you think I was hiding my high-powered rifle?"

He hesitated a moment before revealing, "I thought maybe you were planning to use a lethal injection."

Ruby closed her eyes and sent up a silent bid for patience. "Oh, right. That's me," she said as she opened them again. "I'm on Interpol's ten most wanted list. Code name: Angel of Death."

"Actually, I was thinking more along the lines of code name: The Badger."

Ruby narrowed her eyes at him menacingly.

"Well, you do kind of badger, you know."

"Don't start," she said crisply.

Keaton expelled a restless breath and reached for his own drink. "Look, it was late and I was tired, all right?"

"And also suspicious and cynical," Ruby added.

"Yeah, well, maybe there was a touch of that, too," he conceded. "But if you understood why I—"

Before he could finish the statement, a third, feminine, voice interrupted, "Yes, you are far too suspicious and cynical, Keaton. And you do not wear either of them well."

Ruby couldn't help thinking that the Countess Arabella looked as cool and calm—and as elegant, dammit—as she had the night before as she approached the table. She was dressed this afternoon in a pale lavender sheath of some breezy, gauzy—and doubtless very costly—fabric. Her hair was once again twisted up the back of her head, held in place by some invisible means of support, a few wispy strands dancing about her face with the warm breeze. Grecian-style sandals were laced about her ankles and halfway up her calves, and a translucent, pearl white scarf capered around her neck.

All in all, Ruby felt like a frumpy, mud-covered monkey in the other woman's presence.

"You were not always so suspicious and cynical, Keaton," Arabella added as she folded herself elegantly into the chair opposite Ruby's. "Only since we left Pelagia have you become so. Pass the coffee."

Ruby watched as Keaton immediately complied with her royal decree without complaint, not just passing the coffee, but pouring a cup for the countess as well. He also, without being asked, moved the sugar bowl and creamer within her reach. His good manners, however, left Ruby cold. Well, tepid maybe. Warm, at best. Because where he certainly deemed the countess a paragon of virtue worthy of obedience, he had just confessed that he considered Ruby capable of pumping lead—or at the very least a lethal narcotic—into another living creature.

Men. *Hmpf.*

She found it interesting that Arabella neither thanked nor even acknowledged Keaton for obeying her edict. But she didn't act impolite or condescending, either. Clearly, the woman was simply used to having people do her bidding and not feeling obligated to recognize their gestures.

What must that be like? Ruby wondered. It was her job to do other people's bidding and to not expect anything in return. Though, naturally, she expected a tip. Not that she always got one. But she wasn't supposed to expect one, either. She wondered briefly if Arabella would stiff her should the countess ever come into Frank's. Then Ruby dismissed the idea outright. There was no way Arabella would ever show her face in a place like Frank's. And even if she did, the countess would never be the one paying the bill.

Boy, did Ruby wish she was Arabella.

Of course she'd have to contend with that unpleasant business of being engaged to Reynaldo. So maybe the countess gig wasn't all it was cracked up to be.

"Do I understand correctly that there is a problem with Ruby going home?" Arabella asked as she reached for the cream pitcher and poured a scant amount into her cup.

Ruby nodded. "I can't get into the Bahamas without proof of citizenship. Which I don't have. And I can't get back home unless I can get into the Bahamas. Which I can't."

Arabella looked from Ruby to Keaton. "Keaton?" she asked. "You cannot do something?"

"Like what?" he asked the countess, clearly reining in for her the irritation he had no trouble displaying for Ruby.

"You must know someone here," Arabella countered. "You always know someone. Or your father does."

"Not in the Bahamas," he told her. "This part of the

world isn't exactly the Dannings' playground. Europe and most of Asia, sure. North America, no problem. South America and Africa, little problem. But the Caribbean?" He lifted his shoulders and let them drop again. "My father just never saw fit to cultivate any connections here."

"Then Ruby must telephone someone at home to send her this proof of citizenship," Arabella said. "They can fax it, yes? Or overnight it to *Imperial Majesty* if the genuine article is required."

"We're setting sail early tomorrow morning," Keaton reminded her. "Before breakfast even. We won't be here for her to get it."

Arabella turned a tiny teaspoon of sugar into her cup and began to stir it slowly. "Then we shall stay until it arrives," she told Keaton carelessly.

He eyed her blandly. "Are you going to be the one to tell Reynaldo that?"

"No, I am not," Arabella said. "You will tell him."

Keaton opened his mouth to reply, but Ruby interceded before he had the chance, and before he and Arabella could get into an argument that he would most assuredly lose. Ruby might have been on the yacht for only a matter of hours, but she could already see who wielded the most power around here. And it *wasn't* Keaton. It wasn't the prince, either.

"Uh, guys?" she said to the two of them.

Both Keaton and Arabella turned to look at her, wearing almost identical expressions of inquiry.

"There's one small problem that you don't understand," Ruby told them. "There's no one for me *to* call back home. I live alone. No one has a key to my place except me. And even if I tried to call *home* home— Appalachimahoochee—my mother and my grandmother are in Las Vegas for two weeks."

"What about your father?" Keaton asked.

Ruby wished she could say he was with her mother and grandmother in Las Vegas. Instead she told them the truth. Sort of. "I don't have a father."

Keaton sobered. "Oh, I'm sorry. I didn't realize he had passed away."

"No, it's not that he died," she said, thinking she might as well tell them the whole truth, seeing as how Keaton had a knack for getting that out of her, anyway, even if he never believed it once he had it. "I mean, I don't know if he's died," she corrected herself. "Maybe he has. It's that . . . I've never met my father," she said levelly, her gaze never once veering from Keaton's. "I don't know who he is. My mother isn't even sure about that."

Keaton's lips parted fractionally in response, but his expression never wavered, so she really had no idea how to gauge what he was thinking. What he finally said, though, was "Then I guess you'll have to call the bureau of vital statistics for the state of Florida and have them send you a new copy."

"Fine," Ruby agreed. "But I'll tell you right now that they won't overnight anything to me. I'll be lucky to get a copy of my birth certificate from them before my mother and grandmother get home."

She had a point, and he knew it, and Ruby could see that he knew it. He was a bureaucrat, after all. He knew how that stuff worked. Or didn't work. Whatever.

Keaton sighed heavily. "Let me make some calls anyway. I'll see what I can do."

Arabella smiled with what looked to Ruby like supreme satisfaction. "And in the meantime," she said as she lifted her cup to her mouth for a dainty sip, "Ruby will stay aboard *Imperial Majesty* with us. At least until her papers catch up with her."

* * *

"This should fit you fairly well."

Ruby wasn't sure whether to look at the, ah, garment that Arabella tossed onto the bed in her stateroom or at the stateroom itself. Both were pretty astonishing, though in entirely different ways. The stateroom, however, was undeniably the more attractive of the two, so that, she decided, was where she would focus her attention for now.

Never in her life had Ruby realized how luxurious a boat—a *boat*—could be. Certainly she'd seen for herself last night, both in the lounge and the library, and as she'd wandered in search of a place to escape from the party's frenetic goings-on, that the hallways and such were sumptuous beyond belief. She'd even encountered a spiral staircase at one point that had made her feel as if she'd stumbled onto a miniature version of the *Titanic*. But Arabella's stateroom was the very definition of *sumptuous*.

The walls were painted a buttery shade of ivory, with what appeared to be solid mahogany paneling making up the bottom half. The door and trim, too, looked to be fashioned of mahogany, not to mention the padded bench, the desk, and the chair tucked beneath it. The queen-sized bed was spread with a coverlet patterned in a floral design, dominated by reds and oranges and pinks—Ruby was certain, somehow, that it was silk—identical to the cushion on the bench. A deep, forest green carpet dotted with more reds spanned the room from wall to wall. The recessed lighting in the ceiling was turned off at the moment, but that made perfect sense, seeing as how plenty of sunlight poured in through the ample windows on the far side of the room.

Currently those windows were slid open to allow in the bracing, sea-scented breeze, which mingled with the sweet aroma of freshly cut flowers—lots and lots of freshly cut flowers—that had been collected into a crystal vase on the desk. Oil paintings of landscapes decorated the other walls, offering Ruby the impression that she was not on a boat, but standing in a suite of a luxury hotel. The only thing that made the impression fail was the view outside the window of another yacht berthed next to this one.

The sensation was strange, to say the least.

"Just how big is this yacht, anyway?" Ruby asked.

"I am not sure," Arabella replied. "A little over sixty meters, I believe, because I have heard Reynaldo speak of it in such a way."

Holy cow, Ruby thought. She'd paid close enough attention in high school math to translate sixty meters into about two hundred feet. Two hundred feet. For one boat. The single-wide mobile home where she had lived the first eighteen years of her life—with two other people—wasn't even one-fourth the size of this boat.

"And, ah, and how many people are traveling with you?" she asked further.

"Oh, let me think," the countess said. "There is Reynaldo, of course, me, Marisol, Keaton, the Kurts, Etiènne, the valet, Omar, who sings, a crew of, I think, eight, three stewards, and three bartenders." She shrugged as if what she'd just described was in no way unusual. "Reynaldo insists that someone must be available to make and serve drinks twenty-four hours a day. When he has parties he hires temporary help for those and makes arrangements for their return if the workers accompany him on a cruise such as the one last night." In a very soft, very rapid voice, she concluded, "And there is also aboard, unfortunately, superdolt Dacia."

"And where does everyone sleep?" Ruby asked "I mean, it's a big boat, but . . ."

"Actually, there is room for everyone. Reynaldo, of

course, has the master suite, and Keaton and I each have a stateroom to ourselves. The crew members share cabins below decks. The Kurts and the others also share cabins below. Marisol has a small cabin to herself below."

Arabella didn't mention superdolt Dacia's sleeping arrangements, and Ruby didn't ask about them. She figured it was a safe bet that the model wasn't spending her nights on one of the chaise longues on the Jacuzzi deck.

"That leaves three staterooms vacant," Arabella added. "I will get you settled in one after we have found some things for you to wear. Marisol will not mind you borrowing her clothes until we can find something else for you."

That was three times the countess had mentioned this Marisol person, and she hadn't spoken softly or quickly any of those times. So it was probably okay to conclude that the countess actually liked this Marisol person, and it was all right for Ruby to ask about her.

So, "Marisol?" she asked.

"She is my duenna," the countess said. Said it like Ruby should understand what she meant, too.

"I beg your pardon?" Ruby asked. "She's your what?"

"My duenna," the countess repeated, glancing up from the clothes she had been arranging on the bed. She must have understood how confused Ruby was by looking at her, because she smiled and added, "My companion. My mother and father live in Toulaine, and have many, many obligations. They could not possibly accompany me on this . . ." She sighed heavily. "This endless, pointless, meaningless cruise. But it would be improper for me to travel alone, so I have my duenna with me. Her name is Marisol."

Ruby nodded her understanding. Even though she didn't understand at all. "Why would it be improper for you to travel alone?" she asked. "I mean you're what? Over eighteen surely," she finished with a smile.

"I am twenty-two years old," Arabella said, surprising Ruby again. Not that the countess looked old or anything, but she carried herself like a much more mature woman. Ruby would have put her in her late twenties, at least. Maybe older. She just had the demeanor of a much older woman about her. Most of the twenty-two-year-olds Ruby knew acted more like twelve-year-olds. Then again, twelve-year-olds were usually a lot of fun. The countess didn't seem like the kind of person who had much fun in her life. Probably because she wasn't allowed to act like she was twelve years old. She probably hadn't even been allowed to act twelve years old when she *was* twelve years old.

"But I cannot travel alone because I am not married," she said, confusing Ruby even more.

"I'm not married, either, and I travel alone," Ruby said.

"Yes, and you are in much trouble, are you not?" Arabella pointed out.

"Well. Yeah. Okay. But still. You're a grown woman. Why do you have to have a companion?"

"Because that is how things are done where I come from."

There was a finality in her voice that prohibited Ruby from further argument. So she only said, "Oh."

"And it is very good to have Marisol," Arabella added. "She is very nice, and very easy to talk to and very good company." After a moment's hesitation, Arabella added, "Even if she often falls asleep while I am talking to her. She is nearing eighty, after all."

"Your parents think an eighty-year-old woman is an appropriate companion for you?" Ruby asked.

Arabella nodded but said nothing.

"And they think she's going to keep you out of trouble?" Ruby asked doubtfully.

Arabella shrugged. "So far, so good."

Ruby was fairly certain that the only reason Arabella had stayed out of trouble was that she restrained herself to the point of disallowing any fun or festivity or life in her life. But she didn't say so. Arabella probably already realized that herself, after all. She didn't need anybody rubbing it in.

"And besides, you are lucky I have Marisol," the countess added, "because she is about the same size as you and has something for you to wear. I am certain you would like to change your clothes, would you not?"

"I would *love* to change my clothes," Ruby agreed eagerly. "And I could use a shower, too."

"You may use mine." She waved her hand toward the left side of the room. "It is through that door. Then you may change into these," she added, gesturing toward the, ah, clothes, on the bed.

Reluctantly, Ruby turned her attention again to the assortment of garments. They did appear to be fairly close to her size, but they were nowhere near her style. Not unless she happened to be an eighty-year-old duenna who had a habit of nodding off while people were talking to her. Not unless she *liked* massive muumuus spattered with what appeared to be an Andy Warhol rendition of avocados and pineapples. Not unless she *wanted* to be caught dead in white cotton underpants that were roughly the size of the Pentagon.

"Um, thanks," Ruby said, knowing she was in no position to argue.

Note to self, Ruby, she thought. *Next time you stow away on a royal yacht, in addition to proof of citizenship, be sure to bring along clean undies and a change of clothes.*

She started to collect the garments, trying not to look at the giant underpants, when Arabella stopped her with a question.

"You have really never been out of your country before?" the other woman asked.

Ruby shook her head. "No, I've barely been out of the state of Florida before."

Arabella gaped at her as if she couldn't believe it. "You are joking, yes?"

Ruby shook her head again. "No. I just don't get the chance to travel much. And when I do, I usually go home to visit my family."

"Ah, yes," the countess said with a smile. "I forgot. The grandmother who works in the auto parts store and is having trouble with her nicotine and whiskey habits while working on the chain gang." She grinned. "That was quite a lively tale you made up for Keaton last night."

Ruby glanced down at the clothes she hugged close to herself and confessed, "Ah, actually it wasn't a tale."

Arabella's grin fell some. "Not even the chain gang?"

"Well, that part wasn't exactly true," Ruby admitted.

"Thank goodness."

"It was more like just a road crew."

"Oh. I see."

"It's kind of a long story."

"Yes, I would imagine it is."

"But Grandma Pearl did look really good in that orange jumpsuit," Ruby assured the countess. "I would have sworn that would have been a bad color for her. But it brightened up her complexion a lot."

The countess nodded but didn't probe any further into that particular matter. Instead she asked, "And your family still lives in Florida, yes?"

Ruby nodded. "Yeah. They still live in Appalachima-hoochee, where I grew up."

"Appa-lach-ee-mah-hoo-chee," Arabella repeated slowly. "That is really the name? I thought perhaps you were making that up as well last night."

"Yep. That's really the name. I'm a native Ap-palachimahoocheean."

The countess laughed. "That sounds like it is a painful condition."

Ruby couldn't help chuckling, too. "Yeah, well, it can be at times."

"It is like that for Toulainians, also," the countess replied, her smile falling some.

But she rallied it again, and somehow Ruby got the impression that Arabella wanted to say something more about where she came from. Or else where Ruby came from. Instead she took a step backward and pointed at the bathroom again. "Go ahead and freshen up," she said. "I am going to read for a little while up on deck, and then later this evening Marisol and Keaton and I are going to go ashore for a little while. I will try to find you some better clothes to wear while I am in Nassau."

"You don't have to do that," Ruby said.

"I do not mind."

"I appreciate it. I'll pay you back."

"It is not a concern."

"It is for me."

The moment turned awkward suddenly for some reason, so Ruby quickly jutted a thumb over her shoulder toward the bathroom and said, "I won't be long."

"I will have a steward make certain that a stateroom is made up for you while you are showering."

"Thanks," Ruby said. "After that, if it's okay, I have a

lot of phone calls I need to make, to let everybody know where I am and that I'm okay."

"That will be perfectly fine," Arabella assured her. "Call as many people as you would like."

"Thanks."

Actually, there were only two calls Ruby needed to make, and she tried not to let herself feel too bad about that. As much as she would have liked to have a whole Rolodex full of friends and loved ones who'd be worried sick about her, her life just wasn't that full. No, she only had to call, first, her mother's hotel in Las Vegas, and, second, Frank Tedescucci, her employer. And her mother was just a formality—she probably wouldn't even know Ruby was gone. Frank would be far more concerned about her absence—but only because he was going to have to cover her shifts. Or replace her completely, Ruby couldn't help thinking further, which was likely.

She'd just leave a message with the hotel desk for her mother and grandmother, telling them she'd gone out of town, in case they tried to reach her but couldn't—which actually wasn't likely. Ruby told herself they'd never worried about her because they had so much faith in her ability to take care of herself, and not because they didn't care about her. But she wasn't sure she believed that nowadays any more than she'd believed it when she was a child or adolescent. You'd think with adulthood, she would have come to terms with all that family stuff, but even as an adult, Ruby felt as insecure in her family's affections as she ever had.

But hey, hers wasn't the only family like that on the planet, was it? Lots of people had dysfunctions. And a lot of those dysfunctions were a lot worse in other families than they were in hers. And hey, there were a lot of things in life that were a lot worse than not having someone make a fuss over you all the time.

A lot of things.

"And then after I make my calls," she told Arabella further, "I think I'll probably turn in early. I didn't get much sleep last night. And what I did get was pretty bad."

"It sounds as though your evening is planned," Arabella said with a smile.

Ruby tried to smile back but couldn't quite manage it for some reason. "My evening is planned, yeah. After that, though . . ."

"We will get you home, Ruby," Arabella said, sensing her distress. "I promise you we will."

Ruby nodded. But she realized then that her concern at the moment wasn't generated by any worry she might have about *not* getting home. No, what had her concerned at the moment was that, eventually, she *would* get home. Back to Miami, where she had no connections, no family, no good friends worth mentioning or missing. Back to her tiny, solitary apartment. Back to her dead-end job at Frank's, or another very much like it. And she discovered, with very little surprise, really, that she didn't much want to go home. Nevertheless, she knew she had to. Because what else was there for her? Nothing.

And that, she decided, was the scariest thing of all.

Chapter 8

As he was winding up his afternoon shift and preparing to turn the Jacuzzi bar over to one of the other bartenders, Gus Torrance looked up and saw Princess Arabella coming, realized she hadn't yet seen him going, and decided he didn't have to leave just yet.

"Beat it, Donovan," he told the bartender who was seated on the other side of the bar, enjoying the last of his pineapple juice in the few minutes he had left before he was to relieve Gus. "Take another half hour or so, will ya? I'm not ready to close up shop just yet."

"What are you, nuts, mon?" the other bartender replied in his dulcet Jamaican accent. He tossed his shoulder-length dreadlocks back as he glanced up at Gus, gazing at him as if he had indeed lost his mind.

He was dressed pretty much the same way Gus was, in loose-fitting khaki trousers and a loud Hawaiian shirt, which was the standard nonparty uniform of *Mad Tryst* bartenders. The volume on Donovan's shirt, however, was toned down quite a bit from Gus's—tasteful shades of Caribbean blues versus the bright red background spattered with numerous elaborate liquor concoctions that adorned the one Gus wore.

"You been workin' since ten this mornin' without a break, and you don't want to leave?" Donovan asked further. "We're only going to be on Nassau for the night, you know. Take advantage while you can."

Gus smiled at the other man's choice of words. Or maybe he smiled because he had his gaze trained right on Arabella, and the wind chose that moment to lift the hem of the pearly sarong she had tied around her waist, revealing slim, supple, surprisingly long legs beneath. Her one-piece, pale pink swimsuit, he was sure, was supposed to be modest and unrevealing, but it only jacked Gus's motor straight into high gear. Because he could imagine what lay beneath that curve-hugging garment. Oh, *boy*, could he imagine. In fact he'd imagined it pretty much nightly for the last month as he lay in the tiny bunk above Donovan's. Ever since he'd started working on *Mad Tryst* and taken note of one passenger in particular.

"Oh, believe me, mon," Gus said softly, mimicking his friend's speech, "I intend to take full advantage. Soon. Now get lost."

From the corner of his eye Gus saw Donovan glance over his shoulder in an effort to discover what had captured his attention. "The princess," he said softly. But where Gus always spoke those two words with wistful reverence, Donovan's voice held clear warning. When he turned back around to look at Gus, he shook his head. "You better watch yourself. That woman's body language is screamin' hands off, and you know it."

"Oh, no, it isn't," Gus countered. "If there was ever a

woman who was just begging for a man's touch, it's that one."

"Yah, but it's not your touch she wants, mon."

"Says you," Gus objected, his gaze still fastened on Arabella. She'd appropriated a chaise longue on the far side of the Jacuzzi, had stretched out those long, long legs, and had opened a paperback book to read. She had her back to the sun, a wide-brimmed straw hat shading her shoulders, arms, and neck, the sarong covering her legs. She was no dummy, that was for sure. With skin that fair and delicate, in this sun, at this latitude, even this late in the day, if she wasn't careful she could spontaneously combust.

Of course, Gus thought, his smile changing a bit, there were other ways to heat that tender skin and make her catch fire. And oh, baby, would he like to be there when that happened.

"Even if she's beggin' for a man's touch," Donovan said, jerking Gus from his very fine fantasy back into despicable reality, "what makes you think it would be yours? A woman like that, she got her sights set a lot higher than a bartender."

"Maybe," Gus conceded reluctantly. He met his friend's ebony gaze levelly. "But maybe not."

Donovan rolled his eyes in obvious disbelief. "And even if it was your touch she wanted," he continued, "which isn't too likely, she's not for you, Gus. She's for the prince. He may not act like he wants her, but if he knew what you were up to with his woman . . ." He let his voice trail off, and his dreadlocks danced as he shook his head. "You be food for the fishies, mon. Ol' Reynaldo don't like nobody messin' with his things."

"Then he ought to be taking better care of his things,"

Gus said coolly. "And he ought to stop treating them like they're things."

Donovan lifted both hands in surrender. "Hey, you get no argument from me, mon. I'm just sayin' watch yourself, that's all."

"There are other things I'd rather watch," Gus said, moving his gaze back to the slender blond on the other side of the deck. "Now beat it," he told Donovan again. "Come back in thirty minutes."

Donovan shook his head again, expelled a long sigh of annoyance, then rose and did as his friend asked. Gus wasn't sure, but he thought he heard the other man mutter, "You crazy, mon," as he left. Then again, Gus couldn't exactly disagree with Donovan's analysis. He hadn't felt quite sane for nearly a month now. Not since he'd stepped behind the bar that first night he'd reported for his first shift aboard *Mad Tryst* and seen the Countess Arabella Magdalena Sophia Victoria Genevieve Eugenie Wilhelm of Toulaine standing on the starboard side of the Jacuzzi.

They'd cleared the Port of Los Angeles and were well out to sea, headed south toward Baja. The sun had begun to set and was hovering just above the hazy ribbon that bisected ocean and sky, staining everything on board with bits of orange, pink, and gold. Gus had been preparing a margarita for Supermodel Dacia and had been certain he'd never see a more beautiful woman in his life than she, when he'd looked past Supermodel Dacia and had seen another breathtaking blond on the horizon. And in that moment Gus's heart had begun to hum, his libido had begun to dance, and the sun had seemed to go dim in comparison to the woman's glow.

Arabella's pale hair had been swept up the back of her head in some kind of twist, but the ocean wind had blown free scores of wispy tresses that rushed about her face. She'd been wearing a white cotton dress, simple in design, with absolutely no decoration. But it had bared her shoulders, and somehow that was all the adornment she'd needed. She'd held a glass of white wine in one hand, had curled the other over the rail of the boat, and all of her had seemed to shift in and out of the soft sunset tints behind and above her. She'd turned her head in his direction, and for one brief, delirious moment Gus had thought she was looking at him. Then he'd realized her gaze was off by a bit, and that her attention had actually been fixed on his employer—his employer, the prince, who'd been standing beside Supermodel Dacia, for whom Gus had then suddenly remembered he was supposed to be preparing a drink.

Had you asked him then the name of Supermodel Dacia, he would have been at a loss to recall it, even though he'd had the woman's poster affixed to his bedroom wall when he left home at eighteen. Hell, he wouldn't have been able to tell you his own name at the time. Because his vision, his brain, his life, his soul had, in that moment, been completely overrun by the graceful, cultivated woman who'd stood on the other side of the deck.

Without even realizing what he was doing, Gus had overfilled the margarita glass and spilled a stream of the sticky mixture all over Supermodel Dacia's hands. The prince had been so outraged by Gus's negligence that he'd wanted to fire him on the spot, and doubtless would have if they'd been in port. But they'd been out to sea—Gus in more ways than one—so Reynaldo had had little choice but to keep him on. By the time they'd reached Acapulco, the incident had been forgotten and Gus's employment had been secure.

Not forgotten, however, was the young countess. Nor

was his unprecedented reaction to her the first time he'd beheld her. And neither of those was secure, either, he'd had to concede. Because it wasn't long after Gus's first glimpse of her that he discovered the Countess Arabella Magdalena Sophia Victoria Genevieve Eugenie Wilhelm of Toulaine was already promised to another man. Another man, he'd also quickly discovered, who didn't want her, as insane as such a notion might be.

The countess, however, had seemed steadfast, if not in her devotion to her fiancé, then in her obligation to him. Frankly, Gus hadn't been able to figure that one out. Then again, he'd never been promised to someone by his parents at an early age. Well, not in the same way that Arabella had been, at any rate.

And, God knew, Gus wasn't the poster boy for family values or family obligation by any stretch of the imagination. He'd hoofed it out from under his father's thumb the minute he was legally able and the old man couldn't touch him anymore. He couldn't imagine what Arabella's own upbringing must have been like, to keep her feeling now as if she owed an obligation so great that it meant sacrificing her life, herself.

But that wasn't up to him to understand, Gus told himself now. No, the only thing that was up to him was to follow his instincts and do what came naturally. And, naturally, what his instincts commanded him to do to Arabella was—

Well. What he *really* wanted to do to Arabella wasn't fit for print. Not in any kind of respectable publication, anyway. Still, for now, if he couldn't get what he really wanted from the princess, he'd settle for getting her goat. Her goat, after all, was generally a lot of fun. Eventually, he promised himself, he'd get some other parts of her, too. And he couldn't wait to see what those other parts of her were like. He hoped at least some of them were also animals. At least when the occasion for animalistic behavior arose.

He noted with much satisfaction that the Jacuzzi deck was currently deserted, save for him and Arabella. Everyone else was either ashore partaking of Nassau's many sybaritic opportunities or else napping away the late afternoon in preparation for the party—nay, the bacchanal—that would inevitably come later, and/or in recovery from the party—nay, the bacchanal—that had come the night before. Prince Reynaldo was nothing if not a completely irresponsible hedonist, and he'd had nearly a year of cruising around the world to perfect his mercurial, carousing ways. Why, Gus would bet good money that, at this very moment, Reynaldo and Supermodel Dacia were skinny-dipping in some deserted cove—or else sweating up the sheets in one of Nassau's many resorts—something that left the prince's future wife stranded here on the yacht all alone.

Gus smiled. What incredible bad judgment the prince had shown. And what incredible good luck Gus had found.

Knowing Arabella preferred a splash of lime juice in her club soda, he prepared the concoction just the way she liked it, and garnished it with a lime wheel, a swizzle stick, and a paper parasol. Then he ran a quick hand over his sandy hair, tucked an errant strand back into his ponytail—he wanted to look his best for the princess, after all—and double-checked to make sure all the buttons on his shirt were properly aligned. Then he set the beverage on a tray and approached his quarry with as much obsequiousness as he could muster.

And Gus was extremely good at being obsequious

when he wanted to be. He'd spent the first eighteen years of his life learning from pros, after all.

"Why, Princess," he said jovially as he drew within a foot of her. "How nice of you to gift me with your royal presence this way. I'm honored."

He bent toward her, tray extended, so that she could take the proffered refreshment. And also so that he could enjoy a close-up view of the creamy swells of her breasts just barely peeking over the scooped top of her bathing suit. He saw her stiffen the moment he spoke his preferred nickname for her, saw her clutch the side of her book more forcefully, saw color blossom on her cheeks. Sunglasses shaded her eyes, but not so much that he couldn't see the sheer panic reflected in them when she glanced up to look at him.

Oh, she wanted him, he thought. She wanted him bad. He was—almost—sure of it.

"Your Majesty," he said as he moved the tray closer.

"I am not Your Majesty," she said as she removed the drink imperiously from the tray. "I am not *your* anything, and I am no one's majesty. Even if I were a princess, which I am *not*," she added meaningfully, "I would not be a majesty. I would merely be a highness."

"Heinous?" Gus deliberately misunderstood, because he liked it when she got all riled up. "Oh, come now. How can you say you're heinous? You're not that bad, Princess, honest."

He saw the eyes behind her sunglasses close, saw her jaw clench tight, saw her chest rise as she inhaled a deep, steadying breath, saw the color on her cheeks darken even more. Oh, yeah. She wanted him. No question about that. Now all Gus had to do was make her realize it, too.

When she opened her eyes again, she looked as if there

were a million things she wanted to say to him—none of them especially polite, he would wager—but what she ultimately decided on was a simple, "Do not call me Princess."

Gus smiled. "Okay, Princess."

And then, uninvited, he sat himself down on the chaise beside hers.

She narrowed her eyes at him, arrowing her pale brows down in consternation. "What do you think you are doing?"

He shrugged. "Taking a little break. I've been working since ten without one, you know. Donovan should have been here by now to relieve me. I can't imagine what's happened to him. He must have met a pretty girl on Nassau."

"It is not like him to be late," Arabella agreed, turning her face—if not her attention—back to the book in her lap. "He is a very good worker. Unlike other bartenders Reynaldo has hired." She paused a telling beat before adding, "Honestly, it is so hard to find good help these days."

"Ain't it though?" Gus agreed amiably. He folded both elbows on his knee, cradling his jaw in one hand, dangling the tray between his legs with the other. "So tell me, Princess, when are you and Reynaldo gonna tie the knot, anyway?"

She snapped her head back around at the question, glaring at Gus as if she couldn't believe he had put voice to such a forbidden topic. Then, as if to illustrate further, she demanded, "How dare you ask me such a personal question? You do not know me. It is none of your business, my relationship with Reynaldo."

"Oh, come on," Gus replied lightly. "You can't possibly think it's escaped anyone's notice on this boat that you and he should have been married a loooong time ago. Not to mention how he seems to always be with someone other than you. Someone like, oh . . . I don't know. Supermodel Dacia, for instance."

Arabella sputtered a few times, worked her mouth as if she wanted to say something her gracious upbringing absolutely forbade her to say, then somehow managed a reasonably civil "I cannot imagine what you must be thinking to dare speak to me in such a way. Only a boor and a cad would say such things."

"Hey, I'm not telling you anything you don't already know, Princess," Gus said. "And I'm not saying anything to your face that everyone else on this boat doesn't say behind your back. If that makes me a boor and a cad, then I hate to think what some of these other people on board are."

"I have names for them, as well," she said in as regal a voice as Gus had ever heard. "I am just too polite to say them."

"Yeah, well, maybe that's the problem," Gus told her.

Arabella looked at him again, but curiosity had replaced the animosity in her expression. "What do you mean?"

"I mean you're too polite, Princess."

Her lips parted fractionally in confusion as she gazed at him, and it was all Gus could do not to lean forward and cover her open mouth with his. And then deepen the kiss, tasting her thoroughly, pressing her back against the chaise longue as he did so. Then join her on the chaise longue, aligning his body alongside hers. Then gather her into his arms and cover her body with his, insinuating one of his legs between both of hers, curving his fingers over her hip, and cupping his hand firmly over the soft swell of her bottom. Then push her bottom up, hard, so that her pelvis arched against his, and her legs tangled with his own, and her breasts were crushed against his chest. And then pull aside the snug fabric of her bathing suit with sure fingers, finding that hot, damp, sensitive core of her, playing her, stroking her, penetrating her, until she began to murmur, *Yes, oh, yes, oh, please, just like that, give it to me, Gus, faster, harder, deeper, longer*. And then . . . and then . . . and then . . .

And where was he? he wondered feverishly, snapping himself out of the erotic reverie. Oh, yeah. The princess being too . . . something. Courteous? Decent? Arousing? Something like that. Gus did his best to refocus his attention on . . . whatever it had been focused on before that incredibly graphic little fantasy had taken over. Man, that sun was hot. Hot enough to give a man heatstroke, that was for sure. That must be why he suddenly felt so dizzy and disoriented.

"Uh . . . what did you say?" he asked Arabella. Belatedly he realized he had seen her mouth moving, but for the life of him, he'd been completely unable to process whatever it was she had said. "I was, um . . . I was thinking about something else."

She eyed him warily for a moment, and he wondered if maybe she knew exactly what he'd been thinking about. Then, cautiously, she told him, "I said, what do you mean, that it is a problem that I am too polite? How can someone be *too* polite? If you ask me, the world would be a better place if there was more politeness in it."

Right, Gus thought. They'd been discussing the princess's politeness. Not her decency. Not her arousal. They could work on those later. A lot, if Gus had anything to say about it. For now, though, working on her politeness would do.

"Many people would consider politeness a virtue," she added before he had a chance to say anything. "I spent many years learning how to be polite. There is not enough politeness out there, if you want to know my opinion."

"There's plenty of politeness out there," Gus countered. "And the bulk of it, Princess, rests on your shoulders. You need to let a little go, and let go a little. Trust me. Being too polite gets boring after a while. No wonder Reynaldo doesn't spend a lot of time with you."

She gaped at him fully when he said that, and Gus had to close his eyes tight to quell the erotic images that *that* expression roused in him. *Later*, he promised himself. Later he could lose himself in these pointless—if incredibly entertaining—fantasies about her.

"You are calling *me* boring?" Arabella demanded. "*Me*? The Countess Arabella Magdalena Sophia Victoria Genevieve Eugenie Wilhelm of Toulaine?"

Gus shrugged and nodded amiably. "Yeah, I'm calling you boring. At least five of the seven of you are, anyway. Jury's still out on the other two."

She continued to gaze at him in mystification for a moment, then, "Which two?" she asked quietly.

"Arabella and Wilhelm," Gus replied immediately. "I'm thinking all the rest of those names are kind of unnecessary. And they're weighing down what might otherwise be a perfectly normal, perfectly interesting woman."

She studied him in silence for a moment more, clearly trying to figure him the hell out. *Good luck, Princess*, he thought. Hey, he couldn't figure himself out. Why should she have any better luck with the puzzle?

"I do not understand you," she finally said, her voice threaded with bewilderment. "You do not make sense."

Now it was Gus's turn to eye her silently, because, suddenly, long unused wheels in his brain began to turn. Slowly, methodically, purposefully, igniting a little light bulb he knew he should immediately douse. The hell with it, though, he immediately told himself. This just might be an opportunity that would never rise again.

What would he risk, he asked himself, to spend a little more time with Arabella? Hell, to spend *any* time with her? Would he risk his job? His heart? His neck?

Because Donovan hadn't been too far off the mark earlier with what he'd said about Reynaldo. Even though the prince couldn't seem to be bothered with his fiancée, he didn't tolerate anyone else showing a bit of interest in her, either. There had been an incident in Italy, Donovan had told Gus, that had stayed with the crew pretty well. An American studio had been filming a movie there, and Reynaldo had invited much of the cast aboard for a party. The supporting actor had taken quite a shine to Arabella, even though she, of course, had rebuffed his every advance. According to Donovan, at one point Reynaldo had caught the guy standing too close to the countess—presumably with an arm or some other appendage around her. And then, the next thing anyone knew, the young actor had been going overboard, into waters that, if not shark-infested, had been stinky and oily with diesel fuel, something that had done nothing for the guy's José Eber hairstyle, that was for sure.

And then, the gossip went, the next thing anyone knew, the young actor's part was being written out of the movie. And then, the next thing anyone knew, he wasn't finding any work anywhere in Hollywood. And then, the next thing anyone knew, he was selling shoes at Wal-Mart. And then, the next thing anyone knew, he was nowhere to be found on the planet.

It was all rumor and speculation, to be sure, Gus conceded. But he wouldn't put it past Reynaldo for a moment to do whatever he could to mess up anyone who dared lay a hand on Arabella. Even if he never put his own hands on her himself.

So what was Gus willing to chance? he asked himself. What would he surrender to get close to Arabella, in any way he could? Immediately he knew the answer to that question. And he wasn't much surprised to realize it was—

Everything.

He would give up everything for a chance at her. Not that he had that much to sacrifice, he reminded himself. He made his living as a bartender, had no home to call his own, and had been completely estranged from his family for the last four years—not that his family was any great shakes, either, he had to concede. He had no savings, no investments, no prospects, no future, nothing to offer her save himself. And hell, she was a woman who'd grown up rich and royal, who was used to having everything, every luxury and satisfaction that money could buy. She was engaged to a prince, for God's sake, even if it wasn't some grand, epic romance. Reynaldo was good-looking, rich, famous, charming. Even if he was a big jerk. And Gus . . .

Well. He wasn't a jerk. That had to count for something, right? And, hey, there were one or two luxuries and satisfactions that defied monetary value. And Gus would bet they were pleasures that the countess had never had the opportunity to experience herself. And if there was even the smallest chance that he and Arabella might someday . . .

He stopped the thought before it could fully form, because he knew it was unwise, at the very least, to continue with it. And also because Arabella's expression changed then, and she looked at Gus with utter devastation, as if he'd just told her her cat Muffin had gone overboard and met up with an angry pack of wild dogfish.

"Do you really think that I am boring?" she asked in a very small voice.

Something inside Gus that he hadn't even known existed melted a little bit at the tone of her voice. She really did care about what other people thought of her, even if she put up a good front. Or maybe, he thought further, a little spark of hope kindling inside him, it was just that she cared about what Gus thought of her.

Hey. It could happen.

"No," he told her truthfully. "I don't think you're boring at all, Princess. I think you're—"

"What?" she asked.

But he only shook his head and refused to say. No sense making both of them feel flustered and uncomfortable. "I just think Reynaldo maybe would treat you a little better if he saw you in a different light."

"What kind of light?" she asked.

The kind I see you in, Gus thought. What he said, though, was, "The kind that makes a man take notice."

Behind her sunglasses, her eyes narrowed in clear confusion. "I still do not understand."

"There's a certain kind of woman, Princess," he said, "that men can't help but notice."

"Oh, yes, I do know that," she said readily—and not a little sarcastically, he couldn't help noticing. "They want a woman to be very beautiful and not very smart."

"Actually, it's a fallacy that that's what they want," Gus said.

Arabella gaped at him again, obviously outraged by his remark. "It is *what* that they want?" she demanded, clearly misunderstanding him. "I cannot believe you would say that to me. I cannot believe you would use such a vulgar word in my presence. You should be ashamed."

"Vulgar word?" he echoed, mystified. "What vulgar word? I didn't use a vulgar word."

Arabella's lips thinned primly, but she whispered, " 'Fallacy.' " Her voice returned to its previous outraged timbre as she added, "How dare you use such word when speaking to me?"

Gus chuckled when he realized how completely— and licentiously—she had misunderstood him. "Uh, Princess?" he said. " 'Fallacy' doesn't mean what you think it means. I think you're mixing it up with fella—" Hmm, he thought, cutting himself off mid-word. Probably, he thought, he shouldn't go there. Probably he should just gloss over that for now. So, very gently, he said, "It's a perfectly acceptable word, 'fallacy.' It means something that isn't true."

She continued to eye him warily for a moment, then "Oh," she said softly. "I see."

"I meant it wasn't necessarily true that men like women who are beautiful and stupid. I didn't mean they like to have a woman perform, ah . . ." *Don't go there, Torrance.* "Well, I didn't mean what you were thinking I meant. That *was* what you were thinking, wasn't it?"

Arabella's cheeks burned bright red now. "I would rather not say," she muttered.

"Oh, come on," Gus cajoled, unable to resist the temptation, in spite of his warnings to himself. "You can tell me."

"No, I cannot," she assured him. "I am sorry. You were saying? About beautiful, stupid women that men love so much?"

"Actually, I was saying that men *don't* love that kind of woman. Not necessarily. Not all men. You're the one who brought up the beautiful-stupid combination."

"No, I did not," she countered gracefully.

"Yes, you did," Gus insisted.

"No, I did not."

"Yes, you did."

"I did not."

"You did."

She narrowed her eyes at him again, then asked in a queenly voice that would have put Elizabeth II to shame, "Are you calling me a *liar*, Gus?"

He nodded vigorously. "Yeah. You're damned right I am. You're either lying or incredibly forgetful. I didn't say anything about men liking stupid women. Truth is, any man who's comfortable being a man would demand a woman who's smart."

"And beautiful," Arabella added, sounding sad for some reason. "They always want them to be beautiful."

"Yeah, well, a fair amount of good looks never hurt anyone," he conceded. "Male or female."

"No, I suppose not," she agreed softly.

"But it takes more to attract a man's attention—and keep it—than good looks," Gus asserted. "Trust me on this, Princess."

"I wish you would stop calling me Princess," she said, ignoring the rest of his comment.

"What do you suggest I call you then?" he asked.

She gazed at him in silence for a moment, as if she were giving great thought to her reply. Finally, "Here is an unusual idea," she said. "How about if you call me Countess?"

He smiled. "Can't. Doesn't fit you. Sorry."

She gazed at him with obvious confusion. "And Princess does fit me?"

"As well as anything does right now," he said.

"I do not like it."

"Then give me something else to call you."

She opened her mouth to say something but seemed to think better of it, because she snapped it shut again without uttering a word. Gus nibbled his lip thoughtfully for a moment, then let the moment go. Whatever.

"Anyway," he continued, "it just so happens that I'm an expert in what men want from women."

Arabella laughed outright at that, a surprisingly playful, musical sound. She covered her mouth as the laughter escaped, as if she were embarrassed by it, but no amount of trying would rein it in completely.

"What?" Gus enjoined. "You don't believe me?"

"I think it does not matter what I believe," she said, still laughing quite freely, the sound rippling over him like a warm breeze. "You are obviously what they call a legend in your own mind."

Yeah, so? he wanted to demand. Instead he said, "Listen, do you want to switch Reynaldo's attention from Supermodel Dacia to your own bad self, or what?"

She sobered immediately, resuming her imperious stance. "I wish for him to ask her to leave the yacht," she said, sidestepping the question of whether she wanted Reynaldo's attentions for herself. Gus considered it a very good sign.

"I can help spur that reality along," he offered.

"How?"

"By letting you in on a few secrets."

"What secrets?" she asked.

"Guy secrets," he told her. "Secrets of the brotherhood."

She eyed him suspiciously again. "Once more you are not making sense."

"Tell you what I'm gonna do," he said, mustering the most roguish smile in his ample arsenal. "I, Gus Torrance, who knows women better than just about any other man on this boat—save Reynaldo," he added meaningfully, because it was the truth, and because he knew it would put Arabella in the right frame of mind for what he wanted to offer her, "shall impart to you, Arabella Wilhelm, all of my best-kept secrets on how to attract a man. And I have lots of them," he further assured her, "because I myself have been attracted by many, many women on many, many occasions. I know what men like. Because, in case it's escaped your notice, I just so happen to be a man."

He paused, hoping she'd respond in some way to that final assertion. Respond by, say, sidling up next to him, threading her fingers through his hair, and murmuring in that accent of hers that he found so incredibly arousing, "Oh, it has not escaped my notice, big boy, that you are indeed a man."

Instead she responded by continuing to gaze at him as if she had no idea what he was talking about. Gus sighed inwardly.

"Anyway," he continued, "I can tell you everything you need to know to turn Reynaldo's head away from one Supermodel Dacia and keep his attention for yourself."

Gus had no qualms about revealing such secrets to Arabella. It wasn't that he didn't think she would use them to snare Reynaldo—he was confident that she would use them to do that very thing. But even if Reynaldo *did* turn his attentions to his fiancée—which, in Gus's opinion, wasn't likely—it would only be for a little while. The man had the attention span of a cheese grater. If it wasn't Supermodel Dacia keeping him preoccupied, it would be some other bit of skirt. Of that Gus was certain.

He decided not to dwell on the fact that Supermodel Dacia had been the focus of Reynaldo's attentions for more than a year now, something that suggested the prince's attention span was just a tad better than a kitchen utensil's. Instead Gus dwelled on the fact that this situation would offer him an opportunity to spend a little time with Arabella. That, he reminded himself, was the whole point to this endeavor.

Besides, in revealing his secrets to Arabella, Gus would turn *her* attentions to him, because he would be the one who had information she wanted. And that, for sure, was all that mattered. Because once he had her attentions, he was certain he could keep them. His attention span was *much* longer than a cheese grater's. And so, he suspected, was Arabella's.

"And what is it that you will request in return for this vast cache of wisdom?" she asked derisively. "Surely you cannot mean to share these . . . these 'secrets of the brotherhood' with me without expecting something in return."

"Oh, I fully expect something in return, Princess," he readily conceded.

Pink bloomed on her cheeks again, and Gus was reasonably certain that it wasn't because the sun shone any brighter in that moment than it had before. Probably, he thought, she was thinking about fallacy—or something—again.

"What?" she asked, her voice shallow, her gaze fixed on his. "What is it you will want from me in return?"

A barrage of ideas exploded in Gus's brain in response to her question, none of them in any way appropriate for discussion in polite company. So he only said, "Let me think on that, Princess. I'll let you know."

He noticed then that her chest seemed to be rising and falling in a rapid, irregular rhythm, and that her breathing only mimicked the sudden raggedness of his own respiration. Then he noted how her gaze dropped to his mouth and held there, how her lips parted in that maddeningly erotic way again, and how they, too, seemed to be stained with whatever it was that had darkened her cheeks. He felt the blood begin to race through his body at a dizzying pace, felt how the friction of its passage seemed to heat it to nearly boiling. Vaguely he felt himself moving slowly forward, and for one scant, lunatic moment, he could have sworn Arabella was pushing herself nearer to him, too.

Then, "Gus!" a familiar voice called out loudly.

And whatever odd spell had descended immediately evaporated. Arabella's eyes widened in panic, and she shrank back against the chaise longue and scooped up the paperback she had heedlessly let fall into her lap at some point during their exchange. And Gus spun around on the chaise to find Donovan beckoning to him wildly.

With a long, frustrated sigh Gus stood to make his way to the bar. But he knew he couldn't leave until he had a response from Arabella. "Well?" he asked pointedly.

She went out of her way not to look at him, instead focusing her attention on finding her lost place in her book. "Well what?" she asked. But her voice was a little shaky when she spoke, and she seemed to be having an awful lot of trouble turning the pages with such unsteady hands.

"What do you say?" he asked further. "You gonna take me up on my offer or what?"

She continued to thumb awkwardly through her paperback, still looking for the right page, but somehow Gus suspected she was seeing something other than the book in her hand. Finally, "Let me think on that," she said softly, still not looking at him, echoing his own earlier sentiment. "I will let you know." Then she settled her back against the chaise and steadied her gaze on her book, dismissing Gus with all the interest she might show an overly affectionate spaniel.

Left with no other choice than to retreat—for now—he made his way back to the bar and Donovan. "What is it?" he asked his friend when he got there.

"The prince is comin', and I knew you'd be up to no good, mon, so I came to warn you. And to work my shift. Go on now," he added before Gus had a chance to interject a word. "Before you get us both in trouble."

Gus nodded dispassionately, set the tray he'd nearly forgotten about on the bar, and pondered his options. He had the night off, he reminded himself, and the island of Nassau beckoned. Great beaches, lively bars, beautiful women, endless opportunities. He was certain he could find a willing woman to help him scratch the itch that thoughts of Arabella kept rubbing on him.

For some reason, though, and not too surprisingly, he realized he didn't want to leave the yacht. Instead he found himself wanting only to go below, to the cramped, windowless, airless little room he shared with Donovan and two of the stewards, strip down to his boxers, climb into his bunk, take a little nap, and dream. Dream about things that would almost certainly never come to pass.

With one last glance at Arabella—who, he noted, dropped her gaze frantically back to her book, which made him wonder what she had been looking at—he made his way back to his quarters.

Chapter 9

Keaton sipped his martini as he watched the sun hover seemingly inches above the ocean in the west, splashing a wide trail of pink-gold shimmers over the placid Caribbean. For all his traveling he'd never visited this little corner of the world before, and he didn't think he'd ever seen such serene waters. Nor had he ever seen any so clear, or of such an unusual, vivid blue-green color.

Even Captain Cooki and First Mate Mimi had remarked on it. As they'd left Nassau behind that morning, they'd all gazed over the side of the boat at one point to see a school of small sharks swimming not far beneath the water. Instead of finding the sight intimidating or frightening, however, it had made Keaton smile. Later in the day a school of dolphins had joined them, leaping and diving and chattering at them for nearly a half hour, keeping up with the yacht's—granted, leisurely—speed quite handily.

And now, with the limitless blue/green/pink/gold Caribbean spilling to the western horizon, and some tiny, unidentified island—sunwashed with pinks and golds—to the east, Keaton felt as if he'd tumbled into a dream. A pink/gold dream populated by water nymphs and mermaids and naiads and sirens, all swimming through his head, all quite naked, and all looking very much like—

Ruby Runyon.

Dammit. He had made it through almost a whole—he glanced down at his wristwatch and frowned—a whole fifteen minutes without thinking about her, he conceded. And only then because he'd been focused on finding the Bombay Sapphire so he could fix himself a drink, and then, of course, marveling at the play of color on the water. Still, almost fifteen minutes of engrossment in something other than Ruby Runyon was almost fifteen minutes of engrossment in something other than Ruby Runyon, he reminded himself. And it had been a *good* engrossment, too, by God.

At this point he would take what he could get.

Especially since the better part of his day had been spent making phone calls on her behalf, and, far more unpleasant, pleading with Reynaldo on her behalf, and, most unpleasant of all, trying to jibe all the phone calls with all the pleadings. After much back and forth and organizational hoo-ha—not to mention plying Reynaldo with a good half-dozen Cuba Libras to put him in the proper frame of mind—Keaton had lit on what he hoped would be a workable solution to the problem of Ruby's lack of papers. If things went the way they were supposed to—which granted, was a very big if—a copy of her birth certificate would be waiting for her at the customs office in San Juan, Puerto Rico, when they arrived at that destination. As long as she had a photo I.D. to prove she was who she said she was—like the driver's license she had thank-

fully brought with her—then everything should be fine
and she would be allowed entry into that territory. From
there, she would have no problem catching a flight home
to Miami. *If* things went the way they were supposed to.

He sighed heavily now as he pondered that . . . and
couldn't help feeling they were all doomed.

He pushed the thought away and tried to consider Ruby
instead, engrossment be damned. She had made herself
suspiciously scarce all day, something that had only contributed to Keaton's engrossment, because he'd kept
thinking that as long as she was out of his sight, she could
be up to just about anything. Naturally she hadn't been
able to leave the yacht, but that in itself had been disconcerting enough, because there were any number of ways
for her to get into—or to cause—trouble on *Mad Tryst*.

So far, though, they were still afloat, weren't they? he
reminded himself optimistically. No one had sabotaged or
ruined anything on board, had they? Well, not unless you
counted that disgusting little present Kurt had left in
Keaton's Gucci loafer earlier in the day, but that didn't
bear mentioning. And no, it hadn't been a serving of
Pflaumenkuchen. And, anyway, Keaton was reasonably
certain that Ruby Runyon hadn't been the one who put the
repugnant, ghastly little barbarian up to it. No, he was
quite sure the depraved, scabrous little basilisk had left his
surprise all on his own.

Treacherous, nauseating little miscreant.

And Keaton had checked the tabloids when he'd gone
ashore into Nassau the night before, and after searching
them thoroughly, he hadn't found anything in any of them
to suggest that someone had recently infiltrated Reynaldo's circle and was now feeding information about
wild squid orgies or anything like that to the media. Nor
had the prince been discovered unconscious in his bed

with a suspicious-looking bruise on his hip that might have been the result of a lethal injection.

So there was that much, at least, to feel heartened about.

Still, Keaton had no idea what to do about Ruby Runyon, fugitive waitress—or fugitive whatever. Especially when he turned his attention away from the radiant ocean and caught a glimpse of her stepping out onto the foredeck from the lounge, looking more than a little radiant herself. Because she somehow didn't seem like Ruby Runyon, fugitive waitress, anymore. No, suddenly she seemed like . . .

Well. She seemed like Ruby Runyon, exiled princess.

Good God, what had she done to herself? Keaton wondered, his hand halting his drink halfway to his mouth because he was too stunned to carry through with the action. She looked . . . She looked . . . She looked . . .

Wow. As they said on Pelagia. And elsewhere, too, probably. Still, "wow" seemed to cover it very nicely, in just about any language.

Her tiny, tight black cocktail dress from which she had spilled so freely the night before had been replaced this evening by something that fit much less snugly and much more modestly—a knee-length dress the color of well-aged pewter. It was paired with a short jacket of the same shimmery fabric whose collar was raised chicly over the back of her neck, and whose sleeves reached to her elbows. Her dark hair, which had tumbled liberally past her shoulders before, was now wound up the back of her head in much the same way as the countess wore her hair, though Ruby's long bangs gave her a more impish appeal. Silvery stockings refined the superb lines of her calves, Keaton couldn't help noting, and high-heeled sandals the same sparse color as her dress lifted her to nearer his own height. Not that she would ever come close to seeing eye to eye with him—in more ways than one, he couldn't help thinking—but neither did she seem the smidgen of a woman she had the night before.

Part of him resented the fact that she'd covered so much of herself and bound her hair so tersely. But another part of him—a more restless, more eager part—found himself envisioning, surprisingly well, in fact, what might lie beneath the garment, and how it might feel to liberate her silky hair, and let it fall free, and sift it and twine it and tangle it between his fingers.

And suddenly he felt way too overdressed in his cream linen suit and ivory dress shirt, with the Caribbean blue—coincidence, naturally—silk tie he'd chosen as a complement. Still, he couldn't exactly undress here, could he? Reynaldo wasn't having a party tonight. There would be no naked people or marine life in the Jacuzzi, or anywhere else, save private quarters. Later, however, in Keaton's own private quarters, maybe the two of them could—

Nothing, he assured himself. *Don't even* think *about that*. Don't think about how it would be to watch her skim off that jacket and unzip that dress, then lower it slowly down over a lacy, skimpy confection of bra and panties. Don't think about how it would be to reach behind her and unhook the bra, then fill your mouth with one of those abundant, ripe breasts and lave the tumid peak. Don't think about how it would be to slip your hand between your two damp bodies and find the hot, wet center of her, penetrating her with one long finger as her musky essence flows over you. Don't think about how it would be to have her lush, naked body bucking and sweating beneath yours as you pump yourself in and out and in even deeper than before.

Oops. Too late. He was already thinking about it. And

somehow he was certain he'd never be able to chase the images from his brain again.

Ruby caught sight of him at the same time he caught sight of her, he noticed, but where he took an involuntary step forward, she took one—quite voluntary, he was sure—backward. In fact, the nearer Keaton drew to her, the farther away she seemed to move, until she backed right into the bar behind her. Immediately she spun around and asked for something in a voice too low for Keaton to hear. But he saw Donovan—oh, sure, *now* he was manning the bar, when a beautiful woman was there—draw a bottle of very good single-malt Scotch from the well and pour it over ice, then hand it to her.

And still Keaton drew closer, without even fully realizing he had intended to make the journey.

"You, ah, you look lovely," he told Ruby as he came to a halt beside her at the bar, not quite able to keep the observation to himself, yet realizing even as he uttered it that "lovely" was a pale word compared to what she really was. But he thought she might not have interpreted "va-va-va-voooooooom" in the spirit in which he intended it, had he chosen that, uh, adjective instead. Or worse, she *would* have interpreted it in the spirit in which he intended it, and would consequently have popped him one in the eye. But good.

In spite of the paleness of the compliment, though, she blushed lavishly and gripped her drink more fiercely, dropping her gaze to the deck. Clearly she was uncomfortable with such simple praise, Keaton couldn't help thinking, almost as if she were unused to receiving it. Not that he believed *that* for a minute, of course, but there was something in her demeanor that indicated she had no idea how to react to such a comment.

"Um, thanks," she said with clear discomfort, still staring at her feet. "Arabella bought some clothes for me when she and Marisol went ashore last night. They're not the kind of thing I usually wear, though. I'm sure they were all incredibly expensive. But I'm going to pay her back," she hastened to add, very emphatically, lifting her gaze to meet Keaton's, as if it were very important that he believe her. "She told me not to worry about it, but I *will* pay her back. Someday. Some way. Honest, I will."

And, strangely, he found that he believed her about that. He also noted that she was on the verge of babbling, and he took it as a good sign, mainly because he feared that, feeling the way he did at the moment, he was bound to start babbling himself. Soon. And it would be better if she went first.

"It was nice of the countess to do that," he replied simply, in an effort to curb his babble reflex.

And it had been nice of Arabella, too, he thought further, babble reflex effectively curbed for now. Keaton couldn't recall the last time the countess had done something nice for someone. Not that she wasn't a pleasant person under normal circumstances. In fact, on the few occasions when Keaton had met her before she'd come to live on Pelagia, he'd found her to be a surprisingly charming, open, warm young woman. It had only been since she'd been forced to undertake this . . . this cruise from hell that she had grown so gloomy and dispirited. But considering the appallingly bad behavior of her fiancé, and the utter disregard Reynaldo showed her, Keaton supposed her sullenness wasn't to be unexpected.

Still, in taking Ruby under her wing, Arabella had begun to show a side of herself he hadn't seen for some time, and it was good to see. He hated to think it might retreat once more after Ruby disappeared from their midst. But he couldn't help worrying that it would. And he couldn't help worrying that a lot more might disappear when the fugitive waitress did. Interesting that she should have had such an influence on so many of them after so short a time among them.

"Arabella picked up quite a few things for me, in fact," Ruby continued, scattering Keaton's thoughts. "She did it so I wouldn't have to wear Marisol's clothes for the rest of the trip." Her smile fell some as she added in an uneasy whisper, "I just wish Arabella realized that not everyone thinks thong underwear is comfortable the way she does. I think that's a European thing, you know? But what a choice. The thong bikinis Arabella bought me, or cotton underpants of Marisol's that are roughly the size of Rhode Island. Sheesh."

Keaton squeezed his eyes shut tight at the image that erupted in his brain with the mention of women's underthings. Naturally it was the image of Ruby in a thong bikini that captured his attention most readily, and the vision sent his entire body into overdrive. Immediately he tried to tamp down his growing arousal by picturing her in underpants the size of Rhode Island instead. Even there, though, she looked amazingly sexy. In fact, he thought further, trying to picture her in something even less attractive than giant underpants, she even looked sexy dressed in a nun's habit. And a lumberjack outfit. And a chicken suit. And Lederhosen.

And what the hell was wrong with him, fantasizing about a woman in such a way? he demanded of himself. Worse, of finding her attractive in such a way? Underpants the size of Rhode Island, for God's sake. Lederhosen, for God's sake. Anyway, he was sure Ruby had chosen the thong to wear tonight. He hoped so, anyway. A person should always be open to new experiences, after all.

He wondered briefly if all American women spoke as

frankly as she did about things like underwear. Then he remembered that he knew several American women, and not one of them had ever spoken the phrase "thong bikini" in his presence. But none of them was anything like Ruby.

To dispel the image of her dressed in thong underwear—and nothing *but* the thong underwear—he focused instead on imagining her dressed as Marisol—at least, in more than Marisol's giant underpants. He found that, at last, he'd discovered something to clothe her in that put quite the damper on the thong bikini vision. Well, at least enough to keep him from babbling.

"You were wearing Marisol's clothes?" he asked, unable to stop the smile that curled his lips at the thought.

"Only for a little while," she told him.

His grin broadened. No wonder she'd hidden herself away all day. "Don't tell me. Let me guess," he said. "The red flowered muumuu that says, 'Aloha from Waikiki' in huge purple letters?"

She grinned back. "No, I had on the one with the Andy Warhol avocados and pineapples."

"That's a nice one, too," Keaton agreed with a chuckle. "But my favorite is the one her daughter sent her from Graceland with the guitars and Cadillacs on it."

"Hmmm . . . I don't think I want to know," Ruby said.

"It's just as well," Keaton told her. "If memory serves, that one caused one of the stewards to go blind for two days."

She chuckled, too, at that, seeming to grow a little more at ease. But when she lifted her drink to her lips for a small sip, Keaton noticed that her fingers trembled slightly. She was nervous, he realized. Good. There was no reason that he should be the only one.

"So where are we headed now?" she asked. "I called my mom's hotel in Las Vegas yesterday and left a message for her, telling her I wouldn't be home for a few days. But I didn't want to tell her exactly what happened—"

"You didn't want her to worry," Keaton interjected. "That was a good daughterly thing to do."

"Ah, actually," Ruby said, shifting her gaze to the side a bit, "I just didn't want to humiliate myself."

"Oh," Keaton replied, nonplussed.

"I mean, Mama and Grandma Pearl would never let me hear the end of it if they knew I'd accidentally stowed away on a potentially behanding prince's yacht because I was trying to get away from my possibly Mafia-connected and definitely married boyfriend," she explained. "And they'd tell *every*body back in Appalachimahoochee, and I'd never be able to show my face there again. Not that I really like going back to Appalachimahoochee all that much, anyway, but it *is* home, so . . ."

She let her voice trail off without finishing, but not before Keaton realized how far into babble mode she'd moved. That was why he didn't comment on her explanation, even though he would have loved to know where—and what—Appalachi-whatever was, not to mention request clarification on the "potentially behanding prince" thing. There was no reason to encourage her. Not in her current . . . mode.

"Anyway," she began again after taking a deep breath, "I just told Mama I was going down to the Keys with some friends, and I'd call her when I got back." She swallowed a bit anxiously, and her eyes clouded over with clear worry. "I'm just not real sure when I'll *be* back, you know?"

Oh, Keaton had really hoped to avoid this particular subject for a little while—say four or five days . . . or weeks—but judging by the expression on Ruby's face, he wasn't even going to be able to put it off for four or five minutes. She wanted to know—and had every right to know—where they were going and how much longer she would be stranded aboard *Mad Tryst*. He just wished he could give her the kind of answer she wanted. Instead of the one he would be forced to give.

Hedging, though, he told her, "Well, I spoke to Reynaldo before we left Nassau. I was hoping to get him to go back to Miami, since it's really not that far."

"And what did he say?" she asked hopefully—though, not, he couldn't help noting, as hopefully as she might have, considering her situation.

"He refused," Keaton told her. "He won't go backward, Ruby, won't retrace his steps. It's an allegorical thing with him, though he'd never admit that." Mostly because Reynaldo didn't know what the word "allegorical" meant, Keaton couldn't help adding to himself. "He thinks he has to move forward, even if he doesn't have anything even vaguely resembling a destination in mind. Ever since we began this cruise, he's made sure he never returns to a place he's already visited."

"So then where *are* we going now?" Ruby asked again, looking more worried than ever.

"I did eventually manage to talk Reynaldo into going to Puerto Rico," Keaton told her, still trying to avoid the complete answer he knew he'd have to give her sooner or later. "At first he didn't want to do that, either, but when I explained the situation to him, he finally relented. Better still, I've arranged for a copy of your birth certificate to be sent there by courier, so it will be there when we arrive. And there's a big airport there, with regular flights to Miami."

Her expression grew even more concerned as he spoke. "You 'explained the situation'?" she echoed, her voice sounding shallow and almost terrified for some reason. He found it odd that she didn't voice her relief about the birth certificate business but refrained from commenting. "You told the prince about me?" she continued. "You told him I stowed away? But you promised me you wouldn't do that. Reynaldo won't . . . I mean, he's not going to . . . to . . ."

"Throw you overboard?" Keaton supplied helpfully.

She flexed the fingers of the hand that wasn't gripping her drink with white-knuckled ferocity. "Actually, I was more worried about, um . . . losing a hand."

Oooo, so that was what she had meant by the "potentially behanding prince" thing. Keaton laughed again. Just how primitive did she think Pelagians were? he wondered. Then again, some of the thoughts he'd been entertaining about her over the last forty-eight hours could hardly be described as civilized, could they? Then again, he wasn't a native Pelagian, either, so he didn't have to worry about setting an example, primitive or otherwise, right?

"Don't worry," he told her, banishing those thoughts—for now. "I didn't tell Reynaldo you were a stowaway. And he hasn't cut off anyone's hands for, oh . . . weeks now."

Her expression indicated she wasn't sure whether he was joking or not. "Then what did you tell him?"

Oh, that, Keaton thought. Hmmm . . . That was something else he'd just as soon not go into right now. Not when the two of them were getting along so well. "I, uh . . . I told him you were a, um . . . a friend of mine," he hedged. "A friend who, uh, who needed a favor."

Now she eyed him suspiciously. "Prince Reynaldo is going to go miles out of his way and do something he doesn't want to do as a favor for a friend of yours who he's never even met?"

Keaton nodded uncomfortably, but deliberately said nothing to elaborate.

Unfortunately his response did nothing to curb Ruby's suspicions. Because she continued, "Funny, but from what

I hear about him, he's not the kind of guy who'd do a favor like that, even for a friend of yours."

Keaton bit back a frustrated growl. There was no way he was going to be able to avoid this issue. So, with much reluctance, he said, "All right. Fine. What I actually told him was that you're a woman I picked up in a bar while we were in Miami, and that I invited you to the party the other night, and that we both had too much to drink at the party, and that we disappeared into my stateroom for . . . ah . . . to be alone," he finished discreetly. "And we got so caught up in, uh . . . what we were doing that we didn't realize the yacht had left port."

He hurried through the rest of his story as quickly as he could. "Then the next thing we knew it was morning and we were almost in Nassau, and you couldn't get home, and now I need to get you home as soon as possible because you've become a real harridan and I can't stand your harping and bitching anymore, so could Reynaldo please see fit to point the yacht in the direction of some destination where we can get your papers, so that I can rid myself of you once and for all."

Ruby said nothing in response to his narrative, simply gazed at him in bland silence, as if she expected to hear more.

So Keaton concluded uncomfortably, "That was what I told Reynaldo. And once he stopped laughing raucously and slapping me on the back and saying, 'Way to go, Keaton, old boy, it's about time you left the monastery behind,' he agreed to tell Captain Cooki to take us to Puerto Rico, where I've arranged to have your papers sent by courier," he said again, more meaningfully, hoping for a response.

Ruby continued to study him dispassionately for a moment, and he would have given anything to know what she was thinking about. Mostly he wanted to know if she was going to slap him, so he might have a chance to duck.

"Gee, sort of like *The Love Boat* meets *Fatal Attraction*, huh?" she said flatly, still ignoring his announcement about her papers. Interesting.

But he only replied, "Well, yeah, I guess you could say that." Although he really wished she wouldn't.

"Then I don't suppose I should be standing here talking nicely to you, should I?" she asked, her expression still non-clue-offering. "Me being a harridan and all, I mean. Of course, it would be okay for me to stand here and harass you mercilessly, wouldn't it? I could even throw in some harping and bitching, how would that be? 'Cause now that I think about it, that could actually be a lot of fun. Hey, I have an idea. Why don't I start off by throwing my drink in your face? That would be convincing."

"Now, Ruby," Keaton said slowly, softly, and—he hoped—placatingly, "that won't be necessary." And although he was reasonably certain she was only kidding about that drink-throwing business, he positioned himself to duck, should that, in fact, become necessary.

But instead of throwing her drink in his face, she only lifted it to her lips for an idle sip. "You men," she said after swallowing. "I cannot believe you actually believe the things you say to each other. Oh, well," she added before he had a chance to comment, "at least we're headed for Puerto Rico."

Keaton started to nod, then immediately switched to shaking his head. Ah, hell. He was going to have to tell her the rest of what he had to tell her, as much as he hated to tell her, because she was going to find out sooner or later anyway, and he might as well just go ahead and get it over with, since he was already pretty much prepared to be slapped silly and was ready to duck, should that, in fact, become necessary.

"Um. Yeah. Well." He bit his lower lip as he tried to think of the best way to put this, and couldn't help noting the way Ruby's mouth went slack and her eyes went darker as she watched the motion. Well, well, well. Maybe he could use her reaction to his advantage. Maybe, if she felt even a little frisson of the scorching heat he felt burning up the air between them, she wouldn't be paying attention to the rest of what he had to say. And then maybe, if she felt even a little frisson of that scorching heat, they could retreat to his quarters and . . . do that other stuff he'd been thinking about earlier.

Or maybe she would just slap him silly and be done with it.

He inhaled deeply and tried again. "We are headed for Puerto Rico, where your I.D. will be waiting for you," he confirmed. "Right after we go to Bermuda, which, unfortunately, *won't* have your I.D. waiting for you, and which *won't* welcome you without proof of citizenship."

She seemed not to hear what he had said at all this time, because she just kept gazing at his mouth as if she had some real serious plans for it. Keaton was about to step forward and offer his help in that regard, but, alas, his words did finally seem to register on her.

Because she dropped her mouth open in what appeared to be indignation and cried, "*Bermuda?*"

"I'm afraid so," he told her.

"But . . . but . . . but . . . How long will that take?"

"Not long," he lied. "From here it's like running up to the 7-Eleven on the corner for a quart of milk."

She didn't look anywhere near convinced.

"Except that, you know, the 7-Eleven on the corner is

closed," he continued, "so instead, you have to drive to the other one that's about halfway across the country."

"Halfway across the country?" she cried.

"Three days, tops, to get there at our current speed," he promised, hoping he was right about that. Captain Cooki had been enjoying an Amaretto sour—her third—when he'd asked her about it. "And I'm sure Reynaldo won't want to spend more than a couple of days in port. He rarely does. Then, I swear to you, Ruby, it's back south to Puerto Rico and an airport to take you home."

She gazed at him in silence for a long moment, but for some reason she didn't seem to be quite as outraged as she had initially been about her predicament. "So it's going to be at least a week before I can get off this boat?" she asked.

"Look, I'm sorry," Keaton apologized, "but it was the best I could do. Reynaldo isn't an easy man to convince to do anything. If you have any hope of getting home anytime soon, this is the only way. Trust me."

She gazed at him with that expressionless expression again, but there was definitely something going on in that lovely head of hers. "Yeah, home," she said finally, softly, and, if Keaton wasn't mistaken, a bit morosely. She expelled a long, dispirited sigh. "Gotta get home, after all. Can't just cruise around aimlessly forever, can I?"

"I don't know why not," Keaton replied dryly. "It seems to be working for Reynaldo."

"Yeah, well, if I were a princess, maybe I could get away with it," she countered. "But no. I have to go home."

Keaton cocked his head to one side and considered her carefully. "You sound like you don't want to go home."

She was silent for a moment, gazing thoughtfully into her drink now. Then, even more softly than before, she replied, "No, I do want to go home. Just . . . not back to the one I left. Does that make sense?"

The way she voiced the question made it sound as if she didn't expect a response, so he offered none.

"For some reason," she continued, quietly still, as if she were talking more to herself than she was to Keaton, "suddenly, I realize I really don't miss my home as much as I probably should."

"How ironic," he said. "You're probably the only person on board who feels that way. The rest of us would give almost anything to be able to go back to Pelagia." He neglected to add, however, that he didn't miss the home he'd left behind as much as he probably should, either. Interesting that they would both feel so similarly, coming from such vastly different places.

Still studying her drink, Ruby said, "That's because the rest of you have good lives waiting for you when you get home."

Now that, Keaton thought, was debatable. Not just because many of them on board weren't welcome back home in Pelagia, but because even during the good times, there had been some unrest for some of them, himself included. Although he had no complaint with his prospects back on Pelagia—or, at least, he *hadn't* had any complaint with them once upon a time, back before King Francisco's death and Prince Reynaldo's exile—there had still been a certain amount of dissatisfaction in his life, though he'd never quite been able to pinpoint what exactly had generated that dissatisfaction. And he knew of a certain countess who would probably prefer that things be different—both then and now.

Still, it would be nice if they could all return to Pelagia, in whatever way possible and go back to living lives that were, if not ideal, then at least agreeable. Or else it would be nice if they could find a home away from home someplace in the world, where they all might settle once and for all, and make new lives for themselves in the best way they could. But they hadn't found that place yet, if in fact it existed at all. There were times when Keaton honestly believed he would spend the rest of his life on this yacht and never see a homeland—of any kind— again.

"What's so terrible about your life back in Miami that makes you want to avoid it?" he asked Ruby.

"It's not that it's terrible," she said. "It's just not . . ." She shrugged uncomfortably. "It's not what I wanted. It's not what I planned. It's not what I expected it would be when I left home to strike out on my own."

"And when did you leave home?" he asked. Suddenly, for some reason, Keaton's curiosity about Ruby was more than idle.

"Eight years ago," she said. "When I was eighteen. The day after I graduated from high school."

"And what were your plans when you left?"

She expelled a dubious sound. "Naive creature that I was, I was sure that by now I'd be—"

"What?" he said when she stopped herself before finishing.

"It sounds so stupid now," she told him, obviously embarrassed. "So impossible. I mean, I've been working in dead-end jobs for eight years trying to realize my dream, and I haven't even come close. I don't know what I could have possibly been thinking when I was eighteen."

"Yeah, well not many of us do think reasonably at eighteen," Keaton pointed out.

She met his gaze levelly, and he marveled again at the depth and clarity and darkness of her gray eyes. "What did you want to be when you were eighteen?" she asked him.

He smiled. "When I was eighteen, I fully intended to become prime minister of Pelagia," he told her.

She smiled back, something that sent a strange little frisson of heat shimmying right down his spine, a not altogether disagreeable sensation. "Wow, that's pretty ambitious," she said. "So what were you actually doing when you left Pelagia?"

Now Keaton's smile fell some. "I, uh . . . actually, I was in line to become prime minister of Pelagia," he said.

Her smile fell, too, thereby extinguishing the frisson of heat that had assailed him, and Keaton missed it immediately. "Oh," she said softly. "See? Other people make their dreams come true. Why can't I?"

"Depends on the dream," he said. "There's more to dream about than finding the perfect job. And there are plenty of people who dream about things they can never have, things they never get."

She studied him intently for a moment. "What is it you dream about that you can't have?" she asked.

Oh, if she only knew what he'd dreamed about for the last couple of nights. "I dream about going home," he said evasively, but truthfully. What he didn't tell her was that he also dreamed about someone being there to greet him when he arrived, someone who would make that place feel more welcome.

"Home can be wherever you want it to be," she said. "It doesn't have to be the place you left behind. It can be the place where you're going."

"True," he readily agreed. "I think that's what's been so difficult about this past year. The fact that, in the entire world—and we've traveled a hell of a lot of it by now—there hasn't been one place that's felt genuinely good to me. That's felt comfortable and welcoming to me. That's felt like home." He hesitated only a moment before revealing further, "If you want to know the truth, even Pelagia didn't feel like home to me when I lived there, even though it was the closest thing to a home I ever had."

Keaton couldn't believe he'd just divulged such a thing to her—he'd never once admitted it to anyone else, not even his family. And why Ruby Runyon, of all people, should provoke the confession was beyond him. Somehow, though, confiding in her felt oddly natural, strangely right. She just had a way about her of making a person feel . . . comfortable. Welcoming. Visions of thong bikinis notwithstanding.

"Where do your parents live?" she asked before he had a chance to contemplate the realization further. "Are they still in Pelagia?"

He shook his head. "No, they own Thoroughbred farm in Virginia," he told her. "They wanted to be close to Washington, where my father used to work a long time ago. They moved to Virginia from Pelagia about two years ago, after my father retired from his position as ambassador."

Her mouth dropped open slightly at his revelation. "Your father was an ambassador?" she asked.

He nodded. "The American ambassador to Pelagia, yes."

"Wow."

And Ruby had never met her father, Keaton recalled her saying. She didn't even know who he was. She'd grown up in a trailer park, Arabella had told him, in rural Florida, and had barely ever left the state. Keaton had done his growing up in all the most cosmopolitan centers of the world. Ruby hadn't even attended college, if she'd been working since leaving home. He had four degrees himself, two of them advanced. He wondered if there was any way the two of them could have come from more differing backgrounds than they did. And he marveled at how, in spite of those vast differences, the two of them had landed in exactly the same place.

He remembered then that she hadn't yet told him what it was she had wanted to be when she left home. So he asked her again.

She sighed heavily in response, returning her gaze to her drink. "It just sounds like a really dumb idea now," she repeated. "I'm embarrassed to tell you." In spite of her comment, though, she returned her gaze to his and said, "I wanted to be . . . an actress. In the movies."

It wasn't what he had expected to hear, and he smiled in response. "An actress? Really?"

She nodded and stared down at her drink once again. "Pretty dumb, huh? I just . . . I wanted to *be* somebody, you know? Somebody that people *saw*. Somebody that people listened to. Somebody that people liked to see coming. I wanted to be a comedic actress. I wanted to make people laugh," she finished, her voice dropping to a softer pitch with every word she spoke. After the passage of a heartbeat, she added, "On purpose, I mean."

She uttered that last remark so quietly that Keaton almost didn't hear it. And something told him that she hadn't meant for him to. So he didn't comment, only tucked the remark away along with the other—very telling—things she'd said. And he began to think that maybe, just maybe, there was more to Ruby Runyon than what he'd seen so far.

He shook his head. "It's not so dumb," he said in response to her other remark instead. "Even the most successful actors and actresses all had to start somewhere. I imagine quite a few of them worked dead-end jobs at some point."

"Not for eight years," she countered.

"How do you know?"

She lifted a shoulder and let it drop. "I just think if it was going to happen for me, it would have happened by now," she said. "Or that I would at least be a little closer than I was when I first left home. But after eight years of going to auditions and not being able to even find an agent, I guess I just need to face the facts and admit that I don't have what it takes. Whatever *it* is."

"Maybe you just haven't had the right breaks," Keaton said. "Maybe you just haven't been in the right place at the right time." He wasn't trying to patronize her. And he had no idea whether she was talented. But he suspected that much of success—in any field—was timing. Timing and connections and being in the right place. And maybe Ruby's timing and connections and places simply hadn't gotten in sync yet.

"Well, it is really hard to break into the business," she agreed. "Almost impossible, really. Especially in Miami. It's all about who you know and who they know that might know someone else. And all the people in the know that way hang out in social circles that I sure can't get into. I mean, you have to be a certain kind of person to break into those social circles. Or you have to know someone. Or both. I'll never make it. I'm doomed to be a waitress for the rest of my life."

She looked so forlorn and sad that Keaton found himself wanting to gather her close and tuck her head beneath his chin and simply hold her. Odd, that. Especially since his desire at the moment didn't extend beyond just holding her. Normally, once he fantasized about having a woman that close, the impression didn't stop at comforting. With Ruby looking as she did just then, though, for some reason, all he wanted to do was make things right for her, however he could.

Which might explain how he came to hear himself say,

"I know people in those social circles, Ruby. Maybe not in Miami, but in other places. Places like, oh ... I don't know. New York. Los Angeles. Would you be interested in getting to know anyone in one of those cities?"

Her head snapped up as he offered the comment, and she gazed at him with unmistakable hope. But she said not a word to encourage him, as if she feared doing so might somehow make him change his mind.

"And Reynaldo knows all kinds of people in the entertainment business," Keaton added. "He's pretty much a groupie, if you want to know the truth. You'd be amazed at some of the people he's had aboard this very yacht."

Still Ruby said nothing in response. And still she looked very hopeful.

"And looking the way you look right now," he continued, "you'd have no trouble breaking into those circles." He enjoyed another slow perusal of her from head to toe, liking what he saw very, very much. No, he thought, looking the way she did now, she'd have no trouble breaking into those circles at all.

"Get out," she finally said with much surprise. She lifted her free hand and placed her palm against his shoulder, then pushed him. Hard. Unprepared for the gesture, Keaton stumbled backward a bit before righting himself. "As *if*," she added eloquently.

All right, so she *looked* the part of those social circles, Keaton thought. The minute she opened her mouth—and pushed someone—she'd be tossed out of those circles on her lovely keester. Unless ...

"I could offer you a few pointers about how to infiltrate those circles," he heard himself say further. "Just enough to help you bluff your way through, I mean. Until you make a few connections of your own."

She eyed him warily. "You're joking, right?"

He shook his head. "No, of course not."

She continued to study him in silence for a moment more, as if she expected him to point a finger at her and laugh hysterically and shout, "April fool!" even though it was August. Finally, though, she expelled an exasperated— and not especially socially acceptable—sound and said, "Keaton, I grew up in a trailer park. I don't have anything higher than a high school education. I don't know who my father is. I work as a waitress. The only way I'd fit into one of those social circles would be as an employee of the caterer."

"You also drink very fine single-malt Scotch and have read Marcel Proust," he pointed out.

"I'm a reader," she told him. "I read. And I drink single-malt Scotch because I've seen so many bartenders laugh hysterically at women who order frou-frou drinks."

"Hey, it's as good a reason as any," Keaton said. "And being a reader puts you light-years ahead of the majority of the socially advanced. Most of them never read anything past the part that says, 'Click here for more information about tax shelters.' The seeds are planted, Ruby. We just need to make them blossom, that's all."

"Yeah, but Scotch and Proust . . . that's all just superficial stuff," she told him. "I'm not the genuine article. I never could be."

He gaped at her. "Oh, come on. What do you think social climbing is all about in the first place?" he demanded. "It's *appearance*, not substance. All of it is appearance. All of it is superficial. I've been around social climbing my entire life. And, sweetheart, I can make you look like you're on the highest rung of the ladder. I'm the perfect instructor. Because I can be every bit as superficial as the next person. *More* superficial," he added proudly. "And given a little time, I can make you superficial, too."

She gaped back at him, and he could see that she was trying very, very hard once again not to get her hopes up. "You'd do that for me?" she asked, clearly incredulous. "You'd make me superficial?"

This time Keaton was the one to shrug. "Hey, why not?" he said. "It'll take us a few days to get to Bermuda. Then more to get to Puerto Rico. Instructing you in the finer points of social climbing and superficiality would give us something to pass the time. And besides . . ."

Besides, he thought, he owed her a debt, in a way. Her presence on *Mad Tryst*, however annoying, however exasperating, however maddening it had been up to this point, had also offered him the most welcome—if temporary—distraction he'd had since leaving Pelagia. And every time he looked at her, he felt stirrings inside himself that made him react in ways he hadn't reacted for a very long time, stirrings that made him feel like—

Well. He owed her a debt for that, too.

"Besides?" she coaxed him, and only then did he recall that he had begun to speak his observations aloud.

Not that he had any intention of revealing to her what was going through his brain at that point. Nor what was going through any of his other body parts, either. That, he was certain, would only lead to trouble. Still, he did owe her something resembling an answer.

"Besides," he said again. Then he smiled. "It might even be fun."

Fun, he repeated to himself as Ruby Runyon's responding smile went supernova. Oh, yeah. There was *much* fun to be had in being forced into close quarters with a beautiful, desirable woman he would never, ever allow himself to have, because it would be only temporary and because they both came from two different—too different—worlds. There was *much* fun to be had in having his libido and senses tied in knots, and in playing Professor Henry Higgins to an Eliza Doolittle he never could have seen coming.

Fun. Oh, yeah, Keaton thought again. It would be at least as much fun as a road accident. That was a given.

"When do we start?" Ruby asked him.

He expelled a restless sigh and told himself he wasn't making a big mistake. "No time like the present," he said.

And he had to admit that that was certainly true. Because never in his life had there been anything quite resembling this moment. And he couldn't help wondering if he'd ever have another one like it again, once Ruby Runyon was back home where she belonged.

Chapter 10

When Arabella emerged from the companionway onto the forward deck at just past sunset, she saw Keaton and Ruby standing on the starboard side of the yacht, bathed in the soft golden glow of a lantern burning softly on the bar, clearly steeped in very deep conversation. She smiled. She had not realized even when she chose the dress for Ruby that the other woman would look so beautiful wearing it. But Arabella had wanted to give her something special. Even having met her so recently, she could tell that Ruby Runyon was a kind and gentle person, one who had been denied the opportunity to make the most of herself, her life.

Keaton also obviously appreciated the young woman's new look, if the expression on his face at the moment was any indication. These developments, too, were exceeding Arabella's most fervent wishes and plans. Keaton needed a diversion. He had earned it, having to deal with Reynaldo on a daily basis. The man was suited to much better things than being the prince's nursemaid, but the obligation he felt to the royal del Fuego family ran too deep for him to abandon Reynaldo. And Keaton, Arabella thought, should be rewarded for that.

She had seen the way he had looked at Ruby that first night she had come aboard, and last night, as Arabella had shopped for clothes for the young woman, she had been struck by an idea. An idea that, she thought smugly, seemed to be progressing very nicely at the moment. She paused to thank whatever fateful current had carried Ruby into their midst. Already the stowaway had brought about some welcome changes, not the least of which was simply to improve a few moods. No matter what Arabella had to do to keep her on board for a while longer, she would do it. Even if it meant she had to ask Reynaldo for a favor or two along the way.

Right now, however, Arabella did not have to think about her wretched excuse for a fiancé. Because right now, her wretched fiancé was nowhere to be seen. And he was most assuredly not alone in his absence. She was confident that he and Superdolt Dacia would not make an appearance until dinner was served in a few hours. The two of them generally seemed to be ... occupied ... in the late afternoons and early evenings. Which was fine with Arabella. Today, at least.

Because today there was something very important that she had to do while Reynaldo was ... occupied. And now, she decided, was as good a time as any to do it.

She inhaled a deep, fortifying breath, then adjusted the filmy ivory shawl she had thrown on over the sleeveless, pale pink silk sheath and pearls that she had donned for the evening's festivities. Then she ran that same hand back over her hair to be certain it was well contained in its chignon. In fact, all of her must be well contained tonight, she thought. Because what she was planning to do tonight was anything *but* well contained.

In fact it was madness.

But then not much in her life had made sense for the past twelve months, had it? Which, of course, was not unexpected, considering the fact that her life had gone nowhere for the past twelve months. Oh, certainly Arabella herself—in body, at least—had gone to many, many places, had traveled from one side of the world to the other. But her spirit, her hopes, her dreams . . . All had remained static. Worse than static. All had, in fact, shrunk backward, grown smaller. Some of her, she could not help thinking, had disappeared completely.

When she had moved to Pelagia two months before she was to wed Reynaldo, Arabella had been so hopeful, so excited, so happy about what was to come. Although she had not known her fiancé well—or at all, really—she had been certain that eventually the two of them would find much to like, perhaps even love, in each other. Reynaldo was an attractive, charming man, and Arabella did not think it immodest to view herself as attractive and charming as well. She had many other good qualities, too—or at least she had, once upon a time—and she had been confident that Reynaldo was a good man. His parents, after all, were both lovely people. There was no reason to think they would have raised their only child to be any different from themselves.

But Reynaldo *was* different, something Arabella had discovered within days of arriving on Pelagia to become his bride. He was spoiled, self-centered, and thoughtless. And he had made it clear to Arabella immediately after her arrival, through both his actions and his words, that he had no intention of approaching their marriage with the same hopes and dreams of making it work that she had embraced. In fact he had also made it clear that he was utterly infatuated with another woman—Superidiot Dacia, whom even Arabella could see did not love him.

And yet *still* Arabella had been determined to make their marriage work. She told herself that in time Reynaldo would come to see her in a favorable light, and, even more important, she would grow to care for him. She told herself she could change him. She told herself that once he got to know her, he would forsake Superidiot Dacia and others like her. She told herself that, somehow, the two of them would make everything work.

Arabella told herself many things during that time. She continued to dream the dreams of her childhood about Reynaldo and her life with him. She tried to convince herself that everything would be fine, and that eventually she would be happy. Or, at least, happy enough. But no matter how hard she tried to make everything all right, Reynaldo would have none of it, would have none of her. He wanted Superdolt Dacia instead.

And to Superfool Dacia, Reynaldo was a publicity tool and nothing more. The only reason she was still with him after all this time was that he had not yet run his course in that department. Thanks to all her appearances on all the "Reynaldo Watch" minutes, Supermoron Dacia had found much fame and fortune. And she would stay with Reynaldo as long as that continued. But if something—someone—better came along, Superdunce Dacia would leave Reynaldo, Arabella knew. And Arabella must be ready when that moment came, because she must honor her obligation to marry Reynaldo. She had made too many promises—to her parents, to the del Fuego family, to her own people, to Reynaldo's people . . . to Reynaldo, and to herself—for her to break them all.

Still, if Reynaldo were the one to break the engagement, well . . . There would be nothing Arabella could do but accept his decision. If something happened that caused him to view her in such a way that he would not—could not—marry her, then she would have no choice but to honor his decision to release her. She would have no choice but to walk away and live her life elsewhere, in some other fashion.

As things stood now, however, Reynaldo fully intended to go through with their arranged marriage—someday. He intended to return to Pelagia somehow, and resume what he saw as his rightful seat on the throne. And when he did, he intended to have at his side the queen who had been selected for him. There was enough of the del Fuego honor in him that he was too frightened to undo what his parents had done before they died, in promising him to Arabella. And Arabella was no braver than he—she would not, could not break the promise her family had made to his two decades ago. Instead, she would continue to lie to herself and hide behind her girlish fantasies.

Her parents had been very good to her, she reminded herself, had given her everything she could have ever wanted. She had understood from the day she was old enough to understand such things that because she had been born to the social station she had, there were certain obligations she must meet. She had learned early that in return for all the wondrous things she had been given, she must be willing to give something back. Even if that *something* was herself.

And besides, she reminded herself further, what else was there for her out there in the big, wide world but to be Reynaldo's wife? She knew of no other way to live her life, having had no choice in the matter for as long as she could remember. She knew little of the world, despite being well-traveled. She had no close friends, regardless of her many acquaintances. She was trained for no career, even with her vast education in social graces. The idea of striking out on her own terrified Arabella. She had never been allowed to think for herself, and because of that, she wasn't sure she even knew how. And that, she supposed, was the most terrifying thing of all.

But she was tired of waiting for Reynaldo to either honor his obligation to marry her or agree to a mutual dissolution of their engagement. If both he and Arabella agreed to such a dissolution, then they could reach an agreement with their families that would leave no one looking dishonorable. But as long as one of them insisted the engagement was valid, there was nothing the other could do but honor it.

Unless Reynaldo freed her, Arabella had no choice but to keep herself in preparation to marry him. She owed it to her parents, she owed it to his. She owed it to her country, she owed it to his—even if his was currently in a state of turmoil. Such might not always be the case. A day might very well come when Reynaldo could return to Pelagia as king. And when he did, he would need and want his queen by his side. Even if he did not love her. Arabella had been groomed her entire life to become Reynaldo's wife and queen. To stay by his side, regardless of his circumstances. To bear his children and heirs. And she would do so, if that was what he wished.

But if, for some reason, he did not wish it . . .

Perhaps, with a little nudging, Reynaldo would be forced to make a decision. Now. One way or the other. Arabella only hoped she knew what she was doing in providing that nudge. But yesterday afternoon, she had been presented with an opportunity that might, in some way, make her fiancé realize he must make a choice. Now. He must marry her. Now.

Or he must set her free.

Gus the bartender, for all of his . . . annoying traits . . . had, as they had said in that American gangster film, made her an offer she could not refuse. If he had information that might help her divert Reynaldo's attentions from Supernincompoop Dacia to herself, then Arabella wanted him to impart that information to her. And if that information did not divert Reynaldo's attentions from Supercretin Dacia, then perhaps Gus's presence—Gus's interest—would.

Arabella's stomach pitched as the thought unrolled in her head. Because she had decided not only to take Gus up on his offer to . . . instruct her in the ways of men, but also to use his presence on board *Imperial Majesty* to make Reynaldo see her for what she was—a woman. A woman who had the power and presence to interest other men. She intended to ask Gus if he would pretend to be interested in her in such a way. She did not think he would mind pretending. She could tell by the way he teased her that he liked her. And although she had always before done her best not to encourage him, now, she thought, perhaps she should.

Not that she intended to mislead him. She would tell him immediately that she was only planning to feign interest in him for the sake of, she hoped, making Reynaldo notice her. And she did not for a moment think that there was anything more to Gus's attentiveness to her than simple flirting. He was the kind of man who responded in such a way to all women, she was sure. Perhaps the fact that he was so clearly a womanizer would make Reynaldo even angrier when—if—he noticed Gus's attentions.

Arabella hoped so. Because she could not stand this state of waiting any longer. One way or another, she needed to move forward with her life, whether that meant marrying Reynaldo or having him cast her aside.

Tonight she would begin the process of moving forward. And she hoped it did not all backfire in her face.

Before she knocked on the door of the cabin that she knew Gus shared with three other crew members, Arabella pressed her ear to the cool metal and listened for any sort of sound that might suggest he was not alone. She did not want anyone to see her there, did not want anyone to know it was she who would initiate this . . . this game that she was about to arrange with Gus. She had taken care to make sure that his cabinmates were elsewhere on the yacht before she had come below, but she wanted to be doubly certain before knocking.

A countess could never be too careful.

She heard not a sound from the other side of the door—not even enough to let her know that Gus was present. But he must be, she told herself, because he was nowhere else on the yacht—she had checked that, too. Quickly, before she lost her nerve, she lifted her fist and completed three quick, quiet raps on the metal door. Almost immediately it was answered, and almost immediately Arabella realized what a terrible mistake she had made in coming.

Because she had forgotten until that moment—or perhaps she had merely *allowed* herself to forget until that moment—how she always began to feel whenever Gus Torrance came within a meter of her. She had forgotten how her stomach flamed, how her heart began to race, how her breathing became more difficult to manage. And in that moment it was worse than ever before, because Gus was not as she had ever seen him before.

He had clearly settled in for the evening, because his hair was unbound, the tawny, silky tresses dancing freely about his shoulders—his *bare* shoulders. He wore nothing except a pair of roomy . . . what was the word for the garment? Arabella's mind was a complete blank as she stared at him. "Jams," she vaguely recalled. Nothing but a pair of brightly colored jams. His bare chest was satiny smooth and bronzed, unmarred by the thick pelt of hair she found so unseemly on other men—including her fiancé. A silver medallion of some kind—she was afraid to look at it too closely for fear that she might grow even dizzier than she was—hung on a chain against his breastbone, winking in the pale light that spilled from a single lamp burning behind him. His naked torso was firm and ridged with muscle, and salient biceps in his upper arms bunched and flexed as he settled one hand defiantly on his hip. His forearms, too, were well muscled and well formed, the kind of arms a woman ached to have encircle her and pull her close.

Arabella's mouth went dry as she absorbed this sight of him. Other parts of her body, however, were anything *but* dry. Oh, yes. This was definitely a bad idea, she told herself. She should leave immediately and never come back. Somehow, though, she could not quite bring herself to leave. Somehow, she simply could not look away at all.

His expression, when he saw who stood at his door, went slack for a moment, his amber eyes darkening as his pupils expanded, and his lips parting slightly, as if in invitation. Arabella had to battle the urge to lean forward and tip her head back, then push herself up on her toes to press her own lips against his. Because it would not be a good idea to kiss a handsome, desirable man whom one was planning to use to make one's odious fiancé notice one. That, she was certain, even in all her innocence, would only lead to trouble.

"Princess," he said softly, his voice wrapping around her like the curl of a strong arm across her shoulders. "Gee. To what do I owe this royal visit?"

"Shh," she told him as, without thinking, she pressed her fingers to his mouth.

The moment her skin made contact with his, however, she withdrew her hand, so quickly that she might as well have just been burned. Then again, she thought, she nearly had been burned. She still might be burned. But before she could second-guess herself she pushed her way past him, into his cabin—careful not to touch him this time, which was no easy feat considering the close confines of the tiny room—and closed the door behind herself. To make sure no one entered, she pressed her body flat against it and thrust her hands behind her back, to hold firm the flat metal handle.

"I must talk to you," she said quietly, a bit breathlessly. "There is something I need to ask you."

For one long moment Gus only stared at her in silence, and she could tell nothing of what he might be thinking. She noticed then that he held a book in the hand he had not propped on his hip, and she realized she had interrupted his evening of reading. Tilting her head to the side a bit, she could just make out part of the title and the author's last name, and saw that he held a copy of Ernest Hemingway's *A Moveable Feast*.

Interesting, she thought. She would not have guessed that a man like him would read such things. He seemed more the type to, if he read at all, choose current popular fiction filled with action and adventure and nothing that would tax too heavily the brain.

Arabella was still contemplating the enigma when, suddenly, before she realized his intention, Gus tossed the book onto one of the two small bunks affixed to the left-hand wall of the cabin, then took a step toward her and flattened his hand against the door on one side of her head. With another step he was able to lean his body in close to hers, then press his other palm against the door on the other side of her head. Instinctively she crowded her body backward, away from him, but realized belatedly that the closed door behind her meant that she had nowhere to go.

It was just as well, she told herself, because she did not want him to see how strong was his effect on her. And because she did not want him to see the effect he had on her, she tilted her head back some, to meet his gaze levelly with her own.

He had just showered, she realized as he leaned his body closer still, without—quite—touching her. The sharp, clean fragrance of pine soap surrounded him, surrounded her, and she fancied his skin would still be warm to the touch, from the rush of the water. She closed her eyes for a moment as an image of him standing naked beneath such a hot jet materialized quite vividly. And for that moment her lungs emptied of air, her skin grew hotter still, and her heart very nearly stopped beating. She told herself again, very adamantly, that she was there for one reason and one reason alone—to incur the wrath of Reynaldo and force his hand to either join with hers or release it. She must remember that.

She must remember that that was the *only* reason she had sought Gus out tonight. Normally she would stay as far away from him as possible. He was not the kind of man a woman like her should associate with. Ever. Not because he was a foreigner, and not because he was working class and not because he had no prospects, although certainly her mother would be astonished that Arabella had even spoken to such a man. Arabella was not, however, the social snob that her mother was. Her problems with Gus Torrance had nothing to do with his job or his upbringing or his background. No, the reason she should not associate with him was simple. He made her feel things. Things that a woman like her had no business feeling. Things like what she was feeling right now.

And he always got much too close to her, making those feelings even more intense, more intolerable. He had never touched her, not once, but he came much too close. Physically, emotionally, sexually. Just as he was now.

And sexually was not a way that Arabella was supposed to feel. For *any*one. She had been taught very early that nice, well-bred girls like her were not supposed to have . . . desires. Wants. Needs. Nice girls, good girls, noble girls, girls of good breeding did not experience such reactions to men. Yes, she would be called to perform a duty for her husband, her country, and her people, a duty her mother and duenna had both assured her she would not like. But all women were eventually called to perform such a duty, in one way or another. It was necessary in order to ensure an heir, especially a royal heir who would one day assume the throne for a country. And when Arabella was called, her mother had told her, she must do her duty. She must simply lie back, close her eyes, and think of Toulaine and Pelagia.

Toulaine and Pelagia, though, were not on her mind right now. No, the only thing that was on her mind at the moment was that Gus Torrance was standing much too close to her. And he was looking much too tempting. And he was smelling much too nice. And he was making her feel all those things that she knew she must not allow herself to feel.

She forced her eyes open. And found herself gazing into his. Losing herself in his. Drowning . . . His eyes were even closer now than they had been before. His face was closer than before. And his mouth . . .

Oh, his *mouth*, Arabella thought as a new kind of heat seeped through her. His mouth was very, very inviting.

She wondered what it would be like to kiss him, whether his lips were as soft as they looked. A man like him would know how to kiss a woman, she thought. He would make her feel very—

"Please," she said softly, forcing herself not to think about him that way. Though, truly, she did not know what she was asking—or begging—him for.

"Please what?" he said in response, every bit as softly. His voice was different, too, now, she noted, deeper than before, rougher, heavier. And there was none of the playful teasing that was usually there, only a somber sort of demand that was unfamiliar to her.

"Please," she said again. She swallowed with some difficulty and crowded her body back against the door in a fruitless effort to put some distance between them. "Please help me," she said. "I . . . I need your help, Gus. Please."

"Please" was not a word that Arabella was accustomed to using. It was not that she was impolite. It was just not something that had ever been expected of her at home. She was used to saying things and having them done. "Please" had never been necessary before. But with Gus . . .

With Gus, she suspected there would be many things for which a woman would want to say "please." She did not know what, specifically, these things would be, because no one had ever explained to her such secrets. They were secrets, she had been told, that she would learn from her husband. Strange was the fact that she had never wanted or hoped to learn them from Reynaldo. And yet with Gus, a man she scarcely knew, she found herself hungry to know all of them.

His expression changed again when she spoke his name, and his gaze shifted from her eyes to her mouth.

"My help?" he echoed, his voice a quiet caress that seemed to wash over her entire body, warming parts of her she had not even realized were cold. He lifted his gaze back to meet hers. "My help with what?"

"I . . . I have been thinking," she stammered, "about what you said to me yesterday, by the Jacuzzi. I have been thinking that maybe I should consider taking you up on your . . . your offer."

One side of his mouth lifted into what she thought might be a smile of sorts, but there was something slightly menacing about it, something that made her blood run even hotter than it already was. "And what offer was that, Princess?" he asked.

"Please do not call me that," she said shallowly.

He said nothing for a moment, only continued to gaze into her eyes. Finally, softly, he said, "You know, you keep saying 'please' to me like that, and this night could get very interesting very soon."

"Gus, please," she said again, before she could stop herself.

The other side of his mouth lifted now, too, curling his lips into a grin of smug satisfaction. "I like the way you say that, Princess. I think I'd like to hear it more often. A lot more often."

Telling herself it was pointless to insist he not call her by the name he so clearly did not intend to abandon, Arabella forced herself not to say, "Gus, please" again, and instead repeated, "I want to talk to you about the offer you made to me yesterday."

He hesitated a moment, holding her gaze firm with his. Then, "Refresh my memory," he told her. "What offer was that?"

Arabella found that she simply could not think straight as long as they were as close as they were to each other, with him being only half dressed the way he was. Even though he still hadn't touched her, she felt him all over her body, felt his warmth and scent surrounding her, penetrating her, almost as if his entire body was pushing into hers.

Somehow she managed to banish the image, then began, "Can we . . . Can you . . . I must . . ." She lifted a hand with the intention of pushing him gently backward, but she could not bring herself to place it against his bare chest. So she only flattened her hand and held it, palm out, between them, hoping he would understand. Evidently he did, because he smiled in a knowing way, expelled a single, humorless chuckle, and pushed himself away from the door, taking a step back into the cabin.

"Put on a shirt," Arabella said without thinking.

Gus arched his tawny eyebrows in playful indignation. "Is that a royal decree, Princess?"

She shook her head. "No, it is only a request. Please," she added before she could stop herself—why did she feel the need to say that word to him, over and over the way she did? "Please put on a shirt." She gestured anxiously toward his body. "I am not comfortable being with people who are only half clothed."

"Half clothed," he repeated thoughtfully. "That's sort of a new twist on the optimist-pessimist thing, isn't it?"

"What do you mean?" she asked, confused.

"I mean that thing about the glass being half empty or half full."

"Oh, yes, I understand. I have always thought the glass half full myself."

"Yet you called me half clothed. That sounds kind of pessimistic to me."

"What would be optimistic?" she asked, curious in spite of her discomfort with the subject matter.

He grinned, a very devilish, playful grin, the one that always made her feel a little weak in the knees. "Half naked," he told her. "That would be the optimist's version."

Arabella felt the heat of a blush creep into her cheeks. "I am not comfortable with either," she told him. "Half clothed or half naked. I find them both . . . disquieting."

"Really?" he asked with much interest, hooking both hands loosely on his hips now, offering no indication whatsoever that he would comply with her wishes. "And how long has this half clothed/half naked thing been a hang-up of yours, Princess, hmmm?"

"Hang-up?" Arabella repeated, very confused now. "I am sorry. I do not understand that phrase."

"It's what you say when somebody has an unnatural fear of something," Gus told her, still not putting on a shirt, as she had—politely—requested he do.

"I do not have an unnatural fear of half clothed people," she denied uncomfortably. "Or of half, ah, half . . . naked . . . people, either," she added, stumbling over the words.

Gus smiled that knowing smile again, crossed his arms over his very unclothed, fully naked chest, and took a step toward her. "Really?" he asked. "Then it won't bother you if I decline your royal edict and don't put a shirt on, will it?" Another step brought him right back to where he was before, scant millimeters away from her, his warmth and scent surrounding her again. "See, that's the problem with these crew quarters," he told her. "Interior cabin, no windows, close to the engines. You can't imagine how hot it gets down here sometimes."

Arabella swallowed hard. Yes, she had noticed that it did seem to be unusually warm in the cabin. She had not realized how uncomfortable it must be for the crew sometimes.

"Yeah, there are nights when we're under way," Gus went on, "when the engines are humming, and the boat is vibrating, and the air is thick and hot, and the covers get tangled at the bottom of the bunk, and a man's dreams just go . . . wild. And all I can do on nights like that is think about ways I might relieve that heat. But thinking about that just makes me hotter sometimes, you know?"

Arabella shook her head slowly. No. She did not know.

He smiled again, that same self-satisfied smile. "No, maybe you don't know," he said softly, seeming to read her mind. "Maybe you don't know at that."

"May we please talk?" Arabella asked again.

He lifted one satiny smooth shoulder and let it drop. "Since you asked so nicely, Princess, I don't see why not."

"When . . . when will your cabinmates return?" she asked. "I do not want to be found down here."

"No, of course you don't," he agreed, his voice touched with sarcasm. "God knows you don't want to be caught mingling with the hired help, do you?" He let his gaze travel slowly, deliberately over her entire body, from head to toe, then smiled an almost cruel smile. "Don't want to get your pretty dress—or anything else—dirty."

"It is not like that," she assured him.

"Isn't it?"

"No."

She could see that he did not believe her, but she also knew there was little she could say to make him change his mind. He had decided long ago what kind of woman she was, and, Arabella had to confess, in many ways he was right. She was cool, aloof, standoffish. There were reasons for that. But she was not a snob. She did not think herself better than others simply because of the fortunate circumstances of her birth. She was simply different, that was all. Different in ways he could not even imagine.

"Then why don't you want anybody to know you're down here?" he demanded.

"Because I do not want anyone to know that what I am planning to do with you is nothing but a game. I want everyone to think it is real. So they must not hear us talking about it now, this way."

He eyed her thoughtfully. "You want to play games, Princess? With me?"

She nodded, but could not quite find words to reply any further.

"Sounds like fun," he said, once more in that strange, rough voice. "What kind of game are you looking to play?"

Instead of answering him outright, Arabella said, "I am tired of the way Reynaldo treats me."

Gus expelled a rueful sound. "Yeah, I'll bet you are."

"And I think it is time that he made a decision," she added, ignoring his taunt.

"What kind of decision?"

"He must either marry me," she said, "or he must let me go."

"Sounds like this is going to be a game with pretty high stakes," Gus said.

"Yes. It will be."

"And you're ready to risk everything?" he asked.

"Yes."

"Even yourself?"

"Yes."

"And what if, when this game is played out," Gus said, "ol' Reynaldo decides it's time he married you?"

Arabella swallowed hard, squared her shoulders, and lifted her chin defiantly. "Then I will marry him," she vowed. "It is what I have been preparing for my entire life. That is how the game is supposed to end."

Gus eyed her thoughtfully again. "Even though he doesn't love you?"

She nodded.

"Even though you don't love him?"

She nodded again, with less vigor this time.

Gus studied her in silence for a long, long time, but he said nothing yet to indicate what his thoughts on the matter might be. So, hoping that his silence meant he would help her in this mad scheme of hers, Arabella continued.

"I would like for you to pretend you are interested in me," she said without preamble. "I would like for Reynaldo to think you are a rival."

At this Gus laughed outright. "*Me? A rival?*" he barked. "What the hell kind of a rival could I be? I'm a bartender, Princess. I got nothing to offer you. He's a prince. He can give you everything you want."

"Not everything," she said before she could stop herself.

But Gus must not have understood, because he only demanded, "How can you think he'll feel threatened by me?"

"Reynaldo does not like to have his belongings tampered with," Arabella told him. "If you . . . tamper . . . with me, he will consider you a rival. It does not matter what you have to offer. Reynaldo simply will not like to see you with me. He will not like to see you interested in me. He is like a small child with his toys—he does not want to share them."

"And that's how you see yourself?" Gus asked. "As one of Reynaldo's belongings? As one of his toys?"

Arabella shook her head. "No, I—" But she halted when she realized she could think of no way to describe what she was to Reynaldo. "I only meant that he views the world in a very specific way. What is his is his, and no one should try to change that. And when things do not happen the way he expects them to, the way he wants them to, then he does whatever he has to do to make things right."

"So you think that if I make a play for you," Gus said, "then Reynaldo will turn around and marry you right away, just to make it clear to me that you belong to him. Is that what you're saying?"

"Yes. Or else he will decide he does not want me after all, and he will agree to end our engagement."

He studied her in thoughtful silence for another moment. "Do you really think it's that simple?"

She nodded. "Yes. I do."

"What if you're wrong?"

"I am not wrong."

"And it would be okay with you if Reynaldo cut you loose?" Gus asked after another moment.

Arabella hoped she did not sound too eager when she said, "Yes. I would manage."

Gus was silent for a moment more, as if he were honestly giving her idea some thought. Finally, though, he asked, "And what if, to deal with this dilemma, he just decides to fire me instead of marrying you?"

Arabella had not really thought about that possibility, but now that she did, she realized that Gus had raised a valid point. "Yes, he might fire you, also," she conceded. "But I think he will want to make sure something like this does not happen again, by marrying me."

Gus bit his lip thoughtfully, and she tried not to notice how enticing the gesture was, tried not to think about how much she would like to nibble his mouth herself. "So you're telling me I'm going to lose my job if I help you out, is that it?" he asked.

She realized then what she was asking him to do, what she was asking him to risk. She had not thought that far ahead when she had considered her plan. She did not want Gus to lose his job. She only wanted her life to go back to being what it had once promised to be. She wanted to have a purpose, a meaning, in the grand order. She was tired of being an afterthought to everyone.

"I will make it up to you," she promised lamely.

Gus smiled at that, the most dangerous, seductive, scorching smile Arabella had ever seen on a man's face. Unbidden, her hand crept to her throat, her fingers circling the slender column loosely, as if in doing so, she might somehow avert the heat of his gaze. Then she realized that the heat was coming not from him, but from inside her. And she knew that there was nothing she could do to ease it. Not as long as she was in the same room with Gus Torrance.

"Oh, you'll make it up to me, will you?" he asked softly, temptingly. "I can't wait to find out how."

"Yes, I will make it up to you," she assured him a little breathlessly. "I, ah . . . I . . . I will pay you, Gus. I have money, and I will pay you. And I will help you find work elsewhere."

His smile fell immediately at her offer, turning his expression cool and indifferent. "Don't worry yourself about it," he said, taking a step backward, as if he wanted to distance himself from her physically as well as . . . as well as whatever other way he was attempting to distance himself from her. "I can take care of myself, Princess," he added bitterly. "I have been for a long time now. I can suffer the wrath of Reynaldo. God knows I've suffered worse. And, hell, it'd be worth it for—"

He cut himself off before finishing the statement, and Arabella, in her scrambled state of mind, did not ask him to clarify or explain what he had meant. Instead she began, "But I must do something to—"

"Okay, Princess," he interrupted her before she could say anything more. His voice, too, was cool now, cool and harsh. And she wished more than anything that she knew what to say to bring back that smile he had worn with such heat only a moment ago. "I'll help you bag your prince," he told her. "If that's what you really want."

"It is what I want," she said hollowly. "Being Reynaldo's wife is what I have spent my entire life learning to be. It is my destiny."

But her voice lacked conviction when she offered her assertion. Probably, she thought, because her heart lacked conviction, too. Still, she would marry Reynaldo, if that was what he decided. And of course she knew that that was exactly what Reynaldo would decide. Oh, she did not believe that he would give up Superclod Dacia, or another like her, just because he married. But as his wife Arabella would at last have her role defined for her. She would be Princess Arabella of Pelagia. And if, somehow, they returned to Reynaldo's homeland, she would be Queen Arabella of Pelagia. She would have seen her destiny fulfilled. An entire lifetime of training would have finally been for something, instead of for nothing.

Strangely, though, for the first time in her life, as she gazed at Gus Torrance and his half-naked body, Arabella realized she had no wish to see her destiny fulfilled. For the first time she wanted to see a lifetime of training go wasted for nothing. Because somehow she knew that with Gus, there would be so much more than she would ever have with Reynaldo. Even if it was only for a short time.

"Okay, Princess," he said after another lengthy silence. "I'll play your game with you. Just tell me what you want me to do, and I'll do it."

Chapter 11

"Okay, Ruby, lesson number four. 'Flatware Is Your Friend.' "

Ruby gazed down at the table that lay between her and Keaton and frowned. Never in her life had she seen so many incarnations of knives, forks, and spoons. What on earth were they all for? Who could possibly consume enough food in one meal to require more than three utensils—two, if you didn't have applesauce? Some of those forks on the table were so skinny, they couldn't possibly be good for anything except tridenting sea monkeys. And she'd never seen spoons quite like some of those before, though they did sort of resemble those plastic sporks that used to come with the two-piece dinner at KFC.

Wow. Who would have thought the Colonel was right there at the cutting edge—so to speak—of haute cutlery? Funny, though, how there wasn't a single piece of fried chicken, or any biscuits, or any corn-on-the-cob anywhere on the table. No, in fact, like the flatware, much of the food that was on the table wasn't even remotely recognizable to her. A lot of it, though, did sorta remind her of something. If she could just think what . . . She shook the thought out of her head and returned her attention to Keaton, who seemed to have been speaking to her at length while her mind was wandering—which, now that she thought about it, seemed to have been par for the course during these little "lessons" he'd given her over the last six days.

Six days, she marveled again. In some ways it felt as if she'd been trapped aboard *Mad Tryst* for six months. Of course, being trapped on a luxury yacht for six days—with stewards to wait on one, and a chef to cook for one, and a faithful canine companion to keep by one's side—wasn't exactly a cross to bear. In fact, Ruby had rather enjoyed herself. It had been a long time since she'd had a vacation, and generally those few vacations she'd taken had consisted of little more than a few days in the Keys. This, however . . .

This had been *much* better than a few days in the Keys. She'd had hours to herself—even days to herself when everyone else went ashore in Bermuda—to simply sit on deck with a book and read, or to stand at the rail, and gaze out at the limitless blue horizon while the ocean breeze tangled with her hair. She and Gus the bartender had chatted about their shared experiences pouring drinks for the rich and tight-fisted. She and Omar the pianist had become friends through their shared love of old movies and music—even if she didn't always quite grasp his creative use of English. And she'd taught the culinary Kurt how to make cheese grits, for which, he had told her, he would be forever in her debt. The canine Kurt, too, had benefited from Ruby's instruction. He was now the trans-Atlantic champion for catching a little rubber squeaky ball on a moving vessel. Though he'd learned quickly—the hard way, unfortunately—*not* to retrieve the ball when Keaton threw it, because, for some reason, Keaton's throws always went wild, sending the ball—and, consequently, Kurt—right over the side of the boat. It was the strangest thing. Keaton seemed so focused at other times.

Ruby and Arabella, too, had forged a friendship of sorts over the week. Circumstances had thrown them together, but what had bonded them was the fact that they shared so many similar experiences, in spite of their vastly different lives. Where Arabella had been coddled and pampered since day one, Ruby had . . . not. And where Arabella was engaged to a rich, handsome man, Ruby was . . . not. And where Arabella's destiny, although currently on hold, would have her the reigning queen of a country, Ruby's destiny would . . . not.

Yet in spite of their differences, there were many things the women shared in common. Neither was currently living the way she wanted to live, neither had been offered many choices in life, and neither had been given the opportunity to achieve her full potential. Neither even knew what her full potential was. Both women knew what it was like to be lonely. Both had known unhappiness. Both felt as if their lives had been put on hold indefinitely.

As a result, the time the two of them had spent together over the week had felt like something of a gift. Though, truly, Ruby didn't see as much of Arabella as she had thought she would. The other woman had been ashore both days at Bermuda, and over the last two days, as *Mad Tryst* had made its way to Puerto Rico, Arabella had often disappeared. Presumably to her stateroom, though there had been times when Ruby had knocked and received no answer.

And then, of course, there was Keaton.

Keaton, who, for the last six days, had filled Ruby's thoughts during the day and her dreams at night. Keaton, whom she often caught watching her with eyes that were lit with fire and desire and hunger, even though he had never made a move to touch her. Keaton, who spent hours at a time with her, instructing her in the finer points of social climbing, then disappeared to his stateroom, or elsewhere, in an effort to—Ruby could only conclude—avoid her. Keaton, who, in spite of his obvious interest in her, wanted nothing more to do with her than he had to.

And over the course of the last six days, Ruby had gradually decided—and she was fairly certain Keaton would agree with her on this—that his idea about playing Professor Henry Higgins to her Eliza Doolittle hadn't been an especially good one. Not just because she'd spent the last six days feeling utterly intimidated by all the things he'd tried to teach her, but because Keaton Hamilton Danning III kept making her feel really, really preoccupied. Whenever she was with him—which had been pretty daggone often over the last week, way too often for her comfort and peace of mind—she didn't want to be talking about sporks and sea monkey tridents. No, what she found herself wanting to do with him was . . .

Well, to be perfectly honest, she found herself wanting to wrestle him to the deck and have her way with him. Over and over and over again.

Which, really, when she got right down to it, made little sense. She'd only known him a short time, and the two of them had nothing in common, and she knew she was the last kind of woman a man like him would want. Because Keaton Hamilton Danning III, ambassador's son, Harvard graduate, Oxford graduate, jet-setter, next in line to become prime minister of a country—even if that country had sorta thrown him out on his keester—almost certainly had his sights set a little higher than Ruby Runyon, father unknown, high school grad, trailer park native, comedy club waitress.

Gosh, call her unrealistic, but she just didn't see a guy like him going for a girl like her. And she couldn't understand why she'd want him to, anyway. He wasn't her type, either. No, she wanted, needed, someone who was a lot more grounded in reality, someone who knew what real life was all about. Someone who knew how to change a spark plug, for instance. Someone who *preferred* Cheetos over Camembert. Someone who knew which aisle the beer was in at the grocery store. Someone who could *find* the grocery store in the first place. Someone who could name at least four or five of the members of the original *Survivor* cast. Not someone with whom she had absolutely nothing in common.

But there it was just the same, however little sense it made. Ruby wanted to get into Keaton's groove thang with him, and she wanted to do it as soon as possible. Thankfully, in a way, he'd done nothing to encourage her, ah, preoccupation—except for that business about watching her with fiery, hungry eyes, something that made her pulse race wildly and her blood heat to simmering—so she hadn't done anything foolish. Yet.

And anyway, since he never *did* anything to back up those heated gazes, she was beginning to suspect that the only reason he looked at her in such a way was that he just took his tutelage very seriously. Education, he had told her that first evening he'd adopted her as his social cause, was the very foundation of civilization. And without civilization, he had added, there would be no cocktail or dinner parties. Hence, no opportunity for her to make the social connections she needed to get ahead. Ergo, she must be educated. She must be civilized. At least where the niceties of cocktail and dinner parties were concerned.

It had been sound reasoning, as far as Ruby was concerned. But she still didn't quite feel comfortable with these little lessons. Mainly because she still didn't feel comfortable with Keaton.

This evening was no exception. Because this evening, bathed in the dense, pinkish-golden light of the setting sun, he was way too yummy-looking. Maybe that was because this evening Keaton, just as he had for the last several days, looked less like a jet-setting, potential prime minister and more like a regular, reality-grounded guy. He wore loose-fitting khaki trousers and a short-sleeved shirt almost the same color as the setting sun, a shirt that had a little pineapple stitched over the breast pocket, something she found totally irresistible for some unfathomable reason.

Ruby could safely say she had never been attracted to a man who had a little pineapple stitched on his shirt before. The closest she'd come was a guy she had dated shortly after moving to Miami, one who'd had a half-naked hula dancer tattooed on his arm. Okay, so maybe that wasn't all that close to a little pineapple stitched over a shirt pocket, but at least both were tropical images. At any rate, she hadn't dated the guy long. Only long enough to find out that he had a half-naked hula dancer tattooed on his arm. And she was pretty sure she wouldn't ever have found him and Keaton traveling in the same sort of social circles.

Not that Ruby had much room to talk. In spite of her week-long stay on the yacht, she still felt way out of place on *Mad Tryst*, especially out here on the forward deck at sunset, wearing another one of Arabella's purchases for her, this one a sleeveless, pale lavender sheath slit up both sides to just past her knees. It was made of some creamy soft material that seemed to ebb and flow like water around her legs with every breath of the nautical breeze that whispered her way. She had read on the tag that the garment was silk, and she very much suspected she could in no way afford it on a waitress's budget. All told, the countess had bought six outfits for Ruby while she was ashore—both in the Bahamas and on Bermuda—along with lingerie, shoes, and accessories to complement each.

At this point Ruby had no choice but to become a firm believer in reincarnation. Because it was going to take her at least six or seven more lives to pay Arabella back for all this stuff. The countess had even had Marisol arrange Ruby's hair the way she did Arabella's, so, as had become her new custom, Ruby wore her hair this evening in a sophisticated chignon. All things considered, she almost felt like Grace Kelly, except that Ruby was brunette. And had gray eyes. And was in no way slender. Or willowy. Or graceful. Or famous. And she'd never made any movies with Jimmy Stewart or Cary Grant or Bing Crosby. And she'd never been a princess. Or lived overseas.

All right, all right, so Ruby didn't feel anything at all like Grace Kelly. Which just went to remind her how very out of place she was here in this world.

"So there you have it, Ruby. The seafood fork in a nutshell. Or maybe a clamshell would be more appropriate."

Keaton smiled a little uneasily at his joke—not that she could blame him; it wasn't that great a joke—then set the sea monkey trident he had been holding back down on the table. Suddenly Ruby found herself wishing she'd heard what he'd said about the utensil, because it sounded like maybe you really did use it to trident sea monkeys, and that, she thought, was a skill she wouldn't mind having.

Unfortunately, she hadn't been paying attention. But she hadn't paid much attention to any of his other lectures, either—due to that aforementioned preoccupation problem. So why should this latest be any different? Then again, his previous lectures had claimed titles like "The Hazards of Toe Cleavage," "Manners Make the World Go 'Round," and "Personal Hygiene Is Everybody's Business," in addition to the most recent "Flatware Is Your Friend." So Ruby could have been preoccupied by a hangnail and not heard a word of any of them.

But instead of asking Keaton to repeat what he'd just said about . . . what was it he'd been talking about again? Oh, well. Instead of asking him to repeat whatever it was, Ruby only nodded gravely and pretended she understood, and she tried not to think about how yummy he looked and how nice it would be to wrestle him to the deck and have her way with him.

"Would you like to give it a try?" he asked suddenly.

Panic welled up inside her at the question, because she was pretty sure Keaton was asking her to give something a try that wasn't what she had been thinking about giving a try—namely, him. But since she hadn't actually been listening, there was still an outside chance that maybe he *was* asking her to give something a try that was *precisely* what she'd been thinking about giving a try—namely him. Hence, her panic.

"Give what a try?" she replied cautiously, just in case they *were* talking about the same thing, hoping her voice reflected none of the panic and alarm—and lust and desire—she found herself feeling.

"The seafood fork," he told her, his voice touched with impatience. "Weren't you listening?"

"Of course I was listening," she lied. "I listened to

every word you said. Because I was, you know, listening. Listening really hard, too. I mean, how could I not be listening? You were riveting."

A hint of pink crept into his cheeks, and Ruby bit back a smile at the sight of it. He really was awfully cute. And yummy. And sexy. And enticing. And luscious. And arousing. And hunger-provoking and need-inspiring and damp-palm-inducing and heavy-breathing-inciting and—

"Yeah, well," he said, scattering her thoughts—damn him. "I guess I am kind of an expert in the field. I was pretty much raised on this stuff." She wasn't sure, but she thought he added, under his breath, "More's the pity."

"And, by golly, it shows," she assured him, letting that last, puzzling part of his remark go.

Without commenting, he picked up one of the little forks again and extended it toward her. "Here you go," he said. "Give it a try. Help yourself to a couple of those shrimp."

He gestured toward a silver bowl near her side of the table that was filled with crushed ice, upon whose exterior had beaded dozens of delicate pearls of condensation. Around the entire circumference of the bowl's scrolled lip hung a dozen or so dainty pink shrimp, curling elegantly in on themselves like the petals of a supple rose.

Ruby glanced at Keaton, then at the minuscule fork he held in his hand, then back at those shrimp. Then at Keaton and the fork. Then back at the shrimp. And she realized she had no idea what she was supposed to do, because she hadn't been listening to him, because she'd been too preoccupied with thoughts of him, and thoughts of what she wanted to do with—to—him.

Hey, it's just forking shrimp, she reminded herself. *How hard can it be?*

She accepted the utensil from him, doing her best to

hold it the way he had held it himself, and zeroed in on a particularly scrumptious-looking shrimp. Then, doing her best to be careful but thorough, she attempted to spear it. Unfortunately, her attempt wasn't very successful. Not unless what she'd wanted to accomplish was tumping over the entire silver bowl, and scattering ice and crustaceans everywhere, in which case she was very successful indeed.

The bad news was that she had made a mess. The good news was that Kurt was there to clean it right up. The canine Kurt, not the culinary Kurt. The culinary Kurt, from what Ruby had seen of him, probably wouldn't have cleaned up the mess after seeing her make it. No, he probably would have taken off her hand with a meat cleaver because she'd messed up his beautiful arrangement, cheese grits lesson or no. All in all, she much preferred the canine Kurt for situations such as this one. Especially when he completed the job of cleaning up by licking her toes and making her laugh.

Keaton, on the other hand, reacted quite differently. Not that she would have necessarily minded having him lick her toes as Kurt did, however strange a reaction that might be. He didn't make her laugh, either. Mostly he reacted by muttering something unintelligible under his breath—which, granted, she was probably better off not hearing—and settling loose fists on his hips.

Then, "No, no, no, no, no," he said flatly. "Not like that, Ahab. You're not out here to filet Moby Dick."

"I'm sorry," she apologized. "But I'm getting kind of hungry. I guess my appetite just sort of overwhelmed my etiquette."

He expelled a weary sigh. "Don't worry about it. Let's just try it again, all right?"

"Um, actually, I am getting kind of hungry," she repeated, turning her attention to the overabundance of delectable-looking food that the steward had laid out for appetizers.

One thing Ruby would say for Prince Reynaldo of Pelagia: He might be a pig, but he ate like . . . Well, like a pig, now that she thought about it. But a royal pig. A pig with very good taste. Not to mention an unlimited slop budget.

She couldn't imagine six people being able to consume so much food, especially food that didn't even comprise a meal. But that was the number of guests aboard who had regularly taken meals, and therefore appetizers, together while the boat was under way—one of whom, Ruby couldn't quite help reminding herself, hadn't exactly been invited. So if she wanted to get technical—which she really didn't, but she felt obliged to—then there were five guests and one stowaway who would be enjoying the bounty. Oh, probably the captain and first mate and some of the others were allowed to partake of the banquet, too—eventually—but even at that, this was more food than Ruby saw in her own refrigerator in two months' time. There was all manner of fresh fruits and vegetables and cheeses and hors d'oeuvres and breads and seafood. And again, as she studied the array, she was reminded of something she couldn't quite put her finger on. The food all just looked so incredibly . . . So unbelievably . . . So amazingly . . . So erotically . . .

Oh, God, she thought as a strange warmth began to seep into her stomach and points beyond. It occurred to her then, in a burst of lecherous realization, that the food all looked like . . . like . . . like . . .

Heat flamed Ruby's face as she noticed how the blush on the apricots, along with their . . . unique shape . . . and the way they had been arranged in pairs on the fruit plate made them look just like a man's . . . And some of the peaches, for the sake of garnish, had been sliced in half, the delicate folds and wrinkles on their seeds giving them the appearance of a woman's . . . And there were some canapés made of round crackers smeared with some kind of creamy spread, topped with grape halves in their centers, all arranged in pairs, giving them the look of a woman's, uh . . . And the bananas! Ruby didn't even want to look at the bananas. Not when each of them was displayed by being nestled between two ripe, dewy plums the way they were.

So she shifted her gaze to the rest of the cornucopia, only to feel herself growing more and more uncomfortable—more and more *aroused*—with every new food she noted. There were dried fruits reminiscent of . . . of . . . of . . . of the same thing that the oysters on the half shell were reminiscent of. And there were too many phallic fruits and vegetables to name, olives and pimentos arranged in a way that just looked too suggestive for words. Even the stuffed peppers and sushi rolls somehow gave the impression of rank sexuality.

Boy, either Kurt the chef was *extremely* sexually frustrated these days, she thought, or else—

Uh-oh.

Ruby gazed at the array of food again, then snuck a peek over at Keaton. Then one more at the food. Then another at Keaton. Food. Keaton. Oh, no . . . A ripple of warmth rushed through her body, pooling heat in places she had no business feeling heat—not in mixed and polite company, at any rate—and she realized something with stark and troubling clarity.

It wasn't Kurt who was sexually frustrated.

"Ruby?"

Once again, Keaton's voice interrupted her errant—

and erotic—mental meanderings, and she realized that, as usual, he had been speaking to her at length without her hearing a word of what he had said. When she glanced up to look at him, she immediately wished she hadn't, because suddenly he was just too handsome—too tempting—to bear.

"Are you all right?" he asked.

Somewhere along the line, her mouth had gone all dry, her face had gone all hot, and her brain had gone all—well, her brain had just *all gone*—and an odd sort of tingling had taken over some very disconcerting parts of her body. As a result, all she was able to manage in response to Keaton's question was a silent, awkward nod.

"Are you sure you're all right?" he asked, sounding nowhere near convinced.

Another silent, awkward nod.

"Because you look a little . . ."

"What?" she managed to whisper.

"Flushed," he said. "Are you running a fever?"

Boy, was that a loaded question.

Before Ruby could stop him, he lifted a hand and reached across the table to cup it over her forehead. Instinctively she took a giant step in retreat, because she simply could not tolerate having him touch her when such strange, salacious thoughts were parading through her brain, and such strange, salacious sensations were scurrying to her every extremity.

He dropped his hand back to his side, but seemed not to notice her discomfort. "You do feel a bit warm," he said.

Boy, was that a loaded statement.

"Maybe you should eat something," he added.

Boy, was that a—

No. She would *not* allow herself to think about such things. Because there wasn't a single thing on that table she dared touch—let alone put in her mouth—for fear that she might inflame herself even more than she was.

"The apricots are really nice," he told her. "Some of the most tender you'll ever put in your mouth."

Oh, no. No, no, no, no, no. Not the apricots. No way was she going to even fondle . . . uh, touch . . . those.

"Or maybe," he offered when she didn't respond, "an oyster. Have you ever tried one?"

Oh, no. No, no, no, no, no. She knew there were some women who were into that sort of thing—not that there was anything wrong with that—but it wasn't for Ruby *at all*. Still, she couldn't quite tear her gaze away as Keaton reached for one of the oysters in question and extended it toward her. When she shook her head, though, he shrugged and brought it to his own mouth, tilting his head back and extending his tongue a bit, capturing the pearly little center with the tip of his tongue, toying with it for a moment, then sipping it deep into his mouth.

Ruby's breath caught in her throat as she watched him savor his prize, closing his eyes as he did so, murmuring a soft, contented sound reminiscent of a man who's been utterly, completely, profoundly satisfied. She wasn't sure, but she thought she detected the faint hint of color on his cheek, too, but that might have simply been the result of too much time in the sun, and not the mini-orgasm she suspected was responsible for her own hot, flushed skin.

What on earth was wrong with her? she wondered. All she'd done was watch Keaton have a little, uh, snack, but suddenly, somehow, she felt as if they'd just engaged in prolonged—*very* prolonged—foreplay that had left her wholly unfulfilled, writhing and aching for more, needing his touch, craving his touch, demanding his body atop and inside her own, pumping fast and forceful and furious, hotter, harder, heavier, deeper, as he pressed his mouth to her ear and described all the raw, indecent, nasty things he wanted to do to her, again and again and again, all night long, pumping even faster now, and more forceful and furious, even hotter, even harder, even heavier, even deeper, and . . . and . . . and . . .

And where was she?

Oh, yes. She suddenly felt very, um, edgy. And hot. My goodness, it was hot out here. Why, if Keaton so much as touched her right now, Ruby couldn't say for sure that she wouldn't go right off, in a way she never had before. And having an orgasm at a cocktail party was almost certainly a social faux pas—she didn't even need for Keaton to tell her that. Yeah, there was nothing like a public orgasm to illustrate one's trailer trash roots.

"Oh, I do love those," Keaton said with *much* affection as he lowered the shell and reached for another oyster. "And I always want more. Once I get started eating these, I just can't seem to stop. I enjoy the experience that much."

There was no way—*no frigging way*—that Ruby was going to watch him, ah . . . do that again, so, quickly, she sought to divert his attention elsewhere. "Uh . . . what's that?" she asked, pointing at some other unidentifiable fruit on the table. She really, really hoped he hadn't seen what she saw on those half shells. It would really hinder conversation.

"Ah," he said with a smile as he scooped up one of the halved . . . ah . . . foodstuffs in question.

Too late Ruby realized that what she had directed his attention to, although still not readily identifiable— reminded her way too much of . . . um . . . what the half shells had reminded her of. And Keaton seemed to be fondling it as he held it. And all she could think about was what it might be like to have him fondling her—

"Actually," she said, snatching the . . . whatever . . . out of his hand and dumping it unceremoniously back onto its plate as quickly as she could, trying not to think about what she was holding, "I think this other stuff over here looks kind of good. What are these?"

Finally she had found some food on the table that bore no resemblance whatever to any human sexual organ— well, not as much as some of the other stuff, anyway, although they did sort of look like a man's . . . Ah, at any rate she hastily directed Keaton's attention to them, hoping they didn't remind him of anything at all. In fact, on second look they did appear to be pretty much harmless, even if they were round and rich and loamy, dark in color, soft in texture, and their scent, when Ruby detected it, was earthy and robust.

All right, all right, so they were pretty sexually explicit, too, she thought. At least from where she was standing. They were still way less embarrassing to look at than the oysters and that other stuff had been. Nevertheless, Ruby was totally unprepared for the rush of sensation that washed over her in response to them, a sensation that was as rich and dark and earthy as the objects in question. There was just something about their aroma—and also about their soft, firm, spherical shape—that left her feeling a bit . . . breathless. Hot. Needy. Wanton.

Oh, yeah. It was definitely getting hot out here.

"Oh, now *these*," Keaton said, holding up one of the small, brown orbs for her inspection, "are a very nice delicacy. Truffles. Very rare. Very costly. But well worth both the hunt and the expense. Because they're also very delicious. Here," he added impulsively, extending his arm across the table again, toward her, "try one."

Before Ruby had a chance to decline—not that she necessarily could have declined, because the way he was suddenly looking at her made her voice dry up in her throat—he lifted the truffle to her lips. But he didn't immediately pop it into her mouth, as she would have thought he would do. Instead he waved it under her nose first, so that she could inhale its musky scent more completely. Involuntarily her eyes fluttered closed, and she was overcome by an almost intoxicating sensation that left her feeling quite . . . light-headed. And quite reluctant to open her eyes, too. Which was why it came as such a surprise to her when she felt the truffle skimming lightly along her lower lip, back and forth, back and forth, back . . . and . . . forth . . . again.

She did open her eyes then, only to find Keaton gazing at her with much attention, as if her reaction to the truffle was of great interest to him. Again he grazed her lip with the soft morsel, once, twice, three times, and when she opened her mouth slightly to object, he popped the truffle in whole.

And as she bit down onto the bittersweet delicacy, as her mouth was flooded with its rich, exotic flavor, she heard Keaton say, his voice sounding a bit shallow and unsteady, "They, ah . . . they're also reputed to be a strong aphrodisiac."

Oh, Ruby thought wildly as she savored the dark, sonorous taste that seemed to be spreading now down her throat, into her belly and all points beyond. Oh, no. Where was a napkin when you needed to spit out an aphrodisiac? That was the last thing she needed to be consuming in her current state of unrest. Unable to locate a napkin, however, and not wanting to fail this lesson—whatever the hell it was—Ruby finished chewing and swallowed with some difficulty . . . and immediately felt heat swamp her midsection.

Surely she just imagined that, she told herself. Surely

aphrodisiacs didn't go to work that fast. Surely there were other stimuli at work here that had provoked such a response in her.

She glanced up at Keaton and found him gazing back at her with frank and unmitigated hunger, and the heat in her belly spread faster, farther, furiously, virtually incinerating her entire body. Oh, yeah. Definitely there were other stimuli provoking her response, she thought. Because she'd never felt more stimulated—or more provoked, for that matter—in her life than she did in that moment.

Keaton somehow seemed to be sharing her response, because he continued to watch her in silence for a moment, as if he were utterly mesmerized by her reaction to the truffle. Then, his gaze still leveled on hers, he reached for one himself, eagerly biting into it while Ruby watched him. Just as had been the case for her, he seemed to relish the unusual flavor, hesitating before swallowing, as if he wanted to make it last as long as he could. And the strange warmth that had splashed into Ruby's belly and spread through her body now surged into parts of her she would rather not have, ah, surging.

Oh, swell, she thought as she went a little weak in the knees. Now she and Keaton were *both* going to be under the influence. What would lesson five's title be? "Après Aphrodisiacs"? "Postcoital Courtesies"? Or simply "Wham, Bam, Thank-You-Ma'am"?

Finally Keaton swallowed, slowly, thoroughly, his gaze still fixed on Ruby's face. But his smile faltered some as he watched her. In fact his entire expression changed, his eyes seeming to go darker, his lips fuller, his cheeks ruddier. He opened his mouth as if he wanted to say something, then closed it again before uttering a word. And still he continued to stare at her, as if she were something worth staring at.

And then, without saying a word, his eyes never leaving hers, he took a single step to the side. This step was followed by another around the table. And then another toward Ruby. And then another, and another and another, until he had rounded the table completely and stood only inches away from her. And then, as she watched with an almost detached fascination, he lifted a hand toward her face, as if he meant to touch her.

Instinctively Ruby took a step in retreat, even though what she really wanted to do was move forward, toward Keaton. But something about the way he was looking at her put her on her guard. Probably, she thought, because he was looking at her in much the same way she suspected she had been looking at him over the last few days—as if he wanted to wrestle her to the deck and have his way with her, too.

This, she thought, couldn't possibly be a good thing. Not because she didn't want it, but because she wanted it *so much*. Anything that might develop between her and Keaton out here on the bounding main was bound to be anything but main. No, anything that might spark between the two of them would be chemically based, truffle-inspired, and very, *very* temporary. He wasn't a man for her. She wasn't a woman for him. They didn't belong in each other's worlds—neither would feel comfortable in the other's world. There was no future in this. None beyond a short-lived explosion of heat that flared briefly between them and then fizzled to nothing immediately afterward. It was that simple.

But no matter how many excuses Ruby came up with for why she should discourage what Keaton seemed intent on doing, she found that she just couldn't make herself comply. He didn't seem to share her thoughts on discouragement, anyway. In fact, he didn't seem to be *thinking* about anything, because he was too busy doing. Instead of halting at her retreat, he advanced with more authority, taking two steps closer this time. Again he raised his hand to her face, but this time Ruby just couldn't find it in herself to withdraw. So she stood where she had stopped, willed her blood not to hurtle so rapidly through her body, did her best to tamp down her rising heat, and waited to see what he would do next.

Chapter 12

What Keaton did next was to propel his hand slowly forward, until he was able to brush his curled index finger lightly over Ruby's chin, once, twice, three times, reveling in the silky warmth of her as he touched her.

"You, uh . . . You have something on your, um . . ." His voice—and his thoughts—trailed off as he moved his finger nearer to her mouth, over her lower lip, then to the side, along the line of her jaw. "I'll just, uh . . . I'll just, um . . . I'll just . . ."

But instead of reaching for a napkin to aid him in his ministrations, Keaton couldn't quite keep himself from moving his hand down to her neck, curling his fingers over her nape. Slowly he pulled Ruby closer, leaning forward as he did, then he brushed his lips lightly over the part of her jaw that he had just touched with his fingertips. Her eyes fluttered closed again at the contact, her breath fleeing her lungs in a shallow *whoosh*. Keaton, too, exhaled raggedly when he registered the warmth of her breath dancing along his jaw, and the softness of her cheek beneath his mouth. And then, suddenly, his lips were on hers, brushing gingerly, tentatively, oh-so-slowly, back and forth, back and forth, back . . . and . . . forth . . . because he wanted a little taste of her before sampling her more completely.

"Oh," she whimpered softly when his mouth skimmed upward. And when he brushed his lips gently over the curve of her cheekbone, she sighed, a small whisper of sound, of surrender, that only stoked the fire that had kindled inside him. "Oh, my. Oh, my goodness. Oh, my—"

"Keaton, there you are!"

At Reynaldo's—loud—summons, Keaton sprang away from Ruby as if she had just caught on fire and was about to take him along for the conflagration. Then again, he couldn't quite help thinking that such an idea wasn't far from the truth. If she was burning even half as blisteringly as he was at the moment, then spontaneous combustion couldn't be far behind.

Good God, what had come over him? he wondered as he completed three more hasty steps backward, stopping only when his hip hit the edge of the table. He looked at Ruby's face again and immediately had his answer. Her eyes were huge and sooty and hungry, her mouth full and ripe and potent. Her dress, the color of soft summer violets, hugged every lush, abundant curve on her body, seeming a rampant invitation to come and explore. Her expression, however, was one of innocence and inexperience and uncertainty. Coupled with the passion and pleasure the rest of her promised, it was a combination that no sane man would be able to ignore. Or resist.

Keaton squeezed his eyes shut tight to banish the vision, but she was imprinted at the forefront of his brain, and he suspected she would remain there for a long, long time. What had come over him, he realized, was Ruby Runyon. It was that simple. As much as he wished he could blame his strange reaction on the oysters and the truffles and the fact that all the food Kurt had laid out earlier seemed to have some kind of blatant carnal implication behind it, Keaton knew he couldn't lay all the responsibility there. Mainly because there wasn't an aphrodisiac on the planet that was strong enough to make a man go off the way he just had.

No, it was Ruby, and Ruby alone, who had generated his recent, oh . . . "lapse in judgment" seemed as good a way as any to describe his response. Though "lust for flesh" might have been a little more appropriate. Unable to help himself, Keaton opened his eyes again, only to find, not surprisingly, that his attention focused immediately on Ruby. And he saw that she still looked very much like a woman who was *this* close to losing herself to a mind-altering orga—

Don't think about it, don't think about it, don't think about it, don't think about it, he instructed himself forcefully. And, still unable to tear his gaze away from her face, he added the even more forceful command, *Don't look at her, don't look at her, don't look at her, don't look at her.* Somehow, through some Herculean effort, he made himself glance away from her. But that, unfortunately, presented him with a view of Reynaldo instead, whose presence he'd all but forgotten about. The prince, obviously, had seen what was going on when he emerged from the lounge onto the deck, and he was probably more than a little curious as to why Keaton would be kissing this harridan he had picked up in Miami and was trying so hard to unload.

Good luck figuring out that one, Keaton thought.

Though he wasn't sure whether he was directing the mental remark to Reynaldo or to himself.

Since *Mad Tryst* was currently en route, the prince didn't require anyone to dress for dinner, hence the casualness of Keaton's and Ruby's attire. However, that didn't stop Reynaldo from looking like a Ricky Ricardo rumba reject. His dark hair was slicked back from his face with more hair goo than Bela Lugosi could shake a stick at, and he was sporting a lemon yellow satin shirt unbuttoned down to *there*, and a pair of crepe, wide-legged trousers the color of a conch shell. He'd accessorized the combination with dozens of gold chains and bracelets, and—Keaton shook his head helplessly at the sight—gold sandals.

And to think the man had probably paid thousands of dollars for the ensemble, he mused, money that could have done infinitely more good had he donated it instead to the Clothe a Badly Dressed Member of the Royal Family Fund. Ah, well. It was Reynaldo's money. Stashed in easily accessible, unfreezable Swiss bank accounts. Unlike Keaton's money, which was all tucked nicely away in quite *in*accessible, highly freezable, Pelagian bank accounts. He hadn't seen a nickel of his—not unimpressive—wealth since being forced out of the country, another reason that he couldn't very well abandon Reynaldo. Reynaldo was Keaton's meal ticket until he could return home.

Well, how could Keaton have known the country was going to be overthrown? He'd been too busy cleaning up after Reynaldo to notice anything like Pelagia's state of affairs. And he had thought that since he was destined to become prime minister of the country, the least he could do was keep his money in their banks, couldn't he? And

he did fully intend to get his money back, after all. Someday. When he returned to Pelagia. After the people's anger
at all things Reynaldo-related cooled a bit. And hey, think
of all the interest his money was accruing in the interim.
He'd be even richer when he—eventually—went home.
Provided, of course, the people of Pelagia hadn't already
confiscated his wealth and used it to build more casinos
and hotels to further the tourist trade. And when he *did* go
back and claim his money, Keaton thought, making a
mental note to himself, he would *not* spend it on Ricky Ricardo rumba reject clothes.

So there.

Reynaldo made his way across the deck in a leisurely,
princely fashion, his gaze flickering first over Keaton,
then over Ruby, then over Keaton again. His expression
offered no clue as to what he might be thinking, but
Keaton got the gist of it when he greeted Ruby with a less
than friendly "Hallo."

Reynaldo obviously didn't want her to think she was of
any significance, which was pretty much how he felt
about everyone other than himself. Keaton had seen this
sort of behavior from the prince often enough. Hell, it was
the same behavior Reynaldo had exhibited for the entire
cruise. He'd scarcely given Ruby—or anyone else—the
time of day since she'd come aboard. Though he hadn't
been outwardly hostile toward her, either. Well, no more
hostile than he was with anyone. Reynaldo always wanted
to be sure that the people around him knew their place—
their place being a roughly two-by-three-foot rectangular
space before him, doormat-shaped, that he could wipe his
feet on. Repeatedly.

And, true to his nature, he showed absolutely no sign of
welcome when he spoke his greeting to Ruby. No, in fact,
Keaton noted, Reynaldo was gazing at her now with his

get-down-on-your-knees-and-kiss-my-ring-you-repugnant-peasant look. It was, after all, one Reynaldo used all the time. Damn him.

"Hi," Ruby replied warmly, in spite of her host's coolness, with a genial smile that Reynaldo in no way deserved.

But, obviously having already tired of Ruby's presence, Reynaldo turned back to Keaton to ask, "Still can't manage to give your harridan the slip? You surprise me, Keaton. I would have thought you'd come up with some way to avoid her by now. If it were me in your situation, God knows I would have."

Instead of replying to Reynaldo's question—because the question obviously demanded no reply—Keaton turned to look at Ruby, just in time to see her genial smile go crashing into a hurt frown. He started to say something that might take the sting out of the prince's remark, but was prevented from doing so when she stoically replied for herself.

"My name is Ruby," she said crisply. "Not 'harridan.' "

Reynaldo arched his dark brows in regal surprise at what Keaton was certain he viewed as her disrespect. Which, technically, by Pelagian law, anyway, it was. For one thing, she had spoken to Reynaldo without him speaking to her first—he had directed his question, however offensive, at Keaton. For another thing, she hadn't addressed the prince by his proper title—or any title, for that matter. For another thing, her tone of voice had held almost as much contempt as Reynaldo's had. Which Keaton couldn't exactly blame her for. Nevertheless, on Pelagia, for committing such transgressions, Reynaldo could have had Ruby put in the stocks. That was how old were the laws of the country pertaining to the rights of, and the courtesies due, the royal family. And that was how big a crybaby Reynaldo was about such things.

Instead of having her publicly humiliated, however, the prince only instructed her, "And you may call me 'Your Highness.' "

Ruby said nothing in response to that, and Keaton figured that was probably just as well. Maybe that earlier fear of hand loss she'd mentioned was still fresh in her mind.

"Just what is it you do back in Miami, darling?" Reynaldo asked her then, his voice oozing disdain for the little commoner. "You never have said."

"You never have asked," she replied evenly.

"I'm asking now," he said through gritted teeth.

Not that the prick—er, prince—deserved a polite reply, Keaton thought, but Ruby was poised and courteous as she told him, "I'm a waitress. At a comedy club in Sou—"

"A *waitress*?" Reynaldo interrupted incredulously, clearly unbothered by how rudely he cut her off. And then he disregarded her again in favor of his right-hand man. "Good God, Keaton, what were you *thinking*?" he asked. "Has it been so long between women that you just grabbed the first warm body you saw?" He turned again to look at Ruby, shamelessly inspecting her body up and down before dismissing her again to direct his commentary to Keaton. "I mean, not that this particular body doesn't look warm enough for a tumble, I suppose. It has its own . . . rustic . . . charm. But honestly. You've had actresses and diplomats and socialites and—granted, lesser—members of nobility. Have you no pride at all?" He laughed, but there wasn't an ounce of good humor in the sound. "God, a *waitress*. You *must* have been hard up, old man. Or perhaps you'd just been too long with a hard—"

"*Don't* say it, Reynaldo," Keaton muttered. "I think you've said enough as it is."

In fact, the other man had said more than enough. Because it was right about then that Ruby murmured a soft "Excuse me" and pushed her way inelegantly between the two men. Then she raced toward the lounge entrance and disappeared through it without looking back, leaving both of them gazing after her in silence.

"You bastard," Keaton said to Reynaldo without preamble as he watched Ruby go. Screw speaking before being spoken to. And screw proper address. And screw contemptuous tone of voice for that matter. Hell, screw Reynaldo all around.

"Ah, ah, ah, Keaton," his companion said before lifting his drink to his lips for an idle sip. But his voice was utterly lacking in concern when he added, "You know better than to address your prince in such a manner. I could have you flogged if I wanted to."

Somehow Keaton refrained from belting the sonofabitch. That was a hanging offense on Pelagia. Not that it wouldn't have been worth it for one good pop in the eye.

"Oh, yeah?" he said instead. Still screwing speaking before spoken to, proper address, and contemptuous tone of voice. Still screwing Reynaldo, for that matter. "Well, 'bastard' is a compliment compared to what I'd really like to call you right now. Because trust me, it's not 'Your Highness.' " Your Lowness, maybe, Keaton added to himself. Your Creepness. Your Prickness. Your Bloody-Awfulness.

"You know, the only reason I tolerate you, Keaton," Reynaldo said, "is because you manage to keep order better than anyone I know. But you're by no means unexpendable. Don't forget that."

Oh, the hell he wasn't unexpendable, Keaton thought. If it weren't for him, Reynaldo would have been stripped naked and trotted through Pelagia dangling from a pole a year ago. If it weren't for him, Reynaldo would have been booted out of every respectable country on the globe over the course of the year and told never to return. If it weren't for him, Reynaldo would have been served up as Purina Kurt Chow a long time ago.

"Was that really necessary?" Keaton demanded in as civil a tone as he could manage. He didn't bother to identify what the *that* was. He figured even Reynaldo was smart enough to figure that one out on his own. Barely.

But Reynaldo seemed to be genuinely stumped by Keaton's reaction. "What did I say?" he asked innocently. "You told me she's been harassing you. You told me you wanted her off the yacht. We're going hundreds of miles out of our way just to get rid of her. Then I come out on deck and find you . . ." He shuddered for effect. "Kissing her. And she's a *waitress*. What *were* you thinking, man?"

Keaton expelled a restless growl and ran a hand brutally through his hair. He hadn't been thinking, he realized. He'd only been reacting. But when he'd glanced up and had seen Ruby looking like . . . like . . . like *that*, he hadn't been able to help himself. It was as if there had been a string inside him attached to something inside her, and she'd turned on a widget or something that had begun to pull that string taut. Tighter and tighter the string had tensed, closer and closer Keaton had been drawn, until . . . Until he'd been able to touch her fine skin. And feel her keen heat. And inhale the perfect, womanly scent of her. And taste . . .

Oh, God. She had tasted so sweet.

And okay, so maybe what he'd done hadn't been the smartest thing in the world to do. Maybe he should have thought more about the repercussions of the action before he'd covered her mouth with his and tasted her sweetness. Because he had no idea what he was going to say to her the next time he saw her. And he couldn't exactly avoid her, considering their situation. *Mad Tryst* was a big boat, to be sure, but it wasn't that big. He and Ruby were bound to run into each other several more times before they reached Puerto Rico. Especially since he had another lesson scheduled. Especially since they hadn't completed their lesson today. Especially since, he realized, he really wanted to see her again.

Even if he didn't have any idea what he would say to her when he did.

In spite of everything, though, Reynaldo had had no right to say what he had said to Ruby, or to treat her the way he had treated her. Even if she was a waitress with no more than a high school education who had been raised in a trailer park and didn't know who her father was. It was just simple courtesy to treat all people equally, even if they weren't equal.

"Look, just stay out of this thing with me and Ruby, all right?" Keaton told Reynaldo, suddenly feeling restless and undeserving and mean. "It's none of your business."

But the prince eyed him warily in return. "Do you want her off the yacht or don't you, Keaton?"

Keaton realized he couldn't answer the question right away, and that bothered him a lot. He knew what he *should* want. He should want Ruby gone. Even if she did feel fine and smell womanly and taste sweet, she didn't belong on *Mad Tryst*—for a number of reasons. She had a life to get back to, and Keaton had . . . Well, he had things to do, too. Big things. Important things. Things that needed his absolute, full attention. He couldn't afford to be distracted by Ruby Runyon, even temporarily.

So he was just going to have to stop being so damned preoccupied by thoughts of her. After he apologized to her for Reynaldo's abominable behavior, of course. Because that was one of the big, important things that Keaton had to do these days. Make amends for all the lousy, thought-less things that Prince Reynaldo of Pelagia said and did to other people.

Although he had seen Ruby disappear into the lounge, he didn't find her there. He did see Omar at the piano, playing, naturally, Gershwin. The melody, if Keaton wasn't mistaken, was that of "Nice Work If You Can Get It," but thanks to Omar's unfamiliarity with English, which wasn't quite his second language—or even his fourteenth—the actual lyric the man sang was something along the lines of "Nice Turk if you can get one, and you can get one if you cry." Still, it was rather catchy.

Keaton also saw Arabella sitting at the bar, talking to Gus, something that wouldn't have caught his attention if it weren't for the fact that Arabella seemed to be enjoying herself. Normally she always seemed to be uncomfortable around the bartender, to the point where she didn't even acknowledge the man. Tonight, however, she was smiling at him, chatting with him, seeming to genuinely enjoy herself. Keaton smiled. Good for her. Maybe the countess was starting to shed some of her unhappiness. Maybe there was hope yet for her. Maybe, now that she seemed to be a bit more lively, Reynaldo would even take notice of her. Maybe things would work out well for the countess and the prince after all.

And maybe tonight, while Keaton was sleeping, the Blue Fairy would fly into his room and turn him into a real boy.

He pushed the thought away and scanned the room one last time, but saw no sign that Ruby had ever been there. And just to be on the safe side, he made a quick search for Kurt, too. One should never turn one's back on a wiener dog, Keaton had learned the hard way. They had a bad habit of sneaking up on a person. Of course, they also had a bad habit of breathing, but he supposed there was nothing much he could do about that. But he saw no sign of Kurt, either, so he figured it was probably okay to turn around and leave. Provided, of course, he kept an eye out for the detestable, perfidious little incubus.

A half hour later Keaton told himself he shouldn't be surprised to have found Ruby holed up in the library, with just the hideous, corrupt little malefactor he'd been hoping to avoid. In fact, when he did find her, she was so wrapped up in whatever book she had pulled from the shelf that she didn't even hear him enter. Kurt was sleeping, blissfully oblivious, too, to Keaton's entry, something for which the latter was profoundly grateful. Because it gave him a moment with which to study Ruby in silence, and to try and figure out just what it was he felt.

Not too surprisingly, he realized what he felt was desire. And need. And wanting. He just couldn't quite identify what, exactly, his desire and need and wanting were for.

Well, that should be obvious, shouldn't it? he asked himself. What he desired was another taste of her—a deeper, fuller, more thorough taste of her. What he needed was to lie down with her on some soft surface and fit his body next to hers. What he wanted was the removal of their clothing and the union of their bodies. What he desired and needed and wanted was what he hadn't had with a woman—any woman—for far too long.

That was all.

Now if he could just make it through the next couple of days without it, Ruby would be gone, and so would his desire and his need and his wanting. Because *Mad Tryst* was due to dock at San Juan tomorrow morning, and then Keaton could escort Ruby to the airport and buy her a ticket home—it was the least he could do after the ordeal she'd endured for the past week—and then he could wave goodbye to her plane as it lifted off the tarmac. And then, if he still felt any kind of desire or need or wanting, he could just hie himself to the nearest resort and find an attractive woman who had a few prospects—most notably a willing nature—and scratch the itch that had been dogging him for days.

Good plan, Danning, he told himself. Now if he could just stick to it . . .

He must have made some sound then, because Ruby snapped her head up suddenly and turned to look at him. Her expression, he noted, was one of surprise, but there was something mingled with it that he couldn't quite define, something that gave her the appearance of vulnerability and deprivation, and something else, too, something Keaton couldn't—or perhaps didn't want to—identify. And just like that, all the desire and need and wanting roared up inside him again, simmering just beneath his surface, as if it were mere degrees away from eruption. And damned if he didn't find himself, in some strange way, for some strange reason, kind of enjoying the sensation.

"Hi," she said softly.

He shoved his hands deep into the pockets of his trousers, shifting his weight to one foot as he studied her. "Hi," he rejoined, every bit as quietly.

When he said nothing further, she closed the book in her lap, marking her place with her forefinger, and asked, "What are you doing here?"

"I was looking for you," he said without thinking.

Her expression changed at that, turning hopeful, almost wistful, and, damn, did Keaton like the way she looked at him in that moment. Maybe because he felt a little hopeful, a little wistful himself. Maybe because that hopefulness and wistfulness was for something she hoped for and, um, wisted for herself.

"Why are you looking for me?" she asked, her voice even softer now. "I'm just a waitress."

"Yeah, about that," Keaton began. "I, um, I needed to find you because I needed to apologize for Reynaldo."

Her dark brows furrowed at the comment, and her eyes filled with something akin to irritation. "Why should you apologize for him?"

He lifted his shoulders and let them drop again, and his hands curled into loose fists in his pocket. "Because that's what I do," he told her. "I apologize for Reynaldo."

"But why?" she asked again.

Exasperation welled inside Keaton, mixing with all the other things that were simmering just beneath the surface. "Because it's what I do," he repeated, more adamantly this time. "Part of my job is making sure the prince doesn't leave a mess in his wake. So sometimes I have to make apologies for him."

Ruby studied him in silence for a moment more, her expression now blank and unreadable. "And that's what I am?" she asked. "A mess in the prince's wake?"

"No, of course not," Keaton told her.

"But you just said—"

"That's not what I said, and you know it."

There was another one of those thoughtful silences and blank expressions, followed by Ruby's pointedly asked "Why doesn't the prince make his own apologies?"

Keaton clenched his jaw tight. "Because he doesn't feel obliged to," he said.

"Then you doing it for him is meaningless," Ruby told him.

"It's not meaningless," Keaton immediately countered. "Apologies are never wasted."

"They are if they aren't sincere."

He set his jaw even more firmly and tried to think of

something to say in response. His apologizing for Reynaldo wasn't meaningless, Keaton told himself. She was just still ticked off because of what had happened up on deck. Not that he blamed her, but that was no reason for her to go after *him*, attack *him*, telling him his job was meaningless. Hey, his job was extremely important. It *was*.

"Look, I'm not going to argue with you," he told her. "If you don't want Reynaldo's apology—"

"I don't want it," she interrupted.

Keaton expelled an exasperated sound. "Then what do you want?" he asked.

She met his gaze for a moment, and he thought she was going to say something in response. But she only shook her head once, slowly, then dropped her gaze back down to the book she reopened in her lap. "It doesn't matter what I want," she said softly. "I'm never going to get it."

The actress thing, he concluded. She didn't think she had enough time to learn everything from Keaton she needed to learn to pierce those social circles she wanted to enter. He guessed their lesson *had* been pretty rudely interrupted by Reynaldo, hadn't it? Oh, no, wait a minute, he immediately corrected himself. It hadn't been Reynaldo's arrival that had interrupted their lesson. No, that had happened when Keaton had given her that little kiss. Okay, that not so little kiss. And the interruption had been anything but rude. In fact, it had been pretty damned—

Well. Probably he would be better off not dwelling on that right now.

"We could still finish our lesson," he offered instead. "Reynaldo's probably not on deck anymore. And dinner is an hour off, so the appetizers will still be out."

"I'm not very hungry," she said flatly, her attention still fixed on her book.

"A little while ago you said you were," he reminded her.

"I changed my mind."

Yeah, funny, Keaton thought, how his appetite had changed over the course of the evening, too. He was still hungry. Just not for food, that was all.

"Okay, then maybe we can try again at dinner," he said.

She barked out an incredulous laugh that held not a trace of good humor. "If you think I have any intention of sitting down to dinner with the prince of darkness," Ruby said, glancing up from her book to meet his gaze levelly, "you're out of your mind."

Keaton nodded. He couldn't exactly blame her there, either. "All right. I understand. You shouldn't have any trouble avoiding Reynaldo for the rest of the cruise," he added. "Just lay low tonight, and get up early in the morning." For some reason he had a little trouble saying the rest of what he needed to say. But he made himself continue. "We'll be in Puerto Rico early tomorrow morning, and you can leave the yacht for good, and you won't have to see Reynaldo anymore. Hell, this time tomorrow, you'll probably be on a plane headed for Miami. That ought to make you feel happy."

She dropped her gaze back down to her book. "Oh, yeah. I'm happy. I'm so happy, I can hardly stand it."

Keaton studied her in silence for a moment, noting the despondent slump of her shoulders, the forlorn expression he could discern on her face even in profile, and the way she had pulled her legs up before her on the library sofa, as if she were trying to curl her entire body into a little ball and disappear. And something inside him that had been wound way too tight lately suddenly began to loosen. Something that had been cold for far too long suddenly began to warm. And something that had been shut up in darkness began to crawl out into the light.

"I really am sorry about what Reynaldo said to you earlier, even if he isn't," he told her. "He had no right to say what he did."

"But he had every right to feel it," she said without looking up. "Didn't he?"

Keaton eyed her curiously. "I don't know what you mean."

Still not looking at him, she replied, "I mean even if you don't think Reynaldo should have *said* what he said to me, you do think it's all right for him to *feel* the way he feels about me."

"No, I don't," Keaton replied automatically. But he realized quickly that he didn't reply that way because he knew what Ruby said was wrong. No, the reason he answered the way he did, he realized, was that—and he really hated to admit this—it would have been impolite to respond otherwise.

Ruby continued to stare down at her book in silence. Then, slowly, she lifted her head and leveled her gaze unflinchingly on his. At first he thought she was going to remain silent. Although she opened her mouth briefly, as if she intended to speak, she immediately closed it again, as if she'd changed her mind. But she must have changed it once more, because, finally, she did say something.

And, oh, what a thing she said.

"You agree with him, don't you?" she asked. "You think of me the same way he does. Maybe you're not quite as contemptuous, but deep down, you don't disagree with Reynaldo's opinion of me."

"Ruby," Keaton began to object. He told himself he didn't agree with her. But he couldn't think of a single thing to say to counter her claim.

"You don't think I'm as good as you all are," she continued, ignoring his interjection. "You don't think I fit on

your social level. Hey, you can take the girl out of the
trailer park, but you can't take the trailer park out of the
girl, right? And you can't take away her lack of education,
or her lack of prospects, or her lack of pedigree, or her
lack of anything else. You just don't think I'm as good as
you are, do you, Keaton?"

Keaton said nothing in response to her question,
mainly because he genuinely didn't know what to say. Because, deep down, he *wasn't* honestly sure he could disagree with her. Not about him being better than she was,
but about the two of them being . . . different from each
other. Because they were different from each other. Even
if she had looked like an exiled princess for the last week,
the fact of the matter was that she was really a fugitive
waitress. A waitress who'd grown up in a trailer park and
had no education beyond a high school diploma. A waitress who didn't even know her paternity. Keaton was a
firm believer in equal opportunity for all people, but facts
were facts, and social strata were social strata, and castes
were castes, and . . .

And never the twain should meet.

The fact of the matter was that Ruby didn't belong in
Keaton's world any more than he belonged in hers. And
because his world was filled with infinitely more opportunity and possibility and privilege than hers was, well . . .
That just made the situation even more awkward than it
already was. More difficult. More impossible. Simply put,
there just was no place for Ruby in Keaton's life, or his
lifestyle. His world had more going for it than hers did,
and because of that he needed a woman who . . . who had
more going for her than Ruby did. He wasn't proud of that
realization by any means. But he had to be honest with
himself. And honestly . . .

He changed he subject.

"There should be a little time in Puerto Rico tomorrow before you need to get to the airport," he said. "Is there anything in particular you'd like to see or do before you go home?"

Ruby continued to study him with deep deliberation for a moment, as if she were cataloguing every aspect of his person, every trait and characteristic he claimed, recording every word he had spoken to her and every gesture he had sent her way. Then her shoulders seemed to slump a little more, her expression became even more despondent, and her body curled a little more tightly in on itself.

"No," she finally said, glancing away. "I think I've done—and seen—enough. Thanks anyway. But I think it's long past time that I got home."

Chapter 13

"*O*kay, lesson number one, Princess. The way to a man's heart is through his, ah . . ."

Gus halted before completing the sentence, thinking maybe he was getting ahead of himself with that particular lesson, and that, probably, it was one he should save for a later time. They were just getting started, after all. Even if a full week had passed since Arabella had come to his cabin to ask for his assistance—and to send his libido into overdrive—they were only now getting around to those lessons he had promised her about turning her prince's head. Instead they'd spent the last week doing the other thing Arabella had asked him to do—play a farce that might sway ol' Reynaldo's attentions away from Supermodel Dacia to Supersexy Arabella instead.

But even after a week of Arabella's spending an obvious amount of time in the presence of another man, the only person who seemed to find her supersexy these days was Gus. Of course, Gus had always been the one to find her that, which, quite frankly, was just fine with him. In fact, the more Reynaldo had ignored the two of them, the more Gus had insisted that he and Arabella needed to spend time together. And even if there'd been no noticeable difference in Reynaldo's reaction, there sure as hell had been one in Gus's.

Oh, yeah. After spending a week with Arabella being attentive and nice to him for a change—even if it *was* all phony-baloney attentiveness and niceness—Gus was crazier about her than ever. And that, he knew, was saying something. Because he'd already been pretty far gone on her when she'd proposed this ridiculous burlesque of hers. And now . . .

Gus pushed the thought away. Now he wasn't sure he'd ever recover. Because if this ridiculous burlesque—however illogical—somehow did succeed in bringing the prince's attentions back to Arabella . . . If, however implausibly, Reynaldo did come to the realization that his intended was exactly what he needed and wanted by his side . . . If, somehow, she did wind up marrying the guy . . .

Gus pushed that thought away, too. Right now none of those things seemed likely. And it was up to him to keep it that way. Otherwise he might just be spending the rest of his life in jail for regicide. Or princicide. Or Reynaldo-cide. Whatever.

Still, Arabella had reminded him yesterday that he'd promised to share those secrets of the brotherhood with her, something that Gus couldn't exactly say heartened him any. Because if she still wanted those secrets, it meant she was still determined to recapture her fiancée's interest. And that, Gus knew, he couldn't allow. Nevertheless, he hadn't been able to find it in himself to turn her down. They'd made a deal, after all, and Gus was no welcher. So he'd promised her that as soon as they put in at San Juan, the two of them could begin his promised instruction.

But there was no reason to overwhelm the poor girl with too much information too soon, he reminded himself. It was still early in the day. Way too early to be talking about a man's, ah . . .

And besides, he quickly jumped his own mental track, the entire island of Puerto Rico lay spread before them like a radiant emerald, just waiting to be plundered. Sure, he'd lured Arabella ashore with the promise of teaching her how to bag her prince once and for all—the big jerk— and shed herself of the supermodel who should remain nameless, but really, at the moment, that was the furthest thing from Gus's mind. No, what he wanted to focus on right now was the fact that he had Arabella Wilhelm all to himself for a whole day, and he intended to take full advantage of her.

It, he quickly corrected himself. He intended to take full advantage of *it*. The day. Not the princess.

Not yet, anyway.

No, they were starting off very nicely, if he did say so himself, and he didn't want to mess with a good thing. It wasn't even yet ten o'clock, and the two of them were enjoying brunch at a small oceanside café in Condado Beach, the tawny beach and turquoise water and azure sky fanning before them like a freshly painted watercolor seascape. Gus had donned his best Hawaiian shirt for the occasion—the greens and yellows actually complemented each other on this one—along with a pair of big ol' khaki shorts, the official uniform of a tropical paradise. And Puerto Rico, he had decided right away, was definitely a paradise. And not just because of the palm trees and the ocean, either. No, this place was a paradise simply because of the company Gus was keeping. Then again, Arabella Wilhelm could turn Antarctica into a torrid Garden of Eden.

And my, but wasn't that such an interesting analogy to have pop into his head? Because there was nothing that Gus would enjoy more than playing Adam to her Eve. Or better yet, serpent to her Eve. Oh, yeah. He'd show her some forbidden fruit. And then he'd eat her apple right to the core. Uh, so to speak.

"The way to a man's heart," he tried again, a bit less steadily this time, because he was doing his best to dispel the image of Arabella wearing little more than a fig leaf, her golden tresses tumbling free over silky—naked—breasts, "is through his, um . . . his, ah . . ." Ah, hell. How to begin this thing politely. "Well," he tried a third time. "Let's just say that if you want to command Reynaldo's attention, you're going to need to make yourself more . . . visible."

Arabella gazed at him through narrowed eyes. "I am not visible?" she asked warily.

Hoo boy, was that a loaded question, Gus thought. Hell, yes, she was visible. Way *too* visible, as far as he was concerned. But then, she was never really out of his sight, was she? If he was anywhere in her physical vicinity, he had every last bit of his attention trained on her. And whenever the two of them weren't together bodily—yet another interesting way to put it, he couldn't help thinking—he still always managed to have her front and center in his thoughts. Especially her, ah, her front and center. And today, garbed as she was in a sleeveless dress the color of lemon drops, made of some faint, gauzy fabric that captured the sunlight as if it were a part of her, she was more visible than words could say.

In fact, she was doubtless more visible than she realized, Gus mused, because in capturing the sunlight the way it did, the gauzy fabric of her dress became pretty much transparent, revealing every exquisite outline of her luscious body. It was something he had discovered much to his delight as they'd strode from the yacht club where *Mad Tryst* was currently docked. If she'd had any idea how much of her he had been able to see as she'd walked a little ways in front of him—well, he didn't want to be rude and move ahead of her, did he?—she would have gone running for cover pronto. So naturally he had no intention of pointing out the vitreous nature of her garment at any time during the course of the day. Hey, he didn't want to embarrass her. It wouldn't be polite.

"Oh, you're visible enough, Princess," he assured her with profound understatement. "Just not in any way that Reynaldo would notice, that's all."

"And why is that?" she asked, seeming to be honestly curious. "Am I not attractive enough for him? I have been told that I am beautiful," she added matter-of-factly. "And I do not seem to frighten animals or young children. Surely he cannot be repulsed by me."

"Ah, no," Gus agreed. "You're certainly, um, attractive." He nearly choked on that final word, so inadequate was it. No, a better word for what she was might be "gorgeous." Or "dazzling." Or "enchanting." "Breathtaking." "Flawless." "Radiant." "Magnificent." "Majestic." "Sublime."

Stuff like that.

"But Reynaldo has taken you for granted for a long time now," he pointed out. "I mean, you've been engaged to him since you were . . . how old?"

"Two," she told him.

He gaped at her in disbelief. "You got engaged to be married when you were two years old? Are you serious?"

Her expression indicated she saw no reason that he should find her revelation surprising. "Yes."

"*Two?*" he asked again, incredulously. He wanted to be sure he had this down right.

"Yes, two," she said, sounding impatient, as if she truly couldn't understand his amazement.

He slowly shook his head in wonder. He'd always thought his parents had been totally unreasonable, forcing him to take Lucinda Brewer to the senior prom because her father was friends with his father, and it had been "understood" since the beginning of the school year that Gus would take her because she wasn't likely to get any invitations from anyone else in the class. Not that Lucinda had been all that bad. Well, not too bad. Hey, she'd had a great personality. But Gus had sort of planned on asking Denise Corelli, and he'd never quite forgiven his parents for messing up his social life that way.

But then there were a lot of things he'd never forgiven his parents for. Lucinda Brewer and Denise Corelli weren't even in the top ten. And hey, it wasn't like they'd forced him to marry someone he didn't love, because they'd promised. Especially not when he was *two freaking years old*.

"Jeez, just what kind of place is it you come from, anyway?" he asked Arabella now, surprised to realize that, in all their conversations over the last week, they'd never made more than small talk about likes and dislikes, and isn't the sand in Bermuda interesting, and have you ever seen water so blue. "Does everyone in your country get engaged when they're two years old?"

"No," she told him. "Only those who have a reason to."

"And what reason did you have?"

"Me, I had no reason to become engaged at two," she said mildly. "At two I was concerned with little more than learning how to count and how to hold a spoon. My parents, however, had very good reasons for wanting me to be engaged as soon as possible, to a man like Reynaldo."

"What kind of reasons?"

She shrugged as she reached for her glass of pineapple juice, but her movements seemed anything but casual. Instead of picking up her drink, she ran her finger restlessly up and down the side, making fidgety little trails in the condensation that had collected there.

"Reasons such as a longstanding friendship with Reynaldo's parents, and a tradition of Wilhelms marrying very well," she said softly. She glanced up briefly as she added, "Well above our appointed station. I will be the first, you see, to marry a prince. And also reasons such as many houses and real estate holdings that they wished to keep," she continued before Gus had a chance to comment—not that he really had any idea how to respond to a remark like that—lowering her gaze to the table once again. "And reasons such as many investments, many works of art, many pieces of heirloom jewelry, much money, and a castle that has been in our family for many generations."

Although the list of assets was certainly impressive, it was that last item that most captured Gus's attention. "A castle," he repeated.

She nodded but didn't meet his gaze. Instead she continued to move her finger in restive circles around the rim of her glass. "Yes. A castle. In Toulaine. It is very picturesque, but quite drafty. I did not always enjoy living there."

"You, uh . . . you lived in a castle while you were growing up?" he asked, wondering why he was even vaguely surprised by that.

She offered another not-so-casual shrug in response,

along with more avoidance of his gaze, then followed with a softly uttered "Sometimes. Other times I lived in our chalet in the Alps, or our vacation cottage on the Riviera, or our townhouse in Vienna."

Wow, Gus thought. She really was a princess, complete with castle. He'd joked about that often enough, but the more he learned about Arabella, the more he realized how apt his nickname for her was. Hell, she might as well be an official member of a royal family, so far removed from him was she. The two of them couldn't possibly be leading lives that were more disparate.

Of course, he reminded himself, it didn't have to be that way. There were things he could do that might bring the two of them into social spheres that were, if not equal, certainly closer to touching. Then again, he'd have to make an awful lot of sacrifices and work pretty damned hard if he wanted to elevate himself to her level of cultural and financial sophistication. Arabella was currently engaged to a prince, even if the guy was a royal schmuck. She'd been raised in an ivory tower, and she felt honor-bound to live by the rigid standards other people had put in place for her.

In other words, she wasn't the kind of woman to go for some rootless, penniless, pointless ne'er-do-well, just because the guy asked her to—or even because the guy dropped down onto his knees and begged and pleaded, and whined and cried, and God, please, pretty please, I'll do anything, anything you say, if you'll just—

Ahem.

Anyway, Gus would have to completely forsake his gadabout, no-strings-on-me existence if he had a hope in hell of winning Arabella over. He'd have to think about a future that would involve someone other than himself. He'd have to become a provider, because he was reasonably sure that Arabella hadn't been schooled in anything other than social graces. He'd have to go to college. Hell, he'd have to *graduate* from college. And get a real job. And make something of himself. He'd have to be all those things his family had wanted—expected—him to be, all those things he had sworn he would never, ever become.

Was he willing to do that? he asked himself. Was he willing to turn his back on the man he was now, the man it had taken him five years to realize, and to like? Especially when he'd rejected and walked away from so many other things to become that man? Just how far was he willing to go to win Arabella? Just how many changes to his life and his lifestyle would he undergo to ensure a future with her? He'd told himself a week ago that he would risk anything, everything for her. Only now, though, was he honestly beginning to evaluate just what that risk would involve.

How much of himself would he surrender to be with her? he asked himself again. Especially when there was no guarantee that she would ever reciprocate his feelings? Oh, sure, he knew she was interested in him. He knew she was attracted. He'd be a fool to have missed out on some of the looks she'd sent his way, and how nervous she became whenever he got too close to her. But would she ever *feel* for him the way he *felt* for her? And just what were his feelings for her in the first place? Was she worth such a sacrifice? Was he?

"We have talked enough about me for now," Arabella said suddenly, dispelling his troubling thoughts. "Now you must tell me about yourself, Gus."

Ooo, not a good subject to broach, he thought as he pushed his ruminations about any kind of future with Arabella to the back of his mind—for now. He really, really, really didn't want to talk about himself. Because he really, really, really didn't want to tell lies. There was no way he was going to get personal right now. Getting personal meant revealing things. Things about himself. Things about his past. And although Gus didn't mind talking about himself to a point—hey, what guy did?—his past was a place he absolutely forbade himself, or anyone else, to visit. Ever.

"What's there to tell?" he asked evasively.

She eyed him thoughtfully, a half smile dancing about her lips, her blue eyes bright with curiosity. "Tell me where you come from," she decreed.

"The United States," he replied. Honestly, too, which made him very proud of himself.

"Tell me which state," she commanded.

"Most recently?" he evaded further. "California. I came aboard *Mad Tryst* in LA, but naturally I don't expect you to remember that," he lied.

She eyed him speculatively for a moment, then, very softly, she said, "I remember when you came aboard."

And something about the way she said it made a shudder of awareness ripple right up Gus's spine. Damn. That felt *good*. "Do you?" he asked quietly.

She nodded, her expression taking on a kind of dreaminess that Gus told himself he'd be better off not pondering. No matter how badly he found himself wanting to.

"But you are not from California, are you?" Arabella asked further, her voice, too, now sounding dreamy and faraway. "Because you said 'most recently.' That suggests that there was another state before that one."

"Oh, there was," he assured her. Honestly, too. Maybe he wouldn't have to lie to her after all. "There were dozens of states before California, in fact. I've done a lot of traveling since I left home."

"Then tell me where you were when you began this

traveling," she mandated. "Tell me where this home is that you speak of."

Damn, Gus thought. Had he actually used the word "home"? He was slipping. Big time.

"You cannot evade an answer, Gus," she added when he didn't reply, obviously on to his game. "I will find out what I want to know. I always do."

Something about the way she voiced that remark, too, made a barrage of heat torpedo through him. Gee, if they kept this up, they might just consummate their relationship right here, right now, without removing a single article of clothing or making any body contact at all. But then where would be the fun in that?

"All right," he conceded reluctantly. "I was born and raised in Pennsylvania. There. How's that?"

Arabella smiled, and that barrage of heat speeding through Gus suddenly became a cannon blast of conflagration. "Tell me what city," she dictated.

Gus ground his teeth together hard. And although he didn't want to give her any more of himself than he absolutely had to, any more than he already had, he heard himself reply—honestly, too, dammit—"Philadelphia. Look, why are we talking about me?" he quickly sidestepped. "I thought this day was supposed to be dedicated to your, ah, edification."

"Oh, I am learning very much," she said happily. "Much more than I anticipated."

"My past isn't important," he said. "Not only is it not what we came here to talk about, but it has nothing to do with the present, and it has nothing to do with who I am at this moment."

She made a soft *tsk*ing sound. "That is not true, and you know it. We cannot escape where we come from any more than we can escape where we are going."

He eyed her narrowly. "What's that supposed to mean?"

She shrugged. "Just that the way we are brought up as children is what defines us as adults. You cannot change very much what you are—what you were born to be, what you were raised to be—no matter what you do, or where you go. And where we go is also defined by where we come from."

Gus narrowed his eyes at her, thinking that somehow he understood what she was saying, even though he had no idea what she was talking about. Not that he necessarily agreed with her, mind you, but he did understand. Sort of. Nevertheless, he heard himself respond, "You're making absolutely no sense, you know that, don't you?"

She laughed, and he realized then that it was the first time he had ever heard her do so with such freedom and lack of inhibition. He also realized that the sound was beautiful and lyrical, hypnotic and narcotic.

"Perhaps not to you," she said, still smiling. "But to me it makes very good sense. We are what we are. And we will go where we will go. And we will be what we will be. We have no choice over these things. They just are the way they are."

"Now, see, Princess, that's where you and I differ," Gus said, leaning forward now, folding his arms resolutely over the top of the table. He wanted to make sure she knew he meant business. "Because *I* happen to think that our *choices* are what define us, not where we come from or how we were raised. We *choose* to be what we are. We *choose* to go where we go. We *choose* to become who we become."

"Do we?" she asked him, her smile now seeming indulgent.

"You're damned right we do," he assured her. "We

don't have to be the way other people expect us to be. We don't have to be what other people see us as. We can be whoever—whatever—the hell we want to be. Whoever, whatever we feel like being. Whoever, whatever we *choose* to be."

She said nothing for a moment, only studied him in silence, and Gus got the impression that she was seeing something in him he'd never seen himself—though what that might be, he couldn't imagine. He knew himself pretty well, by God. Certainly better than anyone else knew him. He couldn't imagine what Arabella saw that wasn't obvious to everyone else. What wasn't obvious to him.

Finally she told him, "You speak as if you have tried very hard to become someone—something—that other people did not want you to be."

Damn. In his effort to sidestep his past, Gus had just stepped right into it. Deep. And, boy, it smelled just as bad as he remembered it. "Maybe," he said evasively.

"Definitely," she corrected him with a knowing smile. "But perhaps there is some merit in what you say. Although we may only *think* that we are making choices when, in fact, we are simply following our nature and doing what we have been raised to do. Let me think on this for a little while. I will figure it out."

"There's nothing to figure, Princess," he told her. "I'm an open book. No secrets here."

"No?" she asked. But she was smiling again, even more knowingly than before.

He shook his head. "Nope. Not a one. What you see is what you get."

She didn't look anywhere near convinced. Dammit. "That is interesting," she said thoughtfully, "because you seem to me a man who has many secrets. Only now am I beginning to realize just how many. It is very curious."

Gus jumped up from his seat and tossed a wad of bills onto the table to cover the cost of their breakfast and about an eighty percent tip. "Let's get out of here," he said eloquently.

Arabella stood, too, obviously content—for now—to let their conversation lie. But she still smiled knowingly, and she still seemed to see a lot more than Gus wanted to reveal.

"Yes. We will take a walk along the beach," she proclaimed. "It is very beautiful here."

"It is that," he agreed, as they made their way toward stairs that would lead them down to the beach, grateful for the change of subject, and trying not to notice the way the sunlight filtered through Arabella's dress just so nicely.

He watched as she paused on the last step to slip off her sandals, then dip a perfectly pinkly pedicured toe into the soft sand, amazed at how incredibly arousing the sight of her shin and bare foot was. Gus had watched women perform stripteases just for him before climbing into bed with him, but none of them had provoked an arousal like the one he experienced with just a scant view of Arabella's lower leg. Maybe it was because his scant view of her leg was coupled with his lengthy view of her face when he glanced up at her, and her face bore an expression that bordered on orgasmic. Because as she sank her foot fully into the sand, Arabella Wilhelm looked as if she were being filled herself, by a man who knew just how to fill her.

"Good sand, huh?" Gus heard himself ask. But his voice sounded thick and ragged, even to his own ears.

She snapped her eyes open and locked her gaze with his, and somehow he suspected that she knew what he was thinking. "It is very good," she said, surprising him. "I do not think I have ever felt anything quite as . . . satisfying."

Oh, she knew, he thought. She knew exactly what he

was thinking. And even if she didn't quite have the specifics down—because he'd known for a while now that Arabella was, as they said in Pelagia, a virgin . . . yeah, okay, so they said that in other places, too—he could tell that whatever images were parading through her head, even if they weren't quite . . . explicit, were still good. But that was okay. Because the images parading through Gus's head were explicit—and specific—enough for both of them.

And then he realized something very significant, and very interesting. Arabella was flirting with him. She'd been flirting with him for some time now, too. At least four or five minutes.

This, he thought, was getting good. Slipping off his own sandals, he joined her in the sand—wow, it really did feel kind of erotic—and followed her as she threaded her way through the scattered, sun-baking tourists, down toward the water. And as he followed her, he tried really hard not to look through her dress, honest.

He came to a stop at her side, right at the edge of the water, where the gentle surf lapped at their ankles and cavorted with the sunlight, throwing it back in tiny bursts of diamondlike luster. Arabella gazed out at the ocean as if looking for something specific, her pale golden hair blowing gently about her face, her eyes as blue as the sky beyond her. Never in his life had Gus seen a more beautiful sight.

"So," she said, still gazing out at the ocean, "tell me what it was that you did in Philadelphia."

Aw, dammit, he thought. Just when things had started to get good.

There was no way—no way—Gus was going to answer that question. Nothing he'd done in Philadelphia—absolutely nothing—was worth commenting upon. He'd been a sorry, useless excuse for a human being, just like every other member of his family. He wasn't about to expound on all their misdeeds to a woman like Arabella.

"The best thing I ever did in Philadelphia," he told her, "was leave it behind."

She turned her head to look at him, her expression puzzled. "You have no family there?"

That, he thought, was a matter of semantics. "There are people there whose DNA would match mine if tested, yes. I wouldn't call them family, though."

She continued to gaze at him with obvious bewilderment. "What about friends?" she asked.

"None there."

"No . . . special woman?"

Now Gus turned to look at Arabella, meeting her gaze as levelly as he could. "Not in Philadelphia, no."

She hesitated a moment, then turned her head again to look out toward the ocean. "I see," she said softly.

He shook his head and bit back a bitter laugh. "No, Princess, when it comes to what you might call my family, I don't think you could ever see. And if you did see, you'd run screaming in horror in the other direction. Trust me."

She said nothing in response to that at first, so Gus, too, turned his attention to the vast blue ocean that sprawled before them into infinity. No, not infinity, he immediately corrected himself. On the other side of that blue expanse lay an entire continent. A continent full of people. A continent that Gus could, technically, label "home." Funny, though, nothing on the other side of that ocean called to him in any way. No, what called to him, however quietly, stood right here beside him, on an island he had never visited until today. Strange, that.

Or maybe not so strange.

What was strange was the way Arabella Wilhelm

seemed to have crawled inside him and taken up residency. What was strange was how little he minded having her there. What was strange was that he found himself wanting to do whatever he had to keep her. Never in his life had Gus come close to loving anyone. But there was something about Arabella . . .

Probably best just not to think about it right now, he told himself. Because, right now, Arabella was promised to someone else. Worse, right now, she seemed to think that even though she hadn't been the one who originally made the promise, she had to keep it anyway. Regardless of how badly she wanted something else more.

Pushing his jumbled thoughts away, Gus opened his mouth to tell her they should be going, when she stopped him by speaking before he had the chance.

"I would not run," she said softly. But she never looked his way, never pulled her gaze from the wide blue sea spread before her.

It took Gus a minute to backtrack to where he had left off their conversation and realize what she was talking about. But even when he understood, he didn't allow himself to think too much about it. Arabella had told him up front this was only a game to her. Granted, she wasn't the kind of woman to lead a guy on, but she was also an innocent, one who probably didn't grasp the concept of playing with fire. So Gus only nodded in response and said nothing.

"I mean it, Gus," she replied to his silence, turning now to look at him. "I would not run."

He gazed at her in thoughtful silence for a moment, at the pale blue eyes, so empty of subterfuge and appraisal and guile, at the blush of innocent awareness that tinted her cheeks, at the full, lush mouth, partially open in silent, though probably unintentional, invitation. Then, reluctantly, he returned his attention to the wide expanse of the deep blue sea.

"You wouldn't run, huh?" he asked her.

"No. I would not."

He nodded slowly again. And somehow he kept himself from looking at her, kept himself from seizing her in his arms, kept himself from devouring her in one big, voracious bite. "Well, you know, Princess," he said softly, "maybe I should run. Maybe I should."

Chapter 14

*R*uby had been awakened a little after dawn by the sound of voices shouting outside her stateroom window—voices in Spanish, so she hadn't understood a word of what was said. What she had understood was the rattle of the anchor chain as it slowly lowered, coupled with the hum of the pulleys as the runabout descended, too. *Mad Tryst* was anchoring, and someone was about to go ashore, she'd realized. She had arrived in Puerto Rico. An American territory. Her papers would be waiting for her. She was free to go ashore. Free to go home. Free to start living her life the way she had lived it before.

Great. She could hardly wait.

She'd rolled out of bed and gone to the window of her stateroom, had looked through it to see Keaton, fully dressed, scrambling into the runabout. He'd capably started it and steered it away from the yacht, making his way toward a dock near a stucco structure ashore that she assumed was the local customs house. Once everything was settled, *Mad Tryst* could continue on to berth at a marina or yacht club—she knew the procedure by now—and then she would be completely free to go.

Without much enthusiasm, Ruby had then showered and dressed, slipping on what had looked like the least expensive thing Arabella had bought for her: a bright pink tank dress made of some soft, T-shirt-like fabric—though Ruby was certain it was actually some very expensive material that was only masquerading as T-shirt fabric—that buttoned up the front from knee to scooped neck. Then she'd slipped on plain leather sandals and run a brush through her long hair, opting to wear it loose, the way she had before leaving Miami. She'd told herself she didn't want to bother Marisol so early in the day.

Then Ruby had collected what few things she had amassed over the last eight days—all of them donations of some kind from Arabella—and had packed them in the tapestry tote bag the countess had also given her, insisting she take it as a gift, to carry all the other gifts the woman had given her this week. Of course, there were some gifts that Ruby couldn't pack, even if she did intend to take them with her, gifts that hadn't necessarily come from the countess. And there were other gifts Ruby knew she'd have to leave behind. All in all, she was amazed at how many gifts she'd received in barely one week, and how she'd lived so much of her life in that short span of time.

One week, she marveled again now, as she stood on the forward deck of *Mad Tryst* and gazed out at the marina where they had finally docked after she, too, had gone ashore to collect her I.D. and prove that she was who—and what—that I.D. indicated. Scores of sailboat masts rose like an aluminum forest beyond the yacht, their sail lines pinging like wind chimes in random rhythm as the boats bobbed in the water. The sun was still low in the blue, blue sky, but the morning breeze was warm as it caressed her face. One week, she thought again. So much had happened to her in one week.

She had made more friends in eight days on *Mad Tryst* than she had made during the eight years she had lived in Miami. She'd even found a pet of sorts in Kurt, something she'd enjoyed more than she had realized she would, because she'd never been allowed to have a pet growing up. Not that she thought the culinary Kurt would ever let her keep the canine Kurt, but Ruby would miss the lovable, adorable little sweetheart all the same once she went home to her empty apartment. She had enjoyed good conversations and good company, too, this week, had seen parts of the world—if only from the rail of a yacht—that she had never visited before, had sampled foods she'd never tasted, and had enjoyed a lifestyle utterly at odds with her own.

She told herself she should have felt like a prisoner this week, unable to leave the bounds of *Mad Tryst*, denied the simple freedom of coming and going as she pleased. But she couldn't help thinking she had lived like a princess instead. Then again, she'd learned, princesses—and princes and countesses and prime minister wannabes—weren't at liberty to do a lot of things, either. In many ways, everyone aboard *Mad Tryst* had been a prisoner of sorts this week. In many ways, they still were. Ruby, in fact, was the only one among them who really enjoyed any measure of freedom. She could go home whenever she wanted now. The others, when they left San Juan, would continue on as they had for a year, trapped aboard a moving vessel, searching for a place they might never, ever find.

Now there was an unnatural phenomenon, she thought. Ruby Runyon, waitress—unemployed waitress at that, since she was certain Frank Tedescucci had filled her po-

sition by now—had more prospects at the moment than
Prince Reynaldo of Pelagia, or Countess Arabella of
Toulaine, or Keaton Danning, almost prime minister. All
four of them were pretty much unemployed right now, but
Ruby alone could have another job in a matter of days.
Reynaldo, Arabella, and Keaton would stay unemployed
indefinitely.

Not that unemployment for them carried the stigma—
or impossibility for living—that it carried for Ruby. But
something about the realization made going home seem a
little less distressing than it had before. Still, somehow
she couldn't quite shake the sensation that, once she did
return to Miami, once she did go home, she would never
really feel as if she were *living* there.

Maybe, she thought, she should get a dog. A little dog,
like Kurt, who wouldn't demand much more of her than
the simple pleasure of her company. Then she remembered that pets weren't allowed in the apartment building
where she lived. Cockroaches, sure. The more the merrier.
But no pets. Some of the residents complained about the
lack of cleanliness. So no dog like Kurt for Ruby. No chef
like Kurt to cook for her, either. No Arabella to be her
friend. No Marisol to fix her hair, no Gus to fix her drinks,
no Omar to sing to her, no Reynaldo to remind her that
some people are just a waste of space.

And no Keaton, either.

But Ruby wouldn't think about that. Not now. She
wished she could say, "Not ever," but she knew that was
unrealistic. She would think about Keaton often, and for a
long time to come, she knew. And she would always wonder, *What if?*

"There you are," she heard him say, as if her thinking
about him had conjured him from thin air. She turned
around and saw him approaching from the lounge, his

dark hair still damp from a recent shower, his green eyes lit with a brightness she told herself was simply a reflection of the sunlight. He was dressed casually again, in linen trousers the color of sand and a short-sleeved shirt the color of the sky. He looked very handsome, very relaxed, very prime-minister-on-vacation-y. He also looked very happy. Which made perfect sense, Ruby couldn't help thinking. He was about to rid himself of the pesky stowaway problem once and for all.

"I hope you don't mind," he said as he strode toward her, "but I took the liberty of making a few phone calls for you. I was able to book you on a flight to Miami that leaves tonight at a little before nine. First Class. I charged it to Reynaldo," he added with a smile that didn't look quite sincere. "It's the least he can do for you. You can pick it up at the reservations counter. I wrote down all the information for you."

He spoke his instructions automatically, almost as if he were reading them from a cue card. Then he stopped in front of her and extended a legal-sized envelope. And Ruby couldn't help noticing that there wasn't a bit of hesitation or reluctance in the gesture.

Wow, she thought as she accepted the envelope from him. He'd made the arrangements for her? Already? He couldn't get rid of her fast enough, could he?

"There's some cash in there, too," he said as she noted the additional weight of the envelope. "Enough for cabs to and from the airports, and meals and whatever else you might need. And also some connections."

"Connections?" she asked curiously, confused.

He nodded. "I promised you connections, remember? People I know in LA and New York who might be useful to you, career-wise?"

Oh, that, Ruby recalled. Funny how she hadn't given a

thought to her alleged acting career for days now. Somehow that just didn't seem nearly as important to her as it once had.

"I don't mind you doing all this for me," she lied, forcing a lightness into her voice that she hoped didn't sound as phony to him as it did to her. "Thanks," she managed to add without choking on the word. Though, in spite of his generosity, she felt not one iota of gratitude. "I'll pay Reynaldo back as soon as I can. I'll pay you all back."

"That won't be necessary," Keaton assured her. "I think our debt to you is a lot bigger than yours is to us."

"What do you mean?" she asked, puzzled.

But he only shook his head slowly and said, "Nothing. Never mind."

As she studied his face—because she knew this might well be the last time she saw it—Ruby couldn't help thinking that he looked kind of tired. Like maybe he hadn't gotten much sleep the night before or something. Funny, that. She hadn't gotten much sleep the night before, either.

"That leaves you with a full day—and then some—in San Juan," he added. "Will you be able to find enough to do to keep yourself occupied until your plane leaves? I'm sorry I couldn't get you on an earlier flight."

In other words, she translated, *Scram.* Oh, she'd just bet he was sorry he hadn't been able to get her on an earlier flight. Had Keaton had his way, he would have put her on a plane at dawn.

"Don't worry about it," she told him, certain the remark was unnecessary. The last thing Keaton would ever do was worry about her. And once she was gone, he would cease to think about her. And then he would cease to remember her at all. And then it would be as if she'd never existed in the first place. "I'll just get my stuff," she continued, "and get out of your hair."

She waited for him to say something in response—something like, "Wait! Don't go! I can't live my life without you!"—but he only nodded and took a step to the side, to move out of her way.

Somehow Ruby forced herself to move, too, concentrating very hard on walking across the deck toward the lounge entrance without turning back, and running toward him, and throwing herself into his arms, and saying something like, "Wait! Don't make me go! I can't live my life without you!" That, she knew, would have been embarrassing. Not to mention futile. So she only continued forward, reaching for the door handle as she neared the lounge entrance, telling herself she'd feel better once she got home.

"Ruby, wait."

She halted in her tracks at the softly uttered words, certain she must have imagined them. But just in case she hadn't, she slowly spun back around, in time to see Keaton take a step toward her. But only the one step. When he saw her looking at him, he stopped. And she couldn't quite dissuade herself of the notion that he was looking at her with something akin to yearning.

"Don't go," he told her, speaking as softly as he had before.

Ruby's heart began to hammer hard in her chest as she waited to hear the rest of it.

"Not yet, anyway," he added, something that slowed the pulsing of her heart, but couldn't quite dash her hopes completely. He expelled a quiet sound of frustration and began to walk toward her again. "Maybe we could . . . you know . . . spend the day together. I don't really have anything pressing to do here. There's no reason to cast you off alone like this."

No, no reason, she thought. Except that the only reason he wanted to spend the day with her was that he didn't "have anything pressing to do here," and not because he couldn't live his life without her.

It would probably be a major mistake for Ruby to spend any more time with Keaton than she had to. Just the thought of leaving him behind—which, deep down, she knew she was going to have to do—made something wrench tight in her belly. And she suspected that the wrenching would only get worse with every additional moment she spent in his company. Because she was beginning to think, as ridiculous as it seemed, that she really wouldn't be able to live her life without him.

In spite of her misgivings, however, she said, "All right, I'd like that. I hate doing things alone."

And until she said it aloud, Ruby had never realized just how true that statement was. She did hate being alone. Had hated it for the last eight years she'd spent alone. No, even longer than that, she realized. Because even in Appalachimahoochee, living in close quarters with her mother and grandmother, she'd always felt as if she were alone. And she had never, ever liked it.

"Have you had breakfast yet?" he asked.

She nodded.

"So have I." He smiled again, and this time, somehow, the gesture seemed infinitely more genuine. "Want to have an adventure?"

Ruby couldn't help smiling back, so infectious was his sudden, inexplicable, mood change. "What kind of adventure?" she asked.

He took a few more steps toward her, but he shoved his hands deep into his trouser pockets as he went, as if he weren't quite sure what to do with them. Or maybe, she couldn't help thinking—hoping—it was because he did know what to do with them, but he was trying to keep himself from doing it.

"I did some reading last night about San Juan," he said, preventing her from carrying her thoughts any further, "and I found out there's a rain forest not far out of town." He grinned as he came to a stop in front of her, not quite a step away. "I've never visited a rain forest before," he added. "Have you?"

Ruby grinned back. "Actually, there are times during the summer when Miami feels like a rain forest," she told him, "but if you want to get technical, then no. I've never visited one before, either."

He studied her in thoughtful silence for a moment. Then, very softly, "Could be fun," he said.

She studied him in thoughtful silence for another moment. Then, very softly, "Could be," she agreed.

"And we should be able to make it to the airport in plenty of time for you to catch your plane. Especially since you won't have any bags to check."

She hesitated only a moment before asking, "*We* should make it to the airport in time?"

He hesitated not at all before correcting himself, "Ah, I mean . . . *you* should. *You* should be able to make it to the airport in plenty of time to catch your plane."

She nodded, her heart rate slowing some more, her brain clearing of its fervent fantasies, her hopes fading fast. She reminded herself that she was back in the real world—*her* world—now, and that she had to start looking at things realistically. And, realistically speaking, Keaton Hamilton Danning III wouldn't—couldn't—accompany Ruby any further into her world than he had to. Because he was still trapped in his world. And his world, she knew, would never, ever, overlap hers. Because his world was anything but real.

"We better get going then," she said dispiritedly. "We don't want to be late."

His expression turned puzzled. "Late for what?"

"Late for anything," she said flatly.

Somehow, though, Ruby couldn't help thinking she was too late for it all.

The rain forest was extraordinary, everything the tour book had promised it would be and then some, Keaton couldn't help thinking as he and Ruby stood virtually lost at the center of it. He still wasn't sure what had made him invite her along for the day when he had been certain it would be a hell of a lot smarter to just say their goodbyes this morning and be done with it. But when she'd turned to leave *Mad Tryst*—when she'd turned to walk out of his life forever—something inside Keaton had just . . . rebelled. Something in him had balked at the realization that he would never see her again. And the next thing he knew, he was asking her to join him. Anything to prolong his time with her for just a few hours more.

They had opted not to join a tour group that had been departing for investigation just as they arrived, and instead had set out to explore on their own. Now, having strayed far from the beaten path—literally—they were surrounded by lush overgrowth, and there wasn't another human being in sight. Ruby had toed off her sandals some time ago to go barefoot, and something about the act of utter abandon had appealed to Keaton enough that he had mimicked the gesture, removing his own shoes, and tucking his socks inside, to carry them instead.

Now cool moss pillowed his feet, and massive trees rocketed toward the sky overhead, obscuring it, spanning a canopy of green hundreds of feet above them. Light filtered through the crowded foliage here and there, but not much reached the ground, offering the impression of twilight, though it was barely past noon. The rich, loamy aroma of the earth filled his lungs every time he inhaled, intoxicating him with its fecund heaviness. His skin felt cumbrous and cumbersome, wet and overwarm with the steamy moisture that hung in the air, dampening all it encountered. And although a scant wind whiffled through the leaves and nuzzled his face, an odd, unreal kind of stillness seemed to surround them.

They strode in silence for a while, each lost in thoughts that neither could have possibly ascertained, though somehow Keaton suspected they were reflective of each other. And when they came to an almost undetectable cleft in the dense foliage, when they turned to smile at each other at exactly the same time, in exactly the same way, he *knew* her thoughts were identical to his. In unspoken agreement, they ducked between and beneath dozens of thickly entwined vines, laughing as one when they realized they had entered what looked like a verdant cavern carved out of the lush vegetation—a secret garden that might very well have remained unexplored for centuries, until now.

He sat down to enjoy their discovery and claim a quick rest, tossing his shoes to the side before leaning back on his flattened hands, and stretching his legs out before him. Ruby evidently approved of the idea, because she lowered herself into the damp, springy moss beside him, pitching her sandals so that they landed alongside his Top-Siders. She curled her legs around herself and tipped her head backward, gazing up at the overgrowth that arched above them, offering shade and coolness from what little sun had permeated the trees before. Although it was indeed darker in here than it had been on the other side, enough light filtered through that Keaton could see Ruby quite clearly. But it was an otherworldly kind of light, indefinite and fragile, making him feel almost as if they'd wandered far from reality.

They might as well have been the last two people on earth, he thought, so isolated did it seem that they were. Or maybe they were the first two, he couldn't help thinking further, surprised by his flash of whimsy. There was something primordial about this whole place, something ancient and mystical and abstruse, something that predated time, transcended time. Hell, something that *defied* time. This place might very well have been the Garden of Eden, for all he knew. And right now, he and Ruby could just as well have been completely alone in the world, Adam and Eve and not much else—save forbidden knowledge and sins of the flesh.

And man, oh, man, he really, really wished he hadn't thought that last thought. Because the minute it surfaced in his brain, it lodged there, and no amount of urging would make it go away.

Don't think about it, he instructed himself. *Don't think about what this place might be, and don't think about how beautiful Ruby looks sitting in the middle of it.*

But she did look beautiful. There was no way Keaton could avoid noticing that. In her bright pink dress, she looked like some exotic, succulent jungle blossom in full bloom. And with her hair cascading wildly down her back, dotted by tiny beads of moisture that clung to the dark tresses like small gems, she seemed like a native princess from some faraway culture utterly removed from his own.

And this place . . . This place was a magical, fantastical place, a place where worlds collided and joined, the past mixing with the present, the primitive existing alongside the modern. All the trappings of the real world faded away here, leaving nothing behind but the pure essence of life and all its harvests. There seemed to be no rules here, no laws, no societal morés or expectations. No castes, no roles, no ranks. Just . . . life. Just two people and a world wholly unto themselves. Anything felt possible here, Keaton couldn't help thinking. Anything at all.

"It's amazing, isn't it?" Ruby said quietly, reverently, from beside him. "I mean, just think about it. This is what the world must have been like before human beings got ahold of it and messed it up with all their human imperfections and expectations and demands. This is what the world must have looked like and felt like and smelled like and sounded like before people came along and changed it all. Listen," she instructed further. "It's just so . . . awesome and mysterious and magnificent."

He turned an ear to what he had thought was the silence surrounding them, only to discover that the world was anything but silent here—the very air seemed alive somehow. Birds called to one another from high up in the trees, at once a cacophony of unreal noises and a symphony of wondrous sounds. The wind whispered, then murmured, then sang, then whistled, all the while moving, all the while varying, all the while reminding Keaton of how quickly things could change. And at the center of it all—at the heart of it all—was Ruby.

Whom he would never see again after today.

"I'll miss you when you're gone, Ruby," he said suddenly, softly, only now realizing just how true the statement was. Her absence really would open up a void of sorts. Both on *Mad Tryst* and . . . and elsewhere. "This week has been . . ." He sighed deeply as he searched for a word, discarding one after another that paraded through his brain, because none seemed remotely appropriate. "Extraordinary," he finally finished. Though somehow even that word didn't begin to describe what the last eight days had really been.

At first he supposed he had only thought the sentiment instead of speaking it, because Ruby offered no indication that she had heard him. She only continued to gaze straight ahead, as if she were studying some fascinating specimen of flora she had just discovered. Then he noticed the way her pulse leaped and danced erratically at the base of her throat, the way color had bloomed on her cheek, and he knew that yes, he had spoken aloud, and yes, she had heard what he'd said.

"I'll, um, I'll miss you, too, Keaton," she finally responded. Though her own words were quiet, frail-sounding, as if she'd been afraid to loose them on the world. "I thought the last week was pretty, um, special myself."

But she still didn't look at him, still seemed as if she were almost afraid of something . . . and still looked more beautiful than he could bear.

Keaton didn't know what made him do it, but before he realized it, he was reaching a hand out toward her. She didn't flinch when he brushed his fingers over the silky curtain of her hair, didn't move when he tucked a velvety tress behind her ear. She didn't react when he brushed his fingertips lightly over her cheek, either, but the stain of pink that darkened her creamy flesh gave her away. He smiled then, felt more confident, and pushed himself closer to her.

She did react to that, turning her own body to face his. Her gaze flew to his, her eyes filled with clear uncertainty and something akin to confusion. Keaton lifted his other hand, curving his fingers so that he could cup her jaw in his palm. Then he threaded the fingers of his other hand more deeply into her hair, pushing the heavy mass back over her shoulder so that he could skim his fingers down along the slender column of her throat.

"I mean it, Ruby," he said, fixing his gaze intently on hers. "I will miss you when you're gone."

She swallowed with some difficulty but said nothing, only gazed into his eyes, her own still looking unsure and disconcerted. But there was something else mixed in now, something that looked to Keaton very much like desire. Desire and hunger and something else, too, something that made him want to do things he knew he really shouldn't do. But he suspected he wouldn't be able to keep himself from doing those things. Probably, he knew, because he didn't want to keep himself from doing them.

In a matter of hours Ruby Runyon would be boarding a plane and flying out of his life for good. Well, maybe not for good, but certainly forever. He would never see her again. And although he knew he would be taking a part of her with him—he had no choice in that—it didn't seem like that part would be nearly enough to last him for the rest of his days. He needed something more from her, something he knew he shouldn't want, something he knew he shouldn't take, but he wanted it all the same. Badly. So, her gaze still fixed on his, he leaned forward and covered her mouth with his own.

She melted into him instantly, curling the fingers of one hand into his shirt and threading the others through his hair. A soft sigh of capitulation—or perhaps it was a sigh of command—escaped her as she eagerly returned his kiss. And the moment Keaton heard that sound, the moment he felt her hands on him, the moment he registered the immediacy of her body's response to his, he knew there would be no turning back. He wanted Ruby. She wanted him. There was nothing—nothing in this world—to keep them apart.

So he leaned his body more fully into hers, raked his fingers more deeply into her hair, and captured the crown of her head in his palm. And then he gently urged her forward—or perhaps it was she who moved herself forward—so that he could plunder her more thoroughly, at his own pace. Again and again he pushed his tongue into her mouth, thrusting, parrying, tasting, testing. She tasted of ocean breezes and summer sunsets and velvety darknesses that seemed to go on forever. And something else, too, that he couldn't quite identify, something that drove him to near madness.

She was sweet. So sweet. But with her sweetness was mingled that tangy something else, that something unfamiliar and arousing and irresistible. A spicy something else that stirred him in a way he'd never been stirred before. It made Keaton hunger for things he knew he'd never have, long for things he knew he shouldn't want, and yearn for things he knew he didn't deserve. But he shoved those thoughts ruthlessly away, selfishly kissed Ruby more deeply still, and pretended that everything was exactly as it should be, exactly as it would be forever.

Her hunger and longing seemed to mirror his own, because the more deeply Keaton tasted her, the more intense and heated her own responses became. The fingers in his hair curved insistently into his scalp, urging his head closer to hers, even though they were already as close as two people could be. The fingers twisted in his shirt moved lower and around his waist, splaying open over his back. All Keaton could do was loop his arm around Ruby's waist and jerk her body against his, and when he felt the damp heat of her mingling with his, it was all he could do not to push her roughly onto her back and take her right there in their own little Garden of Eden.

Somehow he managed to tear his mouth away from

hers. But nothing could stop him when he met her gaze levelly and gasped, "Ruby, I want you." He spread the fingers of one hand wide between her shoulder blades, framed the other beneath her jaw. "I want to make love to you," he told her unabashedly. "I want us to be together."

For a long time she didn't respond, only gazed into his eyes as if she were searching for the answer there to a very important question. Her mouth was red and full from his eager kisses, and her cheeks were flushed with her own needs and desires. And her eyes . . . God, her eyes. They were huge and dark and vulnerable, and Keaton found himself almost hoping that she would turn him down. Why, he couldn't have possibly said. But there was something in her expression that just scared the hell out of him.

Slowly, though, she nodded her agreement, and he knew he would never be able to resist her now. "I want that, too," she whispered hoarsely. "I want us to be together. Oh, Keaton, I want it so much. I want *you* so much."

He smiled as the heat that had been winding through his body picked up its pace, flashing to every extremity. "Then take me, Ruby," he told her, pressing his hand more insistently into her back to push her closer to him. "Because right now, sweetheart, I am yours."

Chapter 15

Contrary to his words, however, it was Keaton who did the taking just then, moving his body forward and covering Ruby's mouth with his again. And as he plied her lips with such masterful care, she felt herself growing warm and fluid, as if she might just . . . melt away. As if she would dissolve into the warm, damp mist that surrounded them, so liquid and steamy and hot had her body become.

She had waited so long for this, she thought as she returned Keaton's kiss with equal fire and equal fervor. Waited so long for *him*. Longer even than the eight days that had passed since she had met him. She had spent her entire life waiting for someone who would make her feel the way he made her feel right now—wanted, desired, cherished. And she had waited so long, too, to find someone to whom she could give the love she had stored inside herself year after year, when no one else had been interested in taking it.

Love, she marveled vaguely. Could that really be at the

root of her feelings for Keaton? Did she love him? Was that why she wanted and needed him so much? Was that why she felt so much more alive, more real, more substantial, more . . . more meaningful, when she was with him? Was that why, suddenly, she felt so whole? Because she loved him?

The question faded away unanswered—or maybe it faded away because, deep down, Ruby did know the answer—as she lost herself to their kiss, moving her hand from his hair to curve it over his warm nape and pull him closer still. He responded by pressing his hand more insistently against her back and moving his mouth to the side, brushing his lips over her chin and her jaw and her cheek, nuzzling the hair at her temple before pressing his mouth to the warm flesh there as well.

"You taste familiar somehow," he said as he pulled away from her—though not too far away, she noticed. "Kissing you reminds me of something, but I can't think what."

He stroked her face gently, tracing the pads of his index and middle fingers over her lower lip and chin, down along the sensitive skin of her throat. And then lower still, over the tender flesh of her chest, tracing the scooped neck of her dress, a caress that made her heart slam against her ribs with anticipation. But then he moved his hand back up again, dragging his fingers along the line of her neck and jaw once more. And when he curled his fingers slightly and turned his hand to brush his bent knuckles gingerly across her cheek, Ruby's eyes fluttered closed. A keen heat rushed through her with every gentle brush of his hand, scorching every cell, every atom, every molecule it encountered.

More, she thought. She wanted—needed—more from him. More *of* him. His disciplined touches only teased and inflamed her, rousing a fever inside her she knew wouldn't easily be assuaged. For so many days, so many nights, she had imagined what it would be like to be with him this way. Now they were together, finally, and she'd had only a few tastes of him. It wasn't enough, she thought. Not nearly enough. And somehow she suspected that with Keaton, she never would get enough.

But once, she thought further. Surely she could have him this once. And even if it never happened again, even if she did still have to leave him at day's end, surely that one time would sustain her for a good long while. Long enough for her to get home, where she could relive that one time in her thoughts and dreams indefinitely. Home, where she could tuck the memories of Keaton and this one week with him into a secret place inside her heart, where they would be safe forever. Surely once, she told herself again. Only once.

It *would* be enough, she promised herself. It would be. It would have to be.

"I remember now," he said suddenly, softly, bringing her back to the present, back to where she needed to be.

Reluctant to open her eyes just yet, though, she inhaled deeply, filling her lungs with the dusky, masculine scent of him. Then she urged her body closer to his, to better enjoy the heat of him that encircled her, and to better savor the taste of him that lingered on her lips. And still it wasn't close enough for her. Still she wanted—needed—more of him.

"I remember what it is that kissing you reminds me of," he said further, with a bit more fortitude this time, scattering the mental impressions to which she had hoped to cling.

But when Ruby opened her eyes, she realized she didn't need those subliminal images of Keaton, because he was right there in her arms. She could touch him and taste him at will, hold him and caress him and cling to him. He smiled at her as she watched him, pondered him, a roguish, enticing little smile that made her toes curl into the cool moss beneath her bare feet.

"What is it?" she said. "What are you reminded of?"

His smile grew broader, then, "Oysters," he said in a voice of seduction and secrecy. "Something about kissing you reminds me of eating oysters."

Oh, my . . .

"Eating oysters and also . . ."

But he didn't finish whatever he had intended to say. Instead he leaned forward and covered her mouth with his again, as if he intended to consume her. Ruby opened to him eagerly, cupping one hand over his shoulder, skimming the fingers of her other hand inside the collar of his shirt, up along his nape to weave them into his hair. The silky tresses tangled around her fingers as if trying to trap her hand there forever, just as Keaton wrapped his arms around her waist and pulled her close, as if he intended to imprison her in his embrace for all time, too.

As he deepened the kiss, he pressed his body full against hers, pushing her backward, down, down, down, until she felt the cool crush of the damp moss through the thin fabric of her dress. And as she rested her head against a pillow of lush growth, as she looped one arm around his neck and the other across his back, Keaton arced one arm over her head and settled his body alongside her own. Then he bent his head to hers and kissed her again, long and hard and deep, generating a coarse growl of urgency from somewhere low in Ruby's belly.

He responded with a sound that echoed the neediness in her own, pushing his body half over hers. Then he insinuated one leg between both of hers, crowding his thigh intimately into the juncture of her own. The slender column of her dress prevented Ruby from opening fully to him, but the tightness of their legs only multiplied the erotic sensations that began to pool low in her abdomen. Feeling the pressure of his leg straining so insistently against that part of herself generated a primitive reaction in Ruby, and purely on instinct, she propelled her hips upward to meet him. The tiny friction created by the scant gesture inflamed her further, forcing a savage little cry to escape from somewhere deep inside her.

Keaton responded immediately to that cry, pushing his thigh against her harder, causing her to buck her hips forward again. And again. And again. And as she pleasured herself that way, she felt his hand at her bare breast, and she knew he had unbuttoned her dress and unfastened the front closure of her bra. He covered the tender mound with sure fingers, squeezing, palming, fingering, before raking his thumb over the quickly distending peak. And then his mouth was there, too, wet and warm and wanton, soaking her warm flesh as he tried to pull as much of her into his mouth as he could.

Never had Ruby felt so wanton, so hungry, so *needful* as she did in that moment. Her breath had gone ragged, her vision hazy, her thinking completely frenzied. All she knew was the twin sensations of Keaton's mouth suckling at her sensitive breast and his thigh wreaking havoc at the gateway of her still-covered womanhood.

More, she thought again. *More*. She needed more of him. She needed all of him.

Somehow he must have sensed her urgency, because no sooner had she completed the realization than his hand went to the hem of her dress. She felt him nudge the fabric away, up over her legs, higher and higher, until her legs were bared to the balmy afternoon breeze. A riotous par-rot called out somewhere overhead, giving Ruby the impression that the two of them weren't quite alone, and something about that heightened her awareness of what they were doing, of what they were about to do. Impulsively she lifted her hips from the ground so that Keaton could push her dress higher still, bunching it around her waist, where she couldn't free it. But when she realized how much of her was exposed to him, Ruby made a half-hearted grab at the fabric to push the garment back down.

Keaton halted her hand, circling her wrist with sure fingers and moving them away. "Don't," he murmured. "Don't cover yourself. You're too beautiful."

He pulled himself back far enough to gaze down at her—all of her—and her breath caught in her throat at the heat that burned in his eyes when he beheld her. He was even further gone than she was, she thought. And that was saying something. It was also, she thought as a new heat suffused her, incredibly arousing.

"We're all alone here," he added as he returned his gaze to her face. "There's no one around who can hear us or see us. And I want to look at you. All of you. I want to touch you. All of you. I want to taste you, smell you, hear every little sound you utter. And then . . ."

She was nearly insensate by now, simply from hearing his roughly offered words. Somehow, though, she managed to ask him, "And then?"

He ran his hand from her waist, over her flat belly and the silky fabric of the thong panties she'd had no choice but to wear, along the flare of her hip, down along the outside of her thigh and slowly—oh, so slowly—back up the inside again. A shudder of heat wound through her at the intimate caress, and all she could think was, *More*.

"And then," he said softly, "I want to watch you while you come apart at the seams."

Oh, dear God . . .

Ruby was about to protest, was about to tell him that she shouldn't do this here, she couldn't do this here, she wouldn't do this here. But he skimmed his hand higher again, then beneath her, curling his fingers into the taut, bare flesh of her bottom left exposed by the thong panties that somehow didn't seem nearly as uncomfortable as they initially had.

"Oh, God," he muttered when he realized what she was wearing. "Ruby . . ."

He pushed her hips upward again, toward his own, and when she felt him swell and ripen against her belly, she gasped at the quickness and extent of his arousal. He rubbed his body urgently against hers, and she felt how full he was, how heavy, how hard. Before she realized his intention, he urged lower the hand whose wrist he had circled with strong fingers, pushing it between their bodies, and flattening her palm over that rigid, ready part of himself. Instinctively Ruby cupped him in her palm through his trousers, catching fire at the frantic little sound that erupted from somewhere deep inside him when she touched him that way.

"Oh, God," he echoed his earlier sentiment, this time against the heated flesh of her neck as he buried his face there. "Do that again."

Ruby threw her head back wildly to facilitate these new explorations of his marauding mouth, then stroked her hand over him once more, pressing her fingers even more possessively over him this time. And just as he had that first time, Keaton groaned something feral and incoherent against her neck. So Ruby rubbed her hand over him another time. And another. And another.

"Again," he commanded her when she hesitated.

She raked her fingers obediently—and none too gently

this time—over the long, solid span of him beneath her hand.

"Again," he whispered gutturally.

Once more she palmed and possessed him.

"Again, Ruby, again."

She did as he ordered her, stroking the flat of her hand over his swollen member, until it strained against the fabric of his trousers. Without thinking about what she was doing, she fumbled with his belt and fly to free him completely. Then she tucked her hand deftly inside his pants and opened it over his hot, naked shaft. She palmed the damp head, anointing her fingers with his essence, then curled them around his arrogant staff. And then slowly, deliberately, methodically, she began to pump her hand over his heavy length.

He went perfectly still as she glided her fingers resolutely over him, braced on elbows he had placed firmly on each side of her head. He threw his own head back in abandon, and his lips parted slightly as he expelled one ragged breath after another. His eyes were squeezed shut tight. Unable to help herself, Ruby lifted herself enough from the ground to bury her head against the strong column of his throat, tasting his salty heat as she dragged openmouthed kisses along his damp flesh and possessed him with her hand. When she finally drew back far enough to look at him, she was nearly overwhelmed by the sheer ecstasy in his expression. She was about to multiply her ministrations when, without warning, Keaton clamped his hand over her moving wrist—hard—and put a halt to her motions.

"That," he gasped, "will be enough of that for a while."

"But . . ." she began.

He shook his head weakly. "If you set me off now, sweetheart, the way I'm feeling, I may be witless for days."

She smiled a little shakily. "And that would be bad because . . . ?" she asked.

He leered at her. Positively leered. Oh, my . . . "Because," he said on a soft sough of sound, "then you wouldn't have had your turn."

Ruby tried to say the word "oh," but somehow she wasn't quite able to push the word past her lips.

"Lie back, Ruby," he said simply.

Then, to punctuate the remark, he moved until he was kneeling between her legs, anchoring one hand on the grass beside each of her hips. Silently he loomed over her again, and she realized there was no way she could muster the willpower to refuse him. Mostly because she didn't want to refuse him. No matter where they were, or what was supposed to be happening, or what the world held once they left this fantastic place behind, right here, right now, Ruby wanted Keaton. More than anything. And she saw no reason that she shouldn't let herself have him.

At least for here. At least for now. It was more than she had ever found elsewhere in her life. And somehow she knew it was more than she would ever find once she returned to that life again. She'd be a fool not to take advantage of this opportunity, if only temporarily.

So she settled back against the soft, moss-covered earth, the moisture on her dress now resulting from more than the damp brush she lay against. She reached for the buttons of Keaton's shirt as she went, loosing them one by one as he leaned over her. Then she pulled his shirttail free of his trousers and spread the fabric open wide, reveling in the dark hair scattered across his chest from shoulder to shoulder, arrowing down and thickening as it disappeared into the waistband of his trousers. And then she flattened her palms against his warm chest, marveling at the heat and solidity of the elegant musculature she encountered.

No soft bureaucrat, he, she realized. No, Keaton obviously took great care to keep himself in shape. Because his shape was . . .

Oh. Magnificent. Her fingertips tripped over each ridge of muscle on his torso, skimmed along each refined rib, dipped into the bold divot at the base of his throat. He closed his eyes as she explored him, as if he wanted to savor the sensation of her touch. Then he opened his eyes again, and she saw them darken with his desire for her. A thrill of anticipation shot through her, so strong that it nearly overwhelmed her. Without meaning to, she pulled her hands back, arcing them over her head in silent surrender.

Keaton smiled before lowering his body toward hers again, and she reached for him once more, threading the fingers of one hand through his silky hair and cupping the others around his warm nape, pulling his head down to hers to cover his mouth possessively with her own. But instead of allowing her the control of the kiss that she sought, Keaton immediately usurped her power. Somehow, though, Ruby didn't mind surrendering to him—for now, at least. Later, she promised herself, she would have her turn to command and possess. For now, though, she opened willingly—eagerly—to him, savoring the deep penetration of his tongue and the skillful work of his hands as they meandered leisurely over her.

As he kissed her thoroughly, he curved his fingers over one generous breast, palming it, rolling his thumb insistently over the sensitive peak before capturing it in the V of his index and middle fingers. Then she felt his mouth where his hand had been, his tongue laving her, loving her, with regular, insistent strokes, first along the underside of her breast, then along the top. And then, as he rolled her nipple between his fingers, he flicked the tip of his tongue against it, again and again and again. Ruby groaned at the exquisiteness of the sensation, and he responded by moving his hand and sucking her breast deeply into his mouth. The damp pressure sent shock waves throughout her body, shock waves that only multiplied when he filled his hand with her other breast, squeezing it as he suckled the other. Truly, it was all Ruby could do not to dissolve into a puddle of wanton womanhood beneath him.

And then she felt him moving again, his mouth shifting lower, until he was kissing each delicate rib, dipping his tongue into her navel for an errant taste. Then lower still he traveled, until she felt the soft brush of his lips over her calves, her shins, her knees. She arched her arms drunkenly over her head again, the cool moss tickling her sensitive flesh, then turned her face toward the warm breeze that flitted over them. So lost had she become in the heat that was emanating both outside and within her that she scarcely noticed the direction of Keaton's attentions.

Until she felt the merest whisper of his tongue running along the inside of her thigh.

She gasped as he flattened his palms on her belly and pushed them upward again, filling his hands with her plentiful breasts once more. But the possession was short-lived, only long enough for him to rake his thumbs over the sensitive peaks again, rousing them to hard little buds made even more sensitive by the gentle stimulation of the warm breeze ruffling over her naked skin. Ruby had never made love outdoors before, and certainly never with the prolonged care and ceaseless attention that Keaton was paying her. And at the very back of her brain, she somehow sensed that she would never know anything like this again.

She was wondering vaguely if she and Keaton would ever get to the main event when she suddenly felt his hands at the waistband of her panties, skimming the garment downward. Finally, she thought. Finally, satisfaction. But instead of lifting his body over hers after discarding the garment, Keaton only moved his hands leisurely up over her legs again, his fingers cupping resolutely over the insides of her thighs to push her legs open wide. Then he skimmed his hands down to the undersides of her knees, folding them until her legs were bent, her feet planted firmly on the ground. And then, before Ruby fully understood his intention, he pushed his hands under her bare bottom and lifted her off the ground, moving her pelvis to his waiting . . .

Oh, God. To his waiting mouth.

She cried out wildly at the initial contact, at the damp, gentle caress of his tongue against her. Never had she felt such a keen shot of sensation shiver through her. With the merest of caresses, Keaton inflamed her body, scrambled her brain, sent her libido into stark-raving overdrive. And then his hunger intensified, until the mere caresses turned into eager, ravenous tastes of her. And then the eager tastes intensified, too, as he slipped a long finger deep inside her and continued to feast relentlessly upon her. Ruby writhed and moaned and tangled her fingers in his hair, at once trying to end the onslaught and ensure that it never, ever stopped.

And it didn't stop for a very long time. Keaton, she noted deliriously, was a very hungry man. And he took his time appeasing that hunger.

Eventually, though, he must have satisfied himself— even if he left Ruby feeling anything but satisfied— because he pulled his head back and gazed up at her face. By now she was only vaguely aware of her surroundings, so lost had she become in the ceaseless ripples of pleasure that had been uncoiling with scorching intensity inside her. She saw him smile with what she could only liken to smugness, then shift his body to move it up alongside hers. Her dress was still bunched up around her waist—he hadn't even taken the time to unbutton her—but the moss beneath her naked back and bottom no longer felt cool.

And neither did Keaton when she moved her hands beneath the gaping fabric of his shirt and curved them over his satiny hot shoulders. He said not a word as he moved his body over hers, and Ruby responded with equal silence. She opened her legs wider for him, though, bending her knees more to facilitate his entry, and tucked her fingers beneath his trousers, pushing the garment down so that she might bare and grip his taut buttocks with both hands. He said not a word as he nestled his pelvis against hers, only braced himself on arms he had folded onto the grass on each side of her head. And then she felt him push slowly inside her, pausing when only the head of his shaft had entered her.

"What?" she gasped when he didn't deepen the penetration. "Why did you stop?"

He shook his head slowly as he expelled a soft sound of frustration. "I don't have anything," he told her.

This time it was Ruby's turn to shake her head—in confusion. "You have everything, Keaton," she said quietly. "Everything I want. Everything I need. Everything I—" She cut herself off before she said something she might regret. "Make love to me," she concluded simply. "Come inside me. Now. Please."

"No, you don't understand, Ruby," he said. "I don't have any protection. I don't have a condom. I wasn't exactly expecting us to end up this way today. And without one, you could get pregnant."

Strangely, though, he didn't sound especially disappointed about his lack of preparation and the possibility of her pregnancy. In fact, he almost sounded . . . hopeful? Ruby thought. Oh, surely not. What man in his right mind would want an accident to happen under circumstances like this? What woman in her right mind would want such a thing?

Fortunately she was able to reassure him. "It's all right," she said. "I'm at the end of my . . ."

But she found she wasn't able to finish the sentence for some reason. Even though the two of them had shared and were about to share the most intimate aspects of the man-woman relationship, for some reason she found that she couldn't discuss basic female biology with him. So she only smiled, tried not to blush, and threaded her fingers through his hair. "It won't happen," she told him. And she was absolutely confident of that. "It's not the right time for it."

"You're sure?" he asked.

She nodded. "I'm positive. I won't get pregnant, Keaton." Even if she might be in danger of other, far more hazardous risks, she couldn't help thinking.

Her assurance was evidently all the encouragement he needed, because he moved his body against hers again, sheathing himself completely inside her. Ruby squeezed her eyes shut tight at the feeling of completion that flooded her in their coupling. Having Keaton inside her made her feel whole somehow, made her feel full. His body fit hers as if the two of them had been one at some point in time and then had been viciously divided. Now, though, they were back together, two fragments forming one vessel, two halves completing one whole.

And then they were moving as one, too, Keaton retreating and returning as Ruby launched her body up to meet his every infiltration. They joined more deeply with every penetration—in body, in mind, in spirit, in soul—binding their two separate essences into one unifying element. Little by little their heat multiplied, their speed accelerated, their passion augmented, until one final, incandescent thrust incited the crest of their completion.

Ruby cried out at the dizzying height of that summit, her entire body shuddering as Keaton spilled himself hotly inside her. And he responded with an equally feral exclamation, holding his body rigid above hers for the long moment it took him to empty himself. And then, with a ragged groan, he collapsed beside her, gathering her close, burying his face in the curve where her shoulder met her neck. She felt his warm breath dampen her flesh, registered the savage beating of his heart against her own.

And that was when Ruby realized that she did indeed love Keaton. That was when she knew that making love with him this one time would never be enough, that once would never sustain her for any length of time. That was when she understood that she would want him and need him and love him, to the depths of her soul, and for the rest of her life. That was when she knew she couldn't leave him. Not at day's end. Not ever.

She opened her mouth to tell him that, to reveal to him the intensity of her feelings for him, the extent of her need for him, the fact that she could never, ever, let him go. She started to tell him she loved him. But he spoke before she had the chance, and what he said made the words dry up in her mouth and the feelings go cold in her belly.

"I'll miss you when you're gone, Ruby," he said softly, breathlessly. "I will definitely miss you when you're gone."

The words echoed the ones he had spoken such a short time ago, the ones that had preceded the two of them making love. The first time he'd uttered them, those words had fallen sweetly on Ruby's ears, had sounded like a wistful sort of wanting that might have become more. The first time she'd heard those words, she had thought he'd spoken them because he wanted to keep her. Now, though . . .

Now the words took on new meaning. Because now the two of them *had* made love. And where making love with Keaton had convinced Ruby of just how much she did love him, of how much she wanted to say with him—forever—to Keaton, making love had made no difference. He still expected her to leave at day's end. Still *wanted* her to leave. And he still intended to live his life, quite nicely thanks, without her.

Oh, he would miss her when she was gone. She believed him when he said that. But not enough to ask her to stay. And not enough to follow her wherever she might go. He would miss her when she was gone, to be sure. But he wouldn't stop her from going. Because men like Keaton Hamilton Danning III didn't go through life with women like Ruby Runyon at their sides. Because men like Keaton Hamilton Danning III deserved better. Or so they thought.

You just don't think I'm as good as you are, do you, Keaton?

He had never answered her question that night, she recalled now. He hadn't agreed with her assessment of his opinion of her, but he hadn't disagreed with it, either. And the reason he hadn't disagreed with it was that he *didn't* think she was as good as he was. He'd just wanted to spare her feelings on that score, because he was such a gentleman when it came to good manners. Ruby knew—she'd known all along—exactly how Keaton felt about her. Somehow, though, she had allowed herself to forget that.

He would miss her when she was gone. But he would survive.

Ruby wasn't sure she would, though. She couldn't imagine how she was going to get through the next few minutes without Keaton, let alone the rest of her life. But she couldn't tell him that. Not now. Not after what he had just told her. It would be awkward if she let her true feelings be known. It would be embarrassing. And it would just ruin what few hours the two of them had left together.

She bit back a melancholy chuckle at that. God forbid their last few hours together be ruined because she told Keaton she loved him. So Ruby squeezed her eyes shut tight to hold in the tears, and she clung to Keaton with all the desperation she dared display.

And she told him, honestly but inadequately, "I'll miss you, too, Keaton, when I'm gone. I will definitely miss you, too."

Keaton watched from a window at the airport as Ruby's plane lifted off the ground and soared into a sky smudged purple and black to the east. He'd wanted to accompany her to her gate, but they hadn't allowed anyone without a ticket past the metal detectors. Which was just as well, he thought now. Because once they'd left the rain forest, nothing had felt quite right between them. Oh, they'd returned to the yacht without incident, so that Ruby could collect her things and say her farewells, and he'd ridden with her in a cab to the airport. He'd hung around to make sure everything was in order with her ticket, and then, before she'd gone through the metal detectors, he had kissed her, gently, goodbye.

But even that kiss had felt unfamiliar, uncomfortable, unreal. There had been none of their previous passion in it, none of their earlier intimacy. Only a brief, wistful sort of wanting that had come and gone in a breath of time. And then Ruby had gone, too, and he'd been left alone to watch her move slowly through the metal detectors, never once turning back to look at him, even though long minutes passed before she had cleared the checkpoint. And even after she'd passed through the checkpoint, as he'd watched her stride down the terminal toward her gate, she'd never once looked back at him. Ruby Runyon, he'd decided, was one of those people who just didn't look back. And he'd found himself envying her that.

He would miss her, though, he thought now as he watched her plane disappear into the dark night. He would miss her a lot. And he couldn't quite understand why, the moment her plane was out of sight, he suddenly felt so empty inside.

Chapter 16

Arabella was trying to fall asleep—and not doing a very good job of it—when she heard a soft sound slice through the darkness of her stateroom, making her sit up straight in her bed. Her windows were open to allow in the warm Puerto Rican breeze, and quiet sighs of the harbor whispered through the sheer curtains. But that wasn't the sound that had caught her attention. Cocking her head, she listened closely again and was rewarded by the echo of three brief taps on her stateroom door.

In one fluid movement she pushed off the covers and reached for the bedside lamp, spilling gentle yellow light into her stateroom. Then she reached for the floral silk robe she had tossed at the foot of her bed, donning it over a scant nightgown of the same fabric, before going to the door.

"Who is it?" she whispered at the crack, holding firm the door handle, even though she knew it was locked.

"It's me, Gus," came the not-so-quiet reply. "Open up, Princess. We need to talk. Among other things."

Fearing that he would continue to be not-so-quiet if she did not do as he requested, Arabella opened the door to tell him to shush, and found him leaning insouciantly against the door frame on the other side. He still wore his bartender clothing of khaki trousers and a loud Hawaiian shirt of purples and reds. But the shirt gaped open in heedless concern, as if he had thrown it on as an afterthought and left it unbuttoned, exposing the satiny, muscled expanse of his torso, and the silver medallion he always seemed to wear. His shoulder-length hair was unbound but tousled, as if he had been running his hands restlessly through the tawny tresses again and again and again. And his eyes . . .

Oh, my. His eyes. They were filled with fire and desire and explicit intent.

"You should not be here," Arabella told him. But she negated her own assertion by pulling him into her stateroom and pushing the door closed behind him. She told herself that she was making a terrible mistake in doing so. She knew she should leave him on the other side, but she could not risk having someone hear him out there and finding the two of them together. It would lead to even worse trouble than she was courting by pulling him into her stateroom this way.

Then again, she had made a habit of courting trouble all week, had she not? Why should this night be any different? Because for the last week, she had tried to spend as much time as she could with Gus, in the hopes that Reynaldo would see them together and become upset, and that his reaction might force his hand one way or another. But she and Gus had scarcely seen Reynaldo this week. And on those occasions when her fiancé *had* been in their company, he seemed not to notice—or care—that Gus was pretending to be interested in her.

Perhaps, Arabella thought now, Reynaldo simply could not conceive of Gus Torrance being a threat to him. Perhaps Gus had been right about that. But it had not kept him from pretending to be interested in her all week long anyway. And it had not kept Arabella from enjoying his interest.

And as the week had progressed, she had begun to realize that Gus's pretend interest was not so pretend. Of course, she had always known he found her attractive—he had made no secret of teasing her and flirting with her since he had come aboard. But over the last several days she had begun to understand how much he wanted to act on that attraction. She had sensed in him a new kind of interest, a more serious kind. The kind that might make a man do something he should not do.

Like come to her stateroom in the middle of the night with his shirt unbuttoned and his senses laid bare. And Gus Torrance was the last kind of man Arabella should have in her stateroom in the middle of the night. He was the last kind of man she should be with at all.

No matter how much she might want to be with him.

"What if someone heard you?" she demanded further once he was inside with the door closed firmly behind him. "What if someone saw you?"

He leaned toward her, much too close, then, "What if they did?" he asked without concern, his words tinted with the distinct scent of whiskey.

Arabella frowned. It had not been insouciance with which he had leaned against the door frame, she realized then. No, it was drunkenness. He had been drinking before he came to her.

"You are drunk," she charged.

He smiled as he pulled himself back. "Yeah, I've been drinking," he allowed. "But obviously not enough. Not nearly enough, Princess."

She did not know why, but she heard herself ask him, "Why do you say that?"

He didn't reply at first, only let his gaze drift over her, from the crown of her tousled head to the tips of her bare toes and back again. Immediately Arabella was reminded that she stood before him in her nightclothes, her hair unbound, her defenses lowered. This was not a safe place for her to be, she told herself. Somehow, though, she felt no danger. In fact, what she felt was . . . excitement.

Oh, dear.

"I say that because . . . because I came up here with the express purpose of ravishing you tonight," he said baldly, words that ignited a—rather large—fire in her stomach. "And now that I'm here, and I see you looking the way you look right now, all soft and pretty and warm from your bed, and *God*, so sexy . . . I'm standing here *talking* to you, for chrissake, when I should be pressing you back onto that bed and burying myself deep inside you again and again and again, until neither one of us can think straight."

Arabella's mouth opened in surprise, and heat flooded her midsection as an explicit image of what he was describing exploded in her brain. "You . . . you . . . you what?" she stammered as that heat began to spread to other—more susceptible—parts of her body.

"I came up here to ravish you," he repeated with more gusto. "I came up here to show you what it can—should—be like between a man and a woman. To make you forget about that sorry sonofabitch you say you have to marry, and make you realize once and for all that you really want—"

But he never finished that last statement. And contrary to his bold words, he moved away from her again, retreating to the opposite corner of the stateroom, leaning against the wall there, as if he wanted to push himself right through it. "But now," he continued, his voice softer, less vehement, "looking at you all soft and pretty and sexy, still warm from your bed . . ." He shook his head slowly, as if he couldn't believe his words any more than she could. "Right now I feel the same way I always do around you, and I can't bring myself to do what I really want to do."

Although she told herself not to, feeling dizzy from all that he had revealed, Arabella prodded him, "And how is it that you feel when you are around me?"

He eyed her steadily and, very softly, he confessed, "Scared. Whenever I get close to you, Princess, I'm too scared to even touch you."

"Scared?" she echoed incredulously, taking a few involuntary steps toward him. "Of what?" she demanded. "Of Reynaldo? You are scared of what would happen if he found us together?"

Gus shook his head. "No. Reynaldo I could handle." There was another long, pregnant pause before he concluded, very quietly, "It's you, Princess. I'm scared of you."

"Me?" she sputtered. "But I am not scary."

"The hell you're not." He pushed himself away from the wall and strode now to the other side of the room, as if he were too restless to stand still but wanted—needed—to keep some distance between the two of them. "You're the scariest thing I've ever come up against," he said as he went, not looking at her.

"But . . . why am I scary?" she asked.

He spun around and leveled his gaze on her face, searching her features as if looking for the answer to some grave, puzzling question that had plagued him for a long time. "Because of the way you make me feel," he told her. "You being all soft and pretty and sexy and warm from your bed, I mean. You're scary this way. You're scary no matter how I look at you. Because I can't stop thinking about you. I can't stop wanting you. And I know you don't spend much of your time in the same pursuit. Thinking about me, I mean. Wanting me."

The words were obviously drawn from him with much reluctance, and she could see that he immediately regretted making his confession. Because the moment he finished making it, he drove both hands into his hair, shoving it ruthlessly back from his face. And then he grimaced, almost as if he were in pain. The gesture made his shirt gape open wider, and Arabella's mouth went dry at seeing him in such a state of dishabille.

If only things could be different between them, she thought. If only she had been born a different woman. If only he had been born a different man. If only the whole world would go away and leave them alone to be happy.

If only, if only, if only.

"Ah, hell," Gus muttered, dropping his hands back to his sides. He turned his head away, gazing not at Arabella now, but at the wall. "Maybe I did have too much to drink. I'm saying way more than I should."

Yes, she thought, he had said more than he should have said. Because she was thinking things now that she should not think.

"You are wrong, Gus," she said before she even realized she meant to speak.

He continued to lean haphazardly against the wall, but he turned his gaze back to Arabella's now. "Wrong about what?" he asked warily. "About you being scary?"

She shook her head. "I am not the one who is scary in

this room," she told him pointedly. "But that is not what I was talking about."

He lifted his chin a little, enough to make him look as if he were trying to be defiant, when she could tell that defiant was the last thing he felt. "Then what?" he demanded.

"I meant that you were wrong about me not thinking of you. I do think of you," she told him, knowing she should not, but unable to keep it to herself after all that he had just revealed. "I think about you often, Gus. Much more than I think about anything else. And I—" Somehow she stopped herself before confessing that she wanted him, too. That, she knew, would be a terrible mistake.

He eyed her carefully for a moment, but she could not tell what he was thinking. "Then maybe it's time to stop thinking and start acting," he finally said softly. But he did not sound any more certain of that than Arabella was.

And she had no idea how to reply. She did know, however, that every moment he spent there in her stateroom brought her closer to danger. Closer to doing something she knew she should not do. Closer to being the kind of woman she did not want to be. She must make him leave, no matter how badly she wanted him to stay. And she must make him leave now.

And she must tell him that the two of them should not continue to see each other the way they had been seeing each other. It was pointless. Not just because it had had no effect on Reynaldo, but because it had had too much of an effect on them. And there was no future in any . . . effect . . . they might enjoy. Even if Reynaldo could be convinced to break his engagement to Arabella, Gus was not the kind of man she needed, not the kind of man to whom she should give herself. He had no roots to any-place, no ties to anyone. He was a drifter who did not speak of his past, and who did not look any further into the future than the setting of the sun each day. He was not the kind of man to fall in love with. Because he was not the kind of man who would stay.

"You should go, I think," she told him. "It is very late."

He continued to gaze at her, but his expression was less severe now. "It's not that late," he countered.

"It is *too* late," she insisted.

But he shook his head slowly and pushed himself away from the wall, then crossed the room leisurely and came to a stop just in front of her. "It's not too late," he said. "It's never too late."

"It is too late, Gus," she said again.

But he still didn't seem to share her opinion, because he only studied her face, focusing on her eyes, her mouth, then her eyes again. Before she realized his intention, he lifted a hand and slowly began to extend it toward her. She told herself to move away, that if she allowed him to touch her, she would not be able to resist whatever came after. But no matter how loudly and how often she commanded herself to move, she remained rooted right where she was. And then, suddenly, Gus was touching her, cupping her jaw gently in his hand, threading his fingers lightly through her hair near her ears. Then his other hand joined the first, delving below her hair to curve around her nape, the gentlest, most exquisite caress she had ever felt in her life.

"Oh, God," he murmured. "You're even softer than I thought you would be.

"Do not do that," she said quietly, a bit raggedly, her heart hammering hard in her chest, pumping blood through her body so rapidly she began to feel faint.

But her actions belied her words, because even as she spoke them—and without consciously planning to do it— she found herself turning her head into his palm, to better enjoy his touch, and to grant him freer access to her neck. He took immediate and complete advantage, covering another step so that his body was nearly flush with her own. Then he dipped his head to hers. But instead of covering her mouth with his, as she had thought he would do, he only brushed his parted lips over her temple, nuzzling her hair. And then he took a step away, dropping his hands back to his sides, and she found herself wondering if she had simply imagined the brief caresses.

But his breathing was as uneven as hers was, she noted, and his face was flushed, as she suspected her own was. She had not imagined his caresses. And she could not understand why he had halted them.

"I gotta get outta here," she heard him mutter roughly. "If I don't, I'm going to end up taking you standing, right here, without even undressing you."

Although she suspected he had not meant for her to hear what he said, Arabella had heard. But she could not quite envision what he had described, of him making love to her where they stood. And she realized that many things she had thought about what happened when two people . . . did that . . . were not exactly . . . accurate.

And before she could stop herself, she heard herself saying, "But I thought that when men and women . . . That is, I thought that there was only one way for a man and a woman to . . . I mean, I thought that they only did that . . . in a bed. And only while . . . lying down. I did not know there were other ways to . . ."

She blushed when she realized she was speaking her thoughts aloud, but Gus seemed not to be embarrassed at all by the subject matter. In fact he seemed to rather . . . enjoy it. Because he smiled at her when she stopped speaking. A bewitching smile. A tempting smile. A smile of great invitation.

"Oh, there are *lots* of ways to do it, Princess," he said, his voice thick with suggestion—and seduction. "All kinds of ways. You might be surprised by some of them. Hell, you might be surprised by all of them."

He took a few steps toward her again, halting only when he stood scant millimeters away from her. Then he leveled his gaze on hers, his amber eyes hot with a fire she did not understand, but which she knew nonetheless mirrored the one raging inside her. Somehow she felt as if he were looking not at her eyes, but at some point beyond them, at a place deep inside her soul, where her most secret thoughts and most forbidden fantasies were housed.

"Oh, yeah," he said softly. "You'd definitely be surprised."

He lifted a hand toward her again, as if he intended to kiss her again—only this time, he would make the kiss much more thorough. Instinctively Arabella took a step backward in self-preservation. But where before Gus had always honored her withdrawals, this time he showed no sign of accepting her retreat. Because he took another step forward, larger than the one she had taken back, an action that brought him even closer than he had been before. Arabella tried to take another step backward, but her bed hindered her progress—or perhaps the better word was her "regress"—and she told herself again that it had not been a good idea to invite Gus to her room.

So why had she?

Perhaps, she thought, it was because, deep down, she had known—or at least hoped—that something like this would happen.

So she stopped retreating then and stood her ground, meeting his gaze as steadily as she could. And when he lifted a hand toward her face, she did not try to escape. Instead she held firm and waited to see what he would do.

What he did was . . . touch her hair. Very gently, very gingerly, he ran his fingertip down the length of blond, pausing at the end to wrap the slender tress around his finger. Slowly, slowly, he wound the lock around his index finger, until his hand was even with her face. Then he opened his hand and cupped his palm over her jaw, a completely innocent touch that sent her temperature into triple digits.

How had he done that? she wondered. How had he set her body on fire simply by putting his hand on her face? Instead of struggling to find an answer, however, she only met his gaze levelly and waited to see what else he had planned.

"Like I said, Princess, there's all kinds of ways for a man and woman to . . . get together."

"Tell me," she said shallowly.

His eyes widened at her request, illustrating his surprise at her response, but he quickly recovered his composure. "Most people," he said, taking one final step forward to bring his body completely flush with her own, so that his heat pressed fully against hers, "prefer to do it face to face. Front to front. Usually lying down," he conceded, his voice growing rough now. "But there's a lot to be said for doing it standing up, too. Or sitting down. Or a combination of any of those."

That last suggestion was simply too much for Arabella to consider, so she focused on the earlier one she had tried to imagine instead. "Standing?" she asked, her voice a scant whisper.

He nodded. "Against the wall is especially, uh, stimulating. You can get a surprising amount of depth that way."

"Depth?" she asked, the word emerging as less than a whisper.

"It's best to go deep, Princess. Real deep."

"I, ah, I see." Even though, in truth, she could not. She wanted to ask him what he meant, or, more desperately, to show her what he meant, but he continued before she could work up the nerve.

"But other people," he added, cupping his hands over her shoulders, giving them a gentle push to turn her body until it faced away from his, "like something a little different. They like to do it back to front. With the man coming in from behind. I kinda like it that way myself."

Oh, my, she thought, her body feeling now as if it were about to go up in flames.

"But you cannot see the person that way," she objected weakly. "Why would such a pose be so . . . oh . . ."

She halted when he roped an arm around her waist and pulled her body back insistently against his own. His warm breath danced over her nape as he pushed her hair aside and dipped his head to the juncture of her shoulder and her neck, stringing a line of soft kisses over her sensitive flesh. And then she felt that part of him which made him a man swell hard and long against her bottom, and something deep in her belly exploded, sending heat into parts of her body she had not realized could feel such things.

Then he splayed his hand open over the place where that fire had caught, pushing her back against him so that she could feel the full extent of his arousal. With his other hand he grasped the silk fabric of her nightgown and began to pull it upward, over her shins, her knees, her thighs. And then higher still, until Arabella remembered she was not wearing anything—anything at all—beneath the garment.

Gus discovered that just when she would have warned him to stop. She knew he discovered it, because he gasped against her neck and expelled a sound of utter need and complete longing. And once he made the discovery, Arabella knew, there would be no stopping. Not him. Not herself. Because any objection she might have uttered got stuck in her throat the moment she felt his hand skim over her bare bottom, then lower, stealing between her legs.

Never, ever, had any man touched her in such a way. But Gus moved boldly, without a single hesitation. As he nuzzled her neck and breathed soft kisses along her tender shoulder, he caressed her . . . there. First with one finger, slow and steady, provoking a warm response from deep inside her that Arabella could not help but spill over him. And then a second finger joined the first, pressing more insistently against her, and she could not stifle the soft cry of delight that escaped her in response, or her ragged respiration as she gasped for breath.

She told herself to say something, anything, to make him stop doing what he was doing, because she was enjoying it far too much. More than a woman should be allowed to enjoy anything a man would do to her. Her body was reacting in ways that were completely alien to her, in ways she had not realized it could react. And if she did not stop him, if she allowed him to continue, then she would, she was certain, do all the things she had promised herself she could not—would not—do.

Instead, as that liquid warmth seeped through her, she heard herself murmur, very, very softly, "Oh, now I see. I see why this way would be very . . . exciting."

She had meant for that to be his cue to stop touching her so intimately and release her, but Gus did not take it that way. No, Gus clearly wanted more—much, much more than he had already taken—because he stroked her even more boldly, even more intimately. And Arabella, much to her shock, realized she wanted to give him much, much more. She wanted to give herself to him. All of herself. But she told herself that was something she could never allow herself to do. She was promised to Reynaldo. Even if that promise was hollow and unjust, it was a promise all the same, and she must honor it. She must.

She was about to explain all that to Gus when he drove his finger lower, inserting it inside her, slow and deep. Arabella gasped at the invasion, gasped at her response to the invasion, was shocked at the way her body melted over his hand as he moved his finger in and out of her. And then every word she had been about to utter got lost. Instead her mouth went dry, her brain became muzzy, and a heat flared inside her unlike anything she had ever felt before. She could scarcely remember her name then, let alone an impassioned speech about the preservation of her virtue and her honor and her obligations. Instead, in that moment, she realized she wanted to completely abandon her honor and obligations. More significantly, she wanted to abandon her virtue.

Gus pressed his open mouth to her throat and sucked gently, his breathing coming in short ragged gasps like her own. A strange fire exploded inside Arabella at the twin sensations of his mouth and fingers wreaking such havoc on her body, on her senses. She knew this was madness, knew it was forbidden, yet she still could not find the words to tell him he must stop.

Instead, to her astonishment, she found herself reaching one hand over her shoulder to twine her fingers in his hair. She felt herself rolling her head backward to his shoulder so that he might have freer access to her body. And she noted how her other hand cupped over the one he had spread wide on her belly, weaving her fingers with his.

When she did, Gus moved his hand higher, taking hers with him, until he had cupped both over her naked breast. He palmed her possessively before closing his fingers over the soft mound, and something about joining him in the action made Arabella feel wanton and wicked and wild. She wanted to stay like this forever. Wanted for this moment to freeze as it was, so that she could stay joined with Gus this way forever, feeling these exquisite sensations, for all time to come.

"Oh, God, you're so beautiful," he murmured against her neck. "So soft, so sweet, so perfect."

"No, I am not perfect," she told him weakly.

"You are," he insisted, closing his fingers over her again, claiming her with even greater possession. "You're everything, Arabella. Everything a man could ever want. Everything *I* could ever want. And God, do I want you. More than I've ever wanted anything. Anyone."

"But I am not yours," she said softly, knowing she must make him—and herself—remember that, and trying not to notice the way he had spoken her name for the first time, wrapping his voice so reverently around it, making it sound almost as if he were uttering a benediction. "I belong to someone else," she added, because she knew they were both in dire need of being reminded of that fact. "I belong to Reynaldo, Gus. I do not belong to you."

Gus went perfectly still behind her, his entire body growing rigid. Immediately he removed his hands from her, from her breast and from . . . inside her, and somehow she managed not to cry out her distress at the loss. His actions, though, allowed her gown to fall back down over her body, to cover her, hiding all the damp, heated places that had responded so readily to him. When Arabella turned around to face him, she saw that his expression had gone completely blank. But then she had not seen his expression as he had held her and made love to her with his hands, because he had been behind her. So perhaps he looked no different now than he had only moments ago.

Immediately, though, she knew that was not right. His voice had been thick with his desire for her, and his touches had been incandescent. His expression, she was certain, would have reflected his need and desire for her. Now, though, his expression offered nothing of what he might be feeling.

"Reynaldo doesn't own you, Princess," he said flatly. "No one owns you. You're your own person. Or at least you would be if you'd just realize this is the twenty-first century, and people aren't promised to each other by their parents anymore."

"Where I come from, they are," she said.

"Where you come from," Gus said venomously, "has nothing to do with where you are now. Or where you could be a year from now. Hell, a week from now. If you'd just let yourself—"

But he halted abruptly, clamping his jaw shut tight. His cheeks were flushed, though whether in anger or as the result of his leftover passion, Arabella couldn't have said.

"You do not understand, Gus," she told him. "You do not know what it is like to come from a privileged family. With privilege comes certain obligations. You do not know what it is to have obligations like that. It is different for me. I do not have the freedom that you have."

He expelled a rude, angry sound at that. "Freedom," he echoed flatly. "You think I have freedom? You don't think I understand obligation? Hell, I've spent the last five years of my life trying to escape obligation, trying to find freedom."

"And have you found it?" she asked.

He eyed her silently for a moment, then, slowly, he

shook his head. "No. Not even after traveling thousands of miles. Though, for a minute there, I was awfully damned close." He pinned his gaze on her face. "And so were you, Princess. Whether you'll admit it or not."

She studied him silently for a moment, telling herself he was wrong, and that she should not listen to him. He did not understand. Could not understand. The two of them were just too different from each other. "Perhaps it does not exist, freedom," she said. "Perhaps no one is ever truly free."

He said nothing in response to that, and she could not help thinking that it was because he did not know how to respond. Perhaps he agreed with her. Perhaps he did not believe in real freedom, either. Perhaps it really did not exist.

"I am sorry," she said. "But there is nothing for us, Gus. Even if, for some reason, Reynaldo chose to release me from our engagement, there is nothing for you and me."

For one long, silent moment, Gus only stared at her, his gaze never wavering from hers, his expression never altering. Then, very slowly, almost imperceptibly, he nodded. "I understand, Princess."

Somehow Arabella did not think he did, but she said nothing to counter the remark.

"You think I could never understand what it's like in your world, what with all that privilege and obligation you have. You think it's easy for me to talk, because I can't possibly imagine the sacrifices you'd have to make to go after what you want. You don't think I can appreciate everything you'd give up to come away with me."

Again Arabella said nothing, even though she wanted very much to know if he did indeed want her to come away with him.

"Well, let me tell you something, Princess," he went on

in response to her silence. "I know more than you think. And I understand more than you realize. And trust me. You could walk away from it. You could walk away from all of it. If you really wanted to."

Again Arabella remained silent in response to his remarks. Mostly, she knew, because she did not know what to say. It was not that she agreed with him necessarily, but she could not quite disagree with him, either. She knew she would never be happy with Reynaldo. But at least she would be where she belonged. At least she would have some knowledge of what to expect and what was expected of her. With Gus . . . With Gus there was no guarantee of happiness, either. Because with Gus there were no guarantees at all. She would never know from one day to the next what to anticipate. She could very well end up alone. Alone and having no idea what to do.

So she only watched without speaking as he turned his back on her and strode to the other side of the room. And she said nothing as he opened the door and passed through it, closing it behind him without a single sound. And she wished—oh, how she wished—that she could follow him through it. Instead she remained rooted to the floor. Here in her stateroom aboard *Mad Tryst*.

Where, she thought morosely, she very much belonged.

Chapter 17

*B*y the time *Mad Tryst* reached St. John in the U.S. Virgin Islands, Keaton was fit to be tied. Preferably to a ship's mast, in the teeth of a booming gale, while the sirens sang seductively to him from afar, bidding him come crash his vessel on their lovely hazardous rocks. Because then—*maybe*—he'd have an excuse that would explain why he'd felt so damned nasty and mean-spirited for the past week.

Ever since they'd left San Juan, all hell seemed to have broken loose aboard the yacht. No one—*no one*—had been allowed to voice the words "supermodel" or "Dacia," because a certain member of their yachting party who should remain nameless had met a movie director in San Juan the last night they were there. Then said certain nameless member of their yachting party had proceeded to disappear with said movie director. Then said certain nameless member still hadn't returned to the boat the morning *Mad Tryst* was to have gotten under way, *but* said certain nameless member *had* sent someone to collect her things and tell Reynaldo she wouldn't be back. *Ever.* Because said certain nameless member would be on location in Central America filming what would be her breakout bit part in a major B movie called *Bikini Commandos: Jungle Juice,* the first in what could potentially be a *recurring* bit part in a series of *Bikini Commandos* films, provided the receipts were good, and her character, Bambo, didn't get offed early on in the series.

But as a result of the, ah . . . good fortune . . . that had befallen that certain nameless member of their yachting party, the prince's mood had been a tad, oh . . . mean, ugly, vile, dour—not to mention a host of other four-letter words—for the last few days.

And Reynaldo wasn't the only one.

The Countess Arabella, too, had been in a very bad mood since San Juan, had spoken barely a word to anyone after that first day in port. Kurt the canine had become more intolerable than ever in the wake of Ruby's departure—something Keaton would have sworn was impossible for the foul, nefarious little gargoyle to be—and he'd had no qualms about illustrating his canine displeasure to everyone, especially Keaton, usually by attaching himself to a trouser leg or chewing to bits a very expensive loafer of Ungaro or Gucci descent. Kurt the chef had also been thrown into a bleak, black depression over the last several days, and as a result, his *Pflaumenkuchen* just wasn't the same at all. In fact, Keaton might very well go so far as to say it was *beschissen.* Even Gus the bartender had been in a snit when he had given his two minutes' notice and quit his job—and the yacht—while they were in San Juan. And he had left them shorthanded in the bartender department which, let's face it, at times like these, was the last place you wanted to be left shorthanded.

Keaton wished he could blame the aura of gloom and doom into which *Mad Tryst* seemed to have cruised on the fact that they had, sort of, skirted the edge of the Bermuda Triangle when they left San Juan, so naturally there would be some kind of supernatural phenomenon occurring, even if there hadn't been an actual alien and/or Elvis sighting—and/or an alien Elvis sighting for that matter—to be had. But then he was forced to remind himself that they'd sailed right smack-dab across the center of the Bermuda Triangle when they'd made their passage from Hamilton to San Juan, and they hadn't experienced so much as an inexplicable blip on the radar—or even a vicious mood swing. Therefore, he had no choice but to conclude that the mishaps and general feelings of ill will that had visited *Mad Tryst* of late could be the result of only one—not necessarily supernatural—phenomenon.

Ruby was gone. And everyone noticed her absence. And it left a strange void aboard the yacht that made everyone uncomfortable.

That was what it all boiled down to. Because while Ruby had been aboard, Keaton reminded himself, things on the yacht had been surprisingly good, certainly better than they had ever been since the party had set off from Pelagia. And now that Ruby was gone, things on the yacht were rapidly progressing—or, rather, deteriorating—back to their usual, disagreeable ways. At this rate, by the time they made it to the equator, Captain Cooki would have them all walking the plank at plastic cocktail sword point. And based on his own foul temper, Keaton would be first in line.

Dammit. He had known he would miss Ruby when she was gone. But he wasn't supposed to be missing her *this much*. It was almost as if a part of him had left with her. A whopping great part that he needed for his very survival, the part that had housed his happiness, his contentment, and his hope for the future. The part that had made him want to live his life. Without that part . . .

He sighed fitfully now as he stood at the port rail in his usual going-ashore wear—loose khaki trousers and a white linen shirt—even though he had absolutely no inclination to go ashore. Instead, he found himself gazing out at one of the most beautiful islands he had ever seen—a massive, radiant emerald rising out of a fluid sapphire sea—and he was trying to figure out why he could only view the magnificent vista as a vicious impediment. Something to keep him grounded at anchor when he'd rather be under way, cruising speedily and with great purpose toward . . .

What? he asked himself. Even if they were under way, they'd be headed toward places he'd never visited, places that were totally unfamiliar to him, places where he didn't belong. If it wasn't St. John, it would just be another beautiful bit of paradise making him feel trapped and dissatisfied and anxious. Why was he so ready and eager to move on, when he had nothing to move on to?

"Oh, good, Keaton, there you are."

And speaking of nothing . . .

"Yes, Reynaldo?" he replied dispassionately, turning to find the prince striding toward him.

He had to force himself not to squeeze his eyes shut tight at the sight. Today Reynaldo's wardrobe exceeded even its own usual, ah, flair. He wore pale blue sultan's pants, a shell pink tunic, currently flapping wide open from the waist up thanks to the ocean breeze, and—Keaton had to look twice to believe it—a turban. A silver turban. Which, of course, made perfect sense, because it complemented his silver thongs just so nicely. Reynaldo looked like the cousin no one talked about in Aladdin's family—at a Village People concert. And it occurred to Keaton then—not for the first time, to be perfectly honest—that the Pelagian people would have been insane to ever let this man get near a throne.

"I have a problem," Reynaldo said.

Now there's a shocker, Keaton thought.

"And I need your help."

How astonishing.

"I'm in a bit of trouble with the St. John authorities."

Boy, never could have seen that one coming.

"It seems that I may have overlooked a few rules—"

How unusual.

"—when I started a bonfire last night for a couple of Danish tourists I met."

How unlike him.

"Dagmar and Sigrid."

How very unlike him.

"They're twins."

How very, very unlike him.

"And now the local government—or is it the federal government?—is insisting that I pay a *huge* fine—"

Gee, never had that happen before.

"—just because I burned down a few things."

Excellent. So it was only arson this time.

Keaton expelled a long, lusty, frustrated sigh, and realized he had no idea what to say in response to this latest misdeed of Prince Reynaldo's. Except maybe all the things he'd said to Reynaldo before, hundreds of times, all the things the prince repeatedly ignored, all the things that were so pointless and fruitless and meaningless.

So Reynaldo continued petulantly, "Well, how was I supposed to know that practically the entire island is under the direction of the U.S. Forestry Service? It doesn't say anything anywhere about St. John being a state park."

Keaton lifted a hand to the back of his neck and rubbed at a knot that seemed to have come out of nowhere. "Well, except on the dozens of signs you see all over the place, and all those references in the tourist books," he said. "But I can see where you'd miss that, Reynaldo. It's only obvious to a five-year-old."

"My point exactly," the prince said.

Yeah, he had a point all right, Keaton thought. One that even a silver turban couldn't hide.

"Anyway, I need you to get me out of trouble, Keaton," Reynaldo continued blithely. *Blithely*. Really. And he called himself a man. "I have a date tonight with Dagmar *and* Sigrid." He glanced down at his watch. "I was supposed to show up at some government building somewhere in Cruz Bay about an hour ago, but I was having a pedicure done, and I missed the appointment. Go take care of it for me, would you? I have things to do."

He started to spin around, but Keaton stopped him with a slowly and meaningfully uttered "Oh, I don't *think* so."

Reynaldo halted mid-spin, turning his body back toward Keaton. "What was that?" he said.

Keaton smiled. "I'm sorry. I thought I spoke loudly enough for you to hear. I said, 'I don't think so,' " he repeated. Even more slowly and meaningfully—and loudly—than before. And then, just in case the prince didn't get the gist of his slowness and meaning—or his loudness—Keaton added, "I'm tired of cleaning up after you, Reynaldo. You can do it yourself from now on."

The prince narrowed his eyes at Keaton, and his mouth dropped open in obvious outrage. "How *dare* you speak to me that way," he said.

"Actually, it's not all that hard to speak to you that way, Reynaldo. In fact, it's not difficult at all. What's difficult is being polite to you. Mostly because you don't deserve it."

The other man's mouth dropped open even more, and he turned his body fully to face Keaton now. He fisted his hands on his hips and frowned, but really, it was kind of hard for a guy in a silver turban to look menacing.

"You know," Reynaldo said, "I'd think you'd show a little more gratitude. After everything I've done for you—"

"Everything *you've* done for *me*?" Keaton demanded. Now he was the one to clench his hands into fists, perfectly ready—and willing—to pop His Royal Highness right in the royal eye. "You've done *nothing* for me, Reynaldo. I've always been the one doing for you."

"Oh, please," Reynaldo countered with his usual manly eloquence.

Keaton expelled another heartfelt growl of frustration, opened his mouth to give Reynaldo what for—but good— and then he . . . And then he . . . And then he . . .

And then he experienced a stark, singular, scintillating moment of great epiphany.

Reynaldo really had done nothing for Keaton. Ever. And after everything Keaton had done for the prince— and what he'd done for Reynaldo could fill *tomes*, by God—what did he have to show for it? Not just for the way he had been baby-sitting Reynaldo on *Mad Tryst* for the past year, but even before that, while they were still on Pelagia, when Keaton had been working for the government, for King Francisco, in preparation for eventually becoming the prime minister of the country where he had grown up. What did Keaton have to show for all those years? All that time? All those things he had done and learned and practiced? What did he have?

Nothing. He had nothing. He had no job, he had no home, he had no income, he had no roots, he had no prospects, he had no future. He had nothing. *Nothing*.

God, he was such an idiot. The whole time he'd been with Ruby, he'd told himself he had so much more than she had, had thought he was the one with so much to offer someone like her. He had thought she was the one who had nothing, when all along, it had been he. What good was his money when it was frozen in accounts he couldn't access? What good was his occupation when he had no place to ply his trade? What good was his beautiful house on Pelagia when he couldn't return to his homeland? What good were his roots when they'd never been firmly planted in the first place, and the place where they had been planted was now off-limits to him? And what good was his education when he was too stupid to see the most obvious thing in the world?

Ruby was the one who had everything. She had a family, she had roots in the community where she'd grown up, she had an apartment to return to, she had a job, and she had a regular paycheck. And maybe she didn't have a formal education, but she was by no means uneducated. With all the hard knocks she'd taken, she knew more about life than Keaton had ever learned during his oh-so-much-more-sophisticated upbringing. And Ruby had things even more important than all that other stuff combined. She had sense of herself, and she had the ability to make other people feel better about things. She knew how to make friends and keep the peace. She had a nice smile, a nice laugh. She had . . .

Well, she had a way about her, Keaton thought with a fond smile. Oh, boy, did she have a way about her. And for one week, he'd had a way about himself, too. Because he'd had Ruby. And she, he realized now, had had him. Hell, she still had him. Because now he understood that when she had gone, she'd taken a part of him with her, a part of him he wasn't likely to get back. Not unless he went after her. Not unless he got her back, too. Because whether she realized it or not, a part of her had stayed with him. And now everything was all mixed up.

He had to find her, had to be with her, so they could mix all those parts up again, and combine them and make them one. The way they had been that day in Puerto Rico, in the rain forest, when the two of them had made love. When the two of them—and all their parts—had mixed and combined and become one.

Ruby. God, Ruby. What he'd had with her was the one thing—the only thing—that Keaton had ever had in his life that had any purpose, any meaning. What he'd had with her was the one thing he'd *had* in his life, period. Everything else was meaningless. Everything else was pointless. Everything else was fruitless. Only Ruby had ever mattered, had ever made him *feel* like he was something significant. Something important. Only when he'd had her had he felt whole.

But he didn't have Ruby anymore, either, did he? No, he had let what he'd found with her slip right through his fingers. Worse than that. He had thrown it away. Thrown away the one real thing he had ever had. The one thing that had ever had any meaning, any reality, any value. The one thing that had ever made him feel as if he had a purpose. As if he were something. As if he were some*one*.

Because that, he realized now, was what Ruby Runyon had made him feel. Whole. Complete. Real. She had made him feel as if he had consequence. She had made him feel as if he were integral to the workings of the world. She had made him feel as if he were . . .

Loved. That was what she had made him feel. Loved and . . . in love, too. And that, Keaton realized in that sweet moment of epiphany, was the most important thing in the world.

"I quit," he said to Reynaldo.

The prince gazed at him in dumbfounded silence for a moment, then expelled a nervous chuckle. "You what?"

"I quit," Keaton repeated.

There was another moment of incredulous silence from the prince, then "You can't quit," he said. "You're going to be my prime minister."

Keaton threw his arms open wide. "Look around you, Reynaldo. Prime minister of what? This yacht? Thanks, but I've been that for a year, and shockingly, I do not find it fulfilling. You don't have a country," he reminded the other man. "And if your former royal subjects are smart—which they must be if they ousted your sorry ass from their homeland—you never will have a country. You will never be more than the prince of *Mad Tryst*, Reynaldo. And me, I have higher aspirations than that."

"Higher aspirations," Reynaldo repeated contemptuously. "What on earth could you aspire to be that's higher than what you have now?"

Keaton smiled. Hell, being canine Kurt's kibble-bearer would be a more respectable gig than the one he had with Reynaldo. What he said, though, was "I aspire to be Ruby Runyon's man. If she'll take me."

"The *waitress*?" Reynaldo exclaimed incredulously. "You must be joking."

"At least she earns an honest paycheck and has a permanent address," Keaton said. "Which is more than I can say for some people." He started to turn around, but offered one final parting shot. "And another thing, Reynaldo. She wouldn't be caught dead in a silver turban."

And then Keaton did turn around, walking away from Reynaldo without a second thought, his step feeling lighter than it had felt in years. Every bit of mental energy he possessed was focused on one thing: finding Ruby.

And once he found her, he would . . . He would . . . He would . . .

Well, he would probably fling himself at her feet and beg her forgiveness for being such an idiot. And he would be hers, he thought as he made his way across the deck and through the companionway into the lounge. He'd be hers in a heartbeat, if she would take him.

Problem was, Keaton thought further as he headed below to his stateroom to pack his things and arrange for a flight to Miami, after everything that had happened, he honestly wasn't sure if Ruby would still *want* him. Even if she didn't want him, though, he would still be hers. He had no choice in the matter. He would be hers forever.

He just hoped she'd take him.

It became abundantly clear a few days later that, in addition to not knowing if Ruby would want him, Keaton honestly wasn't sure where she *was*. Because although he had checked out every comedy club in Miami, he hadn't found her at any of them. Oh, she had worked at one of them, Frank's Funny Business, but she wasn't there anymore. Keaton had heard from Frank himself that when Ruby had called in sick one time too many, he'd replaced her with someone infinitely more reliable—and funnier, too. Fortunately—for Keaton, if not for Ruby—Frank had no qualms about giving out the addresses of former employees. Unfortunately—for Keaton, if not for Ruby—she wasn't home when he rang the bell at the squat, dirty little building that was her home.

Keaton shook his head now as he looked at the place. This was where she lived? he wondered. This was her *home*? No wonder she hadn't wanted to come back here. The neighborhood wasn't terrible, but neither was it charming and cheerful, the way most of South Beach was.

Where were the cool Art Deco buildings with bright pastel stucco? Where was the lively salsa music? Where were the chicly dressed, ethnically diverse, hip-hoppin' inhabitants? Where were the mouthwatering aromas of lime and cumin from the street vendors?

This little corner of South Beach was nothing but plain square buildings of crumbling plaster and mortar, grown gray from soot and exhaust. There was no music here, only the wheezing of buses, and the clanking of trash cans, and the yelling of undesirables, who also seemed to make up much of the inhabitants. And instead of lime and cumin, Ruby's neighborhood smelled like . . . Well, never mind what it smelled like. Keaton just couldn't imagine her living here. She didn't belong here *at all*. She belonged someplace where there was color and life and music. She belonged in a lush garden refuge, rich with wonder and spirit and vitality. She belonged with people who knew what it meant to live life, people who loved and appreciated what she had to give. She belonged with—

Hell, she belonged with him. The problem was, Keaton had no idea where he belonged now. No, wait, he realized. That wasn't quite true. He did know where he belonged.

He belonged with Ruby. No matter where she was.

He pushed her doorbell one last time, futilely, he knew. She wasn't home. He'd have to wait for her. He only wished he knew how long it would take her to find her way back.

"You lookin' for Ruby Runyon?"

Keaton turned at the voice and saw a woman leaning out the window closest to the apartment building entrance, her silver hair braided and wound around the top of her head like a coronet. Thick, black-framed glasses sat on the bridge of her nose, and bony arms extended from the sleeves of a red, polka-dot blouse. Keaton guesstimated her age to be somewhere around a hundred and forty-seven.

"Are you the concierge?" he asked the woman.

She shook her head and smiled unabashedly. "Nah. I just like lookin' out the windows and watchin' the neighborhood and stickin' my nose into everybody's business and keepin' an eye on the front door."

Hmmm, where Keaton came from, that *was* a concierge, but he didn't take exception to the woman's explanation. Instead he said, "Obviously you know Ruby."

"Yeah. Nice girl," the woman said. "Makes a wicked Long Island iced tea."

"Do you know where she is?" Keaton asked, smiling in spite of his moroseness. "When she'll be back?"

"She went home," the woman said.

"Home?" Keaton echoed. "But I thought—"

"Her other home, I mean," the woman said. "Up in the Panhandle. Appalachimahoochee. She went to visit her mother and grandmother. She won't be back for a while."

"How do you know?" he asked.

"She told me before she left," the woman said.

"Oh."

"Plus, she gave me her dieffenbachia. What was left of it, anyway. Poor thing looked like it hadn't been watered for a week. She said I could keep it. She knows I'm good with plants."

"Do you know her mother's address?" Keaton asked hopefully.

"Sure," the woman said.

Excellent, he thought. He opened his mouth to ask what it was, but the woman cut him off before he had the chance.

"I can't give it to you, though. You could be a stalker."

Keaton couldn't keep from smiling at that. It was nice

to know *some*one had an interest in Ruby's safety. Some-one besides himself, anyway. "I understand," he told the woman. Besides, he knew her mother and grandmother lived in a trailer park. How many trailer parks could there be in Appalachimahoochee? He'd check them all if he had to. Provided, of course, he could find Appalachima-hoochee. Surely it was on a map. It would be enormously helpful if it was.

"Thank you," he told the woman. "I appreciate your letting me know where she is."

"Home," the woman repeated. "She told me she needed to go home."

She certainly does, Keaton thought. *Just like the rest of us do*.

He lifted a hand in farewell to the concierge who wasn't a concierge but seemed a lot like a concierge to him, and he tried not to dance down the apartment build-ing steps as he descended them. It was hard, though, be-cause, strangely, he really did feel like dancing. Probably, he thought, because he was *finally* going home, too.

He was almost halfway down the block when he heard Ruby's neighbor call out after him, "Listen, when you see Ruby, tell her the dieffenbachia is doing much better!"

Keaton lifted a hand in response and smiled at the words. The dieffenbachia, he thought, wasn't the only one.

Chapter 18

*T*o say Arabella was surprised when Reynaldo asked her to join him for dinner ashore precisely at seven would have been an understatement. What she actually was was shocked. Shocked and amazed. Shocked and amazed and confused. Shocked and amazed and confused and . . .

And reluctant.

Simply put, Arabella did not *want* to join Reynaldo for dinner ashore precisely at seven. In fact, she did not want to join Reynaldo for anything, anywhere, anytime. Which was a very strange reaction, she told herself as she buttoned up one of the dresses she had bought in San Juan, a knee-length sundress fashioned of brightly colored, flowered fabric—much like the shirts that the bartenders on *Imperial Majesty* wore, she realized now that she thought about it. As an afterthought she did not call Marisol to arrange her hair. Instead she wore it down, unfettered. Yes, she rather liked it that way. It reminded her of when Gus had curled a long lock around his finger and—

But she would not think of that, she reminded herself ruthlessly, doing her best to tamp down the heat that spread through her body at the recollection. She did not allow thoughts or memories of Gus Torrance to ever enter her brain. Because Gus was gone. And he would not be back. Just as Supertwit Dacia was gone and would not be back. There was nothing now to keep Reynaldo from marrying Arabella, nothing to keep Arabella from marrying Reynaldo. Nothing. Not one thing.

Except that . . . Arabella did not want to marry Reynaldo.

But that was something else she would not think about. Of course she would marry Reynaldo. She *must* marry Reynaldo. Wanting had nothing to do with it. Expectation and obligation and arrangement had everything to do with it. It was arranged and had been arranged for twenty years. It did not matter that the act of arranging marriages was archaic and heartless and ridiculous. It did not matter if this was the twenty-first century, and women had come a long way, baby. It did not matter if she would love someone else for the rest of her—

But she was not allowed to think about that. About him. She must think about Reynaldo. She must marry Reynaldo. She must. Just as she must meet him for dinner ashore precisely at seven, as he had requested. Even if she did not want to go. She was expected. She was obligated. It was arranged.

But even after Arabella arrived at the resort where Reynaldo had taken a suite of rooms to offer himself some relief from his much smaller quarters aboard *Imperial Majesty*—naturally he did not take rooms for anyone else, only himself—Arabella was not thinking about Reynaldo. Nor was she thinking about expectations. Or obligations. Or arrangements.

What she was thinking about was how very much she wished she was someone else. Someone like Ruby Runyon, who had had the freedom to leave *Imperial Majesty*—eventually—and return to her home, without anyone there expecting anything of her. Without having any obligations to go along with arrangements that had been made for her before she was old enough to understand or give her consent. And Arabella was thinking that perhaps it would be nice to visit her new American friend in America, where people were free to do as they pleased. Before leaving *Imperial Majesty* Ruby had given Arabella her address—both in Miami and in Appa . . . Appa . . . Appa . . . in that other place where she had grown up. Arabella would tell Reynaldo today that she would undertake such a visit.

She found him in the sitting room of his suite—sitting, as circumstances would have it—the table before him already set for their dinner. In fact, Arabella noted further, the food was already there, and Reynaldo seemed to have started—and finished—without her. He had dressed with surprising somberness this evening, she noticed, in white trousers and what she believed was called a poet's shirt the color of a very ripe—she tried not to squint—lime. He was reading the newspaper and she thought at first that he had not noticed her arrival. So she opened her mouth to let him know she was there, only to close it again when he intercepted her.

"I've set a date, Arabella," he said without greeting her, without inviting her to sit down, without even looking at her. "October twenty-third. Since this won't be a formal state affair of national significance, we won't need to put much planning into it. I would like to do it up nicely, though, for the sake of the media jackals. They'll insist on something they can blitz all over cable and satellite TV.

And they have been so good to me, after all. It's the least I can do for them."

"A date?" Arabella echoed, her mind spinning at all Reynaldo had just said. This was the most he had spoken to her since their departure from Pelagia, and she was having trouble processing it all. "A date for what?"

Immediately she realized how ridiculous her question was. What date, after all, had commanded her attention for the last twelve months? For the last twenty years? She had lived her entire life to set this date. No, that wasn't quite right, she thought. She had not actually *lived* her life for this date—her entire life had been *on hold* as she had awaited this date. Reynaldo was setting a date for their wedding. Finally. Why, therefore, was Arabella's first reaction to object? And why was her second reaction to run away and hide?

"A date for our wedding," he told her unnecessarily, over-enunciating each word, as if he were speaking to a child. He turned the page of his newspaper and continued to read.

"You must forgive my confusion, Reynaldo," she said, "but why set the date now when you have put it off for so long?"

Of course, she already knew the answer to that question, too. Because Superninny Dacia no longer wanted him, and he was embarrassed by her rejection and abandonment. He would, Arabella was certain, tell everyone that his impending wedding to his much-cherished fiancée was the *real* reason that Supermoron Dacia was out of his life. He would want it to look as if he were the one who had rejected and abandoned *her*.

Reynaldo did finally glance up at Arabella's last question, eyeing her with what she could only liken to distaste. "Why not now?" he countered. "You've been badgering me for a year to set this date. Now I'm doing it."

Actually that was not true, Arabella thought. She had, in fact, stopped badgering Reynaldo some time ago. About the time that Gus Torrance had come aboard, she realized now.

"By October we can be in Tierra del Fuego, which, considering the family name, would be quite appropriate, I think. A nice sound bite, as they say in the electronic media." He returned his gaze to the newspaper as he continued, "It will be spring there, so the conditions should be good. And you'll have time to alert your family so that they can make travel arrangements."

Arabella waited to see what else he would say, but nothing more was forthcoming. Finally Reynaldo glanced up at her, his expression indicating he was surprised to find her still there.

"That's all," he said. "You can go."

She gaped at him, unable to stop the soft sound of surprise that escaped her. "I thought we were to have dinner," she said.

"Thank you, but I've already had mine," he replied coolly. And then he glanced back down at his newspaper again, as if he had not a care in the world.

Funnily enough, however, Arabella discovered in that moment that she *did* have a care in the world. In fact, she had more than one. She had many cares. And she wondered why it only now occurred to her to voice them.

Maybe, she thought, it was because she had spent every day of her life being resigned to the future that others had mapped out for her, and it was a future that had always sounded like a dream come true. It had never occurred to Arabella to question or be unhappy with what she had been assured was the kind of life that every girl fantasized about having. Someday, she had been told for as long as she could remember, she would marry a handsome prince and go to live with him in his palace and eventually become his queen. Someday, she had been told for so long, she would live a life of leisure and pleasure that others only dreamed of living. She was so lucky, she had heard all her life. She was so fortunate. Any other person would have loved to have the life that she would be living.

And any other person could have it, Arabella thought now. Because now that she thought about it, she did not want to live a life that *others* dreamed of. She wanted to live the life that *she* dreamed of. But she had never been allowed to dream of that life. Not until this moment. And now that she did allow herself to dream, she realized that the life she wanted did not include a palace and a prince. Or a yacht and a prince, either.

No, the life she dreamed of had, at its center, a charming bartender named Gus and not much else. Because she knew that as long as she was with Gus Torrance, wherever they were, whatever they were doing, she would be happy. She would be satisfied. She did not need wealth and society and notoriety to be happy. Those things had never made her happy before. What she needed—*all* she needed—was to love and be loved in return. And the only place she would find that, she knew, was with Gus. Even if he was a rootless wanderer who had no prospects. As long as he loved her—and she was beginning to understand now that he did love her—that was all that mattered. And somehow she knew, deep down, that if she had just told him how much she cared for him before he had left, he would have stayed by her side for the rest of her days, whether she married Reynaldo or not. And somehow she knew that if she found him, the two of them would be as one forever.

Now she just had to find him.

"I will not marry you, Reynaldo," she heard herself say,

surprised by how calmly she delivered the declaration.

At first she thought he had not heard her, because he did not raise his head from his newspaper or offer any sign that he had heard what she had said. She was about to repeat her manifesto, but he muttered something under his breath. Something that sounded like, "First Keaton, now you. What the hell is the matter with everyone?"

Although Arabella did not know what he meant by his words, she at least knew he had heard her. So she waited to see how he would react, waited to see what he would say in response to her proclamation. After a moment he raised his head to look at her, his contempt for her quite obvious. She could not imagine now how she could ever have let herself think she had a future with this man. But then she had not really known him until a little over a year ago. Prince Reynaldo Michael Julian David Lorenzo Constantine del Fuego of Pelagia had been, until then, as much a fantasy as every other image her young brain and heart had formed for her future.

"Of course you'll marry me," he told her calmly. "It's all arranged."

"I do not care," Arabella said. "I do not want you, Reynaldo. I have not wanted you for a very long time. And I will not marry you."

He gazed back at her with confusion, clearly bewildered by her outburst. "Well, what has *wanting* got to do with anything, Arabella? I don't want you, either. But I shall marry you just the same. Need I remind you that it's been agreed upon for *twenty years*?"

"No. You do not need to remind me. But you cannot marry me if I do not agree to marry you," she pointed out. "And I do not agree to marry you. I shall not. I will not."

"But you—"

"Why would either of us want to go through with this

marriage when it is what neither of us wants?" she demanded, cutting him off. "What will our lives be like? Our *lives,* Reynaldo. It is . . ." She lifted her hands, loosely fisted before her, as if she might pull the appropriate word out of thin air. Finally the word she needed came to her. "It is stupid. That is what it is."

He gaped at her for a moment, as if he simply could not believe she was saying these things to him. "But we have to marry," he finally told her. "We must."

"Why?"

"Because it is agreed upon," he said impatiently. "It has been agreed upon for years. We have an obligation, Arabella."

"To whom?"

"To our families. To our people. To our countries."

"You do not have a country anymore, Reynaldo. Therefore you do not have any people. And you do not have any family, for that matter. Your parents both dead. You do not have an obligation to anyone."

He gazed at her in speculative silence for a moment, as if he were giving great weight to what she had said. She was beginning to think she had won him over until he told her, "But you do, Arabella. You do have obligations. To your family, your people, your country. You made a promise."

"My parents made a promise," she said. "It is their obligation, not mine."

"You have an obligation," Reynaldo repeated more firmly. "And you know it."

She nodded once, then lifted her chin defiantly. "Yes. I have an obligation. But it is to one person only."

"Me," Reynaldo said pointedly.

She shook her head slowly. "No. Not you." She jabbed her index finger firmly to her chest. "Me. I have an obligation to myself only. And I do not wish to marry you. I shall not. I will not."

"Arabella, you have to—"

"I do not have to do anything I do not want to do, Reynaldo."

He frowned at her. "And I told you that wanting has nothing to do with any of this."

"Wanting has everything to do with it," she countered immediately. "And I do not want you. I want something—and someone—else. And I will have both."

She had thought he would demand to know the details of the someone else of whom she had spoken, but he only asked, "Even if it means shaming your family? Shaming yourself?"

"I will shame no one by making myself happy."

"Your parents will never forgive you," he said levelly.

"My parents will understand, once I tell them how I feel. They love me very much. They wish me to be happy. They have thought all these years that it would make me happy to marry you. Once I tell them how you really are, and how I feel about you, they will not require me to meet the obligation they made for me. Twenty years ago. Without my consent."

"Are you so confident of that?" he asked.

"Yes," she replied with all confidence, "I am."

Silently she twisted the massive sapphire ring from her left hand, then strode across the room and set it on the table beside his plate.

"Goodbye, Reynaldo," she said softly, with finality.

Then, without awaiting a reply, feeling much better now than she had felt upon her arrival, Arabella spun on her heel and exited Reynaldo's room. She did not stop walking until she reached the hotel lobby, and only then did she slow down because she saw someone she thought

he knew. Or perhaps, on second look, it was not someone
he knew after all, she thought as she drew nearer to the
man. Although he did look familiar . . .

Her movements slowed even more, and then she
topped completely, because she realized for certain then
hat yes, the man was indeed a person she knew. But no,
he was in no way familiar.

"Hey, Princess," the man said as she came to a halt less
han a meter away from him. "Long time no see." He nodded toward her outfit. "Like the dress." He returned his
gaze to her face and smiled. "Like the hair, too. Reminds
ne of a certain something."

Arabella told herself to acknowledge the man, told her-
elf to say something in response to his greeting. But ever
ince she had been a young child, her mother had always
old her she should never speak to strangers. So she said
nothing to him as she stood fixed in place and marveled at
how much he had changed.

"What's wrong?" he asked, his words tinted with
omething she had never heard in his voice before, some-
hing that made her frown. Sarcasm. Yes, that was it. His
mile was forced, unnatural, as he added, "What's wrong?
Don't you recognize me? I recognized you the minute I
aw you leave *Mad Tryst*, even though you look a little
different from the last time I saw you. My cabby had a hell
of a time keeping up with yours on the way here. You
eemed to be in a hell of a hurry to do something, that's for
ure."

Arabella did not even try to smile. Instead she in-
pected him from head to toe and shook her own head
lowly. Because, no, she did not recognize him. This man
vas very different from the one she had come to love.
Where Gus—*her* Gus—always favored those large,
aggy shorts and obnoxiously colored shirts for which she

had developed a very fond affection, this Gus—whomever he belonged to—was dressed in a dark suit and tie. A very expensive dark suit and tie, Arabella noted, one that would have been more appropriate for one of the many hangers-on who had attended royal affairs back in Toulaine. And where her Gus had worn his long, beautiful hair bound at his nape, or hanging unfettered over his shoulders—sometimes his naked shoulders—this Gus . . .

Arabella stifled a gasp when she realized this Gus had shorn his hair off. Instead of bound at his nape, his silky tresses had been cut in a very short and conservative style, obviously by a hand that commanded quite a lot of money for the service. Gone, too, was the mischief that had always sparkled in his eyes, and the knowing smile that had always set her heart to racing. Gone was the casual posture, the cheerful disposition, the irreverent high spirits. Gone was . . .

Gone was Gus, she realized. And in his place stood a complete stranger. One she instinctively knew she would not like. Because he reminded her far too much of the idle, worthless, self-centered people who populated Reynaldo's world. Reynaldo's world, and her own world, too.

"So what do you think, Princess?" the stranger asked when still she offered no commentary. "Think I could pass for high society in this get-up? Think Reynaldo would let me attend one of his parties as something other than the bartender now?"

"Why would you want to attend one of Reynaldo's parties as anything?" she asked. "You do not like him."

"No," the man she had known as Gus agreed. He sobered—not that he had been particularly jovial with his false smile. "But the ol' prince has one or two things going for him that I wouldn't mind having going for me."

"And just who are you?" Arabella asked, as surprised to

hear the question as her new acquaintance seemed to be.

"That's kind of an odd question to ask a man who's been intimate with you, don't you think?"

She shook her head, but heat suffused her cheeks at hearing him speak so casually about the way they had been together, so briefly, that night in San Juan. She could not be casual about that night. And she did not like it that he could mention the memory so carelessly, as if it had meant nothing more to him than a lunch date might have.

"You have never been intimate with me," she said softly.

His eyes flashed fire at her remark.

"You have not," she repeated. "You are a stranger to me. The man who . . . the man who was with me that night, he was someone I cared for. You, I do not know."

"Don't you?"

She shook her head again. "Who are you? I think I deserve an answer to my question."

He bowed his head a bit and said, "Fair enough."

"No, I do not think there will be much fairness in this," Arabella said. "But I would like to know the answer anyway. Who are you?"

He hesitated only a moment before replying, but his eyes never left hers when he did finally answer. "Torrance was my mother's maiden name," he said. "So in a sense, it's my name, too, even if it's not one I grew up with. When I left home, I kind of . . . reinvented myself, and I sort of adopted her last name to use as my last name."

"And Gus?" Arabella asked, her voice sounding— feeling—even more shallow than before. "Is that not your name, either?"

"Not really," he confessed. "It's more like a nickname I gave myself."

"You were not then born Gus Torrance?" she asked, even though he had already answered the question.

He shook his head. "No. I was born—" He halted abruptly without finishing, as if he were afraid to speak his real name aloud for some reason. Finally, though, his gaze still fastened on her face, he told her, "My real name is Augustus Durrett Langley. The fourth," he added dispiritedly. "Maybe you've heard the name before? My father, for instance, Augustus Durrett Langley the third, is something of a celebrity."

· Now it was Arabella's turn to be afraid to say anything. Part of her told herself he couldn't possibly be speaking the truth. But another part of her—a larger part—knew that what he was saying was indeed the truth. Damn him.

Somehow she managed to say, "Everyone in the world who has ever read a newspaper or watched a television has heard of the Langleys. They are often referred to as . . ." She smiled wryly at the irony as she tried again. "They are often referred to as 'American royalty,' " she said.

"Yeah, 'American royalty,' that's us," Augustus Durrett Langley IV said. But he spoke the words with disdain, as if he were reluctant to identify himself with the group.

"Your father is quite a celebrity, as you said. He has lived quite a colorful life. And he is the heir to a petroleum fortune, if I remember correctly."

Her new acquaintance nodded. "Petroleum. Aluminum. Titanium. Uranium. Lots of other metals and minerals ending in 'um.' Among other things."

"And your mother," Arabella continued, amazed that she was able to converse so naturally with this man she did not know, about things she would never, ever have suspected, "she, too, is rather well known in her own right, is she not?"

"Daughter of a former president?" Augustus asked. "Yeah, I guess that makes her something of a celebrity, too."

Arabella nodded. "I have heard much about the Langleys of America. As has nearly everyone in the world. It is a large family, yes?"

He nodded. "My father has four brothers and a sister who all married as well as he did. I have lots of Langley cousins. They're pretty famous in their own right, some of them."

Arabella nodded. "Or perhaps 'infamous' would be a better word," she said. "Many of them do not have good reputations, from what I hear."

"Yeah, well, you've heard correctly," he conceded, again in that bitter voice of disdain. "We've had our share of . . . spots of trouble," he said. "But a lot of what you've heard has been exaggerated by the media. We Langleys are the favorite whipping boys of the tabloids, you know."

Arabella said nothing for a moment, then, "And which whipping boy are you?" she asked softly. "The one who was in jail for selling drugs to a policeman? The one who has been sued for not paying child support for his out-of-wedlock child? The one who is being investigated for killing a woman and her baby because he was driving drunk? The one who is accused of raping his college classmate? The one who—"

"Gee, so you do read the tabloids," Augustus Durrett Langley IV said crisply, clearly as angered by the litany of offenses as she was.

"Reading the tabloids was always the best way I had to keep track of Reynaldo," she told him. "So which of the infamous Langley boys are you?" she added before he could change the subject. "Tell me. I think I have the right to know who I am talking to."

"I'm not one of the Langley boys," he told her firmly. "Not the way you mean. I got out before anybody could turn me into something I didn't want to be. Before anybody could make me out to be something I'm not. Or worse, make me into something like the others. So you see, Princess, I do know a little something about making sacrifices and turning my back on obligation. When the prize for doing it is happiness and self-respect, it's not so hard to leave all that worthless crap behind."

She couldn't help but chuckle at that, however coldly. "Oh, I think you have been made out to be something you are not. But it was not the tabloids that made you that something."

"Arabella," he began.

But she cut him off before he could say anything more. "You are not the man you led me to believe, Gus." Immediately she squeezed her eyes shut tight. "I mean, Augustus. Mr. Langley," she then corrected herself more severely. "You are not Gus Torrance. You have said yourself that that was a name you made up. In fact, I think you are all made up. 'Reinvented,' you said. To me, you are just . . . what is the American word? A phony," she finally said. "You are just a phony."

"Arabella—"

"Why did you lie to me? To all of us?"

"I'm not a phony, and I never lied to you," he said sternly, reaching out to her.

But Arabella intercepted him and took a step in retreat. "You are not a bartender with no roots and no prospects. You are a member of a very old and very well-respected family—though that respect is not so present for your generation—and you are the heir to the family fortune. Or you will be. Someday."

"And you think that's worse than being a bartender with no roots and no prospects?" he said.

"I think it is bad because you are not Gus Torrance. And Gus Torrance is who I fell in—"

She stopped herself before she would have revealed the depth of her feelings for him, but not before Gus—Augustus . . . Mr. Langley . . . whoever he was—understood what she had meant to say.

"I love you, too, Arabella," he said frankly. "And that's why I went back."

She narrowed her eyes in confusion, swallowing hard at his proclamation, wondering if she could believe him about that, when he had lied about so many other things. "What do you mean?" she asked cautiously. "Back to what?"

"Back to the family fold," he told her, the words obviously leaving a bad taste in his mouth. "When I left home five years ago, I turned my back on everything the Langleys had, everything they stood for."

"Why?" she asked.

"Because I didn't want it," he replied immediately, adamantly. "I wanted something else. Something more. Something better."

They were words Arabella herself had spoken only moments ago to Reynaldo, and she realized then that she had no choice but to soften her feelings toward this man, and give him a chance to explain. "And did you find something else?" she asked. "Something more? Something better?"

"I did find it," he replied readily. "I found *her*. But she was someone I knew I couldn't have. She told me that herself. And I knew I'd never change her mind, not being the kind of man I am. The kind of man I *was*," he hastily corrected himself. "Gus the bartender never could have won her. But I figured Augustus Durrett Langley the fourth might very well stand a chance."

Arabella said nothing in response to that. What could she say? She was guilty of doing what he had said. She had not thought Gus the bartender was the kind of man

who understood obligation or privilege or even love. She
had thought him a rootless wanderer who had not a care in
the world. She had not thought the two of them were
suited to each other. Now, of course, she knew differently.
Still, she wanted to hear what he had to say.

But Augustus Durrett Langley IV said nothing for a
moment, only gazed at her in silence, as if he were trying
to memorize every feature, every nuance, of her person.
Or perhaps he was remembering, Arabella thought. Remembering the way they had been that night in San Juan,
the way he had held her and touched her and nearly made
her come apart inside. The way he had made her fall in
love with him.

No, not him, she hastily corrected herself. That had not
been the man to whom she was speaking now. It had been
Gus who had touched her in that way, Gus who had made
her feel the way she had felt that night. This man . . . This
man was someone she did not know. Yet. But perhaps, if
she allowed him to explain, she would find something in
him that was familiar.

"I called my father in Philadelphia the day I quit my job
on *Mad Tryst*," he said. "It was a long, difficult conversation. It's been more than three years since I talked to him.
He didn't even know where I was."

"Why not?" she asked.

"When I left home five years ago," he said, "my father
threatened to disown me if I didn't come home. Then
when I didn't go home, he completely severed all ties, and
I didn't exactly do anything to reconnect them. Not until
last week."

"And what did the two of you say to each other last
week?" Arabella wanted to know.

There was another long pause, then Augustus said, "To

make a long story short, my father told me . . ." He sighed heavily before continuing. "He told me to come home. He told me that all is forgiven."

"It is that simple?"

"Well, not really," he admitted. "But I don't want to stand here all day outlining the terms of my surrender for you."

"I do not understand," Arabella said.

Augustus expelled a long sound of frustration. "In order for things to return to normal with my family—and trust me, 'normal' is by no means normal with them—I have to agree to go to college and get my bachelor's and master's degrees in business."

"That is not so bad," Arabella said. "It would be good to go to university. I would have liked to go myself, but my parents did not think it was necessary."

"Yeah, well, maybe we can enroll together," he said with a sad smile. "I also have to go into business once I graduate," he added. "Even though 'businessman' was the absolute last thing I ever wanted to be. But there's a trust fund my grandfather set up for me," he added distastefully. "I can plunder it at will, provided I use it to further my education and get ahead in business. And if I'm a good boy and do as my father tells me to do," he added, sounding tired and beaten down, "then I'll be welcomed back into the family fold. And once I'm back in the family fold, I'll be in a position to get everything I ever wanted."

"Even the something else you say you have found since leaving that life behind?" she asked softly.

He nodded. "Because now I'm more up to her standards. Now I'm more socially acceptable. Now I'm on equal footing with her. Now she'll have no reason to turn me down."

Arabella looked at him, noted his unhappiness, his dissatisfaction, and his hopelessness. He had surrendered everything, she thought, everything that had ever made him happy, because he had thought it would win her over. He had become the very thing she did not want, because he had thought that was exactly what she wanted.

"Oh, Gus . . ." she said, feeling unhappy, dissatisfied, and hopeless herself. She tipped her head back to keep in the tears that threatened to fall. "I mean, Augustus. You are not Gus anymore, are you?"

"No," he said flatly. "I'm not."

She expelled a heavy, sorrowful sound and realized that no matter how hard she tried, she would not be able to stop the tears. She tipped her head forward again and met his gaze levelly, ignoring the tears that spilled over when she did. "If you are not Gus," she said softly, "then you do not stand a chance with her at all."

He paled at that, his lips parting over a sound of disbelief. "But . . ."

She could not allow this, Arabella thought. She could not allow him to give up his happiness the way he had, but she did not want him to turn his back on his family, either. Family was very important, she knew. But so was happiness. She knew that even better. There must be some way, she told herself. There must be something they could do . . .

And then, suddenly, Arabella had an idea. The woman who had spent her entire life letting others make plans for her, the woman who had never taken a single moment out of her day to think for herself—until today—was suddenly struck by a wonderful inspiration.

"Wait, Gus, I think I have an idea," she said.

He eyed her skeptically. "What do you mean?"

"I mean, I have an idea," she repeated. "For the first

time in my life, I have an idea, an original idea, and it is a very good one, I think."

"You've started thinking for yourself?" he asked. "When did this happen?"

She smiled. "Not long ago. When I told Reynaldo I would not marry him."

His expression went slack at her admission. "You did what?" he asked, so softly she almost did not hear him.

She smiled and took a step forward, one that brought her within touching distance of Gus. Because he was Gus, she realized. Even dressed as he was, even speaking as he was, he was Gus. Her Gus. Because only her Gus would have offered to make such sacrifices for her. Because only her Gus could have loved her that much. At least as much as she loved him.

She extended her hand toward him, to touch his face, but before she could complete the action, he, too, reached for her, meeting her halfway, linking his fingers with hers before pulling her close. Arabella laughed at the sheer joy that went through her in simply being so close to him.

She realized then that she had not yet even kissed him. Not on the mouth, the way lovers should. So she pushed herself up on tiptoe and brushed her lips lightly over his. Immediately Gus pulled her close and kissed her back, again and again and again, taking her mouth with all the passion and promise she felt welling up inside herself.

"I told . . . Reynaldo . . . I would not . . . marry him," she repeated between kisses, threading her fingers through Gus's hair, which she hoped he would someday grow long again, because she had never had the chance to twine it through her fingers when it was long, though she had wondered what it would be like to do so many times. In fact, she hoped there were many things that she and

Gus could go back to. And perhaps, if her idea was as good as she was beginning to think it was, they would go back to those things very soon.

"Why would you tell him you couldn't marry him?" Gus asked, smiling back. He held her snugly in his arms, and Arabella decided it was the most comfortable, most welcoming place she had ever been in her life.

"I told him I could not marry him because I was in love with you," she said, "something else I realized when I finally allowed myself to think for myself."

Gus smiled. "Gee, when you start thinking for yourself, you don't waste any time, do you?"

"No, I do not," she agreed. "Which is why you should listen to me when I tell you I have an idea." She smiled a secret—and she hoped seductive—little smile. "In fact, you would be surprised at what I have been thinking about today. Just in the last few moments."

"Oh, yeah?" he asked. "Does any of it involve me? Preferably me naked?"

Her smile grew broader, and she reveled in the warmth that eased through her body at the freedom with which she might pursue just such ideas now. "Those will come later," she said.

"How much later?" he demanded.

She thought for a moment. "Fifteen minutes. First, I must take a few minutes to dream about something."

"Oh, yeah? That sounds interesting."

"Yes, and dreaming for myself is something I have never done before in my life, so do not interrupt me while I do this dreaming."

"Yes, Princess."

"Do not call me Princess."

"Yes, Your Highness."

Arabella narrowed her eyes at him imperiously, but he

only smiled and did not say anything further. So she then closed her eyes for a moment, and she allowed herself to dream a dream of her very own, for the first time in her life.

And oh, what a dream it was.

Without opening her eyes, she asked Gus, "You say your father told you you must go into business in order to collect your money that your grandfather wanted you to have?"

"Yes," he said, sounding interested.

"What kind of business?" she asked.

"My grandfather never really specified. I just have to go into business."

"Can it be a business you start yourself?" Arabella asked.

He didn't respond right away, and when she opened her eyes, she saw that it was because he seemed to be giving the question much thought. "Yeah, probably. In fact, knowing Grandfather, that's the kind of thing he'd prefer. He was a self-made man."

Arabella nodded her approval. "Then I have just the business for you, Gus." She smiled. "Just the business for *us*. Because I have a little money of my own, you know."

He smiled back and pulled her closer. "I like this dream, Arabella," he said.

"You do not even know what it is yet."

"No, I don't. But you're in it with me. And as long as you're there with me, sweetheart," he said, "it'll be a dream come true."

Chapter 19

*R*uby lay on the roof of the trailer where she had grown up, and gazed at the generous splash of stars that spilled across the vast night sky. She wasn't sure how long she'd been up here, but the cool aluminum beneath her had long ago grown warm from the heat of her body. And from the open air vent near her head, she could hear the sounds of Jay Leno's monologue and Grandma Pearl's coarse laughter, mingling with the sounds of the kitchen faucet and the clinking of dishes as her mother washed them. Ruby was dressed the same way she had dressed on countless other nights she had spent in exactly this way during her life, wearing cutoff blue jeans and a wash-worn yellow T-shirt. God alone knew where she'd left her shoes. When she inhaled deeply to release a heartfelt sigh, she smelled the faint odor of her grandmother's cigarette smoke, her mother's White Shoulders perfume, and the Appalachimahoochee landfill that lay less than a mile to the west.

Really, she ought to feel right at home, so often had she played out this scenario over the last twenty-six years. Strangely, though, tonight Ruby felt more distant and alienated than she had ever felt in her life.

And she wondered, as she had every night for the past week or so, where *Mad Tryst* was, and what everyone was doing, and if Keaton was looking at the same sky she was looking at, at the same time she was looking at it.

Home. Ruby had come home. But it felt no more welcoming or comfortable—or homelike—now than it had ever felt before. She wondered why she had thought it would be a good idea to come to Appalachimahoochee for a visit. Probably, she thought, because she hadn't felt like she had anywhere else to go. When she'd returned to her apartment in Miami, the scant, spartan space had felt even worse than this did.

The moment she had walked in the door, the place had felt smaller, dingier, and lonelier than it had felt before she'd left. And it had felt plenty small, dingy, and lonely then. Ruby had returned from her Caribbean adventure to a home where she felt completely uncomfortable, completely unwelcome. And now, as she lay on the roof of her grandmother's trailer, a position she had claimed hundreds of times over the years, feeling alienated and alone, she couldn't help wondering if she would ever find a place that would feel comfortable and welcome, a place that would feel like home.

Doubtful, she thought now. Very, very doubtful.

Because the only time Ruby could recall ever feeling as if she belonged somewhere—honestly, truly belonged—it had been for one afternoon, in the deepest part of a rain forest, with Keaton Hamilton Danning III. And at this point, she was inclined to believe she had only dreamed that. Because surely nothing could be as perfect, as precious as that afternoon had been.

In fact there were times when Ruby could almost convince herself she had dreamed her entire escapade aboard the prince's yacht. She wasn't the kind of woman who had adventures like that. Wasn't the kind of woman who lived life that way. Wasn't the kind of woman who lived life, period. For twenty-six years she'd just sort of existed, sort of floated from one place to another, aimlessly, pointlessly, meaninglessly.

Except for that one week. That one week she had felt as if she had plenty of aim, plenty of point, plenty of meaning. Now, though . . . Now things were just the same way they had been before.

No, not quite the same, she realized then. Now things were worse. Because before, although Ruby had known her life wasn't full and satisfying, she hadn't known for sure, not exactly, what it was that was missing. She'd felt empty and restless, but she hadn't been able to identify exactly why. Now she could identify why. Now she knew exactly what was missing. Now she could name with complete certainty the source of her emptiness, restlessness, and dissatisfaction.

The thing that was missing from her life was love. The thing that was missing was Keaton. And now that Ruby knew, and identified, and realized, and understood all that, it only made living the way she had lived before worse than it had been. Mostly because she knew she would love and miss Keaton for the rest of her life. And she knew that he *wouldn't* love and miss her. Not the way she did him. Not enough to contact her. Not enough to see her again. Not enough to want to include her in his life.

Not enough, period.

Keaton Hamilton Danning III had bigger fish to fry. He

had places to go. People to see. Things to do. Princes to watch over. He had his life planned and mapped and visualized. He had it all worked out. And nowhere in his equation was there a place for an unemployed waitress with a high school education who didn't even know her paternity. Hey, why was she surprised? she asked herself now. Would she want someone like that in her life? Someone who had no job, no education, no prospects, no background, no future? Of course not.

Not unless it was Keaton Hamilton Danning III, anyway.

At the sound of an approaching car Ruby turned her head toward the two-lane highway that lay just beyond the entrance to the Happy Trails Trailer Park, roughly a hundred feet from her grandmother's trailer. And her curiosity was immediately aroused by the fact that the car didn't keep on going, as cars usually did. No, this car, instead of passing by, turned into the entrance of Happy Trails. And when it turned, her curiosity was even more aroused, because she saw that the car was, in fact, a taxicab. She sat up in surprise. There was no taxi service in Appalachimahoochee, she knew. The nearest taxi was almost sixty miles away, in Tallahassee. She couldn't imagine what would bring one out this far.

Until the taxi pulled to a stop at the first trailer in the park, barely fifty feet from where Ruby sat, and she saw the person who got out. And immediately her heart jumped into her throat.

Two lights illuminated that part of the trailer park— one was a street lamp from which a pale bluish light sputtered halfheartedly, and the other was a neon sign of green and yellow that buzzed and flickered with five burned-out letters. But even in the spastic light available, Ruby had no trouble distinguishing Keaton. He was just that . . . distinguished, she thought with a smile.

Even from a distance he looked exactly as he had aboard *Mad Tryst*, wearing khaki trousers and a tailored, short-sleeved shirt that absorbed the ghostly blue light in a way that made her think the garment was actually white. Her heart withdrew from her throat, but began to hammer hard in her chest as she watched him tug a canvas week-ender bag from the back of the taxi and then stand at the driver's side window to pay the cabby. Then, as the car wheeled away, crunching gravel beneath its tires, Keaton turned toward the collection of two dozen trailers and stared at them. Stared at them as if he had no idea what he was supposed to do now.

Ruby figured he probably couldn't see her from her dark perch, and something—she had no idea what—wouldn't allow her to call out to him just yet. Instead she only watched him as he took a few steps forward, his gaze ricocheting from one trailer to another and back again, as if he were playing a mental game of eenie-meenie-minie-moe. And she smiled when his gaze finally lit on her grandmother's trailer, as if he'd made his choice, and he turned his steps more purposefully in that direction.

She waited until he stood at the foot of the cinder block steps leading up to the front door, then, creeping on hands and knees to peer over the edge of the trailer, she caught him just as he was about to lift his fist to knock.

"Psst," she said from immediately above him.

He glanced up at the sound, his expression surprised and puzzled, until he saw who had summoned him. Then, somehow, his features seemed to go soft and warm all over. He fixed his gaze on her face, his eyes moving from her eyes to her hair to her mouth to her eyes again. And then he smiled at her, and something inside Ruby went all soft and warm, too.

"Hey," she said quietly by way of a greeting.

"Hello," he replied just as quietly.

But neither seemed to know what to say after that. They only stared at each other in silence, as if neither could quite believe the other was real. Maybe he wasn't real, Ruby thought. Maybe she had fallen asleep, and now she was only dreaming him, the way she had dreamed about him every night since leaving him behind in San Juan. But if that was the case, why then, for the first time in days, did she feel as if she were exactly in the place where she belonged? Why, for the first time, did she feel comfortable and welcome and at home? Maybe, just maybe, she wasn't dreaming after all.

"Did, uh . . . did you get lost on your way to Venezuela or something?" she finally asked him, keeping her voice low, because she didn't want her mother or grandmother to hear. She didn't want to share Keaton with anyone. Not yet. " 'Cause I got news for you, sailor. Venezuela is way south of here."

He shook his head. "No, I got lost a long time before I arrived in the Caribbean," he told her. "I've been cruising aimlessly for years. I just never realized it until recently."

Gee, she could really identify with that, she thought. "Maybe you need a compass," she told him.

"Maybe I had one for a little while," he replied.

Her heart kicked up an even faster, even more erratic rhythm. "So, um . . . so what happened to it?"

His expression sobered, but his gaze never left hers. "I lost it," he said. "Worse than that. I threw it overboard."

She inhaled a shallow breath and held it. "Did you?"

He nodded. "So I jumped overboard, too, to look for it."

"And . . . and did you find it?" she asked.

He nodded again. "Yeah, I did. And imagine my surprise to find it on top of a trailer in Appalachimahoochee, Florida. I can't imagine how it got there."

She expelled a single, soft chuckle of delight. "Me, neither," she said honestly. Then, "Come on up," she added. "We need to talk."

"That we do," he agreed. But he eyed the trailer dubiously. "Will that thing hold both our weights?"

"It's survived more tempests than you know," she told him.

"Hurricanes?" he asked. "Tornadoes?"

"Worse," she said. "My puberty and adolescence."

"Ah. Well, if your puberty and adolescence was anything like mine," he said, "then this thing should be damned near indestructible."

"Come on up," she repeated, grinning. "Ladder's on the back."

She had forgotten how his weight would rock the trailer as he climbed up the back, and Ruby's grandmother called up through the open air vent as he did, asking her if everything was all right up there.

"Oh, yeah, Grandma Pearl," Ruby called back down. "Everything's fine." She hoped she was telling the truth. And not just because Grandma Pearl would wash her mouth out with soap if she was caught lying, either.

As Keaton joined her, Ruby settled herself into her original location, lying on her back, head pillowed in her hands, legs crossed at the ankles. And she waited for Keaton to get comfortable, too, though it took him a bit longer to manage it. She smiled when he finally lay beside her. But where she was positioned to look up at the sky, he had positioned himself to look at Ruby—lying on his side, one elbow bent and resting on the trailer's roof, his hand supporting his head.

"I've missed you," he said without preamble.

Her heart kicked up its rapid rhythm again, rushing

blood through her body at a speed that made her dizzy. Or maybe it was just seeing Keaton again that made her dizzy. Maybe it was the swift tide of emotion that flooded her, knowing he was here. That he'd come here for her. That he'd sent the taxi away, as if he intended to stay here forever.

She swallowed with some difficulty. "I've missed you, too," she replied.

"No, I mean, I've *missed* you, Ruby," he said again, more emphatically than before.

He moved his free hand to her face, skimming his fingertips over her cheek, her jaw, her lips. His movements were light, but hungry, as if he just couldn't keep himself from touching her. Not that she exactly minded. And his eyes never once left hers.

"I've missed you *profoundly.* I've missed you physically, emotionally, spiritually . . . in every way that I could miss you. Ever since you left, it's been like there was a piece of me gone, too. Like a piece of me went with you. A big piece."

"That's strange," she said softly, still not moving, reveling in the thrill of sensation that shot through her every time he brushed his fingers over her face. "You shouldn't feel as if a piece of you is gone. Because I left a piece of myself with you."

He smiled. "Maybe we just need to be together, to make those pieces fit right."

"Maybe so," she agreed.

Unable to tolerate not touching him, Ruby removed a hand from behind her head and raised it to his face, too. She traced the rough line of his jaw, one salient cheekbone, his warm mouth. Then she threaded her fingers through his hair and lower, curling them around his nape.

"I think that must be it," he said. "Because suddenly, being here with you again, I don't feel like that part of me is missing anymore. Miraculously, I feel whole again."

"I don't think that's such a miracle," she told him, her heart hammering so hard now, she was certain he must be able to hear it, too. "Because the same thing happened to me, the minute I saw you get out of that cab."

He said nothing in response to that, only studied her face in silence for a moment, as if he were trying to find some change there, something that was different, something that hadn't been there before. But she knew she was still the same Ruby he'd known on *Mad Tryst*. She was the same Ruby she had always been, the same one she would always be. Yes, she loved him, and that was one thing that was different, but, essentially, she was no different. She was still the same woman he had once found lacking, the woman he once thought wasn't his social equal. Unless he had changed over the last few days, there was no reason for her to feel hopeful.

But she did feel hopeful. Suddenly she felt very, very hopeful.

"I went to Miami first," he told her. "I thought that was where I'd find you. And when I didn't find you there, I was afraid maybe you'd left, that you'd gone to New York or Los Angeles to follow your acting dreams. And then I was terrified that I'd never see you again. Not unless it was on the silver screen, after you'd made it big."

She shook her head. "No, I've pretty much abandoned any hope of an acting career," she said with surprisingly little concern. Or maybe that wasn't so surprising, she thought further. Because really, when all was said and done, she hadn't tried that hard to follow her dream in the first place. And over the last couple of weeks, achieving that dream had become less and less important. If it had ever really been important to her at all.

She expelled a soft sigh and shook her head. "I don't want to be an actress, Keaton," she said.

And speaking it aloud that way, she realized how true the statement was. How true it had always been. Her alleged dream of becoming an actress had simply been another empty goal in a long line of empty goals, goals she'd made and discarded because she'd just never really known what she wanted. Not until she'd wandered onto a prince's yacht one night and become an accidental stowaway. Not until she'd met Keaton Hamilton Danning III. Not until she realized what it meant to fall in love with someone. Someone you wanted to keep by your side forever.

"You know," she continued now, tucking her hand beneath her head again, and turning her attention back to the inky sky and its array of stars, "deep down I think that's why I never went anywhere in my so-called struggle to become an actress. Truth be told, Keaton, I didn't really struggle that much. And it never devastated me or anything that I didn't get anywhere. I think maybe that's why I never left Miami to go someplace where I might have had a better chance to succeed. Because, deep down, I don't think I honestly wanted to succeed. Not at an acting career, anyway. That just wasn't what I really, truly wanted. I think I saw it as a means to an end, a way to be somebody, because I'd always felt like such a nobody."

She turned to look at him, meeting his gaze levelly. "But now I realize that being somebody has nothing to do with what you do for a living, or how many people know your name, or what kind of stuff you have. Being somebody means you're a decent person. Being somebody means you care about other people, and that other people care about you."

Keaton said nothing for a moment, then, slowly, he nodded. "Which probably goes a long way," he finally said, "toward explaining why I've never felt like much of anybody myself."

She furrowed her brows down in confusion. "What are you talking about?" she asked. "Of course you're somebody. You're a huge somebody. You're in line to become prime minister of Pelagia. You're Prince Reynaldo's right-hand man."

"I *was* in line to become prime minister," he reminded her. "But the people of Pelagia put someone else in that office after they booted Reynaldo out of the country, someone who's doing a very good job. There's no chance they'd ever allow me to come back and do it. And as for being Prince Reynaldo's right-hand man, well . . . That's hardly something to be proud of, is it? I have nothing in that regard, Ruby. The job I trained all my life to assume isn't available to me now. I think that's why I stayed with Reynaldo as long as I did. Because it was the only place I found any purpose, even if that purpose was just baby-sitting. Everything I've done for the past year, it hasn't been for me. It's been for someone else. Someone who didn't even deserve it."

"Well, maybe not quite everything," Ruby said, smiling. But she couldn't quite keep the sadness out of her voice as she added, "You did something for me. Or at least you tried to. I just wasn't any good at being a social climber, I guess."

He opened his mouth to interrupt her, but she lifted a hand to his lips to stop him from saying anything. She had a point to make, and she needed to drive it home.

"This is me, Keaton," she told him, gesturing down at

her ragged clothes. "I'm not the Barbie doll Arabella dressed in haute couture. And I'm not the Eliza Doolittle you tried to teach some social graces to. I'm a person who grew up below the poverty line, who never went to college, who doesn't know who her father is, and who makes her way in the world the best way she knows how. I never had too many opportunities, and God knows I don't have many prospects." She paused a telling moment before adding, "But you know something, Keaton? At least I don't look at people and assess their value based on *what* they have, instead of *who* they are."

Keaton eyed her in silence for a moment, and in that moment her heart seemed to stop beating altogether. Because for that moment she genuinely wondered if he was going to change his mind about coming, or if the reason he had come was that he had remembered her differently from what she really was.

Finally, though, softly, he said, "And thank God for that. Because if you assessed people's values based on what they had, Ruby, then you'd turn your back on me in a heartbeat."

It was, to say the least, not the response she had expected. "What do you mean?" she asked, puzzled.

"I mean *I'm* the one who doesn't have anything to offer, Ruby, not you. You can get a job any time you want, and you'll always have a regular paycheck. You have a permanent address. *Two* permanent addresses—one in Miami and one here. Hell, I'll bet you even have money in the bank, don't you?"

"A little," she said. "What? You don't?" she added dubiously.

He shook his head and chuckled morosely. "None that I can get to. Not one dime. I'm broke, Ruby. I barely had enough for the cab ride to Appalachimahoochee. I have nothing but what's in the bag I brought with me. I lost my job a year ago, and I have no idea what I'm suited to do now. I don't have a house, or a job, or any prospects. *I'm* the one without a future, Ruby. Not you. *I'm* the one who has nothing. Not you."

He moved his hand to her hair, brushing her bangs out of her eyes, but he didn't come any closer, didn't move his touch anywhere other than her face. And she couldn't help thinking his hesitation came about because he wasn't sure of his reception. Because he was afraid she might very well rebuff him.

"In spite of that," he said softly as he moved his hand back to his side, "I hope you'll give me another chance. Because I really can't imagine living the rest of my life without you."

For a long time Ruby didn't say anything, mostly because she had no idea what to say. She never would have pictured this reversal in roles, though deep down, she didn't think they had switched places. What had happened, she thought, was that they had simply, finally, arrived at the same place. They may have come by different routes, and experienced different things along their journeys, but the important thing was that they were both in the same place now. Somehow, both of them had made it home. And somehow, she knew neither of them would ever leave home again. Not without company, anyway.

"Oh, Keaton," she finally said. "That's not true at all. You have more to offer than anyone I know. I never wanted those other things about you. They weren't what was important to me."

He gazed down at her as if he didn't quite believe her. "They're what everyone else thought was important."

"Well, not me," she replied immediately. "You're much more valuable to me in another capacity."

He still didn't look convinced. "And that would be?"

She hesitated. How could she possibly explain that which defied explanation? How could she make him understand that the reason she valued him was that he made her feel valued? That the reason she thought he was important was that he made her feel important? That the reason she needed and wanted him was that he made her feel needed and wanted, too? That the reason she loved him was that he made her feel loved?

Because Ruby understood in that moment, even if he hadn't said it, that Keaton did love her. He never would have left behind everything he had and spent his last dollar to come looking for her if he hadn't. Good thing she loved him so much, too.

"You know, it's funny," she finally said, dodging his question for a minute, "but when I went back to my apartment in Miami, after all that time of thinking how much I needed to get home, when I finally got home, it just didn't feel . . . right. It felt like I was just visiting someplace that didn't belong to me. Does that make sense?"

He nodded. "It makes perfect sense. I've felt the same way myself. A lot of times."

"And I just . . . I kept feeling this need to go home," she continued. "*Home* home. I kept thinking I needed to come back to Appalachimahoochee, and that when I got *here*, I'd feel better, and I'd be able to figure out what I needed to do next. But when I got here, this didn't feel right, either. It didn't feel like home anymore. Not that it ever really felt like home to begin with, I mean," she added. "But being here has felt as strange as being back in my apartment in Miami."

Keaton smiled, a smile of relief and happiness and . . . and hopefulness, she realized. "I completely understand," he told her. "The same thing happened to me after you left *Mad Tryst*. I found myself wanting to go home, too, but not to Pelagia. Not to my parents' house in Virginia, either. What was strange was that my need to go home led me to Miami, a city I'd only visited once, for a matter of days, where I didn't know anyone. Except you."

Ruby smiled, too, then pushed herself up to sitting, because she just couldn't lie still any longer. She sat facing Keaton with her legs folded pretzel-fashion, and he immediately altered his own position to mirror hers. She reached for him at the same time he reached for her, and their hands met halfway, their fingers twining together.

"And then, when I couldn't find you in Miami," he went on, "when I found out you'd come here, suddenly my need to go home turned into my need to go to a place I'd never visited before in my entire life. And now this place, this place I've never laid eyes on until tonight, somehow feels like home to me." He met her gaze levelly. "Why is that, do you think?"

She smiled. "Maybe because home isn't where you come from. It's where you end up."

He smiled back. "Or maybe because home isn't where you are. It's who you're with."

"Do you think the reason matters?" she asked him.

He shook his head. "No. I think just the feeling matters."

Ruby inhaled a fortifying breath before asking, "And just what is it you feel, Keaton?"

He met her gaze levelly, lifted his free hand to her face, and cupped her jaw in his palm. Very softly, very seriously, very confidently he said, "I love you, Ruby." And then he leaned forward and covered her mouth with his.

It was a wonderful kiss, one filled with promise, and euphoria, and barely restrained passion. It was a kiss that told them both that later they'd say everything else they needed to say to each other, and they'd say it wordlessly, in each others' arms . . .

. . . at a hotel on the edge of town, because there was no way Ruby would be spending another night away from him for the rest of her life, but she didn't have enough money on her for gas beyond the city limits. Right now, though, that didn't matter at all. What mattered was that they were together. And that they would stay that way forever. It was all in the kiss. That and so much more. For long moments they held each other, becoming reacquainted with all the things they'd missed about each other. Finally, though, reluctantly, they parted.

"I love you, too, Keaton," Ruby said as she pulled back—but not too far. "Just in case, you know, you didn't already realize that."

"I did kind of suspect," he told her. "But I wanted to be sure."

"You can be sure," she said. "I love you. And I will love you forever."

"Promise me you'll stay with me, too," he said further. "I want you with me forever. If you'll have me."

She smiled, a wicked little smile that she just couldn't keep inside. "Oh, I'll have you," she said seductively. "I'll have you in as many ways as I possibly can."

He smiled back, a smile that was every bit as wicked as her own. "Starting with on top of a trailer?" he asked.

She laughed low. "Only after I've introduced you to Mama and Grandma Pearl. 'Cause once you meet them, you may change your mind about wanting me."

"Oh, I'll take you, Ruby," he told her with *much* certainty. "No matter what. I'll take you in as many ways as I possibly can."

"Then take me, Keaton," she told him. "Take me home. Take me, because right now and forevermore, I am yours."

Epilogue

Things at the Small World Bed and Breakfast and Cottages on the tiny, privately owned island of Aragusta in the Bahamas were, as usual, hopping, even though it was August and hardly the high tourist season in the Caribbean. Ruby couldn't remember a time when the place hadn't been fully booked. It seemed like within weeks of opening two springtimes ago, the minuscule resort had become *the* place to stay in this part of the Caribbean, and they'd been going great guns ever since.

The island's seclusion and accessibility and breathtaking tropical beauty appealed to the rich and famous, as did the staggeringly high prices of the bed and breakfast and its private cottages, the only buildings on the entire island. For this reason, the Small World was even beginning to see its share of reservations from a handful of celebrities—actors, supermodels, diplomats, royalty, that kind of thing—not that any of them who worked at the Small World were especially impressed by such notoriety, of course. Still, it was good for business. And thanks to good business—and all of that lovely money in Gus's trust fund and Arabella's dowry, which had allowed the newlyweds to buy the island and build the mini-resort right after marrying—all of them had good jobs with regular paychecks, certain futures, and permanent addresses.

And, honestly, what more could anyone want?

"Where is Gus?" Arabella asked as Ruby passed by the reservations desk.

She wore the standard uniform of Small World employees, just as Ruby herself did—big ol' khaki shorts and a Hawaiian shirt. Except that Arabella's garments were a bit larger than Ruby's, due to her being seven months along with her and Gus's first child. Still, even in maternity mode, she was no less commanding now as the director of reservations than she had ever been. Arabella had shown a surprising efficiency for dealing with their customers, especially the more troublesome ones.

"I think our fearless leader is out on the veranda, studying for his economics final," Ruby said. "You want me to summon him?"

In addition to the island and the inn, Gus had purchased a seaplane and hired a pilot, not just to ferry guests to and from the island, but so that he could come and go daily to attend classes at the University of Miami. So far he was three-fourths of the way through his bachelor's degree in business, having made the dean's list every semester. Once Gus put his mind to something, Ruby thought, he really went after it. She smiled when she looked at Arabella again, noting her round, rosy figure.

Arabella shook her head. "It is all right. I will talk to him later. I wanted to tell him my parents heard from Reynaldo last week."

Ruby smiled. "Oh, yeah? Is he going to take that bell-hop position Gus offered him?"

Arabella smiled, too. "He cannot. He is in jail. In South Africa. They arrested him in a local bar for soliciting."

Ruby gaped. Hard. "*What*?"

Arabella nodded. "They thought he was a transvestite prostitute. With Reynaldo, I can see where they might make a mistake. Now he has asked my father to intervene on his behalf, to get him out of jail. Father will do so." Arabella's smile broadened. "Eventually."

Ruby told herself she would *not* be delighted by this news. Really. She wouldn't. Poor Reynaldo. Poor, self-important, thoughtless, egotistical, coldhearted, jerk Reynaldo.

Arabella started to say more, but halted abruptly as one of their newly arrived guests entered the lobby of the bed and breakfast and approached the desk.

"Excuse me," the woman said, "but you told us our rooms would be ready at noon, and now it's one o'clock, and we're still waiting."

Ruby watched as Arabella drew herself up in her queenly way and gave the woman her Catherine the Great look. "No, Mrs. Dennison, as I told you on the telephone when you made your reservation, your rooms will be ready at three o'clock. But I will be happy to check your bags so that you may spend some time exploring the island while you wait."

"You said noon," the woman insisted crisply.

"I said three o'clock," Arabella countered regally.

"You said noon," Mrs. Dennison persisted. Though her voice held less conviction than before.

"No, I did not," Arabella told her.

"Yes, you did," the woman argued.

"No, I did not."

"You did."

"I did not."

"You did."

"Are you calling me a *liar*, Mrs. Dennison?" Arabella asked imperiously.

Immediately the woman backed down. She smiled a bit nervously. "No, of course not. I would never do that. I suppose you did say three o'clock. And truly, I'm just grateful we got rooms here in the first place."

"Yes, you should be," Arabella told her without a bit of obsequiousness. "We had to turn down Mick Jagger last week, even though he insists he is wearying of Mustique. Aragusta is very much in demand. It is because we here at the Small World Bed and Breakfast and Cottages are so accommodating."

"Ah, yes," Mrs. Dennison said. "I could see that immediately."

"And also," Arabella added, "because our chef makes the best *Pflaumenkuchen* in all the Caribbean."

"Oh, Mr. Dennison and I are so looking forward to dinner tonight," the other woman added, seeming much less irritated now. "I understand his midnight buffet is amazing, too . . ."

Ruby smiled and, realizing that Arabella, as always, had things in the lobby well in hand, went in search of the general manager, who also happened to be her husband. She found him in the kitchen, nodding in agreement with the culinary Kurt over the evening menu selections. The canine Kurt, Ruby noticed, was affixed to his left trouser leg, growling as he tugged at the khaki.

Some things, she thought, would never change.

"Oh, darling," she called to Keaton, who glanced up

when he saw her approaching, giving his leg a little shake to dislodge Kurt. "I need your help with the Land Rover. It won't start."

He and the chef exchanged a few more words in German, then, pysching out the dog with a feint to his right, Keaton freed himself of the canine and made his way toward Ruby. He looked so cute in his Hawaiian shirt, his dark hair looking a bit shaggy and way overdue for a cut, streaked with gold from time spent in the sun. His eyes were full of laughter, his skin was burnished bronze, and she'd never seen him looking so happy. They lived in one of the Small World cottages, which wasn't a whole lot bigger than the trailer where Ruby had grown up—five rooms, very cozy. But where that trailer had always felt stifling and close, her home with Keaton felt limitless and liberating. Within its walls, after all, the two of them had everything they could ever want. Because they had each other.

And, of course, the ocean view sure beat the buzzing, fractured neon sign of Happy Trails, and the sea breezes were way better than the smell of the Appalachimahoochee landfill. All in all, Ruby couldn't imagine a place more comfortable—or welcoming—than this one. As far as she was concerned, she had found her way home.

Keaton followed her out to the Land Rover and lifted the hood, peering inside. Immediately he found the problem.

"Well, here you go," he said, "it's a spark plug. But don't worry. I can change it. It'll just take a minute."

Ruby narrowed her eyes at him, a wave of déjà vu washing over her. For some reason this scenario seemed familiar somehow . . .

"You can?" she asked suspiciously.

He nodded. "Sure. No problem. And listen, tomorrow one of us needs to fly into Miami with Gus for a beer run.

But be warned—the Piggly Wiggly has moved it to aisle eight. And whoever goes needs to pick up some Chee-tos, too. I've had a real hankering for some Chee-tos lately. A man can only handle so much Camembert, after all."

Ruby narrowed her eyes at him even more. This was definitely a familiar scenario. "Hey, Keaton, did you, by any chance, ever watch the original *Survivor* when it was on?"

"Oh, sure," he said. "I couldn't get enough of that whole Colleen and Greg thing. Never could figure out those two. And that fight between Kelly and Susan? Was that enlightening or what? And I couldn't believe Gervase wasn't a better swimmer than he was! I mean, a guy like that. And I felt so bad for Jenna that day she didn't get any pictures from home, didn't you?"

Ruby chuckled, thinking she was the luckiest woman alive. Although she'd thought that a lot, so why was today any different?

"What's so funny?" Keaton asked.

She sighed with much contentment. "You. You really are amazing, you know that?"

Keaton smiled back. "Not really. I'm just a regular guy."

"That's what's so amazing," she told him.

"Yeah, well, with me, Ruby, what you see is what you get. Take it or leave it."

"Oh, I'll take it," Ruby said as she moved beside him and wrapped her arms around his neck. And as she pushed herself up on tiptoe to cover his mouth with hers, she added, "I'll take you, Keaton, because, baby, you are mine."

The weather is getting warmer, and things at Avon romance are getting hotter! Next month, don't miss these spectacularly sizzling stories . . .

....

MARRY ME by Susan Kay Law
An Avon Romantic Treasure

Emily Bright has found a place to call her home, but imagine her shock when she is awakened in the middle of the night to discover a tall stranger who claims she is sleeping in *his* bed! Should she marry Jake Sullivan and make this claim come true?

MY ONE AND ONLY by MacKenzie Taylor
An Avon Contemporary Romance

When Abby Lee strides into the office of Ethan Maddux and begs for his help, he barely agrees to give her ten minutes out of his busy day. So how *dare* he ask her to spend time with him at night? Abby knows that when business and pleasure mix—look out!

A NECESSARY HUSBAND by Debra Mullins
An Avon Romance

He's the long-lost heir of the Duke of Raynewood . . . she's a delectable society lady who learns it's her role to turn him into a proper Englishman. Of course, there are rules about these things . . . but sometimes the rules of society are meant to be broken.

HIS SCANDAL by Gayle Callen
An Avon Romance

Sir Alexander Thornton has a reputation as the most dashing— and incorrigible—man in England. He wagers he can win a kiss from any lady in the land . . . but that's before he meets proper Lady Emmeline Prescott.

REL 0402